Always
Green

A Novel

WITHDRAWN

Patti Hill

BETHANY HOUSE PUBLISHERS
Minneapolis, Minnesota

Always Green
Copyright © 2005
Patti Hill

Cover design by Koechel Peterson & Associates

Published by Bethany House Publishers
11400 Hampshire Avenue South
Bloomington, Minnesota 55438

Bethany House Publishers is a division of
Baker Publishing Group, Grand Rapids, Michigan.

Printed in the United States of America

Library of Congress Cataloging-in-Publication Data

Hill, Patti (Patti Ann)
    Always green / by Patti Hill.
        p.   cm. — (Garden gates ; 2)
        Summary: "The Garden Gates series continues with a glimpse at how God's promises
lead one woman through a season of loneliness. Both thought-provoking and fun, this
second-chance romance features colorful characters, light-hearted humor, and moving
spiritual themes"—Provided by publisher.
        ISBN 0-7642-2938-9 (pbk.)
        1. Widows—Fiction. 2. Single mothers—Fiction. 3. Women gardeners—Fiction.
I. Title II. Series: Hill, Patti , (Patti Ann) . Garden gates ; 2.
        PS3608.I4373A79   2005
        813'.6—dc222005008955

TO MY MOM,

Hazelle Kretlow,

A WOMAN OF DYNAMIC FAITH

and abundant love.

*B*ut blessed is the man who trusts in the Lord,
whose confidence is in him.
He will be like a tree planted by the water
that sends out its roots by the stream.
It does not fear when heat comes;
its leaves are always green.
It has no worries in a year of drought
and never fails to bear fruit.

JEREMIAH 17:7–8 NIV

JULY

9

Hot, hot, and more hot to come!
This is day 5 of temperatures over 100° and
nothing but 100s are forecasted to come.
Leaf scorch everywhere. How long, O Lord?

I stepped on something soft and squishy, and it wasn't a sandy beach.

A voice came over the public address speakers. "Folks, we'd like y'all to mosey on over to the barn. The livestock auction starts in five minutes."

"Wait here," Greg ordered as he closed the corral gate behind him.

I scraped what I could from the bottom of my Birkenstock onto a fence rail while Greg joined the owner of a brown horse in the middle of the corral. The men exchanged a volley of horse-speak, and the owner coaxed the horse into a trot at the end of a rope. The horse's coat gleamed with sweat by the time Greg raised a hand to stop the show. He shook his head and spat near the owner's boot.

Strike two. No spitting on the first date.

Strike one had been telling me to wait in the sun. I wiped the sweat from my face with the hem of my T-shirt, creating a reddish smear on the hem. I'd probably smudged my face with dirt, too. *Oh well.* My brain screamed, *Get out of the sun, silly!* I looked for a place to sit down.

My prize was a sliver of shade that fell across a hay bale. I cleaned the treads of my shoes, and then I twisted my hair into a knot and stuck a pencil through it to hold it off my neck. The water in my bottle was too warm to satisfy my thirst, so I rinsed the dust out of my teeth instead. *If I sit very still, maybe the heat won't roost on my shoulders.*

From the center of the corral, the pristine whiteness of Greg's shirt blistered my eyeballs. Translucent with sweat, the shirt was snapped shut at the collar and wrists. If that was cowboy fashion, they definitely needed to revise the dress code of the West. A glint of sunlight flashed off his silver belt buckle as another owner brought his horse into the corral for Greg's scrutiny. I inwardly cheered for the horse, a leggy red with muscled thighs, a kindred spirit.

Greg's face remained expressionless as he inspected each hoof. I turned away from the scene when he shook his head at the horse's owner. One comet of spittle per day satisfied my limit, thank you very much.

After the auction, we ate complimentary burgers at the Western Colorado Emu Society barbecue. The umbrellas above the plastic tables proved useless against the low rays of the afternoon sun. It was too hot to eat or move or even think thoughts faster than a trot. The first bite of the burger sat in my stomach like a stone.

Greg approached his emu burger with the same stoicism he'd expressed while buying horses, so I eavesdropped on the conversations of other diners, all spoken with an economy of words to avoid exertion. A man with a red gingham shirt said, "I stole that horse." His wife replied, "We'll see about that" and took a long drink of iced tea.

At another table, a man bragged to his dining partners, "Greenhorns. California. Didn't know enough to look a horse in the eye. Dang fools." A chorus of grunts agreed with him. A girl of about ten stuffed the last of her burger into her mouth and asked for permission to go see the new mare. She ran off before her mother had a chance to answer. More than anything, I wanted to follow her.

Greg crushed a bundle of French fries into his mouth and gestured toward my plate. "Want 'nother?" he asked, which marked the beginning and end of our supper conversation. He walked off to get another free burger.

Sitting on the edge of a stockyard collecting dust in my teeth and watching a man I barely knew sweat and spit, I realized that dating at thirty-six would be a lot like playing the lottery, something I'd always considered as reckless as eating potato salad left out in the sun. I'd come to dating needy, knowing my chances of striking it rich were, at best, improbable. But there had to be a winner. Why not me? I couldn't win if I didn't play. The same desperation that drove people to buy fistfuls of lottery tickets fortified my optimism. There were men out there, good men; I just knew it. That's why I'd accepted a blind date arranged by a client with her sister's grandson's hunting buddy.

We leaned side-by-side against the rails of the corral watching Greg's new horses nuzzle a bale of hay. I wore a hat I'd folded from the center page of the auction guide. Around us, people loaded horses, cattle, and emus into trailers and drove off trailing plumes of dust. I couldn't think of one good reason why we were still standing there, unless Greg was working up the courage to ask me out again. I prayed he wouldn't. Really, how could he ever hope to top the romance of a livestock auction?

He wiped his brow with his sleeve and fidgeted with his hat.

Uh-oh.

He cleared his throat. "I'm looking for a woman with good teeth, a strong back, and one who don't complain much."

I fit the profile, all right, but stifled the urge to volunteer. "It sounds like you'd be happy married to one of your horses." I smiled broadly so he would know I was kidding—mostly.

His eyes finally opened wide enough to show his eye color, chestnut brown. Big surprise there. He rubbed his chin, worked his hat into place, and spat in the dirt.

Strike three.

"Let's go, then," he said.

Red dirt swirled around the cab of his truck and needled my skin as we drove the fifteen miles back to Orchard City. The air-conditioner control pointed to off. I felt some pride that, even though I'd been edged out by a horse, I didn't complain. I inched toward the open window to catch the hot breeze.

The sky was a faded chambray shirt, dull and lifeless, and for all its many washings, still tinted pink, as if it had been washed with red socks when it was new. Smoke from fires throughout the West and a dust storm as far away as Mongolia flattened the Book Cliffs to gradient shades of gray and collected at the base of the Grand Mesa to obscure the eleven-thousand-foot mountain completely. Only one cotton-ball cloud teetered on the Colorado Plateau to the southwest. In the single-digit humidity, the inconsequential cloud was destined to evaporate before one drop of moisture touched the earth. The bank's digital temperature sign read 105 degrees. That seemed understated.

Greg's truck rattled to a stop in front of my house. He leaned over and pushed my door open. "Much obliged."

~~~

Andrea's eyes glistened with tears as Louise pulled a strand of hair through the frosting cap with a crochet hook. "She sharpens that thing," Andrea said as I walked into my kitchen. "Look, my ear's bleeding."

Andrea is my stepdaughter. She came to Orchard City the summer after Scott's death, looking for the father she had never met. For whatever reasons, my deceased husband had never told me about his first wife and his baby girl. Fortunately—and I mean that with all my heart—Andrea found my son, Ky, and me. God set her in our family as surely as He sends any child into a family by birth, and with at least as much labor. She had returned to San Francisco and her first year of teaching at the end of the summer. Now she was back with us to recuperate from the popping, patching, and pilfering of her great expectations.

Louise is my neighbor and friend, but mostly a self-appointed ministering angel. When my husband, Scott, was killed in a cycling accident, she lowered herself into the dank well of grief I called home to hold my head above the water. She is the bravest woman I know.

A wannabe hairdresser, Louise worked on Andrea's hair within a circle of electric fans and welcomed me with a private smile. "You look hotter than a sinner at church on the Fourth of July. Pour yourself some iced tea, sugar. We can't wait to hear about your date with Clint Eastwood. Didn't y'all just love Clint in those lasagna westerns?"

Andrea and I shared a knowing glance. "*Spaghetti* westerns, Louise," Andrea said.

"Really?"

According to Louise, no task was too insignificant to dress accordingly. Today, she wore cropped black leggings and a royal-blue smock with her name stitched in white above the pocket. To complete the thematic ensemble, a sterling silver earring in the shape of a comb swung from one ear and a pair of scissors swayed from the other. The trim fit of the smock emphasized Louise's new figure. Her red wig lay discarded on the counter.

I petted her downy head on the way to the refrigerator. "Just like a baby."

"Manley says I look like Sinead O'Connor."

Manley is Louise's husband. And I agreed with him. Her features had sharpened with weight loss, first from the chemotherapy and then from an anti-cancer diet, but it would take more than a bald head to make anyone mistake Louise for a nettled rock star.

"Are you sure he didn't say the Marquis de Sade?" Andrea asked.

Louise rested her hands on Andrea's shoulders. "Do y'all want me to stop?"

Andrea bit her lip.

"That's what I thought." Louise poked through the plastic cap and dug for another strand. Andrea swallowed hard but didn't say anything.

A collection of silver loops, no two alike, edged Andrea's ears, and a tiny garnet nestled in the fold of her nostril. Below her delicate collarbone, a tattoo of blue stars floated in her milky complexion. Just recently, she'd added a pointed stud in the fleshy fold between her bottom lip and chin.

She fingered the stud. "At least they numbed my chin first."

Louise pushed Andrea's chin to her chest and worked at pulling the hair of her nape through the cap. I told them about the auction and the supper and the quiet ride home. Then I told them about Greg's dream wife.

"Better not get tied to his hitching post," Louise drawled, not even trying to cover her delight in her own cleverness. "Why, he's tighter than bark on a tree."

It had been this way since Louise returned from a trip home to Louisiana. After a week of talking to her aunties in the weighted air of the bayou, her speech flowed like an alluvial stream of honey, slow and sweet and littered with colloquialisms and mixed metaphors. She punched the crochet hook through Andrea's cap.

"Ouch."

Louise inspected the crochet hook. "The tip's dull again." She sharpened the point on a stone and tested it against her finger. "That should do it."

"I can't believe that Neanderthal had a list of requirements," Andrea said. "I'm surprised he didn't ask for a dowry of cattle—or emus. Louise!"

"Sorry, sugar." Louise rested her hands on Andrea's head as she spoke. "Having a checklist isn't such a bad idea. Seems to me a thinking woman would know what kind of man she wants in her life—and the life of her son."

"No way. Where's the romance in that?" countered Andrea.

In the shadowed places where my dreams huddled, shaken and jumbled, I had a checklist, but it needed revision. I added *thoughtful* and *good conversationalist* to the bottom and crossed off *strong, silent type,* which had lingered on the list unchallenged from my teens. And you couldn't overestimate the value of a working air-conditioner, especially in what was proving to be one of western Colorado's hottest summers on record.

Andrea winced in pain again, so I excused myself.

She beseeched me with her eyes. "You're coming right back, aren't you? I want someone here in case Louise nicks an artery."

I assured her I'd be back as soon as I changed into shorts.

Louise called after me, "You'd best check on Ky. He skipped dinner to play a computer game."

The evaporative cooler clattered valiantly at the top of the stairs, but it was losing the battle against the heat. With each stair, the temperature climbed another degree. By the time I stopped at Ky's door, the heat encased me in its woolly grasp. He sat at his computer; the monitor's glow lit the room. I knocked on the doorframe with no response and entered.

"It's sweltering in here." I lifted the blinds and opened the window. A shaft of sunlight illuminated the chaos of a fourteen-year-old's life.

"Hey!"

"Son, Louise says you didn't eat."

Ky looked at me and I stifled a gasp. He could have been his father sitting there. When had his face narrowed and his nose lengthened and his blond hair dimmed to a muddy brown, just like Scott's? His ears—they were huge—and beads of sweat clung to the coarse hair of his lip and sideburns. When had facial hair appeared?

"You won't believe what she cooked for dinner. She called it tofu aspic, said it tasted like meatloaf. I thought I was gonna spew." He turned his attention back to the monitor.

I promised Ky some decadent macaroni and cheese when Louise went home.

"Thanks, Mom."

I crawled into Scott's closet and closed the door behind me. In the dim light, the world's dizzy dance slowed. Staring up at Scott's golf shirts, a revelation surprised me. Love would be different, if it showed up at all, the second time around. Greg may have understood that better than I. Second love was more practical, and a draft horse shouldn't be excluded so easily. That was depressing.

In the twenty months since Scott's death, I'd tiptoed through all of the anniversaries and holidays and birthdays, most of them twice. Anniversaries were now would-have-been anniversaries. Last August would have been our sixteenth anniversary, but no one had asked. When I'd turned the calendar to April, there was no need to hunt for the perfect birthday card with an innuendo only Scott would've understood. There was no one to notice when I took three ibuprofen tablets for a headache, or when I sighed over the credit card bill, or when I slammed a car door harder than necessary. And when Ky had bulleted a throw to home plate to make the last out, Scott hadn't been there to squeeze my hand in a way that meant *We sure have a great kid.*

Just because Scott was dead didn't mean he was absolutely gone. He still showed up whenever I presumed his opinion about a news story or a neighbor's house paint or the way an intersection had been reconfigured. Sometimes his presence was so real, I'd have to say good-bye to him all over again, but that was happening less and less, and I wasn't sure how to feel about it. Part of me wanted to hold him closer; part of me wanted to shoo him away; part of me wanted to scold him for being so careless with his life. And the part of me that insisted on thinking about all of this stuff was driving me crazy.

It wasn't like I didn't believe I would see Scott again. I did. I believed in heaven. Scott was there now, and someday, I would be too. For now, though, I only got to see the hurting side of death. That was faith, Louise kept telling me, to see one thing before my eyes but to live with a certainty that there was something better beyond my seeing. And someday, she promised me, I would bubble with joy just thinking about our eventual reunion. Until then, my greatest sorrow bisected my greatest hope.

A knock on the closet door startled me.

"Are you in there?" Louise knocked again. "Mibby, are you in there? Open up, now."

I obeyed because experience had taught me, if nothing else, Louise knew the meaning of perseverance.

"Honey lamb, you've got to stop doing this."

I couldn't argue with that, not in the heat and not after a date with Hopalong Cassidy.

Louise knelt before me. "Let me help you empty out this closet. You know, don't you, that Scott is clothed in righteousness, walking on golden streets with Jesus, the only light he'll ever need? If Scott plays golf in heaven—and why anyone would think hitting a teeny tiny ball a zillion times is fun—" Our eyes met, and whatever she saw stopped her cold.

"Oh, sweet pea, I'm so sorry. All I'm saying is Scott has a generous clothing allowance in his Father's house. He wouldn't mind one bit if you got rid of his golfing togs or his skateboard."

The skateboard was Ky's, off limits until school started again because he'd forgotten to wear his helmet. "Maybe after Ky goes back to school this fall."

"When you're right, you're right, sugar. Fall is a perfect time for fresh starts and new beginnings. First, we'll clean out Scott's closet, make sure these things get to someone deservin' and all, and once that's done, we'll purge your closet of denim and hippie sandals, which means we'll have to wrap you in a towel to go shopping."

The timer on her apron buzzed. "Phooey. I better go get Li'l Miss Tender Head neutralized. You'd think someone with that much metal in her head would be a lot tougher." Louise stopped to look at Scott's golf clubs in the corner of the room. "For heaven's sake, Mibby, there are cobwebs all over these golf clubs."

"I was going to—"

Louise covered her mouth with her hand. "I honestly don't know where my heart is today. I'm so sorry. Don't you go worrying about cleaning out Scott's closet. When the time is right, you'll know what to do." She closed the closet door on me and whispered through the crack. "If you keep the clubs so close to your bed, you might want to check the bag for spiders. I heard a story about a gal in Beauregard Parish who died when a nest of black widow spiders hatched in her hair."

Finally, some information I could use.

Her steps receded down the hallway and then returned. "Listen, Mibby. Manley's at that plumber's convention in Orlando all week. Do y'all mind if I ask Andrea to stay with me? The house is so quiet."

"No problem."

~~~

I woke up craving shish kebabs, but the hankering faded once I removed Scott's golf shoe from under my back. No light shone under the closet door. A happy thumping by the door told me Blink, my faithful black Labrador, was posted outside.

"I'm coming out," I warned him. His broad tongue lapped the sweat off my cheek. He deserved a belly rub for his kindness.

I found Ky in front of his computer. "Hungry?"

"I ate." He laughed at the monitor and typed frantically.

"What's up?"

"It's Salvador. His sister ran the car through the garage. Oh man, this is good."

The computer pinged. Over Ky's shoulder I watched another install-ment of Salvador's story appear—sans punctuation—on the screen, some-thing about his dad grounding Theresa for the rest of her life. Ky leaned forward with his hands poised to respond.

"I'm going downstairs for some ice cream. Want some?" I asked.

Ky typed a response to Salvador and waited.

"Ky? Did you hear me?"

"What? Uh, yeah. I said no thanks."

I knew better than to argue with him. It was one of those guy things. He honestly believed thinking something meant he'd said it, especially when talking to his mother. The *Living and Thriving with Teens* book I was reading said I had two choices in situations like this. I could be flattered that my male teen thought I was telepathic or be angry over his rudeness. The latter seemed a more genuine response, but sometimes my genuine responses stirred a hornet's nest.

More pralines and caramel for me.

In the kitchen, Ky's dinner dishes filled the sink and an empty box of cheesy macaroni mix lay by the stove with an empty carton of milk. I scooped some ice cream into a bowl and then attacked Ky's mess. On the way to the sink, I stepped in powdered cheese sauce, but the thought of confronting him about the mess, especially after a long, hot day with my fellow beasts of burden, seemed overwhelming. Besides, I was the one who had broken my promise to fix him dinner. I filled the sink with soapy water and massaged the growing headache over my eyes.

A mound of bubbles rose in the sink, but my arms grew leaden. Soon, the tears flowed. Since when had dishes in the sink demoralized me? Or for that matter, the dried rings of iced tea on the counter? Or a bill com-ing the day after I'd paid the others? Or the dust on an end table? Or a recall notice from a car manufacturer?

I was God's right-hand woman on Crawford Avenue. He kept the planets and stars in their places, and I did the rest, or so it seemed. Everything that happened in the Garrett household happened because of me or by me. And sadly, it wasn't enough. No breaks, no bouncing of ideas, and absolutely no divvying of chores. I would have ended up back in the closet for sure if I'd allowed myself to think about the dwindling bank account.

I'm so tired, Lord.

Blink lapped at the ice cream that had melted into praline soup. I shook my finger at him. "And you'd better put that bowl in the sink when you're finished, young man."

Right.

Day 7 of temps over 100. Ugh. Watched hummingbirds feed at low-growing Zauschneria garrettii. I love this tough little bloomer—fiery orange trumpets crowd the stems most of the summer. It's not named after me, but I wish it were. Common name is hummingbird trumpet, but that's not nearly as much fun to say.

I dreamed I was at the circus, the shabby kind with faded colors and beleaguered animals. A man in a red satin cape and top hat told me to lie on a bench and not move a muscle. He sounded like Ben, the guy I'd let slip away the summer before. When I turned for a better look, he was gone. A clown with a painted frown pounded out a drum roll. Scott? Dread tumbled in my stomach. In the audience, Ky ate popcorn and laughed with Salvador, but they were watching the dancing dogs in the next ring. Louise, dressed in pink tights and a sequined tutu, snapped her whip above Andrea's head. Andrea cringed and pulled a stocking cap over her eyebrows.

The drumming stopped when an elephant with a feathered headdress lumbered into the ring. Someone told me to close my eyes, but I didn't. The tent went black. I blinked, willing my eyes to adjust to the dark. Above me, the elephant trumpeted a warning. A soft pressure to my chest turned solid and crushing. My lungs burned for oxygen. I opened my mouth to call for help, but dream rules are strict: No yelling! The clown drummed faster and faster.

"Get off, Blink!" Louise said. "Mibby, wake up and make this ol' dog mind." Louise pulled on Blink's collar. "I can't believe you're sleeping with this mangy thing. Blink, get off!"

I moistened my teeth with my tongue. "Blink, it's time for breakfast." That did it. He swiped my cheek with his tongue and headed for the kitchen.

"He has more germs in his mouth than a chicken has feathers." Louise stood over me, hands on hips. "Tell me you don't let that dog kiss you on the lips."

"That's how he says good morning."

Since Louise's diagnosis of breast cancer, she'd turned to clean living, become a guru of healthy eating, and appointed herself captain of the nutrition police. No more fat-rich treats or white flour or red meat for her. All comfort foods—especially the fried ones—had been replaced with colorful vegetables and fish, hardly the kinds of food that would coax me out of bed.

Not wanting to suffer alone, she had recruited me as recipe tester and fitness-walking partner. Honestly, I would eat roadkill to help her, and the results hadn't been all bad. My form was decidedly less pear-like, but getting up before the sun to walk was pure torture. That's why Louise had a key to the house. It took a boatload of cheerfulness to rouse me out of bed at five thirty.

"I brought you one of my tofu energy bars, sugar."

"Maybe later," I said. To stay in the sheets for a moment longer, I told Louise about my dream.

She wrinkled her nose. "I only need to know one thing. Could you smell that ol' elephant?"

"No."

"You best get dressed while I think on this."

While I rifled through the laundry basket for walking clothes, Louise made the bed. No turning back. Once she'd smoothed the quilt into place, she sat on the edge of the bed.

"Sugar, there's no great mystery here. You're as tired as a plow mule at the end of the day. The elephant represents the things that demand your attention. No one can be as tired as you and feel up to tackling the world."

She stood up and adjusted her waistband. "It's a good thing I'm here to lead you to the Rock, Mibby girl. We'll give that stinky ol' elephant to Jesus. He'll tame the beast. Now put on your walking shoes. Daylight's a-wastin'."

We stepped into the darkness and let Blink set the pace. The morning wore an old flannel shirt, light but warm. Louise blotted her face and offered her water bottle. "I bet I looked ravishing in those pink tights."

<center>~~~</center>

Before starting the work day, I stopped by the growing yard—a fancy way of saying a small patch of gravel behind the garage—to walk through the flowerpots I'd designed and planted for Margaret and Walter's wedding. Margaret was one of my garden maintenance clients from the very beginning of my business, Perennially Yours, so I wanted the ten pots she'd ordered for her garden wedding to be perfect.

Although the flowers had to be delicate and color-perfect, they couldn't be sissies to survive August's heat. I chose the tough guys of the flower world. The theme came from Margaret's wedding suit, pink with a white lace overlay, and the strawberry pecan wedding cake. I'd thumbed through countless plant catalogs with a swatch of her dress in hand to find the pinks that ranged from baby's blush to Pepto-Bismol and hold-the-phone fuchsia.

I'd wanted the pots to have the form and style of a florist's arrangement, so I used variegated maiden grass to spray like a fountain beside a prolific petunia the color of raspberry stains. Barbie-pink *Argyranthemums* with yellow centers sidled up beside white geraniums with pink throats, and white starlike *Bacopa* spilled over the rim with *Calibrachoa* tainted with enough orange to be coral, but not too coral.

The real joy for me was their compliance. They grew. They branched. They budded. They bloomed. They thrived. On an unremarkable patch of ground, a miracle went unnoticed by everyone but me. Like God in the garden after all His toil, I looked at the pots and patted myself on the back.

It was very good.

Not as often as before, but more often than I appreciated, the sight of my work truck could be a whammy o' grief, one of those links to Scott that hurled me back to the moment when the cold steel of grief first entered my chest. As cartoonish as the old truck was with its pea-green paint and red bucket of daisies sitting on the cab, it had been Scott's vote of confidence in my success as a garden designer. The Daisy Mobile, as he'd christened the truck, had been waiting for me in the driveway at the end of my first week of business. As I'd rounded the corner to our house that day, I'd been thinking of a way to bow out of entrepreneurship gracefully. But seeing Scott beam with pride over his surprise convinced me to give the business another week or two. That was almost four years ago.

I wiped my nose on my sleeve and pumped the Daisy Mobile's gas pedal. When I'd coaxed a soft idle out of the old truck, I backed down the driveway and headed for the Harlan Chandler residence, my first maintenance client of the day.

Mr. Chandler opened his screen door just enough to hand me a check. I wiped my sweaty palm on my overalls before taking it.

"I'm tired of paying out all this money and not having anything to show for it," he said. His dog, Buttons, yapped in agreement.

Mr. Chandler was one of my fussier clients. I'd talked him out of firing me before. He just needed a fresh perspective. "Mr. Chandler, I know—"

"The warranty is up on those shrubs. I'll have to buy the replacements myself."

"There's a reason for—"

"The guy with the blue truck came by. He says what you've done here is pure neglect."

"I told you to change the settings—"

"And don't you think I won't tell all the neighbors how irresponsible you've been."

"Mr. Chandler. We've talked about your lawn. In this heat—"

"I knew you'd try to blame me. Git! And don't come back." The door slammed shut.

I explained his problem to the door. "Mr. Chandler, when it's this hot, you must water your lawn and shrubs more often but not every day. They'll drown."

~⌒~

"This will make you feel better," Margaret said, serving me a piece of cake.

"You won't tell Louise about the cake, will you?"

Margaret wiped my tears with the hem of her apron. "Our little secret," she said and winked. "Let me make a fresh pot of coffee."

She heaped coffee into the coffeepot's basket. Coffee wasn't on Louise's new diet, either. "You have to tell me honestly how you like the cake," Margaret said. "It's the recipe I'm testing for the wedding. Walter's mama made it for his birthday every year, but I don't think she wrote down all the ingredients, if you know what I mean."

From the beginning, Margaret and I had shared the triumphs and trials of only sons. And since Scott's death, we'd shared being widows, too. If I could build my own family, I would make Margaret my grandmother.

The screen door squeaked open. "Sunshine, I brought you some flowers," Walter called. The satiny folds of Walter's face tinted pink when he saw me. Margaret slipped her arm around his waist and kissed his cheek. He thrust a bouquet of Shasta daisies into her hands. "Here."

"What happened to you?" he asked me.

"Now, don't give her a hard time, Walter. She's been crying. I told her Sonny won't be paying for her services once we're married." Margaret served Walter a generous slice of cake. Her gray hair flowed in sparse strands over one shoulder, and when she smiled at him, I glimpsed the girl she'd once been.

She massaged her gnarled knuckles. "I tried to convince that no-account son of mine I needed your services more than ever. Some days my hands hurt so bad, and Walter's knees was just operated on last winter." She batted her aggravation away with a flip of her hand and asked earnestly, "How you liking the cake, Mibby?"

I worked the cake over my tongue and closed my eyes to concentrate. "There's a sweet but delicate strawberry flavor, and I like the strawberry bits in the frosting. Something's missing, though. I can't put my finger on it."

Walter collected the last of the crumbs between the tines of his fork. "Perfect, never tasted better."

Margaret's eyes sparkled with mischief. "Does it taste like your mother's?"

"Exactly, only better." He held up his plate for another piece.

Margaret obliged. "Walter, didn't you notice I forgot the pecans?"

"Never liked pecans much."

She giggled and poured the coffee. Walter busied himself with stacks of embossed invitations and silver-lined envelopes. He tidied the piles, set the pens parallel, and opened an address book.

Margaret waited with my cup and saucer in her hand. "You weren't just crying over losing my business, were you? There's something else."

"You know me too well," I said, hoping my acquiescence earned me the cup of coffee. But it didn't.

"This doesn't have anything to do with Greg, does it? He didn't do nothing, you know, ungentlemanly on your date, did he?" Margaret cocked her head and waited. I hated cold coffee.

"No," I said, "he was the perfect gentleman."

"He said you told him to marry his horse."

Walter coughed into his napkin, and his eyes danced with amusement. He showed promise.

I told Margaret and Walter about my date with Greg. She bent close and whispered, "Greg was Walter's idea."

"Now wait a minute—" he started.

"Now, you get busy with them wedding invitations before I change my mind."

"Again?" he said, smiling.

"Just leave the groom line blank," she said. "Me and Mibby are going out to the garden. Someone I like better might walk by and ask me to marry him."

Walter's shoulders sagged.

"Oh, baby cakes," Margaret cooed.

Feeling extraneous, I slipped out the screen door. At the Daisy Mobile, I hitched on my tool belt, slathered my freckles with sunscreen, and pulled a broad-brimmed hat to my eyebrows. Before I sharpened my pruners, I doused myself in bug repellent. I caught my reflection in the driver's window and added zinc oxide across my nose.

Margaret's yard needed some urban planning in the south bed. The coreopsis pressed aggressively into the bloody cranesbill and paprika yarrow. I couldn't do much about that now, but I would return in the fall to divide the plants, paid or not, my wedding present to the newlyweds. I snipped the browning blossoms of the coreopsis to encourage another bloom cycle before the wedding. The bucket brimmed with trimmings by the time Margaret joined me.

"I forget how tenderhearted that old sweetie is," she said, offering one of the stools she held. "But it sure is fun making up." She hummed "Wonderful Grace of Jesus" as she clipped at the yarrow.

Margaret and Walter had been neighbors for over forty years. With their spouses they'd weathered good times and bad—births, deaths, children sent off to war and children lost to war, mine closings, more than one drought, and of course, the deaths of their spouses. When Quentin died, Walter took a closer look at Margaret. He liked what he saw but knew Quentin would be a tough act to follow, so he staged an act of vandalism against Margaret's roses. Walter wanted Margaret to look to him for protection and more. Since it was Louise, Andrea, and I who discovered Walter's misguided attempts at courting, Margaret doesn't know about his attack against her roses. The four of us swore a vow of secrecy to give love a chance to grow. That was Louise's idea. Margaret and Walter were marrying in seven weeks. They would have married sooner, but Margaret had wanted her daughter to be at the wedding.

Margaret added her clippings to my bucket. "I'm sorry Greg wasn't the one."

I scooted my stool to the next coreopsis plant. I followed the stems from the spent blossom down to its base and cut. An ache burned in my lower back, and sweat pasted my T-shirt to my body. A broad expanse of flowerbed still awaited my attention. Margaret mopped her forehead with her sleeve.

"Margaret, you don't have to be out here today. It's awfully hot already, and I know Walter would love your company."

"He's okay. He has his little job to do." Margaret touched my shoulder. "It's you I'm concerned about."

I would have loved to set her mind at ease, told her I was over the worst of it, but I wasn't.

"Mibby, I have a secret to tell you. Walter wasn't my first choice. Another man at church caught my eye a while back. I wanted him bad. He was good-looking and had a real nice pension and a condominium on the golf course." She waved off my protest. "I know, those sorts of things shouldn't matter. That shows you how petty I can be.

"I watched my Casanova at potlucks to see what he liked to eat," she continued, "figured I'd woo him through his stomach. He ate everything but the tablecloths, I tell you. That didn't worry me a bit. In my courting days, back when I pined for Quentin, I always baked a Passion Fruit Blossom Cake. The pastor of the country church we attended renamed it Proposal Cake because all the boys feigned a proposal after taking one bite. All of the boys except Quentin, I might add."

Margaret frowned and squinted down on her memory. "Where was I? Let's see. Oh yes, I figured I had a secret weapon no man could ignore in that cake. At our next potluck, I parked that cake right in the middle of the banana nut breads and packaged brownies and waited. I should have paid better attention. Casanova was a chocolate-loving man. I don't know how I missed that little detail. He fell for Edith Connor's Chocolate Truffle Cake with Raspberry Sauce, and then he fell for Edith. They married a while back. They took a cruise to Tahiti for their honeymoon."

Margaret paused to watch Walter empty the trash and give her a shy wave. "All the while, Walter lived right there, working with all his heart to meet my needs. When I finally realized that, I discovered I'd loved him for a long time."

As Margaret talked, she combed her hair with her fingers and twisted it into a bun at the nape of her neck and fastened it with a clip from her pocket. She caught loose strands around her face in a tortoiseshell comb, one on each side of her head. There was my Margaret, right out of a black-and-white movie, soft cotton and rose water. My heart trembled at the thought of not seeing her regularly.

"I'm going to miss you, Margaret."

"Don't talk like that. We'll see each other." She frowned. "Mibby, did you hear what I said about that Casanova?"

"Sure I did, but I'm not a very good cook."

She groaned. "Now listen carefully. I almost missed the love I had right next door. I'm telling you, don't do that. Keep your eyes open to all the possibilities. Your Prince Charming may walk by your house every day."

Margaret's heart beat in the right place, but the only single men in my neighborhood carried Sesame Street lunchboxes or earned senior discounts at Pizza Man. Things were bleak. The way I saw it, going AWOL from the whole dating mess would be safer than entering the fray, especially with all those Hopalong Cassidys out there looking for beasts of burden.

"I'm not really looking for a husband, Margaret. I've had my one true love. I don't want to be greedy."

"Honey, you talk about love like you can use it up. Not even you can do that. True love flows from God's heart to yours." I conceded her point with a smile, although I doubted anyone but Blink would love me anytime soon. I worked silently, moving on to the purple coneflowers and the remnant of Shasta daisies Walter had left behind.

Margaret cleared her throat. "I told a nice boy at the market about you."

～⌒

When I drive up a bachelor's driveway, leading to the home where he lives in sweet ignorance of all things whimsical, I don't expect to see certain things, like birdbaths and gazing balls and fairy statues strategically placed among the spirea and viburnum. Patio furniture, mismatched and shabby, would sit on the front deck. You'd be lucky to find a chair without a rusty puddle on the seat or a broken leg that needed propping just so. My prejudice probably sounds sexist, but I've seen it too many times to believe otherwise.

Ben Martin's patio furniture sat arranged for conversation, and the chairs were festooned with puffy chintz pillows in stripes, florals, and checks, mismatched yet harmonious, the hardest decorating style to pull off. Either Ben was more in touch with his feminine side than I'd realized or the unthinkable had happened—a woman, *another* woman.

Ben had asked me to design a memorial rose garden for his deceased wife the previous spring. Spending time with another griever had been the last thing I wanted to do, but his garden was so pitiful and his compassion so compelling that I buckled to his request easily. And yes, it was true; he was some kind of gorgeous with those bittersweet chocolate eyes of his.

"Coming in?" And there he was, Ben, clearly enjoying my astonishment.

I didn't care. His military haircut had grown unruly waves to touch his ears, and his eyes, as delicious as ever, beckoned me. I had an irresistible urge to bake a warehouse full of pies from scratch, the impressive kind with lattice tops sprinkled with sugar. He looked that good. I was so glad I'd showered and washed my hair when I'd gone home for lunch.

"The yard looks great," I told him, getting out of the Daisy Mobile. "Just great."

He gestured toward the house. "I had some help. I don't know anything about decorating stuff. Claire helped me."

Uh-oh.

I shouldn't have been surprised. I'd seen less and less of Ben over the months until his visits stopped altogether. I reasoned it was for the best, in the same way you would reason a broken leg gave you time to rest. After all, we both needed time to heal from our losses. His wife, Jenny, had died only several months earlier, Scott not much earlier than that. No matter how warm Ben's hand had felt in the small of my back, a romantic relationship wasn't right just then, so I'd asked him for some time. But now that another female was challenging my position, I struggled against the urge to raise my hackles and reclaim Ben like a fallen caribou.

I abandoned all primal property rights when Claire came out of the house carrying a tray of lemonade. She was Aphrodite in a business suit—blond, tall, polished. Even in heels, she walked effortlessly across the gravel driveway. Ben took the tray and introduced us.

She took my hand and met my gaze. "You're such a talented designer. I love the memorial garden you designed for Jenny."

"Thanks." Her eyes were a tranquil ocean. No danger of a rocky shore, no riptides, no rogue waves. Ben could depend on her.

"Great socks," she said. "I wish I could dress for work like that. You're so lucky."

Lucky? Me?

I wore Snoopy on one foot, Scooby Doo on the other. Both were dogs, so I guess I matched. That hardly made me lucky. She was the one with a safe place for Ben's heart.

Claire pointed to my nose and frowned. "You have something white . . ."

While I abraded the zinc oxide off my nose, Ben and Claire talked quietly about their dinner plans. She excused herself to clean the kitchen before returning to work. "I won't bother you two anymore." And to Ben, eyes smiling, she purred, "I'll see you later."

The fight-or-flight response quickened my pulse. As usual, I chose flight, although what professionalism I could muster in doggie socks compelled me to look at the ailing rosebushes Ben had called me about.

I knew at a glance the roses of his wife's memorial garden were infested with spider mites. Their ravages had left the leaves stippled and silvery, and if you looked closely, the webs on the underside had collected garden gunk. Spider mites alone loved the pressing heat, so they'd dominated gardens all summer, including mine.

"Don't tell Claire about the spiders," Ben said. "She really hates spiders."

"They're pretty small. She won't be able to see them unless she uses a magnifying glass."

"That's good." He ran his hands through his hair. "Can I get rid of them?"

I assured him he could. I knew I was being silly, but his cavalier attitude irritated me. Where was his concern for the plants? He needed to understand the gravity of the situation.

"You've got a pretty bad infestation here. Could be lethal," I said.

"Really?"

Now we could talk pest control. "Give the plants a cold shower with a powerful spray of water every day for a week or two." It seemed like good advice for him, too. I stared down at the struggling plants, thinking I'd stumbled into the twilight zone of male-female relationships, only there was no script, so no one knew what part they played. Was I the meddling neighbor or the alien pretending to be human? Most likely, I was the castoff. I decided to exit stage right.

Before I could move, Ben swept my bangs off my sweaty forehead. "I like your hair down, Mibby. It looks like fire."

His words fed the smoldering fire burning in the fallow place between my stomach and my heart, deepened my regret, even tumbled my resolve.

"I know," I said, turning to leave. "I sweat a lot in this heat."

I don't know what Ben thought would happen when I arrived at his invitation and Claire served lemonade that she'd oversweetened. I wanted to believe she had caught Ben off guard, that she'd shown up unexpectedly, that she'd presumed too much from a casual lunch date arranged by friends. Maybe he barely knew her. Better yet, she wasn't quite right in the head. Too bad none of that was true.

I said a silent prayer the Daisy Mobile would start on the first try. The starter complained but turned the engine over.

Thanks, Lord.

Ben leaned on my open window and looked down the driveway. "I wasn't expecting Claire to be here today. I was going to tell you . . ." He gestured toward the house and garden. "I'm sorry."

Me too.

The pot of plastic daisies on the roof of the truck rattled noisily as I sped away from Ben's house. The road undulated through alfalfa fields and dairy farms. Breathing got more and more difficult. Ben had moved on to a new . . . what? A new girlfriend? A soulmate? A fiancée? I pulled over in front of Harrington's Dairy. A herd of milk cows lifted their heads to watch me gulp for air.

"What are you looking at?" I scolded the closest heifer.

I should have known Ben needed someone else, someone whole, someone with matching socks, for crying out loud. Nothing personal, I told myself. Of course, choosing Claire was as personal as it could be. He chose someone who was not me—very, very not me. He could have found someone a tad battle-weary, someone who walked with an emotional limp when a storm threatened. But he hadn't. Never mind that I'd done nothing to encourage him. He'd moved on and so had I, only not quite as far.

And what was with the sweeping-the-bangs-off-of-my-forehead thing? *My hair looks like fire?*

I put the Daisy Mobile in gear and waved good-bye to the cows. Knowing the door to Ben's heart had been bolted was a good thing, I rationalized as I ground the truck into third gear. A woman taking charge of her life needed to know when the key had been removed from the lock and thrown into the moat. Ben was behind a locked door. At a stoplight, tears began to spill onto my cheeks.

Ben is behind a locked door.

The heat settled on me as if I'd been buried in sand. I twisted my hair into a ponytail and pulled it through the hole in my Rockies cap. Evaporating sweat cooled my neck for a whole nanosecond. And then my face burned with embarrassment. Of course Ben had noticed my hair. Let's face it, when it came to my hair, ease had eclipsed my drive for style long ago. Arriving at his house with carefully coifed locks was like shouting, "Hey baby, come see about me!"

Oh, brother.

The light changed. At the next red light, I wrote myself a sticky note to call Virginia, my hairdresser, and stuck it to the dashboard.

~⌣

I found Blink lying in a cool nest he'd dug for himself under the lilacs. Hollyhocks feathered his bed. He avoided looking at me and hunkered low. In his predator's mind that still sparked and sputtered now and then, if he didn't move, he didn't exist. I learned that on Animal Planet. Fortunately, I was higher up on the food chain.

"Blink, what have you done?"

He worked his jowls nonchalantly.

"Blink?"

I knew better than to expect him to take responsibility for his actions. He'd already forgotten he'd dug up my majestic, tall-as-me, transplanted-from-my-grandmother's-garden, absolutely favorite, always-anticipated, hot-pink hollyhocks. Then why did he look so guilty?

"Blink, you picked a very bad day to be a naughty dog."

He crawled to my feet and rolled over to reveal his muddy underside. I added giving the dog a bath to my list of things that wouldn't get done that day. I sat with him on the damp earth and rubbed his crusty belly.

"I've had a hard day, old pal."

Blink wiggled closer. I lay beside him playing a mental game of "What if?" At the end of the game, losing two accounts, Margaret's and Mr. Chandler's, meant there was still too much money going out and even less coming in. And, oh yeah, my heart had been drop-kicked into oblivion.

I closed the book and turned off the light while trying to avoid reading the clock on the nightstand. One-twenty. Only four hours until Louise came to walk. I turned the light back on and reached for yet another parenting book, *You Only Think You Remember What It's Like to Be a Teenager*. The book was big and heavy and completely void of pictures. By the third paragraph of the introduction, my breathing slowed and my lids burned with sleepiness. I reached to turn off the light.

Tap, tap, tap.

"Mibby?" Andrea whispered through the door. "Are you awake? There's something you better see."

She led me to the basement. "I got home an hour ago. I wanted to take a shower, but the water didn't get hot. I waited awhile and tried again. The water was like ice."

I didn't like where this conversation was going. Something wasn't working, and when something wasn't working, it cost too much to get it fixed.

"So I thought I'd check the water heater," she said, leading me through the dark house. "I had a real old one in my last apartment. The pilot light went out all the time, usually at the worst possible time." Andrea flipped on the basement light. A lake lapped against the bottom stair. As I waded to the water heater, she asked an excellent question: "Should I turn off the electricity?"

JULY

13

Tomatoes are a no-show. Nights aren't cool enough for fruit to set — or for me to sleep. I noticed about a third of the tomatoes at Kobayashi Farm are infected with curly top. Mine too. A summer without tomatoes? It's too terrible to consider.

"Pick up the pace, Mibby. I have a new guest coming in ten minutes." Beside me, Louise swung her arms broadly and extended her stride.

"But it's six o'clock in the morning."

"I'm up. Besides, it's Connie McManus."

"Connie? Connie has cancer? I didn't know."

A secret army of cancer patients marches just out of view of the everyday world. I'd entered the fray with Louise. I had driven her to chemotherapy, where she would sit for hours with an IV drip of drugs designed to kill fast-growing cancer cells, only they weren't very discriminating. Within weeks, Louise had lost her hair and the light in her eyes had dimmed.

Louise insisted that God had a reason for her suffering. Until she knew what it was, she said she would keep busy loving the Lazy Boy Brigade, the patients who sat with her tethered to their own IV poles. She shuffled from recliner to recliner reading Scripture, telling jokes, and mostly listening to the patients' stories. If they let her, and most did, she held their hands and prayed for heaping portions of blessings for them.

Along with the other family and friends who accompanied the patients, I became an honorary member of the Brigade's community. We shared each other's triumphs and setbacks. Joe brought pictures of his new grandson. Kay's daughter made chintz caps for the ladies when they lost their hair and sporty driving caps for the guys. And when Frieda died from a virulent colon cancer, we even mourned together. Later, when the chemo drained Louise's energy, I tucked a quilt under her chin and let her sleep. As she slept, I did a pitiful imitation of her ministrations. The Lazy Boy Brigade was too polite to complain.

At the conclusion of her treatments, Louise reopened her bed-and-breakfast as the Still Waters Inn for folks who traveled from across the region to Orchard City for their treatments. She liked to tell folks she'd taken the name from the Twenty-third Psalm. The Still Waters Inn gave people a place to feel at home and find refreshment for their weary souls and bodies. I guessed that meant Connie McManus now, too.

Connie was one of those ubiquitous women of the church. Whatever the need, large or small, Connie eagerly met it. She baked, cleaned, taught, collated, and prayed, all with a contagious smile. After Scott died, she brought plates of food and only spoke to apologize for not having brought a bouquet of dahlias. Whenever I saw her at church, she asked me about Ky. I loved her for that. Although I wasn't sure I wanted to hear the answer, I asked Louise about Connie's prognosis.

Louise's answer kept time with her steps. "Caught early. She'll be fine. Chemo's hard. Larry wants . . . her watched."

"Her son?"

"First service. Sits in back. Very tall. Beard."

Like I would go to the first service. "I thought he lived in Virginia."

"That's right. Moved home . . . to help. It's been . . . over . . . a year."

"A year? I don't think so. I would've known."

"Sugar . . . you've been . . . distracted."

Truer words had never been spoken. But while I'd never met Larry, I'd known about him for as long as I'd known Connie. If she was whistling, it was because Larry had sent her flowers for no reason at all, and she'd shown me at least a dozen greeting cards from Larry—some flowery and some bitingly funny. She mentioned more than once that he'd received a commendation from the university where he worked, and there were a few times she'd asked me to pray for him because he'd gotten down on himself. It had been a while since I'd talked to Connie about Larry. *But a year?*

As we turned the corner to Main Street, a Sweet Suzy delivery truck stopped at the curb in front of Louise's house. Just the thought of all those Sweet Suzy Strawberry Cream Balls in the truck made my stomach growl.

"Is that you?" Louise asked.

"I'm *hungry*."

A tall man with broad shoulders and a full beard helped a dark-haired woman out of the passenger side of the van. That had to be Larry delivering Connie into Louise's care. The biggest tabby cat I'd ever seen waited for them on the sidewalk.

"Double time," demanded Louise. "I want to greet them." Blink caught sight of the cat and pulled hard on the leash. I trotted behind him.

Larry stooped to support Connie with an arm around her waist as they walked slowly up the front walk. Louise rushed to greet them at the porch steps. I hung back with Blink but not far enough. He barked wildly at the cat until I got his attention with a jerk of the leash and a command to sit. To my amazement, he did what I asked. I wrapped the leash around my wrist anyway.

Connie stood up straighter and greeted me with a question about Ky's baseball season. Wasn't that like Connie to be asking about my son when she was wading in her own dark waters? And then she introduced me to Larry, who wasn't at all the man I'd pictured him to be. I blinked away the image I'd held of him as a tweedy professor. The man before me was lumberjack material, congenial and self-assured, and from the length of his hair, he'd been out in the woods a tad too long. Evidently, the university had a forestry department. What was he doing working as a Sweet Suzy deliveryman?

I was about to ask Larry if he had any Strawberry Cream Balls in the van when the cat sauntered up to Blink and arched its back. Blink cried pitifully and gave me a look that meant, *Mom, let me eat the kitty, please.* The cat hissed. The tremor of Blink's muscles traveled through the leash.

"Blink," I warned.

"Don't worry," Larry said. "Goliath can take care of herself."

Oh really?

Blink inched closer to the cat and I let him. For a moment, Goliath allowed Blink's nose to touch hers, and then the cat pummeled Blink's nose like a punching bag. We all laughed until Blink bolted with a yelp. The leash went taut and my legs buckled under me. And then I was staring up at the sky, my lungs burning for air.

Louise called to me. "Sugar baby, are you all right?"

From nearer, a man's voice, calm and deep, told me about his tomato patch. "I'm trying those Sweet One Hundreds. I didn't do so well with Early Girls last year."

Huh?

Before I knew it, my lungs filled with air and I was wondering why he hadn't planted my favorite tomato, a sweet and persistent Fantastic.

Larry's face filled my field of vision. His eyes were impossibly green. "Better?" he asked, smiling with amusement.

A warm flush worked its way up my chest toward my face, so I started to sit up. With a hand to my shoulder, Larry stopped me. "Wait a minute. You had a pretty hard fall."

"I'm *fine*."

Louise's and Connie's faces pleated with concern, but I pushed away Larry's hand and stood. The world teetered, spun, and slid out of view. All I saw was blue sky again. Larry caught me, and this time, I lay back down without complaining. The ground was solid and reassuring.

"Gracious sakes, should I call 9-1-1?" Louise said.

"That won't be necessary," Larry said, chuckling.

What's so funny?

"She just got the wind knocked out of her," he said.

"I need to find Blink," I said. Traffic had picked up in front of Louise's house, and I lay there as conspicuous as a bad haircut. I wanted out of there.

"You know Blink's gone home," Louise said. "He always does."

That was true. I closed and opened my eyes to see if the world had stopped leaning to the left.

Connie spoke with authority. "Larry, when Mibby's ready, you're giving that girl a ride home."

I sat up. "That won't be necessary. I'm fine, really. My house is just across the alley." The horizon remained stationary, so I stood. Larry held my elbow. I stepped out of his grasp. "Why don't you help your mother into the house? I got up too fast, is all."

"I think Connie's right," Louise said. "I don't want you walkin' home. You might fall and hit your head on something sharp and lay in the alley until who knows—"

"*Louise!*"

"Well, you *could.*"

There was nothing more morbid than a Southerner's imagination, and I wanted to prove her wrong, but honestly, my legs were feeling rubbery. I lingered near the stair railing.

Louise touched Larry's forearm the way she does when she wants to speak to a person's heart rather than his head. She looked positively elfin looking up at him. "Don't you worry over your mama one bit. God's in the business of restoration. Connie's headed for the still waters where she can drink deeply and rest in the Shepherd's presence. Before you know it, she'll be sportin' exercise togs and running circles around all of us. But we'd best get started." Louise and Connie turned to walk up the stairs, stopping briefly after each step to rest. To see Connie bent under the weight of her treatments made my chest tighten and my throat ache.

I called after her, "I'll be praying for you, Connie."

As soon as I sat down in the passenger's seat of Larry's truck, the sweet scent of his cargo made my mouth go juicy and my stomach growl again.

Larry laughed. "I have that kind of effect on women. Try one of these." He handed me a package of oatmeal date bars from an opened box behind the driver's seat. That explained the mild softness of his middle.

As unsettling as the morning had been, I needed more sugar. "You wouldn't happen to have any Strawberry Cream Balls, would you?"

While Larry shuffled boxes to find the cream balls, I looked around the cab of the van. Not one gum wrapper sullied its floor. The only personal items, besides Goliath and her bed, were a jumbo-sized cooler, probably his lunch, and a book about Emperor Hirohito flagged with multicolored Post-it notes.

Huh?

Larry checked for traffic in his mirrors and pulled away from the curb. I looked out the window, willing the morning's misadventures behind me and hoping Larry wasn't the talkative type. Before we'd moved beyond Louise's driveway, Goliath jumped onto my lap.

"Goliath isn't much of a people cat," Larry said. "She must like you."

I smiled, but I was pressing against her, hoping she would return to her bed to leave me with my cream balls. Goliath played with the flesh of my thigh with her claws, so I gave up trying to open the cellophane package and stroked her fur—until she tried to nip my hand. *Fine!* I tore open the cream balls and reached the creamy center with my first bite.

"You know, now that I've saved your life, you're indebted to me." Larry said this with a broad smile that crinkled the corners of his eyes.

So, he was a kidder. I could handle that. Better than that, I could dish it out. "Funny, I was thinking the opposite. Since your cat nearly killed me, you owe me a week's supply of Sweet Suzy Strawberry Cream Balls."

At the stop sign, we waited for a break in the traffic streaming toward downtown. I sucked the filling out of the second cream ball.

"Your life is worth more than a carton of pastries, don't you think? How about a nice steak dinner at the Riverbend? If we hit it right, we might even get to watch the sun set behind the Monument."

First Hopalong Cassidy and now the Sweet Suzy man. I didn't like the way this trend was headed. And I didn't trust men with beards, unless, of course, we were talking Jesus or Santa Claus, because beards were nothing but fuzzy masks. Who knew what a man was hiding under all that hair? Besides, Larry had quite an ego for someone who wore a pink-striped shirt with Sweet Suzy's face embroidered over his pocket. By the time I'd decided to tell Larry I wasn't dating at the time, which technically wasn't a lie, the traffic held his undivided attention. I hoped that somewhere in the back of Larry's brain a buzzer had gone off and the dinner invitation had timed out. Thank goodness men had such short attention spans.

Then I remembered the odd question he'd asked when I'd been lying on the ground. "Why'd you talk to me about tomatoes when I couldn't breathe?"

His smile widened. "To distract you. It helped, didn't it?"

I had to say it, but I didn't have to like it. "Thanks." I barely waited for the truck to come to a stop before I shoved Goliath off my lap and stepped onto the curb in front of my house.

"Mibby—"

"I sure hope your mom is feeling better soon."

"The invitation's always—"

"Thank you. Thank you so much. That's so nice of you. Really. Have a nice day." And because he had given me a ride home, I gave him some good advice. "The best slicing tomato is a Fantastic."

Once inside the house, I peeked around the curtain on the door to make sure he drove away, but he was leaning over the passenger's seat, grinning and waving. I dropped the curtain.

"Who are you growling at?"

I jumped at the question, but I was getting used to Droop's unannounced morning visits. Since taking a job remodeling my next-door-neighbors' Dutch Colonial, there were days Droop hunkered down in our kitchen until the Morgans drove off for work.

"Nobody," I told him.

"*Nobody* sure made your face red."

"Louise and I walked faster today. I had to get her home in time to welcome a new guest."

"Is that so?" Looking over his reading glasses, he asked, "This doesn't have anything to do with your dog running home like his tail was on fire, does it?"

While I poured coffee, I told Droop the whole story. "And then Larry the Sweet Suzy man actually asked me out." Saying that out loud made my desperate reality play out before my eyes. All of the Scott types were happily married long ago and would stay that way. The Bens, after a brief period of mild dementia in which they dated women evolved from middle-school wallflowers, recovered quickly and moved on. That left the Hopalong Cassidys and the bearded Sweet Suzy men for me.

"That isn't strawberry cream on your chin, is it?" asked Droop.

Droop—short for his full nickname of Droopy Drawers—had entered our lives almost two years earlier as a master craftsman when Scott and I decided to add on a family room and remodel the kitchen. We'd done most of the restoration work on our no-frills Victorian ourselves. Droop was our extravagance and the expression of our self-doubt, not necessarily in that order. We got more than a carpenter. Droop became our plain-talking uncle and resident philosopher, a man who did not economize on opinion. And, like me, he couldn't say no to a sweet treat. I rubbed the sticky cream away with my sleeve.

"Another cup of coffee?" I asked.

"Sure 'nuff." While I added cream and sugar to my coffee, Droop complained about my neighbors. "Besides not owning a coffeepot, all they do is bicker, bicker, bicker. Each and every morning, without fail or time out for national holidays, they fight about which way is up."

I reminded him that he had Louise to thank for their business, not me. I needed to be in his good graces. It would take more than words. I poured animal crackers onto a plate and set it beside Droop. "I need a favor."

He pushed his glasses up the bridge of his nose. "Are these mangled jungle creatures s'posed to soften me up? Now, if you got any of them Magnum P.I. muffins Louise bakes, we can wheel and deal."

I offered to bake him something myself.

"I'd rather you didn't. What's up?"

I showed him the water heater, drawing out all the details of cleaning up the mess to stir his sympathy.

"No can do, Mibby." He drank the last of his coffee. "I got the water off next door for most of the day, so I have to finish plumbing out the powder room before they get home and start bickering again. Besides, Honey's brother is visiting with his newest wife. They expect me to get them to the bingo parlor the moment the doors open." Droop removed his painter's cap and crumpled it over his heart. "You know I'd do anything for you, as long as it don't get me in hot water with Honey. You best call a plumber." He settled his cap back on his head. Before he left he couldn't help offering a piece of advice. "You best lock the door before you go walking in the morning. There's some real kooks out there."

I didn't have the heart to agree with him.

The phone rang. Kathleen, a clerk at Walled Garden Nursery, greeted me cheerfully and listened to me complain about the heat.

"It's really cut into our business, too," she said. "Nobody wants to be out in their gardens. But I have a referral for you. Sorry it's not a design job. This sweet old man needs some rock work done."

Rock work meant muscle work, but I stifled my disappointment. The money would come in handy to cover the cost of the new water heater. I wrote down the man's name and phone number and asked Kathleen how she was getting along with the new owner.

Her voice stood up straighter. "We have a great selection of cactus. You won't be disappointed. Thanks for calling Walled Garden, the distinctive place to shop for all of your gardening needs. We dig your patronage. Good-bye."

The dial tone hummed in my ear.

~⌒

The plumber handed me the estimate. Once I saw the number circled at the bottom, I stopped listening and started scheming. If I didn't pay the utilities until the day they were due and I paid the auto insurance late but still in the grace period and sold all the living room furniture . . .

"Thanks for coming so quickly," I said, ushering the plumber to the front door. "I'll call you."

He stopped and planted his feet. "That'll be fifty dollars, then."

"For what?"

"For the house call."

"What did you do?"

"I gave you an estimate."

This man would never have made it in the garden design business—no design, no money. Come to think of it, I wasn't making it in the garden design business, either. "Listen," I said, "I can't afford to have you do the work, so I sure can't pay you for showing up and writing an exorbitant number on a piece of paper."

The man hugged his clipboard to his chest with beefy arms. "Time is money. My boss expects a signed work order or a check for fifty dollars from each house I call on. I can't afford to make him mad. Kids like to eat; wife likes to shop."

Naiveté had worked well for me in the past. I made my last stand. "No one said anything about a fifty-dollar estimate."

He shrugged. "S.O.P. Standard operating procedure, ma'am."

I wrote a check for fifty dollars.

I stood behind Ky watching cadaverous creatures on his computer monitor lurk behind crypts and ooze green slime. As far as I could tell, those were the bad guys. A bug-eyed boy with a metallic hairdo hunted the creatures with pulsating balls he carried in his pockets. When the boy decapitated an old woman with a sliding fast ball, I protested.

"That's disgusting."

"It's only a game, Mom."

"Ky, that stuff will be rattling around in your brain until the day you die. Is that what you want?" What a dumb question. I knew his answer before he said it.

"I don't care."

"I do." I remembered how much my mom's caring meant to me at fourteen. I shifted my strategy. "Ky, it's ten thirty in the morning and you're still in your pajamas. Have you fed Blink?"

He clicked something and the macabre world on his monitor froze in place.

"Okay," he said, barely hiding his contempt. "I'll feed him."

When he stood, I had to look up at him. "Wait a minute. Blink depends on you. From your tone, I hear you saying this game is more important than Blink. Maybe that's the problem."

He stomped out of his room. "I said I'd do it."

My fatal flaw, and I knew it, had not been setting ground rules for the computer earlier. One more thing was slipping through my fingers. If I didn't set limits, it wouldn't happen.

"Ky, wait a minute."

He shifted his weight and gave me the long-suffering look of having to placate a mother with dwindling cognitive function. I pointed an accusatory finger at the monitor. "Come back here and turn this off. From now on, you need to get your chores done before you get involved in anything else. Besides, Ky . . ." I wanted to give him a compelling reason to turn that game off, but nothing came to mind. So I told him to turn it off because I'd said so.

"That's not fair. You don't even know what it's about."

"You're right; I don't. But I know I don't want those images in my home."

"It's my home, too."

Oh really? I goaded him with sarcasm down the stairs and through the house to Blink's bowl. Blink, of course, followed behind eagerly. His glee only fed my angst toward Ky. "Are you prepared to make the mortgage payment this month? Maybe you noticed the windows need washing? Or the laundry needs folding? Better yet, will you be installing a new water heater today? And how about the bathrooms? If this is your home, you're probably dying for a chance to chisel the toothpaste out of the sink."

I would have stopped right there if Ky hadn't shifted his weight again and crossed his arms with a sigh.

"When you're ready to carry the responsibility of the house's mortgage and maintenance, you can play any computer game your heart desires. Your brain can putrefy into slime and drip out of your ears. Until then, you live here by my good graces, and to do that, the game goes."

Oh, how I wish I had remembered how quickly the sweetness of sarcasm sours.

"Fine, just fine," Ky hissed. "You really know how to make a kid feel wanted. Thanks a lot." He bounded out the back door, mumbling under his breath. I only heard phrases like *on the street, leave me alone, some vacation.*

I couldn't let him have the last word. From the porch, I yelled, "Stop right there." And he did.

Now what?

"I'm leaving to meet a client in a few minutes, and I have a hair appointment after that. I should be gone an hour, maybe an hour and a half. I want your bed made, the trash taken out, your clothes folded and put away, the dog fed, and—"

"Don't worry. I'll *do* it."

"*Before* I return," I called to his back. "Do not turn that computer back on until we can talk about it nicely."

And I supposed that meant me, too.

~~~

"It's a little dated," Roseanne said as she showed me her kitchen. Over her shoulder, her daughter, Phoebe, watched me with the wide-eyed wisdom of a toddler and smiled coyly when she caught my eye. A pang of longing squeezed my heart when I remembered Ky at that age. I would have to beg his forgiveness when I got home.

"When I paint the cabinets and change the countertops, it'll be like a new kitchen," Roseanne said.

Her cottage in the college district was a far cry from the *Architectural Digest*-worthy home she'd shared with her then-husband Daniel. The whole cottage was smaller than her previous kitchen but warmer, like Roseanne. She had painted the living room a Mediterranean gold, like the sun softened by sea breezes. Plantation shutters cast stubby bars of shadow and light on the deep-hued oak floors. A loveseat and two club chairs faced a glass-topped coffee table smeared with pudgy handprints.

"It's cozy, don't you think?" she asked.

I wanted to plump myself and sit in the corner of her sofa like one of her tasseled pillows. "Oh yes, I could stay here forever."

Daniel had left Roseanne for another woman. Right there, you had to know the man was one pickle short of a bushel, as Louise would say. Roseanne's beauty reflected the shimmering warmth of an autumn afternoon, the dance of windswept leaves and smooth caramel, and all that loveliness resided in a hospitable heart, one that had cherished her husband and nurtured their tiny daughter. It all went to show his infidelity had nothing to do with what he possessed but with what he wanted, because he had left Phoebe, too.

Phoebe was Italian cream with roasted coffee-bean eyes and impetuous shafts of dark hair—too much for such a small child. She rubbed her eyes and buried her head in her mother's shoulder.

"Let me put her down," Roseanne said. "I'll be right back."

We sat on her covered patio looking out on what was possibly the saddest garden in the city. No trees. No lawn. One dead lilac. Lots of weeds and crusted soil. An uneven sidewalk divided the yard in two and led to a sagging gate and the alley beyond. Perhaps someone had tested nuclear devices there in the fifties. Perhaps worse, a long string of college students had called the cottage home over the last three decades.

Roseanne popped open two Diet Pepsis. "Can this yard be saved?"

"The cure may be worse than the disease, but yes, it can be saved."

"Have shovel, will dig," she said, clinking her can against mine. "I don't want Phoebe cheated out of a pretty place to play because her mommy and daddy didn't stay married. I want birds and butterflies to love living here, and I want a big sandbox for her to play in. Do you think I could build a playhouse? It won't be as nice as her fairy village at the old house, but—" Roseanne stopped abruptly and smiled broader than the occasion demanded. "But nothing, it'll be great."

After we measured Roseanne's yard, I sketched and talked. "When Ky was Phoebe's age, we installed a sand pit instead of a sandbox for him. We lined a shallow hole in the ground with weed barrier fabric and poured in the sand. Then we placed several boulders around the edges. For Ky, the boulders provided great cover for G.I. Joe commando raids, but he also leaned against them to read. By planting some boy-proof ornamental grasses, the sand pit became an integral part of the garden, not just a piece of equipment. I can still see him out there with a pile of books." I handed her the sketch. "How does that look to you?"

"I love the idea, but I worry about Phoebe playing out in the sun." Roseanne pointed to a spot behind the boulders on the sketch. "Could we plant a shade tree here?"

"Of course." I told her I would plant several shade trees but not to expect much shade before Phoebe started school. "I've been encouraging people to use the new cantilevered umbrellas. They give absolute shade and you can swivel them to an adjacent play area."

"That's why I love working with you," she said. "You think of everything."

We agreed the playhouse belonged on the north end of the vegetable garden so it wouldn't shade the tomatoes. Roseanne wanted a rose to climb up the side of the playhouse and another tree for afternoon shade. I penciled in a golden rain tree a bit north and west of the playhouse.

I explained how the drought and increasing demand on our water resources had made it important to design gardens to be water-thrifty.

"I don't want a garden full of cactus."

"If we use xeriscape design elements, you can have a garden that's colorful and soft. It means grouping plants with similar watering needs and choosing plants that are suitable for our climate. It also means downsizing, or even eliminating, the lawn."

Roseanne frowned.

"Trust me?"

"Yes . . ."

"Lawns for toddler play areas are overrated. When they're sitting, they're digging. That's what the sandpit is for. When they're walking, they want to be pulling or pushing something. A hard surface is better for wheels."

Her smile returned. "Go for it."

When I finished penciling in a few ideas, we moved to the air-conditioned house to put our feet up. I asked Roseanne how she was doing, knowing full well my question might open a floodgate.

"I won't try to kid you that it's been easy," she said. "Almost hourly I fight the pull of despair, and worse, this foul-tasting bitterness that seems to pop out of nowhere. Sometimes I fail miserably. When Daniel left me . . ." She shuddered. "It's always a choice. I can let the anger shape me into a pitiful remnant of myself, or I can exact the best revenge of all— live a happy, meaningful life full of good friends and maybe a true love." She ran her fingers through her hair. "I choose the good life." Again we clinked our pop cans.

She laid a brochure on the table. "Speaking of the good life, I have a great opportunity for you. Do not say no until you've heard me out."

Inside the brochure, a couple silhouetted by a sunset leaned toward each other. In another photograph, a man and woman danced on a terrace lit by moonlight and tiki torches. Whoever had created the brochure had found clip art for the hopelessly romantic. I steeled myself against Roseanne's spiel. Whatever she was selling didn't really exist.

"I know the dating scene hasn't exactly been wonderful for you. But this is totally different. It's a Table of Ten event I'm putting on at my church," she said.

Greg's face flashed before me and I said, "I don't think so, Roseanne."

"Don't make up your mind until I tell you about it. Okay?"

In my book, right after lottery tickets and warm potato salad, singles events occupied slot three of things to be avoided. But this was Roseanne, so I folded my hands over my satchel to listen, just to be polite.

"I went last month," she said, her voice airy with excitement, "and now I'm helping to plan this month's event. For one thing, I can promise you the food will be much better."

She noticed me squirm. She folded the brochure and got down to business. "This is how it goes. Five men and five women meet at the church and sit at a large round table. There's no pairing up of any kind. We sit boy-girl, boy-girl to encourage interaction, but that's the extent of the planning. I've booked a new caterer in town, Moroccan Dreams— very exotic, great authentic Moroccan food. The Symphony Guild used them for their fundraiser in May. The food was great. But that's beside the point. The important thing is all of the awkward stuff is eliminated. No wondering if you should meet him in a public place or give him your address and phone number. There are no decisions about where to eat or what to order. If you can't make conversation with the guy to your right, talk to the one on your left, or forget the men and talk with another lady. When it's time to go home, you offer your card to anyone you would like to call you, but then you get in your car and leave. The bottom line? You cast your net in new waters without any of the weirdness."

I wiped my palms on my pants. "I don't think so."

"I'll be there."

I rose to leave. "Small talk isn't my thing,"

"Then just listen, but you have to know that everyone's in the same boat. At last month's Table of Ten, we talked about the weather all through the appetizers. But by the time the soup came—a dreadful broth they called onion soup—you would have thought we'd been friends for years. I haven't laughed that much in a long time. I came home with a card from a guy, and we decided on the phone that we probably weren't a good match. So you see, the people attending are sincerely looking for a life partner. They're being very careful. An added bonus for me was meeting another gal with a baby Phoebe's age. We've baby-sat for one another and met at the park for a play lunch. She's really become a good friend. She understands completely what I'm going through."

"I don't know . . ."

"Mibby, you have to be an active participant in your own life. You have to look to find."

I tried to picture myself schmoozing with other singles. Instead, I saw Ben and Claire, heads together, making dinner plans. "I can't, not yet."

"I want it short, boyish, no care, maybe an inch long all over my head."

"Does this have anything to do with a man?" Virginia asked, shifting her weight from one stiletto-heeled boot to the other.

When Ben had complimented my hair days earlier, he'd made me believe I was at least as interesting as a pregame show—and it wasn't the first time. Truth be told, I had let it grow knowing Ben preferred my hair long. That was why I'd fussed over it and put on a clean T-shirt before going to his house to check on his roses. But then Claire had been there. The hair had to go. Cutting my hair was my way of declaring, *No more Ben.*

"It's the heat," I told her.

"It is a man, isn't it?" Virginia held my gaze in the mirror. "Isn't it?"

"Sort of."

Virginia's bracelets jangled as she patted my shoulder. "Look, honey, no man is worth self-mutilation."

She didn't know Ben.

Virginia had one foot in the sixties and one in the present with laced boots that put her in the nosebleed section. She wore a gauzy blouse of pink and brown with a suede miniskirt. A cameo hung from her neck on a velvet ribbon. I was about to ask her if she knew the way to San Jose when she demanded to know what the man had done to me.

When I finished the story about meeting Claire, the stylists on both sides of Virginia's station and their clients cooed sympathetically.

"You're going about this all wrong, girlie girl." With a curling iron lifted high, she declared, "This is war."

In one short hour, the miracle of modern chemistry had transformed me into Loretta Lynn's stunt double. "I like it," I said, sucking in my bottom lip to stop it from quivering.

"Now that your light is shining, you'll attract more wildlife, if you know what I mean." Virginia winked at me in the mirror.

Exactly. Birds could build their nests in the safety of my bangs and woodland rodents could burrow into the voluptuous waves. I paid her and left with thoughts of a hairspray-dissolving shower and shampoo. And then I remembered the broken water heater. Loretta Lynn and I shared more than a coiffure. I wailed like her, too.

～～◞

Blink lay staring at his empty bowl, and the contents of the waste-basket threatened to topple onto the floor. Obviously, Ky had ignored the list I'd given him. But I couldn't ignore the list of disappointments and setbacks I'd accumulated through the day, including the prospect of another cold shower. The anger that ignited and grew in my chest seemed completely justified.

"Ky!" I yelled from the mud room.

In the kitchen, an empty frozen entrée box lay on the counter with an open liter of Pepsi. The food tray, empty except for the green beans, marked Ky's lunch spot at the island along with a bag of potato chips and a popsicle stick lying in a puddle of orange syrup.

"Ky!" I yelled from the kitchen.

"Mibby?" Andrea, breathless and still dressed in her black-and-white uniform from the Pampered Cow, met me in the hall.

"Where's Ky?"

"Mibby—"

"Where *is* he?" I took the stairs two at a time, knowing without being told that he sat mind-numbingly close to the computer, but I enjoyed the heat of the question in my throat.

"Mibby, you should—"

I turned to face Andrea on the stairs. "This place is a mess. Has it ever occurred to you to ask Ky to clean up after himself or that maybe sitting in front of a computer all day might not be the healthiest thing in the world for a fourteen-year-old boy?" I pounded up the remaining steps before she had a chance to answer. Even in my anger, I knew Andrea wasn't to blame. It was my fault. Ky was my son, no one else's.

"Ky!" I shouted from the landing, and for effect, I bellowed his name again just short of his bedroom door. From in front of his computer, Ky and Larry gaped back at me.

"Mom?"

I breathed deeply to flush out the anger, but my heart still raced and my eyes burned with tears.

"Ky, Blink's waiting for you to feed him," I said as evenly as I could.

He tapped his keyboard and ran out of the room apologizing.

"And please take out the trash while you're down there."

"Hard day?" Larry asked.

"What are you doing here?"

"Trying to help."

"Distracting Ky from his responsibilities isn't helping."

"You're right about that. I better get going." He slipped past me and started down the stairs. He stopped halfway down and said, "I couldn't help noticing Ky's baseball gear. I coach the church's softball team. We have a few games left. We could use a ringer. Have Ky give me a call."

Over my dead body. "I'll think about it."

When I started to follow him, Andrea stopped me with a finger to my chest. "Larry installed a new water heater for you today. Ky helped. You might want to thank him. It seems like a healthy way for a fourteen-year-old boy to spend the afternoon."

I caught up to Larry at the garden gate. I took a breath, intending to beg his forgiveness and thank him profusely. All that changed when he smiled smugly.

"What made you think it was okay for you to invite yourself into my life? I'm perfectly capable of getting the water heater repaired," I said.

"When I came to pick up Mom at Louise's, they told me you needed some help, that things were a little tight for you. I thought I'd make this one day a little easier for you."

"Well, you didn't."

"Maybe you'll change your mind when you take a shower tonight."

He had me there. "I can't pay you for a couple of days, maybe longer."

"I'm okay with that."

"Good."

"Have you always had a hard time accepting help?"

When I'd had the crazy notion that I was a capable adult, accepting help had come easily. "No, not always."

"Then just say, 'Thanks, Larry,' and I'll be on my way."

"Thanks, Larry."

Before closing the gate, he turned to say, "You know, if we were sweethearts, you'd qualify for a fifty-percent discount."

I pitched a dirt clod that hit the gate dead center.

He grinned at me over the fence. "Your hair looks real nice."

I touched my hair, stiff with hairspray, and I hardly recognized my own head. Larry disappeared before I found another dirt clod.

～∽

I sunk my teeth into one of the Strawberry Cream Balls Larry had left with Ky. "Thanks, Larry," I said again, but only Blink heard me. I put the remaining cream ball into my nightstand drawer and took it out again. With the ceiling fan on high and the window open to the night songs of crickets, I munched in the dark and prayed.

"This was not my best day, Lord. Have you noticed that the road through the dark valley hasn't gotten any lighter? How about one good day, a day of mercy with no humiliation or being fired, or cranky clients, or arguments with Ky, or unpaid bills, or—dare I hope it—hairspray? A few hours of sleep would be nice, too. Twenty-four hours of smooth sailing. That's not so much."

I brushed the crumbs off the sheets. Blink jumped onto the bed and exposed his belly to the fan.

And because even God deserved a pat on the back, I thanked Him for the blessings, too. "Ky's healthy. That's one. The breeze from the fan feels nice. That's two. It's exciting to see Andrea awakening to your presence. That's awesome beyond belief. And yes, the Strawberry Cream Balls taste great. Thanks for those. And Larry? Listen, Lord, I don't appreciate how he just waltzed in here and took my water heater on as a good deed."

Every good and perfect gift is from above, coming down from the Father of the heavenly lights.

"Thank you for sending Larry to install a new water heater. Amen."

JULY 14

Temperature at six this evening was 105°. Even I stayed inside today when I should have tidied the flowerbeds. Be brave, daylilies! Keep the faith, coneflowers! Shine on, gaillardias!

I downshifted the Daisy Mobile into third to crest the hill above Walled Garden Nursery. The sturdy adobe home with its sheltered patio and rows upon rows of potted trees and shrubs filled a shallow depression. I parked near the scrolled iron gates that stood open and welcoming. There were only a couple of other cars parked in the customer parking lot. I congratulated myself for being an early bird.

Inside the stuccoed walls of the garden center's patio, long plant tables branched off the tiled walkway that led to the front doors and sales area within. Summer-blooming perennials filled the tables on the left—blanketflowers, asters, black-eyed Susans, and electric blue salvias. Annuals crowded the tables to the right—petunias, geraniums, and of course, tried-and-true marigolds. It had been several years since I'd worked at the garden center, but I couldn't stop myself from straightening a row of marguerites. I noticed the patio was quiet. Not one fountain gurgled; not one wind chime sounded. The metal hooks where lush baskets of petunias and sweet potato vines had hung in past years were empty.

That's strange.

"I want a million of these," said a woman using her pregnant belly as a shelf for small pots of zinnias. "My aunt grew them all along her front porch."

The woman's husband set down a clipboard to return four of the potted plants to the bench. "Maybe we should start with half a million."

"But they're cheaper by the dozen. Maybe we should get a cart."

"Maybe we should move into the house first."

In the checkered shade of the latticework, a tug of war between passion and temperance played out.

"They'll be gone by then," she said.

The husband said, "Carol," soft and deep. Her face went all satiny, and I knew she'd heard him say her name that way many times before. She returned the flowers to the bench, and they walked hand in hand through the door to the sales area. I stopped to realign the zinnia pots she'd disturbed and to allow my heart to settle back into its place before I followed the couple inside.

The couple stood before my former workmate. Being with Kathleen was like sitting under a catalpa tree on a hot day. Catalpas—sheltering, solid, and lush—are known as tornado trees in the Midwest because they bloom at the start of the violent-storm season. But here in the Southwest, the blooms mark the onset of sun-baked summer days and weightless summer nights. People tended to linger with Kathleen. That was a problem.

The husband unfolded a poster-sized paper that showed the outline of a house on a lot. His voice had stepped up an octave. "We're moving into our new house in a few weeks, and our baby is due about then, too. The lot's huge and I've never even mowed a lawn in my whole life."

I opened my mouth to pitch my services, but he said, "We don't have much money left for plants and all, but our parents offered to buy all the lawn stuff as a housewarming gift."

Never mind.

Undaunted, Kathleen said, "Don't worry, putting in a lawn's not that hard."

No, but it took a long time to explain how to do it, so I mouthed,

"Be right back" and headed outside to load the Daisy Mobile with petunias.

Each year, as the heat of summer peaked and perennials stalled in their blooming, I planted twelve flats of petunias for Gloria Langston. I showed up with the petunias, planted them in an hour or so, and sent a bill, which, this year, would come close to covering the cost of the water heater.

Thanks, Lord.

Back at the sales counter, several more customers now waited to be checked out, but Kathleen still instructed the couple on how to seed their lawn. I sipped water from the drinking fountain, perused the seeds for interesting varieties, straightened a rack of books, and revisited the drinking fountain before I eavesdropped on the conversation again. They hadn't gotten to the part about mowing yet.

"What do you recommend for amending the soil?" the husband asked.

I searched the greenhouses and the area around the potted trees and the bulk soils bins to find another salesclerk, or maybe the owner, to wait on me. Oddly, Kathleen worked alone that day, so I returned to the sales counter. I'd lost my place to a man in overalls carrying a concrete garden gnome. The man cleared his throat, but the husband pressed Kathleen for more information.

"My dad said we could get the manure cheaper from a dairy."

Oh brother. Now Kathleen had to deliver the spiel about the high salt content in fresh manure and the advantages of aged and shredded manure. The day was only getting hotter.

I helped myself to a piece of scratch paper to write Kathleen an IOU. I listed what I'd taken: twelve flats of petunias, one small bale of peat moss, and a packet of Salad Rose radish seeds. To make it official, I signed and dated the paper, added my resale number, and taped it to the cash register.

~⌒

At Gloria's garden gate, I offered her ancient spaniel a rawhide chew bone to distract him from my legs. He took the bone and disappeared into the house through a doggie door. That bought me an hour or so to plant all of the petunias. No time to waste.

I winced at the sight of Gloria's backyard. A fringe of dead grass edged the expanse of lawn and seeped inward where the green was tinged blue from the stress of heat and too little water. And worse, leaf scorch dulled her shrubs and perennials. Some of what I saw could be blamed on the heat, but most was evidence of neglect. Gloria had had a tough year of loss and health concerns. I hoped the petunias would cheer her up.

Listening to Michael W. Smith on my headset, I planted the flowers in tight groups of six to intensify their immediate impact. I had tamped the soil around clusters of red, white, and almost-blue petunias at the base of the flagpole when Gloria tapped me on the shoulder.

"Mibby, for heaven's sake, what are you doing here?"

"What?" I shielded my eyes against the sun to look at her. Despite the heat, Gloria was dressed in a mint-green blazer and pants with a silk confetti sweater underneath. It made me hotter to look at her.

"Didn't your son give you my message?" she asked.

"Message?"

"I don't see how I could possibly fuss with petunias in this heat—and the drought. It would be throwing good money after bad. Have you seen the lawn?"

My relationship with Gloria went back to the early days of my employment at Walled Garden. New to the area, she'd hung on every word I'd said. The result had been a garden she displayed proudly and a friendship we both enjoyed.

If I explain to her—

"You'll have to dig them up—all of them," she said.

I reminded Gloria how dependable our irrigation water was, even with the drought, and how her mulch would keep additional water requirements minimal, but she was determined to fulfill her civic duty to conserve water. How could I argue with that? I offered to leave the petunias I'd already planted, hoping she'd pay for them and the time I'd spent planting them, but she hesitated. Perhaps, like Mr. Chandler, she didn't trust me to do a good job.

Before she was forced to invent another excuse, I said, "Don't worry about it, Gloria. I'll remove the petunias and take them back to Walled Garden, no problem."

Gloria left for her bridge game and I dug up the three flats of petunias I'd managed to plant—two hundred and sixteen of them. I worked fast so I could return the petunias that remained in their flats to Walled Garden before they had a chance to wilt.

You couldn't even tell I'd been there.

The cell phone rang as I drove over the Colorado River. "He's been in the pool for an hour," Sarah, my neighbor to the west, said. "I thought he'd get out and go home on his own. I'm so sorry I had to bother you while you're working. Frankie wanted to go swimming, you see."

I assured Sarah she'd done the right thing by calling. "I'll be right there."

Blink lay in the muddy water of Sarah's three-year-old daughter's wading pool, more statue than dog, hoping we would forget about him and leave him to soak under the scant cover of a young ash tree.

Frankie, wearing a pink bathing suit and yellow flippers, clung to her mother's leg. "Bad dog go home," she said, shaking her finger at Blink. When he didn't move, she stepped away from her mother and put her hands on her hips. "Blink, it's time to go *now*."

Blink, unmoved by Frankie's pleading, remained statuelike. Behind him, a Blink-sized tunnel under the fence connected Sarah's yard to mine. And while mountains can be moved with a mustard seed of faith, it would take more than that to move Blink. I had to be wily.

"Blink, do you want to go bye-bye?" I said in my cheeriest voice.

Of course he did. He always did. He stepped out of the pool, trotted to the fence, and squeezed through the tunnel to search out the Daisy Mobile. I helped Sarah empty and clean the pool before I plugged Blink's tunnel with empty clay pots and an upturned wheelbarrow. Who knew when I would get around to backfilling the hole.

It was moments like this I regretted not having repaired the Daisy Mobile's passenger window. Since the window was stuck at half-mast,

Blink stood to squeeze his head out the window. That put his less alluring end at my eye level. Only a dog treat could entice him to sit. I filled my pocket with Bacon Treats from the glove compartment. That got his attention. As I lectured him on what did and did not constitute best-friend behavior, I fed him the treats. When I finished, he shimmied, covering me and the cab with a peppering of mud.

"Shaking in the truck is *not* best-friend behavior, Blink, and I could use a best friend right now. One of your adoring stares would mean a lot to me, old pal."

Blink whined at the open road. I shoved the gearshift into first and pulled away from the curb.

"No more ice cream soup for you."

~~~

Back at Walled Garden, I stood before Christopher Stohl's desk feeling like a naughty child in the principal's office. Kathleen had sent me to his office to discuss the IOU I'd left. She had also warned me to watch my back. Christopher hung up the phone, so I cleared my throat to explain. He punched the button for line two and started talking again.

I looked around. I hardly recognized the place as Judith's old office. Gone were the exposed studs where she had stacked anything too valuable to throw away but not important enough for her desk, things such as promotional paperweights from fertilizer and pesticide companies and coffee mugs filled with unsharpened pencils. Now, framed motivational posters covered faux painted walls, and Judith's industrial-grade office furniture had been replaced with an expansive cherry wood desk and matching credenza. Not one particle of dust dulled the furniture's gloss. I tried brushing Blink's artwork from my clothes.

Christopher said into the phone, "Make sure it gets here when you promised this time. I'm trying to run a business here." And without saying good-bye, he hung up.

That was my cue. "I guess there's been some kind of misunderstanding about—"

He held up one finger while he wrote notes on a legal pad. When he turned the page and kept writing, I sat down. Since he'd replaced Judith's fan with an air-conditioner, I decided to be patient and give him a chance.

Be pleasant.

Across the desk, Christopher looked like a new book with a pristine cover and stiff pages, never read. Pressed creases ran the length of his sleeve and down each breast of his hunter-green polo shirt. The name of the garden center was embroidered over his heart with the addition of *the distinctive place to shop* in gold letters below. The dark shadow of his beard stood out sharply against his pale skin. His pores looked too small to sweat, and his doughy hands made mine look like they belonged to a Norwegian fishing boat captain, so I sat on them. When he finally looked up from his writing, his gray eyes scolded me even before he spoke.

"Mrs. Garwood—"

Be pleasant. "Garrett, but you can call me Mibby. That's what Judith called me."

"Mrs. Garrett, I think it's best to keep a professional distance in business relationships. Now—"

"That's wise, Chris. I'm here about a misunderstanding with my purchase this morning."

His jaw tightened, and he drummed his desk with a pen. "I think it's more than that, *Mrs.* Garrett. You stole those petunias from me."

I waited for a smile, but it didn't come. "I did no such thing. I left an IOU."

"Mrs. Garrett, this is a business, so I must run it like a business. That means using recognized accounting principles for all transactions. The shoeboxes are gone. No more loosey-goosey business practices." His oblique reference to Judith quickened my heart rate. To give my anger a chance to cool, I studied the wall behind him. A triple-matted framed diploma hung just above his head. In elegant script it declared that Christopher Phillip Manchester Stohl III had successfully completed the course of study to earn a Master of Business Administration. I needed a magnifying glass to tell if CU stood for University of Colorado or Curmudgeon U.

There were other garden centers in town, but none with the reputation for quality or selection of Walled Garden, and the plants at the big-box stores arrived from the southeast too lush to survive our hot summers. Until that changed, my association with Christopher Stohl remained important.

"Do we understand each other, Mrs. Garrett?"

I bit down on my answer.

He opened a file drawer and pulled out a printed document. "This is the new credit application. I'm requiring all of my charge customers to reapply. On the third page you'll find a list of required documents and references. Trade references. Credit report. Personal financial report. Collateral. Letters of reference from clients and your banker. The usual."

His gray eyes turned to me again, and I wondered if I was looking at the ash heap where Perennially Yours would expel its last breath. Was Christopher Stohl the lethal hitch in all of my planning? Maybe the time had come to let the business die. My resources had dwindled to nothing, and what grit I had left would only irritate, not cultivate. How had I missed the call of code blue? Had my dream been worthy of my devotion? Had it been ordained by God or was it a flight of fancy?

"Mrs. Garrett? Did you hear me?" Chris had come around the desk to stand over me with the application in his hand.

I took it.

Just then, Blink trotted into the office with his head wet to his shoulders. He'd been looking for rocks in the irrigation ditch, no doubt. Chris moved behind his desk and eyed Blink nervously, which only enticed Blink to take a closer look.

"What's a dog doing in here?"

"Blink's with me."

Chris's face bleached three shades, and he mewed, "Please get it under control."

"Blink, come," I commanded, but Blink chose to act like a dog. He couldn't resist one good sniff and a friendly bark.

Chris whimpered and barricaded himself behind his chair, and he hadn't even noticed the smudge of dog snot and mud on his khakis yet. He pointed the way to the door. "If you ever bring that dog on this property again, I'll call animal control."

Besides the cost of the three flats I'd planted and unplanted for Gloria, Chris charged me a twenty-five percent restocking charge for the remaining petunias. All in all, *not* planting Gloria's petunias had cost me over a hundred dollars.

Then there was Ky to deal with. Taking a message, important or not, was the least he could do. I cycled through anger, hurt, purely vengeful thoughts, and back to anger again all the way home. But by the time I parked in the driveway, the whole mess fell back into my lap where it belonged. It was me who needed to do a better job with Ky, spend more time with him, teach him his part in making Perennially Yours work.

One more thing to do.

~~~

A note on the dining room table in Andrea's handwriting said that Ky had gone channel cat fishing with Droop. He'd be back after midnight. "I'm at Louise's, so y'all come on over," she wrote.

I walked out the back door and across the alley to Louise's, hoping against hope she had lapsed back into my personal sweets chef. She welcomed me at the back door dressed in calypso wear, a ruffled peasant blouse with a thin slice of belly showing and embroidered capris. Rhinestone pineapple earrings dangled from her ears. Nice touch. She offered her downy head and I rubbed it.

Andrea sat in a rosy chintz chair with her knees drawn to her chest and her purple toenails curled over the cushion's edge. I couldn't help thinking of a delicate bird. A Bible lay open on the tea table beside her.

"It's too hot for ice to melt," Louise said. "I have a pitcher full of mango passion fruit juice." She also offered a gluten-free brown-rice-and-honey cookie, but if I'd wanted a chew stick, I would've borrowed one from Blink. I declined as politely as I could.

Andrea unfolded herself from the chair and pulled me into her seat. "You look so tired. Take off your sandals and socks. I'm treating you to a foot massage." She headed for the kitchen. "I'll be right back with some warm water."

Inside my Birkenstocks, my feet still burned with the day's heat, and if my disappointment had settled in the low points, I hated to think what such a combination would smell like.

Louise looked up from her magazine. "If you're thinking that you're going to refuse her foot massage, you better think again. That sugar lamb wants to give something back to you. Lucky for you, it's her love."

Andrea returned to the living room carrying a plastic tub of soapy water and a towel. She set the tub at my feet. "First, we soak." She emptied an envelope of lavender seeds into the water. "The lavender will help you relax."

My thoughts were as unruly as a tree full of monkeys fighting over the last banana, so relaxation seemed a bit lofty. The monkeys had started their chattering before I opened my eyes that morning. "It will take a lot more than lavender to help me relax. I've got a serious case of monkey mind going on."

"Racing-monkey-head syndrome? I get that, too."

"You do?"

"Yep, and monkeys hate lavender."

I bent to remove my Birkenstocks again, but Andrea stilled my hands with a touch. "Let me do that for you. You just relax." She met my eyes. "Those monkeys will be quiet before we're done. First, you need to keep your thoughts in this room. Stay here with the warm water and the lavender and the soft chair and Louise and me. Don't let your mind go back to visit your problems—not even Ky. You can think about him when we're done." She lifted my bare feet and lowered them into the water. "I have to go back to the house to get some lotion and stuff. While I'm gone, throw the monkeys a banana and send them out for recess."

From across the room, Louise watched me, so I closed my eyes and leaned back. There, in the privacy of my mind, I let the monkeys run free. It was much easier that way—they weren't housebroken. I saw the bulging veins in Harlan Chandler's neck again, I heard Margaret say, whisper really, that she could no longer afford my services, and I prayed her son's miserliness was the real reason she canceled my services. My pulse quickened when I remembered Chris Stohl's contempt as he accused me of stealing. And the weather—how could I fight against the drought? Maybe I should get a job, a regular job, paycheck included. But another job would never give me the same freedom. My throat tightened, and tears threatened to spill.

Louise interrupted my thoughts when she cleared her throat. I focused on the soapy sweetness of the lavender wafting up from my footbath. A field of lavender Scott and I had stumbled upon in Provence came to mind. Heartened, I commanded the monkeys to hightail it, and their chattering stopped.

Bubbles tickled my ankles, and the pages of Louise's magazine crinkled with each turn. A light breeze from the ceiling fan raised goose bumps on my arms and legs. But in the time it takes to peel a banana, the monkeys were pounding on the door again, calling out my list of disappointments one by one. Louise's voice cut in when I moaned over the check I'd written at Walled Garden.

"Just how serious are you about quitting Perennially Yours?"

"Probably not serious enough."

"Sweet pea, your talent is a gift from God. You can't go hiding it in a hole. You bless people with beautiful gardens on His behalf."

"Shouldn't my clients be a little more grateful?" Then I asked the real question, the question the monkeys at the door wanted to ask. "If I'm working with God on this, why is making a profit such a struggle? Would it bust His budget to pull a few strings for me?"

Louise closed her magazine and smiled with her eyes. "Haven't you gone and asked the burning question? It's about time you did."

A sermon was coming, I knew, prepared just for me, and whether I'd meant to or not, I'd invited it with the right—or wrong—question. On the squirm meter, Louise's sermons ranked a ten out of ten. But on the love-you-to-death meter, they ranked a thousand, so I paid attention as well as any thick-headed, fear-mongering, stone-poor woman could.

"I don't like boats much," Louise started, "not since Haskell LeJeune, the preacher's son, rowed me out to the middle of Carson's Pond at a Sunday school picnic. Haskell was about as coordinated as a three-legged dog on a tightrope, and that was on dry land. If I hadn't set my mind to make John Peter Paul Thibodeaux jealous, I wouldn't have trusted Haskell to help me across the street, let alone row me across a lake. I do believe the first time that boy had ever sat in a boat was on that very day. He rowed like a wounded goose. First we'd circle one way and then the other. And the splashing!

"'Haskell,' I finally said, 'put the oars in the water and leave them there. Sit there and look at me like I'm the most ravishing thing you've ever seen. John Peter Paul is probably watching us right this very second.' Haskell fixed a stare on me, all right, and in no time at all, a fire lit in his eyes. I hadn't planned on that, but who could have blamed him? I'd flipped my hair like Sandra Dee, only better. Haskell lurched at me without so much as a hidey-ho. I'm not sure to this day if he kissed me or baptized me. I gave him one good shove, and he reeled back and tried to right himself, and the next thing I knew, we were swimming with the turtles. So much for the Sandra Dee coiffure and my new eyelet sheath. Worse yet, every fair eye, John Peter Paul's included, from the Firm Foundation Bible Church Sunday school watched me as I trudged out of the pond trailing duckweed. John Peter Paul went home with Pookie McCallister. I haven't been on a boat since."

Louise went back to reading her magazine. The clock ticked. The fan whirred. A gnat landed in my lemonade. "Was God teaching you humility?" I asked.

"Humility? Me? What are you talking about?"

"John Peter Paul? The pond? Duckweed?"

"Duckweed? What on earth are you—? Sorry, sugar. I guess I let this article about anti-inflammatory eicosanoids distract me a teensy bit."

Whatever eye-causing noits were, I knew they wouldn't taste anything like Louise's buttery lemon scones. "You were saying?"

Louise cleaned her reading glasses, pulled the hem of her top down to cover more of her belly, and frowned at the ceiling. "Sugar, you're going to have to give me a teensy-bitsy hint as to what I said. Since I started taking tamoxifen, I don't have enough estrogen to float a thought."

I repeated her adventure with Haskell and prompted her with all the details, but she still frowned at me. "Did it seem like I was saying something important?"

"Something to do with boats, I think."

"Boats?" Louise's smile relit. "I remember!"

"Are you getting a boat?" Andrea asked as she walked in carrying a bulging canvas bag. She sat before me on the ottoman.

"Girls, have I ever told you about the night before my mastectomy?" Louise asked.

What about the boat?

Andrea leaned forward. "Go on."

"It was the bleakest night of my life. Fear made me prickly from the spine out, but I didn't let on. I was worried about Manley's heart. I didn't want to add one ounce of weight to what he already carried. That sweet cherub's face had been puckered with worry since I'd found the lump.

"I waited in bed that night until he started snoring, about two minutes is all. I slunk downstairs and sat in the dark. In less than a minute, I had visions of myself wasting away, lopsided as an old barn, with a hospital gown hanging on me like I was a wire clothes hanger. Then I chose songs for my funeral, but honestly, I couldn't think of one pitiful enough. Poor me. I sat there for a long, long time enjoying an eight-course meal of self-pity. Wasn't very satisfying, though, so I ate three lemon scones smeared with Devonshire cream and raspberry jam."

Yum!

"It wasn't until I imagined Miss Pookie McCallister decked out in a buttery Yves Saint Laurent suit and batting her eyes at Manley at my funeral that I finally remembered to consult the Comforter.

"I prayed and opened my Bible to the story of Jesus and the disciples crossing the Sea of Galilee. I'd hoped for a healing story, not one about a group of whining sailors, but that's what I got, so I read about the crowd pressing in on Jesus and how the disciples followed Him onto the boat and how the storm came up unexpected like. That's when the disciples started crying about their doom. The way I figured it, the disciples did everything right. They stayed with Jesus when things got crazy and followed Him without question. But when they told Him they were about to die in the storm, Jesus scolded them for their lack of faith. That didn't sound like my Savior at all.

"I thought I must have missed something, so I read the story again. Jesus was being terribly unreasonable, I thought. The waves nearly swamped the boat, for crying out loud. And darlin's, the waves were crashing over me, right here in the Rose Room, so I read the passage again. Nothing. I read it again.

"Then I complained to Jesus about His attitude." Louise shook her finger at the ceiling. "'And listen here,' I said. 'I need to hear from you. This is the last time I'm reading this here story.' And there it was. Do y'all know what I'd missed?"

"The lifeboat?" I asked.

"This isn't a time to get flip, Mibby. We're gettin' to the summation."

I apologized.

Andrea's voice was breathless with anticipation. "What did you miss?"

"In the very first line of the story, Jesus tells the disciples they're crossing to the other side of the lake."

Louise squinted at me through her glasses. "He didn't tell them to go to the middle of the lake and drown," she prompted. "What He says will happen, and He said they were going to the *other* side of the lake. That storm didn't change a word He'd said. They would arrive on the other side of the lake safe and sound. Period.

"That's when I knew I had a choice to make. I could cling to the mast, paralyzed by fear, and let the waves of pity wash over me, or I could go down into the hold with Jesus and take a nap. We're on our way to the distant shore, Mibby girl, and we won't be takin' easy street to get there. If you take a refreshin' nap, y'all will look a lot better when you get there."

Louise leaned into her chair and closed her eyes. I waited for the punch line. I recognized myself in the story, all right. I was the one saying, *Hey, is this storm really necessary? Could you cut me some slack here? I'm rowing as hard as I can.*

I went on the offensive. "Louise, I've lost three clients in three days, and the summer is shaping up to be a scorcher. The reservoirs are lower than they've been in decades. No one knows if we'll have enough water to last the summer. If the river level drops below the intake valves for the irrigation systems . . . Louise, I have a mortgage to pay and food to put on the table."

Silence.

"She's sleeping," Andrea said. "She's been dropping off like that. She's still busted from the chemo, I think."

How typical that Louise equated her trials with too much water. My life was a dry lake. The bottom lay cracked before me in a million pieces.

I could walk to the other side. No boat was needed and no waves threatened my survival, just more of the same emptiness day after day.

Andrea dumped some misshapen candles from her bag and set them on the hearth and tables and windowsills. The fan fluttered their flames into dancing shadows on the flowery wallpaper of Louise's parlor. Next, Andrea draped the lampshades with silk scarves. The room glowed rosy and the shadows softened. My eyelids surrendered to their weight. On the stereo, Andrea played a Yo-Yo Ma CD.

"Mood is everything," she said.

The cello's mournful song mimicked my lament.

"Maybe I should have picked something a little more cheerful," Andrea said.

She dried my feet and rubbed her hands together to warm the oil; still, I jumped when she took my foot in her hands.

"Relax, Mibby. One of my roommates was a massage therapist. She did this for me all the time."

I let my head sink into the chair's cushion and reminded all of my muscles to put down their worries, if only for a short time. *Don't worry,* I told them, *if we lose these worries, we can always find some new ones tomorrow.* In the dim light, I listened to Louise's soft snores and soon my breathing matched hers. Within moments my feet felt like they'd been filleted.

Andrea kneaded the muscle of my right calf, finding sore spots I didn't know I had. "Wow, these are super tight," she whispered. She pressed deeper. At first, my muscles hoarded their pain, but she coaxed them until a flush of warmth flooded my calf. She took my other foot into her hands.

She leaned forward and whispered, "I love to listen to Louise talk about God. It's like He's in the room with us."

"Really?"

"But there's so much I don't get. Sometimes I'm so sure. I mean, I really, really know that God exists. I look at something and I just know that God made it. And I'm totally surprised by my own knowing. It's cool."

My heart fluttered, and I wondered if Andrea could feel my pulse in her hands.

"There were times this last year when I felt His presence. Once it happened, and this was kind of funny, but I didn't want to feel His presence just then. I wanted to say, 'Not now, God. This is not a good time.' But I couldn't shake it—Him, God—you know, the feeling that nothing else mattered." She laughed. "That was kind of hard to explain to the guy I was with. I mean, there we were . . . and all I could think about was God at a time like that. The guy was totally weirded out. He left and didn't even take his shoes. And it was okay. I mean, I'm not sure I want to even be with someone who gets weird when I mention God."

My heart burned to introduce her to her abiding Father, her Creator, her Redeemer, the passionate Lover of her soul, but it was as if someone had erased every tender thought I'd ever held about God. I had nothing to say to her, not one word. So I said the only thing that was so cemented into my lexicon, nothing could remove it. "Cool."

Later in bed, remembering my missed opportunity with Andrea, I stared at the ceiling fan and added disappointing God to my list of failures. Things couldn't get any worse than that. But the idea of curling up next to Jesus to take a nap appealed to me. It was becoming clearer to me that the storm wasn't going to blow over any time soon. If I was going to ride it out, I would need my rest.

I closed my eyes, and with little effort I imagined myself on the rolling deck of a fishing boat, just like the one Jesus and His followers had taken across the lake. I was ten years old again. My sodden clothes and the inevitability of my own doom froze me in place. Any comforting light the moon and stars could have offered was obscured by the storm. The rain stung my face, and a wave crashed over the rail. I grabbed the mast. A surge of water pulled my feet out from under me and strained my grip. The deck roiled under me, and the hatch to the hold swung open. A golden light beckoned me to go inside, but the boat pitched and the hatch slammed shut again. A wave towered above the deck, and I tightened my grip. The mast seemed too puny to hold much longer. The boat slid into the deep trough of the wave. The hatch blew open again, and again the light beckoned me to join Jesus within, but that meant releasing the mast and walking across the bare planks to the opening. I wanted to go. I took two steps toward the door. Out of the corner of my eye the sharp edge of a wave's crest curled toward its plunge across the deck.

Enough!

I sat upright and opened my eyes to the familiar darkness of my bedroom.

JULY 19

Hancock coralberry is being ravaged by spider mites! I hard-sprayed them with water. Now the plants are completely denuded. On the brighter side, planted Salad Rose radishes in a pot. In this heat, they should sprout in a week.

I slid two over-easy eggs onto my plate and checked the garden walk for any sign of Louise. The coast was clear. I patted the bacon with a paper towel—my half-hearted salute to healthy eating—and opened the box of glazed doughnuts I'd bought at the day-old bakery.

I had fifteen minutes before Louise finished her weekly phone call to her Aunt Pansy, after which she would be free to saunter over for a cup of coffee, her one remaining vice. By then all traces of bacon grease had to be eliminated, or she was sure to assign another chapter of her nutrition book to read. I had more important reading to do. The night before, I'd picked up another parenting book, *Boys Will Be Men: A Mother's Guide to the Teen Years*. So far, it had been authoritative and informative, just what I needed. I revved the exhaust fan over the stove to high and opened the window.

The phone rang. I sopped up the rest of the yolk and grease with my doughnut and popped the whole thing in my mouth. "Helro?"

"Mibby, are you eating?" asked Margot. "That's disgusting."

Talking to my sister on the phone was like being one of those tin ducks in a carnival shooting gallery. I collapsed with each shot, only to pop up to be shot at again. Addressing me by name was atypical enough, but that morning, her voice trembled when she'd said my name.

"Is something wrong?"

"It's been a month since Mother's contacted me," she said. "I'm not worried . . . too much. She usually calls once a week to let me know where she is. Has she called you?"

We both knew how unlikely that would have been. In an attempt to distance myself and Ky from my mother's unreliability, I'd minimized contact with her. Now she was missing for the umpteenth time, and I was once more tempering my heart against the pain of her absence.

"No, she hasn't called."

"I walked the pier and the farmers' market. I went to all the bead shops within fifty miles of Santa Monica. The owners knew who she was, but no one had seen her lately. I even went to a shelter to ask some street people if they'd seen her." Margot cleared her throat. "They're such pigs. Their teeth, good grief, couldn't they brush them once a year? The thought of Mother . . . Do you think I should call the police? The hospitals?"

Never in all the years of our childhood or adulthood had Margot asked me for an opinion, much less for permission to do something. "You've done all you can. Maybe you should."

Her voice rattled with panic. "Let's not get hysterical."

Her dread was contagious. "We have to know. Do you want me to call?"

Margot wasn't happy to have her little sister taking the initiative, even in panic. She shifted into her role as protectorate. "Forget it. I'm here. Let me do it. I'll call when I know something." The dial tone moaned in my ear.

~~~~~

Enough light slipped around the edges of the room-darkening shade for me to watch Ky sleep. The sight was disappointing, really. The pouting lips and rosy cheeks of a sleeping infant had been replaced by a gaping mouth with crusty deposits of dried spit in the corners. And what was that odor? I hoped he hadn't taken up collecting crawdad shells from the irrigation canals again.

I took the opportunity to look around his room. Ky's dragon art had been replaced by posters of sports heroes and snowboard logos—none that I knew and some that looked downright menacing. He didn't draw anymore. There was no place to draw if he'd wanted to. The artifacts of his life, including enough empty pop cans to clad a small battleship, left his desk too cluttered for artwork. The floor functioned as a depository for piles of dirty clothes and stacks of magazines and fishing gear and, of course, a scattering of all things baseball.

I stifled the urge to scream, took a deep breath, and tapped his shoulder. "Ky?"

He opened and closed his eyes.

"Too late. I know you're in there. I'm putting a list of chores on the island that need to be done by noon. Ky? Do you hear me?"

I took his groan as affirmative and continued. "It's extremely important that you water the flowerpots for Margaret's wedding. They're drying out fast in this heat. I watered them once this morning, but they'll need watering again. You'll have to check them."

His breathing slowed.

"Open your eyes so I know you're hearing this."

Two slits opened.

"Are you listening?"

"I said *yes*."

The *Boys Will Be Men* book warned that sarcasm threw down the gauntlet and started a battle that would only lead to a full-blown war, so I spoke evenly. "Water all the flowerpots in the growing yard. Fill them to—"

"I *know* how to water."

Stupid book. "Like you know how to take a phone message?" I held my breath. Part of me—the part of me that still stung from the Gloria fiasco—wanted him to pick up the gauntlet so I could spew my anger back at him. The other part of me—the part that had dodged bullets

77

downrange from Margot's rapid-fire sarcasm—prayed he hadn't heard me. No such luck.

He rolled toward the wall. "I'll *do* it."

Oh, how I wanted to believe, had to believe, he would. "Right. I also need you to mail this envelope for me today. It's very important. I've paper-clipped enough money for the postage. The walk will do you good. Ky?"

"No problem."

"I'm putting it on your keyboard. See? Ky, look."

He rolled toward me and one eye opened.

"Thanks, bud. Okay, have a good day. I'll see you at lunch."

Outside Ky's door, the weight of the morning settled on my shoulders. I leaned against the wall to pray. Ever since I'd noticed that the best whiners and complainers of the Old Testament had books of the Bible named after them, I'd found my voice.

"Can I be perfectly honest, God? It isn't even eight in the morning and I'm not sure I want to participate in this day. I resent my son for sleeping all day and smelling like dead things. I resent my mother for disappearing. What's with Margot? It's not like Mother hasn't done this a hundred, make that a thousand, times before. And if I'm going to be completely honest, I'm not too happy with you, either. What? Did you think I'd have too nice of a day without losing my mother . . . again?" Even as I asked the question, my chest tightened and tears burned my eyes. "Oh God, please find my mother."

⁓

I called my sister seven times throughout the day, but her assistant never put my call through to Margot's office. I finally left a message to say I would wait for her call, as usual. I found a box of Sweet Suzy Coconut Dream Cakes leaning against the back door when I got home. A note from Larry asked how the water heater was working.

The kitchen was quiet when I poured a glass of milk and tore open a dream cake. While I ate, I read the note from Larry again. His handwriting was more precise than I would have expected. He'd offered to adjust the temperature and double-check the sweat joints of the water heater. That was nice, and the dream cakes were very nice. The last time I'd had a steady supply of Sweet Suzy treats was in the fifth grade. Bradley snuck them into my lunch bag every day for a week. When he'd tried to claim a kiss in payment, I'd kicked him hard in the shins.

With a shudder, I asked myself what Larry might expect in return for fixing the water heater and for providing the steady stream of treats. He lived with his mother, for goodness' sake, and he was at least five years younger than I, which just as well could have been a hundred.

Blink whined at the box of remaining dream cakes perched on top of the kitchen trash. I hesitated, my size nine Birkenstocks poised over Sweet Suzy's face. The automatic icemaker filled with water and the compressor hummed in the refrigerator. When I put my foot back on the floor, Blink beat my leg with his tail and inched closer.

"I guess Larry meant them as a gift. No harm in that," I said.

I read the note he'd left attached to the box one more time. "Seems innocent enough, doesn't it, boy?"

Blink stepped on my foot.

"Ouch."

A squiggle in front of Larry's name caught my eye. "Is that a heart?" I stomped Sweet Suzy deep into the wastebasket.

"I can't afford his gifts, old friend."

Blink barked his disagreement.

"Don't sass me." I held his muzzle in my hands, thinking all that was needed was a little eye contact for Blink to see my point of view. "Really, that woman's-best-friend thing would mean a lot to me right now. Are you with me on this?"

There was no mistaking the defiance in the *tap, tap, tap* of his claws as he trotted away from me and disappeared through the doggie door.

"Fine," I said to the swinging door.

Now that my core temperature had returned to normal, I took a better look at the kitchen and knew I had another problem. A plate, my grandmother's Havilland pattern, one of the remaining four dinner plates, forbidden for unsupervised use for the last fourteen years, lay encrusted with a mortar of refried beans and cheese in the sink, and a carton of orange juice was warm to the touch by the refrigerator. My left eye twitched. The corner of the chore list I'd left for Ky peeked out from under a block of cheese, also warm, also hardening.

At the top of the list, I'd written, *Take out the trash*. What else had he forgotten? Blink's food and water bowls were empty, and something told me Ky's floor still lay hidden under a sea of refuse. I yelled out for him with the indignity of ruined food and a forgotten doggie friend. No response.

I clomped up the stairs, dreading the confrontation, knowing where I'd find Ky. The scene was getting too familiar. I yelled his name at the back of his head.

He tapped the keyboard to freeze a ghoul in mid-prowl on the screen. He turned. "Mom, is something wrong?" He still wore the clothes he'd slept in. His hair was pressed into a half pike any skateboarder would have been proud of.

I inhaled deeply to gain control, which proved to be a huge mistake. The air smelled like something had died under his bed. "Have you been at the computer all day?" As dumb questions go, that one entered me instantly into the stupid question hall of fame, parking space and full benefits included.

"No."

"Making a mess in the kitchen and retrieving pop from the refrigerator doesn't count," I clarified. From his bewilderment, I guessed he hadn't strayed any farther than the kitchen. Stupid question number two, "Did you do *any* of the things I asked you to do?"

"What things?"

"The list I left for you on the island."

"I didn't see it."

"You didn't have to see it. I told you about it."

"When?"

"We talked about it before I left this morning."

"I don't remember."

"How convenient." If the parenting book had been within reach, I would have eaten it in one bite. "Let's get this straight. All in one day, you forgot to feed Blink and give him water?"

A flash of surprise passed over Ky's face.

"And how about the value of refrigeration in July? Poof! Gone! And despite the obvious stench coming from your room, the concept of a wastebasket has also been erased from your memory?" The momentum carried me irresistibly on. "Amazing, Ky, just amazing. I guess you're ready for gingko supplements and adult diapers." I wiped sweat from my forehead. "And would turning on the air-conditioner have overtaxed your mouse finger?"

His eyes narrowed and his face flushed a deep red. Part of me wanted him to blow. I wanted a fight, a hard place to hurl my frustration, maybe to break it into more manageable pieces. The thought of using my son that way made me queasy—until I remembered the last thing on the list. "Ky, tell me you watered Margaret's pots."

He grimaced. I had my answer. Like a woman going into a dressing room to try on bathing suits, I left Ky's room to face the inevitable disappointment. He demonstrated admirable courage by following me—albeit at a safe distance.

Down the stairs and through the house to the back door and along the garden path, I thought of all the time I'd spent poring over plant books to find flowers to match Margaret's dress. The false starts. The overnight deliveries. The receipts awaiting reimbursement. Finally, after countless phone calls, bloom time, color, size, shape, and heat tolerance all came together for the perfect arrangements to encircle her garden wedding. Now, in the hundred-plus heat, all of my work had baked, most certainly, into potpourri.

I stopped before turning the corner to the growing yard where the flowerpots had made me so proud only hours ago. Ky's steps halted several paces behind me. He sucked in a breath. So did I.

Plants lived or died by the laws of their Creator. By His design, they required sunlight and carbon dioxide and water, no exceptions made. Single digit humidity only intensified their needs. That was why I stopped dead in my tracks.

"Mom?"

The geraniums, the gentle pink of a conch shell, stood in regal authority over the graceful bow of the trailing *Bacopas*.

"Are they all right?" Ky asked, his voice earnest with caring.

I felt the soil in the closest pot. It was spongy, cool, hydrated. I walked the length of the growing yard, testing the soil of each pot with a touch, marveling and oh so very grateful. The *Agryranthemums,* a big name for the sweetest little pink daisy ever, smiled back at me, and in front of the tall tufts of variegated maiden grass, the geraniums glowed with health. Their leaves opened to the sky like little hands reaching for a gift.

Lord, did you do this for me?

"They look great, Ky. I don't know what happened."

He was beside me now. "Maybe Andrea?"

"She's working two shifts."

"Louise?"

"I water *her* garden."

We stood face-to-chin—my face to his chin. One moment, we'd been crushed by the weight of survival, the next we were reminded that our well-being mattered to God. My tummy tingled.

The worry on Ky's face had been replaced with wide-eyed wonder. "Do you think . . . God? Maybe?"

"I think God, absolutely."

"Cool."

"Real cool."

Ky stood with his head down and his hands deep in his pockets. As in Jesus' story about the man whose huge debt had been forgiven by the king, I needed to pass the same grace on to my debtor, my son. My heart flattened in my chest. "Ky, I'm so sorry."

He watched his toes wiggle. "Yeah. Me too."

"Things have to change, Ky. We agreed when Louise took on her special guests and Andrea doubled her work hours that you'd have to make smart decisions on your own, carry your part of the load. You assured me you could handle the responsibility."

"I know."

"I have to be able to trust you to do—"

"I *know.*"

"Ky, I—"

"I know I screwed up, okay?" He stomped off.

Huh? I changed my mind. If I'd held the parenting book, I would have doused it with lighter fluid and struck a match. "Excuse me, young man."

He kept walking.

"Stop right there and turn around." I caught up to him and I did what small dogs do to compensate for their size; I barked. "You're not off the hook that easy. Divine intervention or not, your behavior has been pretty irresponsible. Make that very irresponsible, and your attitude stinks."

He shifted his weight and crossed his arms over his chest. I eased onto the balls of my feet and squared my shoulders. If he dared to tilt his head, I couldn't be held responsible for my actions. There it was, the head tilt.

"Get in the house. Start at the top of the list and work your way to the bottom. If the computer is still on when I come in the house, my foot's going through it."

"You wouldn't—"

"I would."

He swallowed hard and studied me.

More than I wanted to admit, I enjoyed the effect I was having on him. My voice got pleasant, or was it sadistic? "And while you're in the house, I want you to know, I'll be out here in the blazing sun watering the pots one more time. I need the time to consider how I'm going to help you regain your memory, so don't bother offering to do the watering for me. I'm glad to do it."

"Mom," he said, and it was a complaint as well as a plea.

"No, Ky, I insist. I'm your mother, and I should be the one to help you develop skills for success." This was getting fun. "Besides, the heat makes me creative."

He turned to leave. "You're not funny."

"Blink thinks I am." And bless his heart, Blink barked, so I yelled to Ky's back, "Feed the dog first, and when you're done with the list, take a shower and comb that rat's nest you call hair." I told Blink, "You better follow him."

Boy and dog walked toward the house, Ky like a badly maligned, terribly misunderstood rebel without a cause and Blink bouncy with anticipation of his kibble. By the time they reached the porch steps, I was filled with self-doubt.

No time for that.

I attached the watering wand to the hose and cranked the tap to full open.

"You're mean."

I whirled around. Larry beamed at me over the alley fence.

"You have no idea," I said, moving on to water the next pot. There was no way I was going to let Larry get under my skin.

Larry wore sunglasses and a Raiders cap, something considered dangerous in some parts of Colorado. I added *reckless* to his list of aggravating behaviors. He had a nice smile, though, full and white, and yes, it was unguarded enough to keep him from looking like the Unabomber. There had definitely been some orthodontic work in his past. The flowerpot I was watering overfilled and water spilled over my foot.

"What's Ky facing, ten to fifteen with time off for good behavior?" he asked.

"He'll be lucky to see the light of day by the time he's thirty. And since Blink didn't get his kibble today, hunger and deprivation will be involved."

"Good for you."

Good for me?

"Hey, did you find the Coconut Dream Cakes I left for you this morning?"

I moved to the next flowerpot and pinched a spent *Bacopa* blossom. "I threw them away."

"Why'd you do a thing like that?"

I fully intended to tell him I wasn't interested in his gifts, or his attention, or his handyman capabilities when I heard Connie's voice through the fence. "We thought Ky might like a treat."

Connie? I wanted to run into the house and put my head under the sofa cushions. Instead, I opened the gate and promised Connie I'd give the Coconut Dream Cakes to Ky, but I didn't tell her they'd been embossed by my Birkenstock.

"Can I show Mom your flowerpots?" Larry asked. "Louise said you wouldn't mind."

Connie leaned against Larry as they walked through the growing yard. "These are gorgeous. They look like something out of a magazine."

Connie's maintenance-free curls had been transformed into a smooth chignon sprinkled with glitter and held in place with a rhinestone comb. The style screamed Louise, but the glitter? I wondered if Andrea had anything to do with that. Beads of sweat formed at her hairline.

"Connie, it's awfully hot out here. Do you want my hat?" I asked.

"And mess up Louise's hard work? I can't do that. I won't be out here long."

"Doesn't she look pretty?" asked Larry. "We're heading out to Big Valley Steakhouse after a little rest. I have to show my best gal off."

Connie blushed and batted away the compliment, but she squeezed Larry's arm and leaned into him.

Would Ky ever . . . ?

"Thanks for showing me your flowers. They're so pretty they take my breath away." With her hand over her heart, Connie sighed, "Barbie would love to have one of these flowerpots by her front door."

"She sure would," Larry said.

I offered to make a list of all the plants I'd used to make the flowering pots. "Does Barbie live with you?"

"Yep," Larry said, "all three hundred of her."

"Three hundred and *one*," corrected Connie.

"Mom has been designing dresses for Barbie, the doll, since my sister started walking. She just couldn't bring herself to part with a few hundred of her favorites."

Larry and Connie exchanged looks and laughed.

A small ache pulsed in my chest.

"You'll have to come by and see them sometime—and Larry's dahlias, too," she said. I assured her I would.

"It's a good thing Larry came by to deliver the dream cakes when he did. He said the soil in the pots was bone dry. The geraniums and petunias would have wilted for sure in this heat if he hadn't gotten them watered for you."

"*You* watered the pots?" I asked.

He flashed a toothy grin, and this time I wasn't so impressed. I cut a bouquet of *Argyranthemums* for Connie and the Barbies. "You should get your mother out of this heat," I told Larry.

Connie's head rested on Larry's broad bicep. "This heat has pulled my plug. Take me home, son."

Mother and son walked slowly across the alley to Louise's garden gate. After they'd gone, I sat on an overturned pot in the shade of a viburnum, and the heat sat on me. I wasn't ready to go back into the house to face Ky. More than likely, he was sulking anyway. No doubt about it, my bluster had waned, and all I really wanted was to know Ky liked me again. Since such an affirmation seemed unlikely, I decided one skipped meal and no computer for a couple—or even one day—would get the point across. To soften the blow, I planned on a run to the grocery store for some Cocoa Puffs. More than once, Scott had teased Ky about eating the people kibble. Hopefully, Ky would remember that, too.

And then there was Larry to think about.

I'd liked the idea of Jesus lugging a hose around my garden, stopping to water each pot and to admire our partnership and anticipating my joy at His intervention. Three billion men lived on the planet. Any one of them could have watered my pots, but God sent Larry. What was that about? Just because all of the farmer types I could think of—Old Mac-Donald, the Jolly Green Giant, Johnny Appleseed—were figments of someone's imagination didn't mean there wasn't someone else out there with flesh and blood who knew how to handle a hose.

Nothing works off angst like tending to a neglected garden. I worked counterclockwise, deadheading and weeding and snipping misplaced sprouts. The compost pile swelled from my offerings. A bedraggled columbine almost received last rites, but everyone deserves a second chance and a good long drink of water. I filled a terra cotta donkey pot with soil and sprinkled the Salad Rose radish seeds on top. Before I watered the seeds, I moved the donkey to the back porch, where I could see it and water the germinating seeds several times a day. While I had the hose in my hand, I cranked the spigot wide open to hard-spray spider mites off of the Hancock coralberry shrubs. Three leaves remained. At the porch steps, I turned to inspect my work. With the spent blossoms gone, only the toughest of the summer bloomers displayed their colors. I couldn't blame the rest for deferring their blooms for milder temperatures.

Rest well, my pretties.

Only the Ky-shaped lump on his bed let me know he lay within. With his computer off and the shade drawn, the room was inky dark. I turned on the hall light for my first look at his cleaning efforts. His books stood orderly on the shelves. His game bag lay plump and zipped at the end of his bed. Not one Pepsi can marred the order. And since I hadn't specifically told him to do his laundry, a heap of clothes rose from his hamper and threatened to avalanche to the floor. In Ky's mind, the floor was clear. Mission accomplished.

"Your room looks great," I said to the lump.

He grunted from the darkness. It was as much of an *entre nous* as I was going to get, so I walked toward the lump and had to smile. The air reeked of sweetness and spice. Ky had found the air freshener.

"Blink asked me to bring this up for you," I said.

"What is it?"

"Your kibble." I handed him the bowl of Cocoa Puffs and explained that Blink had wanted to send him a peace offering. I expected a groan and a half smile followed by some eager eating. Instead, he handed the bowl back to me.

"Not hungry," he said and turned to the wall.

I held my breath and let it out slowly. The corners of my motherhood bag of tricks held nothing but lint. Time to go direct. I sat on the edge of his bed.

"Help me understand what's going on with you."

"Nothing's going on."

"You're not yourself anymore. All you want to do is play that stupid game. That's not healthy."

No reply. Silly me, I thought I'd given him a conversation opener, but I hadn't formed it as a question. Fortunately, I'd come armed with more than kibble. I opened the Orchard City parks and recreation catalog. "Is there anything else you'd like to do?"

"I want to go to the skate park."

"You know how I feel about that. If I could trust you to wear your helmet and if you agreed to only go when I could—"

"Never mind."

"We could go on—"

"Never mind."

"Okay." *Keep it moving.* "The rec department has all sorts of stuff going on, or maybe you could help with Vacation Bible School again. The kids loved you last year."

"No VBS."

"Okay. That's a start. We're getting a clear picture of what you don't want to do. How about golf lessons?"

"No."

"Swimming? Diving?"

Grunt.

"Is that a no?"

Moan.

"That's a no." I flipped through the catalog. "Hey, tennis is fun."

"Too hot."

I'd managed to keep sarcasm out of my voice to that point. I deserved some slack, some coming together, or at least a complete sentence. After our earlier skirmish, it was probably too much to hope for, so as long as I was careening toward futility, I decided to take the express route.

"Look at this, Ky," I said flipping on his bedside lamp and showing him an opened page. "Clogging! They have junior clogging lessons. You could meet some girls and get a great cardio workout all in one place. I think you'll like the shoes, too. Very snappy. It's you, Ky."

I wasn't getting the reaction I'd hoped for, so I upped the enthusiasm. What teenager could remain nonplussed by dance fever?

"We could do this together. Matching outfits. Hours of practice on routines. Some patriotic music. And to raise money for all the workshops we'll want to attend, we could hire ourselves out for anniversary parties and shopping center openings—the clogging Garretts. How 'bout it?"

"I don't need anything to do. I'm fine. I only need you to leave me alone, *please*."

Please?

Please wasn't a word you used with "leave me alone." You used please for minor inconveniences like "please pass the butter" or "please call when you get to your destination." Saying please with leave me alone was like stabbing someone in the heart and asking for your knife back, *please*. The choice became clear. I could go to bed hurt or I could go to bed angry. Anger wasn't the best sleeping aid, but I knew I could cry myself to sleep, no problem.

"G'night, Ky."

Never one to miss an opportunity for revenge, I returned to his doorway after I'd showered and dressed for bed.

"Set your alarm for six. You're spending the day with me."

I turned off the light to say my prayers. *Lord, remember that mercy I asked for last night? This would be a great time to answer that prayer. But if that's too much, how about some . . .*

I almost asked for normalcy. Not good enough.

How about a day or two, longer would be better, of something predictable? Go to work. Please my clients. Get paid. Come home to a tail-wagging dog and a smiling teenager. And I would love to sense your presence. Amen.

The phone rang. It was Margot.

"Are you in bed already? Never mind. Mother called. Left a message. She's alive, somewhere. I'll call again when I know more."

I fell asleep knowing God had been listening after all.

JULY

Patchy clouds raised the humidity but that's all. Tough year to keep potted plants happy. Next year, add polymer granules to the soil. Good news: pincushions and butterfly flowers blooming well in the heat. Yay!

When I walked into the kitchen, Ky was hunched over a bowl of Cocoa Puffs, fully dressed, and reading a book. He turned the page but didn't look up.

"Morning, Ky," I said, pouring myself a cup of day-old coffee.

He filled his mouth with a heaping spoonful of Cocoa Puffs. No reply. I punched the touch pad of the microwave harder than I needed to and reminded myself to be patient. At least he was out of bed and reading a book. Right? I poured the hot coffee into a travel mug.

"Be sure you clean your mess up when you're done."

Again, no response. The few times when Ky had copped an attitude, it was Scott who had stepped in to right the pecking order in the Garrett house. There was yet another reason to miss Scott.

"Ky, I forgot to ask, did you mail that big envelope I gave you yesterday?"

He poured more Cocoa Puffs into his bowl.

"Ky?"

"What?" He turned to me, his eyes cloudy with contempt.

I'd read a chapter the night before from yet another parenting book, *A Monastery Isn't the Answer: Parenting Teens in the Twenty-First Century.* The author drove home the point that parents cannot control the attitudes of their teen. Parents only have jurisdiction over their own attitudes and feelings, so I chose to be pleasant and insistent.

"Did you mail the envelope yesterday?"

"What do *you* think?"

"Ky!"

"Yes, I mailed it. *Okay?*"

What had the author said about episodes of flagrant disrespect? Eat your young? No, that had been a *National Geographic* special. Be a chump? Don't turn your back? Choose the hill you want to die on? I sure didn't want to die in my own kitchen.

"Thank you, Ky. That was a help to me."

He turned the page of his book, and I could see that it was a play book for his computer game. As I filled my lunch cooler with Diet Pepsi and energy bars, I counted the years until he went to college, which reminded me that he had laundry to do. "Do your laundry today, too, and don't forget about getting the garbage to the curb."

He finally looked at me. "It's already out there."

Wow. "And Blink?"

"Done."

"Thank you." And lest he think his random acts of responsibility canceled out having to do his laundry, I reminded him again it needed to be done by the end of the day. "You know, I can smell your shirt from here."

He sniffed at his shirt. "I can't smell anything."

"Wash it. Today."

I was almost out the door when I heard him grumble something unflattering about my intelligence. I slammed the kitchen door behind me and huffed my way to the Daisy Mobile. If the bluebird of happiness had landed on my shoulder, I would have brushed him off. I was that angry—angry at myself for being so weak and angry at Ky for changing from a sweet child to a sullen teen. And as pointless as being angry at Scott for dying was, my heart raged against him, too. What could have distracted him from the first rule of cycling safety: Look both ways?

Then I remembered why Ky was up so early. The thought of working with him all day was sadly unappetizing. It wasn't like staying home let him off easy. He had his laundry to do. On the other hand, I didn't have to read a parenting book to know that saying what I meant and meaning what I said mattered. Ky settled any indecision I had on the issue. He waved me down as I backed down the driveway. When I stopped, he climbed in.

"How much are you going to pay me?"

"As much as you're worth."

"That means nothing, right?"

I backed into the street and headed for the business loop. Ky stared out the passenger window the whole way to the Morleys.

I was standing in front of the refrigerator, looking but not seeing that the water pitcher was empty. It had been a very long day. The phone rang. "Sugar, could you sit with Connie while I pick up a new guest? Connie has visitors coming. I'd feel a whole lot better knowing you were here to watch over her. I don't want her getting tuckered out."

My head throbbed, and my feet burned inside my Birkenstocks.

"I just made some lemonade, just like Mammy's," she said.

Ky lay on the couch scowling at the ceiling.

"I'll be right over."

Louise had forgotten to tell me she'd made one minor change to Mammy's lemonade recipe. She used half the sugar. While I stirred the contents of two sugar bowls into the pitcher, Connie chatted with her visitors at the kitchen table. The mother and her little girl sat stiffly in the high-backed chairs. In a dress two sizes too big and two decades out of date, the mother stared at a suncatcher that splintered sunlight around the room. Angel, the little girl, only had eyes for a purple velvet box on the table.

"Do you have your money with you, Angel?" Connie asked.

Angel slid a dime across the table to Connie, and Connie made a show of opening her coin purse and dropping it in. "Before you see your Barbie, we need to talk about how to take care of her."

"My sister's Barbie can't be up past eight-thirty on a school night, but during the summer, she's up until nine," said Angel, a girl of about eight, with hair the color of butter.

"That's right," Connie said. "Barbie wants to do well in school, so she has to be rested. Have you given any thought to your Barbie's career?"

"My sister's Barbie wants to be a fashion designer, but you have to move to New York City to do that. That's too far from Mommy. I think my Barbie will be a teacher. That way, she can come home for lunch every day. She wants to teach second graders like me. Fifth graders are too mean."

"Anything else?"

"She has to eat good food, like green beans and applesauce, and no dating until she's sixteen. My Barbie's going to wait longer, 'cause she doesn't like boys much."

Connie winked at me. "Anything else?"

"I forget."

Connie explained the importance of reading to Barbie every day and keeping her clean and neat. "She takes care of herself and others."

Angel brushed a strand of hair out of her eyes. "Sometimes my sister forgets to read to her Barbie, but I won't. Tiffany talks on the phone to her friends."

"Barbie depends on you. If you don't read to her, no one else will."

"I know."

"One more thing. Do you remember what it is?"

Angel looked at the velvet box with longing. "Oh yes. Barbie goes to Sunday school every week."

Connie turned over a sketch of a flouncy evening gown with soft drapes of purple and pink. "This is the gown we designed together. Take a good look at it. I want you to make sure I did as you said. Ready?"

The girl nodded and leaned in, and so did the mother. Connie lifted the velvet box to reveal Angel's Barbie dressed just like the picture. The girl reached out but withdrew her hands quickly. "I have to wash my hands."

I helped Angel pull a chair to the sink to wash her hands while Connie talked with the mother.

"Thank you so much," the mother said. "Tiffany's done so much better in school since she got her Barbie. Angel's been practicing reading. We went to the library to get books Barbie would like. She's been so excited. She asked a million times if today was the day. I told her she had to wait."

"Are the girls getting to Sunday school?" Connie asked.

The mother's eyes dropped. "The neighbor lady takes them."

"You're doing a good job, Crystal."

Angel showed Connie her clean hands. "Can I hold her?"

"She's your Barbie, bought and paid for."

With last good-byes and final instructions, Angel and her mother left. Connie sighed.

"Let's get you to bed," I said. "Louise won't be happy if I let you get worn out."

We made our way to the bedroom with Connie leaning on my arm. I helped her take off her shoes and got her situated in the bed, laying a chenille throw over her. "You make such a difference in little girls' lives."

"I've been making doll clothes since I could thread a needle, but it wasn't until I started making clothes for my daughter's Barbies that my creative juices got flowing. And once I started, I couldn't stop. It's not brain surgery, but I guess God can work through baubles and bangles, too. When the girls leave with their Barbies, they feel like the princesses God intended them to be. They stand straighter and smile brighter."

I'd spent all day cajoling Ky into being helpful. I'd been less than successful, so if Connie had a doll in her collection to make Ky feel more like a prince, or at least fearful of the queen, I would pay more than a dime for it. In his present frame of mind, Ky was more likely to use a doll for target practice.

When I complained to Connie about his sulking, she said, "Sons are such a blessing, aren't they?"

I knew Connie hadn't meant to open a debate, but I couldn't help myself. "Are you sure about that?"

"Definitely. I couldn't imagine getting through this illness without Larry. He's such a help."

Maybe she *was* looking for a debate. "I could say the same thing about Ky until about two months ago. In some ways, he did a better job taking care of me than I did of him. Now I'm invisible to him."

Connie patted the bed and I sat down. "I remember that age," she said. "When Larry turned fourteen, I practically ran down to the humane society to adopt the ugliest dog they had. I knew a dog like that would love me for no better reason than I filled its water and food bowls every day. Once I got Scrounge home, that dog watched every move I made, even followed me to the bathroom. The little guy loved me and I knew it. There's not a better antidote to teenagers than a wagging tail. My only mistake was to let Larry name him." She frowned. "But you have Blink, don't you?"

Sure, I had Blink, but from his recent escapades, I suspected he was stuck in perpetual canine adolescence.

"Don't you worry too much about Ky," she said. "I've had him in Sunday school twice. He's deeply rooted in his faith. I've watched him, and he's nothing but kind when he helps with the toddlers. He sits on the floor with them, reads them stories, and lets them chase him around the tables. They adore him and so do I. Just last week, he sat next to me after the service and asked me how I was feeling. He seemed real interested. That says a lot about a young man."

Getting Ky to church that week had been like pushing water uphill.

"It's nothing but the sourpuss stage, as normal as a pimple on prom night. Once he agrees to grow up, he'll snap out of it."

"And if he's a budding Peter Pan?"

"That's what the military is for. It sure helped Larry. He's downright useful now. He did most of the sewing on the evening gown for Angel's Barbie."

No matter how hard I tried, I couldn't picture Larry stitching Barbie evening gowns. I changed the subject. "Can you tell me anything about the new guest Louise went to pick up?"

"She's a young girl, thirty-something. She and her mother are from Ridgway or Telluride . . . or somewhere down there. It's just the two of them, no husband or dad mentioned. The girl had just found her way back to her mother. Then the cancer hit . . . breast, I think. But it doesn't matter. It's all over the girl. She doesn't have long."

"Shouldn't she be in a hospital?"

"Her mother wants her to stay in the hospital, but the girl's begging to go home. Coming here is a compromise."

"Is Louise up to it? I mean, she's only a few months out from her own treatment."

"Louise has learned to lean on Jesus for her strength. I wouldn't worry about her."

It wasn't Louise I worried about.

People who live in the high desert spend a lot of time doing arithmetic problems in their heads, especially in the summer. Every night, unless clouds hold the heat in place, the temperature drops thirty degrees from the day's high. If the daytime temperature was 95—pretty typical for July and the first weeks of August—in the hour just before dawn, the temperature would sink to 65 degrees, great for strenuous exercise and better for sleeping. That day, the mercury had topped 105 degrees while Ky had watched me saw through a sycamore branch as big around as my thigh, so by dawn, the temperature would dip to 75 degrees. Still tolerable. Unfortunately, Scott and I had skimped on insulation in our bedroom walls to save money for an incredibly romantic four-poster bed. The bed had seemed like such a good idea at the time, but now I had to add seven degrees to the low to compensate for our flight of whimsy. The mental arithmetic added up to a miserable night of tossing and turning on hot sheets. Why even try?

I showered and dressed in the coolest thing I could wear in public, the orange and white hibiscus muumuu Louise had bought for me on her anniversary trip to Hawaii. She'd denied buying the muumuu at the airport, but it was too garish for anything but an impulse buy. I didn't even towel my hair dry. I'd hoped the wetness would cool me, but it only made my neck itch.

I joined Andrea on the front porch. She kept the porch swing going in an easy rhythm while we waited for her friends, who were going to pick her up at nine o'clock. Her cello leaned against the railing like an attentive boyfriend. Blink lay at our feet with his belly exposed to the night air. The heat had distilled our conversation to only the essentials until our talking evaporated completely, but not my curiosity. Andrea seemed different. I counted her earrings, noted the garnet stud in her nose and the pointed stud in her chin. All metal was present and accounted for. A car slowed to a stop in front of the house.

Her fingers, light and dry, rested on my hands. "You don't have to worry about Louise," she said. "She'll be all right. She thrives on this sort of thing." Andrea stood, and I almost asked her not to go. Over her shoulder she called, "Remember how much she loves doting over us."

That was true.

With Andrea gone, I turned out the porch light and watched Mr. and Mrs. Fellhauer come out of their house to walk their Boston terriers, Bella and Mabel. Blink moved to the steps to protect his territory. The darkness deepened. Blink cried to go inside, so I let him in.

"You're making me sorry I didn't get a cat," I told him.

Walkers, alone and in pairs, sauntered by unaware that I watched them from the porch. I folded myself to lie down on the swing. The crickets' songs intensified. Traffic noises hushed. I considered going inside, but Ky's mood had seeped through the house, dimming light bulbs and leaving the air too thick to breathe. A mosquito taunted me, so I stretched the muumuu to cover my toes and pulled my arms out of the sleeves. Safe in my muumuu cocoon, I slept.

The hollow beats of footsteps on the porch woke me. A man—Ben!—held a large book under his arm. I blinked at the darkness, and soon I could see by the glow of the streetlight that he was tapping his foot and shifting his weight as he waited for the door to open.

What are you doing here? Go home!

He cupped his hands to look in the sidelight. Whatever he saw encouraged him to knock again harder, and when no answer came, he leaned the book against the door. He wore Birkenstocks, barefooted, of course, a comfort I'd introduced to him. This was no time to weaken. I sucked in a breath and squeezed my eyes shut.

The scent of Ben's cologne reached me. My pulse quickened. *Get a grip!* The thinking woman part of me had gotten it right. Ben was trouble. This guy worked too hard to keep his options open. *The door is closed. The door is closed. The door is—*

"Aloha," he said, standing over me. "Weren't you even going to say hi?"

"I must have dozed off," I said, sitting up to put my arms back in my sleeves.

Even in the dark, I saw the flash of his smile, the one that puckered his dimples, unseen in the darkness but fully remembered. "Mind if I join you?"

I tried to run my hands through my hair, but it had dried into a matted mess.

"I'm sorry for coming by so late," he said. "I've had this book in the truck for weeks. I thought I'd better drop it by." He handed over the book, a glossy monolith too bulky for anything but collecting dust.

I lit a citronella candle and tilted the cover to read the title, *Rose Gardens of the World.* I flipped through the pages as politeness required and cooed approvingly at the impossibly beautiful rose gardens, but inwardly, I was wishing for a hairbrush and a butterfly clip. *Don't forget, the door is closed.*

I pulled my hair into a ponytail and tied it in a loose knot. "Thanks for the book. It's very thoughtful. I love it."

"I also wanted you to know I'll be out of town for a while."

"Oh?"

"You're not going to believe this. I'm on my way to Ecuador, of all places, with Flying Missions. It's a short-term thing. They're desperate for pilots, especially with high-altitude experience. The recruiting director spoke at my church's mission fair a couple months ago. We got to talking, and the next thing I knew, he'd handed me an application."

"How short is short term?" What I really wanted to know was why he was on my porch, late at night, bearing gifts. His presence had reignited my hope, and soon, without any encouragement from me—or Ben, really—the flame burned brightly. I wiped my palms on the muumuu.

"I'll be gone six weeks. I know it's crazy, but it feels right, the best I've felt about anything in a long time. Maybe that's why I came tonight, to let you know and to thank you, I guess. I never would have gone back to church if I hadn't wanted to impress you. I thought you might warm to me if I was a good Christian boy like Scott."

A rush of blood flooded my heart and heated me from within. *The door . . .*

"Going back to church was the best thing I could've done," he said. "I went once, and it was like going home. Week after week, I'd find myself in church, very surprised at myself, I might add. In fact, I'm on my way home from a Bible study now. If my wingman could see me now . . ."

Oh my. In an instant, the loneliness of the past months gained meaning as the mysterious workings of God unfolded. It was perfectly clear. Ben needed the time to revisit his faith and grow into a man able to shepherd a family. My family? And now that he had entered back into the fold, he came back to where he knew I waited, open armed and open hearted, to welcome him.

That is so cool, God.

Claire's name pestered me like a mosquito, but I shooed it away.

Ben rested his arm on the back of the swing. I leaned back, and although I couldn't feel his arm, I knew it was there and my shoulders warmed at its nearness. We rocked back and forth. A soft breeze fingered my face.

The new future I envisioned with Ben made my skin prickle with excitement, but I was utterly content at the same time. A piece of my life had been settled. This was how I'd felt when I found out I was pregnant with Ky and earlier when Scott had asked me to marry him, but this didn't seem like a good time to bring up Scott. It was settled. Ben and me. The squeak of the chain serenaded us.

"How are you doing these days?" he asked.

"Great." Losing clients, alienating my son, owing Larry a bundle of money, and being called a thief all seemed trivial, hardly worth mentioning. The world had become a safer place, just like that.

"Ky?"

"He's going through some typical teenage turmoil right now. He needs a course correction is all. He's such a resilient kid. He'll snap out of it in no time."

"That's good. That's real good." Ben squirmed. "How about Louise? How's the recuperation?"

"Typical Louise, really. She's already looking for ways to turn her pain into triumph." I explained about the Garden House becoming Still Waters Inn. "And today, a woman and her mother moved in. Such a sad story."

"If I was sick, I'd stay with Louise and eat her blueberry streusel muffins three times a day."

Everyone had a favorite.

"Blink?" he asked.

When a man asks you about your dog's well-being, you have to wonder if he isn't avoiding the real issue, as men so often do. I hoped the real issue had something to do with waiting for him to return and a fresh start to our relationship, but my hope ebbed. Ben had never flinched at saying how he'd felt about me. Why would this night be any different?

He leaned forward, his elbows on his knees, to study my porch floor. Louise and I had painted the floor last fall, and it looked nice, but I doubted Ben could see our workmanship in the dark. I steeled myself, again.

"I think the world of you."

Uh-oh.

"You saved my life. You forced me to move on. When I couldn't see how foolish it would be to get involved in a relationship, you knew better."

Foolish? Did I say foolish?

"You knew we needed time, and somehow you knew I needed to reconnect with my Savior. For that I will always love you."

Like a friend?

"I met Claire at a group they have for singles at my church. I almost didn't go. The whole singles ministry sounded pretty lame, pretty desperate. My mom called every week to see if I'd given it a try."

A golf-ball-sized lump stuck in my throat. *How could I have been so stupid?*

"Claire had just moved here from Phoenix. We hit it off right away. She loves to fly, and she actually knows my sister from Montana State. That's weird, huh?"

Weird was a cat with six toes, a black widow spider eating her mate, the reappearance of bell-bottoms and wide collars. Hearing Ben say Claire's name like a prayer was more like watching my own heart monitor go flat for the third time, and there was no one to blame but me.

"Totally weird," I said.

Ben stared into the darkness. "We're pretty serious. I thought I should tell you."

Somewhere close by, a siren startled the night.

～⁀◡

The full moon cast a blue light that splayed long shadows across Louise's garden. We'd been sitting on her iron settee long enough for my bottom to go numb. After Ben had left, I'd made a beeline to Louise's back door. As it so often happens between friends, one heartache trumps the other's.

Louise blew her nose and wiped her tears on the flounce of my muumuu. "Having that girl here has been like ripping open an old wound. I thought my heart had healed long ago, but when I saw her lying there as empty as a root cellar in July, I saw my own dear son. At the end of Kevin's treatments, I had to look deeper and deeper to find him. Finally, his light receded too far. I couldn't find him, even though he was right there."

Kevin was Louise's son who lost his battle with leukemia at the age of ten. I squeezed her hand tighter. "It was unfair of the mother to bring her daughter here when she was so very sick. The hospice folks should have been notified."

Louise sighed heavily and turned her face to the moon. The pure light caught the red and green facets of her cherry earrings. "I can't help but wonder if I missed something that would have caught Kevin's disease sooner, and if I had, he would be alive today. He would have a wife and at least ten darlin' towheaded children, and he'd bring those rambunctious cherubs to dinner on Sundays with his precious wife. I know he'd come over on Saturdays to help Manley change the oil in the car every three-thousand miles or to repair shingles on the roof—guy stuff, you know. If only—"

"Louise, you did all you could have done."

"But you don't know . . . you just don't know." And then she fell into my arms again, sobbing on my shoulder. Like a couple of synchronized swimmers, our shoulders shook, and we gulped for air only to return below the deep waters. Manley peeked at us through the curtains and disappeared quickly. Smart man.

Louise straightened herself. Her voice, deepened by her sorrow, continued steadily on. "Kevin complained of a fever, so I gave him Tylenol and told him to go to bed like I always did when he'd caught a cold. But that time, sleep wasn't enough. I knew something was terribly wrong. The doctor said not to worry, Kevin was fighting an infection, was all. I pointed out his bruises and how very pale he was. Doc Hanson had an answer for everything, blamed my concern on first-time mother hysteria, and he even said I needed another child so Kevin could get about the business of being a little boy without me interfering. I should have insisted on blood work. I certainly thought about it, but I guess I wanted to believe the doctor more than I wanted to hear anything bad about Kevin. Oh, Mibby, I actually told the boy he was lazy."

We sat in the moonlight for a long time. A barn owl roosting in the Morgans' garage hooted his monotonous call, and the crash of metal disturbed the night as train cars hooked together across town. I prayed, asked God to give me words to comfort my friend, but nothing came. Then I remembered that even God had cried when His Son died.

Louise's breathing eased. She blew her nose and wiped her eyes again. "And if revisiting the dark days of Kevin's illness hasn't been bad enough, I can't help thinkin' it should be me on the way to the hospital right now instead of that girl. She's only thirty-seven years old—"

"I'm almost thirty-seven," I whispered.

"I know, sugar. I shook like a scared puppy when I thought of that, too. She's so young, she'd never even thought of having a mammogram. If I hadn't done my self-exam; if I hadn't gone for the mammogram; if good ol' Doc Wilcox hadn't insisted on a biopsy to be absolutely sure, it most certainly could have been me. And that upsets me more than I'd like to admit."

I trembled at the thought of losing Louise and held her tighter.

"Maybe it's a little soon for you to be taking in sick people. No one would blame you—"

"Don't you worry. I'm going to be all right. The Lord has always given me the strength to do what He's asked me to do. This won't be any different."

Louise pulled her wig off to fan herself. "Enough about me. What are you doing out so late?" The last thing Louise needed to hear was my lovelorn tale, but she insisted. "You can tell me about it, sugar."

Her mascara had left trails down her cheeks. In the moon's spotlight, Louise's skin was cool porcelain, like one of those clown dolls sold in magazines. I had no power to resist her. My own voice sounded strange to me, like every word weighed too much for me to hold.

I told her about Ben's visit and how easily I'd abandoned my good sense with one good whiff of his cologne. "There's nothing as pathetic as a desperate woman in a muumuu."

Our eyes met and blubberfest round two commenced. By the time we'd finished, the hem of my muumuu was damp with tears.

Louise pulled her wig back on and stood up. "Get the keys. We're making a run for some first aid." In the intimate language of friends, that meant a trip to Dairy Queen for a Peanut Buster Parfait. When a friend breaks a diet, one intended to keep the evil C at bay, you know you're loved.

Fifteen minutes later, with chocolate coursing through our veins, Louise offered a prayer. "We're partners in misery tonight, Lord, but we want you to be our joy in the morning."

Amen.

~~~

Every time I closed my eyes, I saw Ben walking down the front walk to his truck, so I threw back the sheet and headed for my drawing table in the family room. Regret didn't inspire me any better than desperation. I drummed my fingers on the drawing board, hoping to evoke a creative thought. The white expanse of paper mocked me. I drew Roseanne's property lines and the exterior walls of the house and garage that represented the simple transfer of numbers and angles to a page—mindless stuff. Then I stopped cold. There was nothing like a broken heart to kill the muse.

I wrote Ben's name in the corner, outlined it with a cloud, shaded the cloud until it foreshadowed a storm, and then drew in dense lines of rain. Not good. I switched to elaborate scrolls and curlicues, sunshine and daisies, a cube, an eye with a tear.

No cigar. Try again.

I drew arrows following arrows up the margin to bubble letters saying, "Peace be with you and you and you."

I closed my eyes again. A pond. A crescent of flowering shrubs. Those adorable twinspurs that never stop blooming. I sketched the arrangement I'd envisioned next to Roseanne's small stoop. Would she consider a French door in her bedroom? I rubbed out the stoop and outlined a patio the length of the house, erased it, and redrew it again with rounded edges and added a winding path to the garage door. Then I drew a pond and a cluster of circles to represent plants. The doodles had worked their magic. The mild resistance of lead against paper had loosed my creativity.

Blink trotted by and out the doggie door, and I willed my thoughts to stay in Roseanne's garden, not to follow the dog out to the poop deck, the only patch of lawn in a yard otherwise covered in flowers.

I erased the pond—too much of a hazard for Phoebe—and changed it to a cobble fountain, no standing water, lots of great sound. Next, the trees. Roseanne had insisted on two of her favorites, a Forest Pansy redbud and a Redspire pear, but they were both thirsty trees, so I neighbored them with other water gobblers, like the hybrid tea roses Roseanne loved. The plan needed another tree. Something feminine? Weeping birch? Too sad and too thirsty. Washington hawthorn? Better, but unapproachable with all those thorns covering its trunk. What was I thinking? I needed something sturdier. I erased the circle and drew a slightly larger ring to represent a burr oak, a stately, even majestic tree. Excellent shade. At home in dry conditions.

Blink stuck his head in the doggie door.

"So, you're polite in the middle of the night, are you? Come on in."

He squeezed through the door and trotted over for an ear scratch.

"That's enough. Go lie down."

He didn't move.

"Not now, Blink. I'm working."

He collapsed to the floor, stretched, and closed his eyes. Before I turned back to my work, his snores, more like moans, filled the room.

I finished Roseanne's plan just before four in the morning. To anyone else it would have looked like a mess. Erasures. Tentative lines. Bold lines smeared by my hand. Scribbled plant names. But the energy of the marks reassured me because they meant ideas worth keeping still percolated behind my burning eyes.

I considered making a pot of coffee and getting an early start to the day, but my maintenance clients—and their neighbors—wouldn't appreciate my predawn industry. Before going to bed, I looked at the plan one more time, changed a variety of butterfly bush near the fountain, and exchanged a heliotrope for a star zinnia. Better.

The doodles caught my eye. I reached for an eraser but stopped. The tension I'd felt over the expanse of white paper mirrored the taut dread of perching on the edge of my own future—so many minutes, months, and years to fill. With what? Not Ben, that was sure. Other than that, I didn't know. I had to doodle in my life, do some safe stuff, experiment with a safety net to find the courage to step into the whiteness. When I delivered the plan to Roseanne, I would tell her to count on me for the Table of Ten party.

JULY
21

The red badge of courage goes to First Love dianthus. Still blooming, knee high with serrated hot pink petals. What a trooper!

Under the shower's stream, I worked hard at keeping my thoughts off of Ben. It wasn't easy, so I formulated a strategy for repaying Larry. The phone bill was due on the first, trash and sewer on the fourteenth. Half of Roseanne's fee would cover those, and the rest would go for groceries next month. Maybe a yard sale? No time for that. Pawn broker? We hardly ever ate in the dining room . . . *No way.* That was my grand-mother's table. Sell the computer? That would solve two problems in one—rescue Ky from the crypt and pay off Larry. *Arrivederci,* Larry! Having settled my financial troubles, my thoughts went back to Ben like a compass to north.

The d-o-o-r is closed.

I reached for the shampoo, but something seemed awfully familiar about the bottle. Had I already washed my hair? I couldn't remember. To be safe, I sudsed up again. Reasonably sure I was clean, I wrapped a towel around my hair and dressed.

In a small porthole I'd toweled on the foggy mirror, I gave myself a pep talk. "Listen up, girl. You can't be getting lost in the shower. Folks are depending on you. Straighten up. Get it together. You're not in high school anymore. Ben loves Claire, not you." The woman in the mirror winced and considered going back to bed. "Lord, help!"

~~~

Andrea looked up from her cello and smiled without interrupting her warm-up. The notes stepped up and down the scales with a lively bounce, terribly inappropriate for the hour and my mood. I hoped she'd slip into something ponderous and brooding soon.

She stopped midscale. The unfinished exercise hung in the air like an Escher drawing. "Isn't that what you wore yesterday?" she asked.

I scratched at a crusty spot of refried beans on my overalls. "All better."

Andrea frowned. "Maybe you should change into something . . . er . . . more professional, say a black skirt and blouse, something silky. You could borrow one of mine."

I was a garden designer, not a vampire. "Overalls are professional when you pull weeds for a living." The doorbell rang. "Who could that be?" When I moved to answer the door, Andrea stopped me with a hand to my shoulder. "Why don't you put your shoes on before you answer the door?"

An exchange of male voices at the front door startled me. Andrea's eyes smiled as if they held a wonderful secret. "Go ahead. You look great."

Droop was at the door, but he wasn't alone. Behind him stood a man, my height or maybe a little shorter, who struck me as round—small round eyes, round-tipped nose but not so round as to be clownish, and a round, dimpled chin. Over his belt, a paunch completed the theme. He wore dress slacks and a short-sleeved white shirt with a shades-of-blue striped tie. He would have been inconspicuous anywhere, even on my porch at seven in the morning, except for his comb-over. Never had so little hair been asked to accomplish so much and failed so miserably.

"I'd like you to meet one of my fishing buddies," Droop said. "This here's Crenshaw . . . What's your last name again?" he asked the man.

Crenshaw cleared his throat with a volley of shallow coughs before answering. "Crenshaw is my last name. That's what I go by. For those who want to know, my first name's Hollis."

"Hollis? Really?" Droop asked. "I had a dog named Hollis."

The conversation stopped as if a sinkhole had opened in the porch. Droop nudged Crenshaw with a hard jab at the ribs, but by then I'd figured out I didn't want to hear what either of them had to say, so I told Crenshaw it had been nice to meet him, and I started to close the door. Droop stopped the door with his boot.

"Crenshaw here has something to ask you."

The man's face flushed crimson, and a new spell of coughing began. The least I could do was offer the man a glass of water.

"Thanks, no. It's just a cough. Had it for years. Be fine in a minute."

Droop winked at me, and he wasn't the winking kind. Now I was worried. "What time is it?" I asked. "I . . . I . . . I want to beat the heat. Nice to meet you, Crenshaw."

Andrea giggled behind me.

Droop nudged Crenshaw harder, which only intensified his coughing. Crenshaw took a plaid hanky out of his pants pocket to wipe his forehead and a stiff arc of hair stood out from his head like an antenna. "I was thinking, Mrs. Garrett, seeing how you're a widow and I'm a widower, that it would be nice to go out for a bite to eat for the sake of a little company sometime."

He watched me, unblinking, waiting for an answer and coughing into his hanky. He was so very not Ben—nor Scott. The leap was too big. My imagination froze under the challenge of declining his invitation. Instead, I yammered.

"Sometime? Sure. Sometime would be good. Right now, though, I have to finish getting ready for work. Hair's wet. Need to put on a little makeup, some clean clothes. Need to be professional, you know. This isn't exactly a good time. But sometime later. That would be good. Thanks for coming by. If you'll excuse me, I have to be going."

This time Droop let the door close.

I raced through my maintenance clients. I needed to talk to Louise and get a little Southern-style commiseration. A lemon scone would surely calm my nerves. But instead of Louise, Larry held her back door open. He'd unbuttoned his Sweet Suzy shirt to reveal his white undershirt.

"What are you doing here?" I asked.

"Hello to you, too. I'm here to pick up my mom. You look thirsty." He poured two glasses of iced tea from a pitcher in the refrigerator. His familiarity with Louise's kitchen irked me.

"Where's your mom? Is Louise here?"

"Relax for a minute," he said and pulled out a kitchen chair for me. "Have a seat. I hear you have a date."

I looked into the parlor to see if Louise had fallen asleep in her chair. "I do?"

"Crenshaw?"

"Crenshaw? Him? No, I don't think so. I told him to call sometime, but I don't think he will. He coughs a lot, seems pretty nervous."

"I would." He said it softly.

Larry seemed determined to unnerve me, but I wasn't about to give him the satisfaction. I pretended not to hear him. Instead, I asked him again where I could find Louise.

"We'd have a good time, too."

"What?" I asked coyly.

He leaned back in his chair and took a long drink of tea. The smile had faded from his eyes. "She's upstairs with my mother packing up that gal's things, the one they took to the hospital last night."

I hated to think what that could mean. "I guess I better come back later." I downed the iced tea and put the glass in the dishwasher.

"Want some advice?" he asked.

Not really.

"I can see that you don't, so I'm going to tell you anyway. You'll thank me someday." He patted the chair beside him.

I leaned against the doorway to the dining room.

"Come on, you've got time to sit down." He held my gaze.

I knew this wouldn't be over until I listened to him, so I sat down on the very edge of the seat and sighed.

"When Crenshaw calls, make a lunch date. They're shorter. And don't let him pick you up. Meet him at the restaurant. That way, if you get uncomfortable, and I mean uncomfortable for any reason at all, you can get out of there. Then go home and lock the door."

"Like I said, I have no plans to go out with Crenshaw, but if I did, I don't think he's anyone I need to worry about. Droop says he's the nicest guy he's ever known." Actually, he'd said he was a straight shooter, which hasn't been important to women since Daniel Boone courted Rebecca.

"I don't care if he's Mr. Rogers. He's a man, so I'd worry."

"I can take care of myself."

Larry tapped his temples. "Watch his eyes. If he's saying one thing and his eyes say another, get out of there, especially if he waggles his eyebrows."

Waggles his eyebrows? "What are you talking about? Cartoon characters waggle their eyebrows. Real men don't waggle their eyebrows. I'm outta here." As the screen door hissed closed behind me, Larry couldn't resist yelling instructions after me. "And carry some cash. Be prepared. Do you have a pepper canister for your purse?"

Oi vey.

"And tell Ky I really need a pitcher!"

I'd fallen in love with Scott the moment I saw his house and not one moment sooner. Before that, I'd noticed he was good-looking, the way you would notice the nuance of color and light in a Vermeer painting. I had no hope of ever owning one, but that didn't diminish my enjoyment. Scott was nice and funny, had a great smile and eyes the color of the ocean before a storm. Everything else about him was a wheat field in late summer—golden, no storm in sight. His age bothered me. The fifteen years between us was a wide chasm of confidence and experience. I liked my men—boys—malleable.

We met at the La Mesa True Value store where I worked after college graduation as a management trainee in the garden department. I'd taken the job out of desperation. Art majors were plentiful and didn't eat very well, but the building boom in San Diego County had fueled the horticulture industry to a fevered pitch. As long as there were bare lots in the county, I would be able to pay the rent. All of my time in my grandmother's garden had finally paid off.

I'd just broken up with Gary, a fellow artist who modeled his life after Picasso and accused me of emulating Grandma Moses. I was hiding—though I wouldn't have admitted it then—among the azaleas and camellias when Scott wandered by reading plant tags and scratching his head. He sighed with relief when I offered him assistance.

That first Saturday I coached Scott on how to clear his lawn of clover and how to reseed the bare batches where the grass had been killed by the previous owner's dog. A few weeks later, he came in, flush with success, wanting to know what kinds of flowers grew well in the shade. He left with a truckload of perennials and annuals, only to return the next week for a *Photinia* to screen the view of his neighbor's RV and two bougainvillea vines—one deep pink and one a vivid orange—to cover an ugly block wall. He came to the store like that week after week. By late summer, I greeted him with, "What now?" I thought I'd rescued him. Later, Scott told me I'd worn my sadness like a wool coat and he wanted to hang it up for me.

When he'd bought enough plant material to reproduce the Royal Botanic Gardens at Kew, he asked me over for a cup of coffee and a tour of his yard. I declined at first. He was older. A little gray streaked his temples, and his clothing was more than a tad conventional. He never wore the same golf shirt twice. In short, he looked like a J. C. Penney model, kind of starchy and a bit glossy. His shopping had, in part, however, boosted my sales numbers to make me eligible for my first promotion, so I eventually agreed.

I followed him in my rattling VW down a palm-tree-lined street. He pulled into a driveway and I parked on the street, but I didn't, couldn't, get out of the car. His house, a squat Spanish-style bungalow with a red-tile roof and arched doorways, mesmerized me. It was painted algae green—that would have to be changed—but the house was weighted, a part of the earth, unshakable. And that made Scott secure, too. I saw myself waving from the doorway, although in my mind the house had already been painted butter cream.

Now I sat across from Crenshaw at Denny's on Highway 6 near the airport. "Sometime" had not been indefinite enough for Crenshaw. He'd shown up at five o'clock, saying now was good for him, and in one of those strange convergences of events, my mind refused to manufacture an excuse to turn down the date. Even Ky encouraged me to go.

"Have fun, Mom. Don't worry about me. I'll mow the lawn or something."

I changed into a denim skirt and a T-shirt, stepped back into my Birkenstocks, and off we drove in his Neon. Going out with Crenshaw was a nice thing to do. His self-confidence needed a boost for all those other women he would be dating. We would have a quick meal and an even quicker good-night. *Ta-da*. A good deed done.

Crenshaw cut an oversized bite of pancakes with his knife and jabbed a hunk of sausage with his fork. I wondered what it would take to make me fall in love with someone like Crenshaw. I'd already ruled out the Taj Mahal and the White House and the czar's Summer Palace. How could Droop have been so clueless about what a woman wanted in a man?

"Aren't you going to eat?" he asked around a mouthful of food.

"I had a late lunch."

He coughed. "Do you mind if I eat your bacon?"

So far, we'd talked about the weather, we'd speculated on the newness of the upholstery in Denny's, and he'd explained how much he liked eating breakfast for dinner. He wore the same clothes I'd seen him in that morning, only after a full day of work his shirt was a map of stains. The continent of Africa covered his chest. His cough worsened by the minute.

"Where do you work?" I asked.

Cough, cough. "IHOP, but I like the sausage here better."

The waitress refilled his water glass.

"I'm sorry." More coughing. A sip of water. "I'm a little nervous."

"You are? Don't worry, I'm having a nice time." I reasoned that wasn't a lie, because I loved hashbrowns, and if I'd been home, I would've felt compelled to do the laundry.

113

"You don't understand." Cough. "It's been a long time since I've been with—" Crenshaw's coughing turned spasmodic and drew attention from the other diners. After another long drink, he started over. "I haven't been with a woman in a long time."

"You're doing fine, really. Relax."

Cough. "No, I mean *with* a woman." And this time, he waggled his eyebrows when he said *with*. "Together. *With*. You know, later?" Cough.

Later? With? Oh . . . *with*! "Excuse me, I have to go to the restroom."

As I slid out of the booth, Crenshaw grabbed my hand and waggled his eyebrows again. "I'll pay the bill and meet you in the car."

Inside the bathroom stall, I checked my wallet for cash. Only nineteen cents in nickels and pennies. Not even enough to make a phone call. No pepper spray. No whistle. I didn't even have my nail clipper. And there was only one way out of the restaurant. I waited, hoping Crenshaw took the hint and went home.

The door to the women's bathroom opened and closed. A pair of scuffed tennis shoes stopped in front of my stall. A husky female voice asked, "Are you Libby?"

Close enough. I unlocked the stall door. A woman in a Denny's apron stood with her weight on one hip. Her face had the vitality of a wet pair of jeans. Her nametag identified her as Yvonne.

I whispered, "Is there a problem?"

Yvonne's voice boomed in the tiled room. "There's a guy wants to know if you're in here."

"Would it bother you to tell him I'm not?"

She stared at me as if someone had pushed her pause button. Finally, she said, "Okay, wait here," and shuffled out the door

I put my back to the stall door and prayed the prayer of the irresponsible. "Lord, deliver me from this mess I've made."

Just outside the door, Yvonne yelled, "Tell him she says she's not in there." A male voice said something I couldn't understand, and then Yvonne yelled again. "I'll do it myself!"

Groan.

I waited, counted to a hundred, and recited the alphabet. I promised myself I'd leave the restroom, head up, shoulders back, after I said the

Pledge of Allegiance and the Lord's Prayer three times each. Only then would I be ready to face Crenshaw.

The restroom door opened again. "Come on out," Yvonne said. "He left. Wasn't too happy, neither. Taxi?"

Thanks, Lord. I explained my cash situation and asked her to call Louise.

"Sit at the counter, hon. I'll pour you an iced tea."

"I think I'll wait here."

Within the cramped boundaries of the stall's laminated walls, the true torture of solitary confinement came to me—my own taunting voice. Last summer, when I'd cooled my relationship with Ben, I told him I needed time to help Ky through the dark valley of grief and that I'd promised Ky I wouldn't date until he was ready, too.

Eleven months later, Margaret suggested a date with Greg, and it hadn't taken all that much prodding for me to accept. Loneliness was the dragon, and I was nothing better than a damsel in distress looking for a knight, and Greg had a horse. That seemed promising. I'd forgotten all about my promise to Ky. When my conscience caught up to me, I'd justified that going out with Greg wasn't a real date, not to a livestock auction, anyway. It was a cross-cultural experiment. And now I was hiding from a squat man with a class-A comb-over. The lesson was clear. The damsel had to return to the castle for a little chat with the prince.

Yvonne returned with a message that Louise couldn't come but a ride was on the way. She smiled, and for a compact moment, energy snapped in her eyes. "This is just like high school."

Since high school hadn't been as good for me as it apparently had been for Yvonne, I got out my mini New Testament with Psalms and Proverbs and searched for a prayer pitiful enough for the situation. I found what I needed at the beginning of the thirteenth Psalm. *How long, O Lord? Will you forget me forever? How long will you hide your face from me? How long must I wrestle with my thoughts and every day have sorrow in my heart?*

Poor David. Poor me. I got out a pen and underlined the passage.

Once Larry was convinced that nothing indictable had happened between Crenshaw and me, we drove in silence, except for Goliath. She mewed plaintively from the backseat of Larry's Datsun 510, which rode like it had lost its suspension years earlier. I looked sideways at Larry. His head grazed the car's ceiling. He didn't belong in a Datsun. Larry was more of a kilt-wearing guy, the kind who gathered with other kilt-wearing guys and tossed telephone poles around. I would have guessed a Land Rover for Larry, a really old one.

Goliath batted the back of my head. By the time I turned around, she was looking out the window like an angry grandma. Only the tip of her tail twitched.

Larry's silence was full of accusations, so I composed his lecture in my thoughts. *What were you thinking? How stupid can you be? You can't date just anyone. Every man who comes into your life is a candidate for Ky's father. Be choosy. Learn to say no. Have some standards!*

I answered him out loud. "I know. I know."

He looked over. "I didn't say anything."

More silence.

As we turned onto Crawford Avenue, I conceded defeat. "You were right. The waitress hadn't even offered the dessert menu before Crenshaw waggled his eyebrows at me."

Larry spoke words so surprising, so soft with compassion, I almost didn't hear them. "I'm sorry your date wasn't what you'd hoped."

～

Ky jumped when I said hello. "You're home early."

"Can we talk?"

He clicked the mouse and a cloudy sky filled his monitor screen. "What's up?"

I moved a frozen-entrée tray from the bed to his dresser and sat down. "I need to apologize to you about something."

"What? I'm okay."

"Well, I haven't exactly been straight with you about dating. I promised to wait until we were both ready, and I didn't even talk to you about it. I just jumped in." Never mind that the water was too shallow to swim. "I broke my promise. I'm so sorry."

"No problem."

"No problem like I'd rather not talk about this right now, or no problem like I think dating is an okay thing for you, my beloved mother, to be doing?"

"I wasn't so sure about you dating at first, but Andrea told me that dating was an adult thing and that I'd have to trust you to do the right thing. And I do."

"You do?"

His eyes said, *I'm enthralled with this conversation with my mother,* but his twitching legs told the truth. He wanted me to leave so he could finish his game. His attempted deception warmed me.

"Just don't do anything stupid or act weird or anything," he said as he turned to the monitor.

Starting now? "You got it."

"Good 'nuff."

I rose to leave and kissed the top of his head. Then I remembered I wouldn't see him before I left in the morning. "Tomorrow's Wednesday. We agreed your room would look like a magazine spread by four."

Ky wagged his cursor on the screen. "We agreed the floor wouldn't be a fire hazard."

"And . . . ?"

"I don't smell anything."

"And . . . ?"

"And the room wouldn't smell like dead things."

Louise had warned me recently that males went through an additional developmental stage in which the olfactory glands switched on. Only then would Ky be able to smell himself and his surroundings. She said I would know the new plateau had been reached when the water bill tripled and he requested deodorant. Incessant calls from giggling girls would follow promptly. Ky wasn't there yet.

The glow of the monitor filled his room. "Good night," I said. But Ky the monster slayer had already saddled up and headed out on his quest.

The cricket's song echoed out of the floor register far from the reach of the flip-flop I kept under the bed to smash the likes of him. I increased the speed of the ceiling fan from medium to high in hopes of muffling the cricket's ardor. No such luck. The sheet over me felt like an old horse blanket after a long ride, so I kicked it off. The improvement wasn't noticeable. The clock read 2:43.

Think of something else.

I saw Ben smiling at me.

The . . . door . . . is . . . closed. What else?

Crenshaw's clammy hand on my arm.

Nope. Try again.

That Larry—

Don't go there. Think of something else, something cool.

The air-conditioner in Larry's car was the coolest thing I'd encountered all day. But thinking of Larry's car meant thinking about being rescued from Crenshaw and how foolish I'd been.

"I'm sorry your date wasn't what you'd hoped."

What hope? I hadn't hoped anything. I just didn't, or couldn't, say no when I wanted. Valid or not, I had enough hope to believe another invitation would come. But when that chance came, would I be woman enough to say what I meant? I imagined myself back at the front door at five o'clock. Crenshaw stood in the penetrating heat, shiny with a day's worth of oil and sweat, expecting me to go out to dinner with him. He said, "So, where ya wanna go?"

Instead of looking to Andrea and Ky for the answer like I actually had, I squared my shoulders and said, *No thank you. You're much too roundish for me, and what's with the hair?*

No need to be insulting.

All right, then. *No thank you. I have to keep the crickets company tonight.*

Tell the truth.

No thank you. I'm looking for someone who looks like Brad Pitt, has been nominated for several Nobel prizes in different categories, is certified in CPR, and has coached a Little League team to the World Series. Furthermore, I require an unauthorized biography that is boring but reassuring. I want a gourmet cook, and, oh yeah, anyone I date has to live his faith. He should also know which end of a toilet brush to use. Don't go yet, there's more. Never been married. No kids. Hates cats. Willing to die for my son.

I wanted to say no to the man, not demoralize him. How about a plain and simple no thank you? No insults. No excuses. No lies. And no atomic bombs to the male ego.

"Lord," I said out loud to drown out the cricket, "this is so not high school or college or one bit anything I ever wanted to do. If there's another way to find Mr. Right, part *deux,* I'd appreciate a guiding hand. Otherwise, help me to date as a woman with a spine and a heart."

And since I was still wide awake, I decided to pray for all my neighbors, starting with the Morgans. "Bless them with every good thing, especially your love, and grant them peace and . . ."

JULY
25

No more Jupiter's beard! What a pushy plant. It totally dominates the perennial bed by the bench, and it slouches. Only polite plants, like Shasta daisies or white coneflowers, allowed.

"Today? You want me to come today?" Gloria's request surprised me, but I also wanted to be sure I'd heard her correctly through the static of my cell phone.

"I know it's a lot to ask," she said, "especially after how crazily I acted about digging up the petunias the last time you were at the house. All I can say is it had been a terrible morning, and I'm so sorry."

I switched the phone to my other ear to downshift for a stoplight. "Don't think another thing about it, Gloria. I figured something was going on."

"You're a dear, but I'm crazier than ever today."

The light changed, so I cradled the phone with my shoulder and shifted into first. "What's going on?"

"Emily called last night to tell me she's getting married next weekend, here, at my house, in the garden. Her fiancé has been put on alert to go to Iraq. They want to marry before he leaves. Oh, I hope he comes back." Gloria gasped. The static snapped in my ear until she'd composed herself.

"We live in a crazy world, but love keeps finding a place to grow," she said. "It's so sweet they want to come home to get married. It's been a dream of mine since Emily wore diapers to have her wedding in the garden. I can't complain if my dream is coming true a little sooner than I'd anticipated.

"Anyway, the wedding is this Saturday morning, early—nine o'clock. Any later than that and I'm sure the plastic chairs would melt. There's so much to do and only five days to get it all done. I have people coming and going all week. Today is the best time for you to plant the petunias, and I think we better double the number you usually plant to really make an impact. As far as the drought goes, if we run out of water, so be it. The petunias can die where they're planted as long as they look good for the wedding."

As she talked, I reviewed my schedule. Three maintenance clients expected me that morning. Two weeks would pass before they came up on the schedule again, which equaled three unhappy clients if I put them off. Not a good idea. After lunch, I was presenting Roseanne's preliminary plan inside her cool house. I was proud of the plan and couldn't wait for her to see it. But still, in a pinch, I could put off Roseanne. Mr. Schluter was the real problem. I'd already rented a cement mixer, and the man who'd hitched the contraption to the Daisy Mobile had emphasized the rental shop's no-refund policy.

"Gloria, I can't come today, but I'll get there before the sun is up Friday, I promise." The phone went quiet. "You don't even have to be there. I'll come, plant, and be on my way."

"The fence repairmen will be here that morning."

I assured her I could work around them.

"And the caterers will be here at one to set up their tents."

"I'll be done by one."

"I knew I could count on you, Mibby. You're a real friend."

"Don't let yourself give another thought to the petunias. I'll take care of it. They'll be beautiful."

"Do you think you could get some of those marigolds, the ones that look like pom-poms? As a little girl, Emily brought them to me all the time. I hate to think about where she got them."

Roseanne bounced Phoebe on her knee while I cleared a flower arrangement from her kitchen table to make room for my portfolio. "Your yard is narrow but deep, so I didn't have any trouble incorporating everything you wanted, plus the strawberry patch is bigger than we'd hoped."

"Hear that, Pheebs? We'll have strawberries for our cereal." Phoebe smiled at the attention her mother gave her. Roseanne rewarded her with a snuggle, but the baby's face reddened again and she grunted. Roseanne resumed the bouncing. "That means giddyup. Aren't I well trained?"

I laughed with her, but inside I ached for the days when bouncing Ky on my knee made us both happy. "Before I show you the plan, I wanted to remind you that we talked about eliminating the lawn. But if you don't like what I've done, I'm willing to change the plan."

"Show me. I can't wait another minute."

I opened the portfolio and let Roseanne study the plan without my yammering at her, but I couldn't stay quiet long. "You'll have plenty of green. In fact, you'll be surrounded by green and every other color you can imagine. Throughout the garden, I've created paved sitting areas nestled into peninsulas of plantings. When the plants mature in a few years, each seating area will be an outdoor room, nice and cozy and very private."

With her finger Roseanne traced a sandstone path that wound past a Chinese lilac. "I like the shape of the path."

"Right, and once you've experienced the freedom of lawn-free living, you'll want me to rip out the grass in the front yard, too."

Roseanne's bouncing stopped. "We'll just have to see about that."

"There's another issue, the drought. This is the fifth year. Even if the weather pattern goes back to normal next year, it could be years before the water supply is stable. What I've designed is a xeric garden—"

Phoebe, unimpressed with the discussion, grunted for another giddyup.

"Should I even be planting a garden now?" Roseanne asked, resuming her bouncing.

"Locally, our water rights are secure. There will be water, but demand will increase, too. The responsible thing is to plan a garden that isn't water-greedy. "

"Roses are xeric, aren't they."

Words wouldn't convince Roseanne, but her eyes could. I opened the portfolio to the rendering I'd painted of her new garden. She brightened. I took Phoebe into my arms. Her dark eyes studied me while her mother saw the backyard as it would be in three to four years.

"Wow, it's so lush. . . . And the colors . . . I love it."

"Are you sure?"

She looked at me. "Of course, I'm sure. This is so much more than I'd hoped for."

This was the magical moment I lived for as a garden designer.

"I love the way the path winds back to the playhouse," she said. "It's so*ooo* cute, and you made the patio bigger. Is this a fountain?"

"Yes, and here's the sandpit we talked about. The ornamental grasses among the boulders will naturalize the area but won't attract bees to the play area. I've grouped plants with similar watering needs together. That's why the roses you wanted are here, next to the burning bush you had on your wish list. The perennials in the rock garden thrive in dry conditions. You'll be sipping tea every morning on your chaise longue, watching the hummingbirds and listening to your gurgling fountain."

"You've completely forgotten what it's like to have a toddler, haven't you?"

"Don't forget, I have Blink."

"There's no comparison." Even with nonstop knee bouncing, Phoebe's gurgles turned plaintive. "Let me put her down for a nap," Roseanne said. "Then I can give your plan the attention it deserves."

While Roseanne was out of the room, I looked over the installation contract I'd prepared, including the thirty percent I usually required before starting a project. Such a self-protective requirement might insult a friend like Roseanne. I turned the contract face down on the table, no longer sure I would even ask her to sign it.

When she returned, we changed several plant selections and discussed fencing options. From her crib, Phoebe sang a mournful song that slowed and sputtered before it stopped altogether. "Ah, quiet," Roseanne said, leaning over the plan. "This is so exciting. I can't wait to see it done."

"Once you decide what you want for the patio surface and the walkways, we're done. I drew in the sandstone path, but you can pave it however you want."

"How about with good intentions?" She laughed at her own joke but only briefly before her eyes hardened. "I'm sorry. That unprovoked jab has nothing to do with you or the plan. It was for Daniel." Roseanne excused herself. When she returned her eyes had softened and I'd slipped the contract back into my satchel. She handed me a glass of pink lemonade. That sealed our partnership.

"Don't forget, Table of Ten is this Friday night."

I groaned. "I don't know, Roseanne . . ."

"There's no backing out now, sister. You're registered."

I told her the whole pitiful story about Crenshaw.

"That horrid little man."

"I don't think he's horrid. He's been watching too much television is all. And to be fair, I didn't want to go out with him. I just couldn't think of an excuse fast enough."

"You don't need an excuse."

"I didn't want to hurt his feelings. The man has a cough."

"He's a grown-up. Be polite but firm."

She made me repeat after her, "No thank you. I have plans."

"And then you keep your mouth closed, Mibby dear. Above all, you need to trust your instincts."

"I think I lost those around my third anniversary. That's why dating men I don't know is a bad idea."

"Okay then, list all the unmarried men you know—besides Ben."

"Not fair."

"Name them."

"Let me think a minute." There was Ben, but Roseanne was right. It didn't do me any good to dwell on him. There was Walter. Too old and too engaged. How about Mr. Schluter? Too fussy. Greg? Too . . . what? Too horsey. Larry? Too much of a know-it-all—and too much of a guy, a guy who lived with his mother and sewed Barbie clothes.

"It's a very short list," I said.

"See? Getting to know men is what dating is all about." Roseanne put her hand on mine. "Besides, Table of Ten isn't dating; it's meeting people. You only date the men you like. This is very different from your handyman matching you up with his fishing buddy. The dinner is sponsored by my church. Don't you think that implies the men attending intend to date in an honorable and gentlemanly manner? Please say you'll come."

"Okay. Why not?" *Let me count the ways.*

After leaving Roseanne's, I spent the rest of the afternoon shoveling Mr. Schluter's scoria into a cement mixer to agitate it clean. Mr. Schluter was kind enough to supply a colander to sift out anything that wasn't rock before I shoveled the clean rock back into the scalloped beds. It was the first time I remembered ever hating my job. Mr. Schluter liked the results enough to add a three-dollar tip to the check he handed me. What was left after paying my expenses would almost repay Larry.

When I arrived home, my spine still reverberated from the rumble of the stone in the cement mixer. The effort of setting the parking brake nearly drained me of consciousness. I was that tired. I pushed open the door of the Daisy Mobile but didn't move. Only the hope of a cold Diet Pepsi got me out of the truck and to the refrigerator. Before I opened the door, I read a note taped to the screen door: "Gone to the mall for pizza and video games. Be back by eight. Love, Ky and Andrea."

The only liquid I found in the refrigerator was in a pickle jar.

I was standing at the top of the stairs waiting for the fire in my thigh muscles to cool before I headed for the shower when the phone rang. I fell across the bed to grab the phone. The bed felt nice.

"Hello, gorgeous."

I sat up. "Larry?"

"Hey, you know my voice."

"I know your style."

"I taught Romeo everything he knows."

I got up to walk down the hall toward Ky's room, knowing, most likely, I'd be disappointed by what I found. "I'm pretty tired . . ."

"Hard day?"

Was today harder than any other day? "Not hard, just more physical than usual."

"Crenshaw hasn't been bothering you, has he? I'd be happy to talk to him for you."

I pushed a pile of laundry with the door to enter Ky's room. The smell coming from his wastebasket qualified the room as one of Dante's rings of hell for mothers. And what was floating in the aquarium? I pulled the door shut.

"Mibby?"

"Huh?"

"I'll talk to Crenshaw if you want."

I leaned against the wall. "There's no way he's going to call again, not the way I acted."

"If he does—"

"I'll let you know. Look, Larry, I'm awfully tired."

"I wish I could make your life easier for you."

"Yeah, well, that's really not your job."

"No, I suppose it isn't. But if you let me, I might have something for Ky. Like I told you, I coach the church's softball team. We aren't very good, but we have a lot of fun. From the trophies in Ky's room, I figure he's pretty good. We could sure use someone who knows how to pitch . . . and catch . . . and it wouldn't hurt to have someone who could hit, either. I'd like to invite him to join our team, but only if you agree."

Ky had missed or ignored the deadline to have his room clean, so I'd be confiscating the modem. Who knew what a vacuum like that might suck into a boy's life. Getting him outside and active would only help.

"How often do you practice?" I asked.

"Twice a week, on Tuesdays and Thursdays at seven. The game days vary but usually it's a Friday night or a Saturday. I can pick him up."

I draped a towel on my grandmother's damask chair and slumped into its softness. "That won't be necessary. I'll take him."

"That's good, real good. Ky will be a great addition to the team. Can I talk to him?"

"He's not here. Besides, I should talk to him first. He's been a bit surly lately." And when Ky saw that I'd moved his computer to the family room and hidden the cable modem he'd be unfit for human conversation.

"You know you're a very good mother, don't you?" Larry said.

Do I?

"You do, don't you?"

"I'm trying." One encouraging word deserved another. "You're a good son."

"Someday that young man of yours will treat you like a queen."

My bottom lip quivered. "Do you have an estimated time of arrival on that?"

He laughed. "I can't predict the weather, either."

When the conversation stalled, I knew I'd given Larry an opening to say something stupid about the two of us. Maybe it was because he had offered something positive for Ky to do, or because he'd said I was a good mom that I planned on playing along.

Larry sputtered and then said, "You know, if we left for Denver now, we could catch the opening curtain at the Beull Theater. I think *Phantom of the Opera* is opening tonight. We could go for a late dinner afterward. Marlowe's grills a mean rib eye."

"Sorry, my beaded chiffon evening gown is at the cleaners."

The phone went quiet for a minute. *He was kidding, wasn't he?*

"There's a full moon tonight," he said. "How about a romantic stroll on Waikiki Beach?"

"I did that last night, sorry."

"A small town in Arkansas has a pink tomato festival going on this week. We could go there."

"A pink tomato festival?"

"We've missed the parade and the Miss Pink Tomato contest, but there's time to catch the talent show."

"Are you making this up?"

"Nope, the Pink Tomato Festival is the last week of July in the friendly town of Warren, Arkansas."

"Have you ever gone to the Pink Tomato Festival?"

"Just once. The folks are real nice. The food's great, too. You'd like it."

I'd always wanted to grow a pink tomato, but that meant starting the plants from seed, which meant planning ahead. "If we've missed the parade, it's hardly worth going." I almost added, "Maybe next year," but I didn't want to encourage him. "Listen, Larry, I need to get ready for a photo shoot with Louise. I better get going."

I knelt by the one rose in my yard that wasn't looking beleaguered from the heat or my neglect, a Tropical Sunset. Louise held the camera to her eye. "Put the hat on your head this time, sweet pea." She lowered the camera. "Do you have a hat that's a teensy bit feminine, something with flowers on it, and maybe with long ribbons to trail down your back?"

The hats in my closet were purely functional. "No, nothing feminine exactly."

Louise enjoyed playing fashion photographer, especially since she got to dress for the part. "Just call me a shutterbug," she'd said when she came to my door wearing black shorts and a red T-shirt with black polka dots. In case I didn't make the connection, she'd pointed out the puff-paint ladybugs swarming over her red tennies and the strings of enameled ladybugs swaying from her earlobes. Her fingernails alternated red and black. Even for Louise, she was over the top. But how could I complain? She was making good on her promise to help promote Perennially Yours. The pictures she took would be used for brochures and mailers.

She looked through the viewfinder again. "Would you reconsider changing into the yellow shirt? Pink is not your color."

"This is red."

"Not anymore it's not. Now it's pink, and red would be worse. Roll up the sleeves a couple times. All the models do."

It was useless to argue.

"No, that won't do, either. Your sunburn makes you look like a red-and-white '56 Chevy."

I unrolled the sleeves and smiled at the camera.

"Is that broccoli in your teeth?"

"Louise, I need to water the pots."

"Okay, okay. Don't get twitterpated. Forget smiling. Look down at the plant. Hold the trowel in your left hand. Shoulders back. Head tilted to the right. Too far. That's right. Now, look rapturous."

"Are you reading romance novels again?" I asked through my teeth.

"Pay attention, now. You're as distractin' as a squeaky door at midnight."

"Huh?"

"Something my mammy used to say." She cocked her head to study me. "Try looking contemplative. No, that's pain or constipation, and neither will do. Come on, I need you to work with me. I want every freckle on your sweet face to convey confidence. Try riddling over something important, like the meaning of life or where to shop for shoes." To Louise, those topics were more closely related than you could imagine.

"Hold steady now. Push the trowel slightly into the soil. That's right. Hold it." She moved in close and told me to look at the camera. "Uh-oh, too close. Hold that pose. Let me move back a teensy bit. Much better. You look like an angel." The camera beeped and whirled. "Perfect!"

She pocketed the spent film. "I'll have these developed by tomorrow. Goodness gracious, it's comin' onto seven o'clock."

"It's almost time to go to bed."

~~~

Lying in Scott's closet had been a bad idea. I felt like a day-old bagel left in the toaster. The decision to move the computer to the family room had been all mine and so would the consequences. When I heard Andrea and Ky come through the front door, I was mustering the energy to take my third shower of the day.

Ky bounded up the steps and down the hall to his bedroom. "Where's my computer?" he yelled. Back down the stairs he went. His muffled complaints reached me in the closet. And then he was pounding on the closet door.

"Mom! What's my computer doing downstairs? Where's the modem?"

Thankfully, I'd read the chapter on conflict resolution in *Be the Parent Your Teen Needs*. I opened the door. "May I help you?"

"Where is it?"

"You're going to have to calm down, Ky, so we can talk."

"Where's my computer?"

Behind him, I saw Andrea slip into her room and close the door.

"Four o'clock came and went," I said. "Your room posed a fire hazard."

He hit the doorjamb hard with his open hand. "Oh, man."

"We'll talk when you get yourself under control."

Ky shifted his weight from side to side and took quick, trembling breaths. "All right. I'm cool. We can talk now."

"Can we?"

He stood still. "Yeah, I'm okay."

"First of all, the computer stays in the family room. You've been isolating yourself too much with that thing."

"I need it quiet to concentrate on the game."

"But you're not concentrating on your responsibilities around here, and—" would he care about maintaining a relationship with his mother? From the scowl on his face, I doubted it—"staying in touch with your family."

"It's *my* computer. Dad gave it to me."

"He did, and we both know he never intended for you to spend all day, every day, playing hideous games."

"You don't know anything. This is a problem-solving game. My algebra teacher plays it. You can call him."

"Can you talk about this with me in a respectful manner?" I asked as I'd practiced in the closet.

"Where's the modem? Salvador is waiting for me to play."

"You can earn the privilege of using it for one hour by keeping your room clean for three days."

Ky slapped the wall. "Three days? An hour?"

"Besides your room, there'll be some other stuff for you to do, but I don't want to talk about that now. I'm too tired. We can talk before I go to work tomorrow."

He stomped off toward his room. "I want my modem now!"

Who let the two-year-old back in the house?

I followed him. "Sorry, Ky. I'll consider giving it to you when your room's been clean for three days, not before. I'll start counting the seventy-four hours—"

He spun around to face me. "Seventy-*two*. Three days is seventy-*two* hours, not seventy-four."

We locked eyes. A pulse of anger pounded in my chest. I decided against defending my mathematical honor to stay the course. I smiled and said, "Right. I'll start counting the hours when your room is clean."

Ky disappeared into his room and slammed the door. He was entitled to his frustration. At least it wasn't mine anymore. Besides, I'd done it. I'd stuck to the battle plan and emerged somewhat victorious.

So why did I feel like I was I standing alone on the hill checking for missing body parts? I'd won the battle of the wills with dignity, but there were no troops shouting accolades, only a self-righteous teenager bumping around his room like a captured bear cub. I replayed all that I'd said, measuring each phrase for its worth. Yes, I'd done even better than I'd hoped.

But the exchange had brought me to a place where time walked slower, where the chasm between angry words and reconciliation seemed unbridgeable. Scarier still, while I slept and worked, the vanquished—one said teenager—had plenty of time to sulk over his counterattack.

～～

The phone rang. A cough answered my hello.

"Hello, uh, this is Crenshaw."

I considered hanging up.

"Are you there?" he asked.

Was I? "Yes."

"I thought maybe we could go out again."

I remembered the phrase Roseanne taught me. "I'm sorry. I have plans."

"I haven't told you the night yet."

I'd promised myself I'd be a woman with a spine and a heart. "I don't think we're a good match."

"You're probably right."

The correct response would have been, *Thanks for calling. Good night.* But I didn't want to leave the man bleeding. "It's nothing about you, really."

"I'm not too good at this stuff. I was married a long time."

The way he rode the word *long,* I figured he'd counted the years of his marriage as dog years. I felt sorry for him. Maybe with a little coaching . . . "Would you like some advice?"

Cough. "I really wanted to go—" cough—"out with you."

He definitely needed coaching. "Why? I treated you terribly. I hid in the bathroom. I acted like a child."

"Yeah, but you're real pretty. I like redheads."

"But I wasn't very nice."

"My wife wasn't very nice or pretty."

I was too tired to be diplomatic. "I'm not too good at this stuff, either. But you can't expect to be *with* a woman just because you buy her dinner."

"I should have waited until after dessert, huh?"

"No amount of apple pie would have made the difference, because there's a lot that has to go on between a man and a woman before they're *with* each other."

"That's not how I see it on TV."

"TV isn't real life."

"You got a point there."

"If you're really serious about finding love, don't watch anything on TV but C-SPAN or the Weather Channel or the Food Network, as long as it isn't Valentine's week. That means no sitcoms, and especially no reality shows or beach dramas."

"Wait a minute. I better get a pencil." The receiver clunked on a hard surface, and the sound of rustling papers and mild cursing came over the phone. "I got it. What was that about the sports shows?"

I explained to Crenshaw that TV wasn't the place to learn about how to have a good relationship. They skipped all the important parts, like friendship and marriage. "You want to be loved by someone special, don't you?"

After a short pause, he answered enthusiastically, "Yeah."

"Then you're going to have to invest some time and effort into this."

"How long?"

A good teacher knows when to be ambiguous. "As long as it takes."

"What's the first step?"

Since the dawn of time, men have needed a goal to accomplish anything. They risked life and limb to bring down enough game to last the winter and ate their boots to become rich with beaver pelts. Long before that, they slept with camels to conquer the known world. None of that matched the motivational power of conquering the female heart. Consider Helen of Troy. Crenshaw needed a goal.

"Do you know a special lady?"

"There's a waitress at the Hop . . ."

"Go on."

"She's not so pretty as you, but she's more substantial, and she preps her tables without me having to ask her all the time."

"Okay then. The first step is to be friends with her."

"Just friends?"

"Just friends. Ask her questions. Find out what she likes and doesn't like. Care about how she feels. Talk about the weather."

"That could take a while. It gets pretty busy at the Hop. Maybe I should ask her out."

"Absolutely not. No asking out until she knows you care about her as a person."

"Will she tell me?"

"Probably not." At that moment, I knew I'd started a journey I wasn't likely to finish. There was too much ground to cover, and I was too tired to go on. "I'm going to pray for you."

"Huh? Okay. Sure."

Click.

I read the day's meditation verse for the third time. The words were English, simple, even familiar, but they made absolutely no sense. I let my head get heavy in the pillows.

Andrea came in and flopped down onto the bed. "You're still up." She held a place in her Bible with her finger.

"Only because I'm too tired to turn off the lamp."

"Roll over. I'll give you a back rub." Of course I complied. She walked her thumbs up either side of my spine and kneaded the tight muscles of my shoulders. "I see you're still wearing Dad's T-shirt."

"It's comfy."

She worked the muscles of my right arm in her hands. "Are you up to answering a Bible question for me? And don't suggest going to Louise." She imitated Louise's southern drawl. "Sweet pea, your questions have stirred my head like a fox in a henhouse. I don't know nuthin' about trees. Y'all go ask Mibby."

She'd worn Louise down? "I'll try."

"Louise told me to read through the Bible, so I started reading in Genesis a couple days ago. I've asked Louise a few questions along the way, like why did God make Adam first? And why would God need to rest if He was so powerful? Things like that. Anyway, she told me not to get bogged down in the details but to read the Bible as a love story, and that helped for a while, until I got to chapter three. And finally, there was a story I knew, or I thought I knew. It's the story of the serpent and Eve."

"Is Adam in the story, too?"

"Yeah, sure he is. Didn't I say so? Anyway, there's this tree in the middle of the garden. God tells them they can eat of all the trees in the garden but that one. Like, how could they resist that? Was God setting them up for failure or what? I mean, all they did was eat a little fruit. They didn't kill anybody, but then I guess there wasn't anybody to kill yet. And this Bible you gave me, is it a real Bible? There's nothing in here about an apple."

Be prepared in season and out of season.

"Hand it to me." I propped two pillows against the headboard and invited Andrea to join me. I opened her Bible to Genesis. "Maybe you skipped over this part." I read about God telling Adam to avoid the tree in the second chapter. "The tree is no ordinary tree," I told her. "It's the tree of knowledge of good and evil. It represents stuff only God needs to know. In His love, He was protecting mankind—"

"*People*-kind."

"—people-kind from knowing things that were too big for us to handle."

"Like what?"

"Like . . . I don't know, just stuff."

"That's kind of childish, isn't it?"

I was beginning to believe all of the important things you have to say in life come when you're least prepared. *Holy Spirit, come.* "Not if you're God, and all you do is motivated by love. Andrea, faith isn't like a test you study for. It's a relationship. Say you meet a guy at a concert. He smiles as you talk, even nods with approval as you tell him about your dream to play in the San Francisco symphony. Then he tells you his dream. He's a musician, too. After you've talked for a while, he asks you to go have a cup of coffee—"

"Is he tall?"

"But not too tall."

"Is he cute?"

I smiled.

"What?"

"You're getting distracted by the details. Stay with me. What's the most important attribute of a friend?"

"That they care about me, Andrea, the person."

"Exactly. Think about it. God loves you enough to step down from His perfect home where everyone agrees He's in charge, to come to earth and hang out with smelly fishermen and other undesirables of the age, not to mention to die on a cross, all so word of His love could travel through generation after generation to you. Does that sound like someone who cares about Andrea the person?"

A pin dot of light reflected on the inky pools of Andrea's eyes. "This is all so new to me. I don't want to change my whole life and find out all of this God-is-love stuff is all a lie."

"Andrea, you traveled a thousand miles in a rickety Toyota to find a man who had, for good or bad reasons, written himself out of your life. You have a heavenly Father—who traveled a lot farther—waiting to be welcomed into your life."

She ran her fingertips along the stitches in the quilt. "So, starting a relationship with God is like going for coffee?"

"Pretty close."

JULY
27

Another fire on the Book Cliffs. That makes three plumes of smoke around the valley. Radishes have sprouted, but even my bravest bloomers—rose of Sharon, trumpet vine, and dinner plate hibiscus—seem timid this year. Come back when it's cooler, girls!

The sun baked my back as I stood with Margaret admiring her vegetable garden. There would be no walking away from the heat that day, and the futility of hoping for escape settled on me as I thought of the long days of August and September that lay ahead. I pushed my hat back to shade my neck.

Focus!

Margaret's garden was more watercolor painting than horticulture. In my mind, I loaded my paintbrush with raw umber for the soil. The zucchini blossom was cadmium yellow with only a speck of alizarin crimson. Broad strokes of sap green, almost transparent with wetness, shaped the leaves.

"There's enough zucchini here to feed the whole county," Margaret said, "only no one wants it. We watched some chef on TV make squash blossom soup. Walter didn't like the looks of it, said it looked slimy. He's funny about what he'll eat sometimes. Anyways, the freezer's full of zucchini nut bread, so that's what we're having instead of the strawberry pecan cake for the wedding."

139

Margaret laughed at a memory and brushed strands of hair off her forehead. "Of all the things, Walter and me had a tiff over zucchini bread, for goodness' sake. He saw all them loaves in the freezer and said he'd always wanted a brick fireplace. He knows now that I take my nut breads seriously. He won't make that mistake again." She fished a grocery bag out of her apron pocket. "Take all the zucchini you want, dear. The rest will be going to the soup kitchen."

I thanked her, but Ky was funny about what he would eat, too.

"Take a look at them tomatoes for me. They aren't doing nothing but growing a pretty vine. Do you see any of them tomato worms on there?"

Shriveled blossoms littered the ground around the plants. "It's the heat," I told her. "Tomatoes don't mind the hot days, but the nights aren't cooling down enough for fruit to set."

"So that's it? Guess there won't be any tomato juice in January. It's a good thing I'm in love or I'd really be upset." Margaret shielded her eyes against the glare. "Speaking of love, how are you doing in that department?"

I used a hoe to chop at the spurge growing at the base of her zucchini plants. "I'm thinking that marrying a horse isn't such a bad idea. They're strong, good looking, and they'll do anything for a bucket of oats."

"Don't you dare give up on love. The soul thirsts for love . . ." She took a stack of coupons out of her apron pocket to fan herself. "It's awfully hot already, isn't it?"

I remembered the heat advisory I'd heard on the radio. "You should get out of the sun."

"Just a minute now. I got something I'm trying to say."

Blink panted in the shade of a honey locust tree. I regretted bringing him along. He would have been much more comfortable at home where he could have hijacked the neighbor girl's wading pool or destroyed my flower garden. Margaret followed me as I refilled his water bowl. Blink lapped at the water before I set the bowl on the ground.

"I've got it," she said. "The soul that thirsts for love loses its blossoms in the heat."

One poorly constructed metaphor deserved another. "Margaret, most single guys are wounded frogs, not princes."

"You mean the frogs ain't Scott, don't you?"

When I hesitated, she continued. "Of course you do. That's natural. But you wouldn't want another Scott."

Oh yes I would.

"Sit down with me in the shade. The spurge can wait." She led me to the stairs on the west side of the house. "Scott will always be the love of your youth, the one you loved as a girl. Most of us marry for the silliest reasons when we're young, usually out of fear of one kind or 'nother. As for me, I wasn't the prettiest peach in the bushel. I feared I'd be a spinster like Old Lady Anderson, so when Quentin winked at me, I fell in love immediately, or what I thought was love. Truthfully, I didn't truly love Quentin until we'd been married over thirty years. I'm a slow learner, all right. It took me that long to realize no movie star could ever love me as much as he did.

"Now there's Walter, a little sour at times but devoted as the day is long. The difference is me. In case you hadn't noticed, I'm a mature woman, and a mature woman is a cultivated garden. The large stones and sticks have been raked out, and experiences have been tilled in to enrich my soul. And then along came Walter, and a seed of love was planted. With a little water and warmth—and that's the fun part—roots took nourishment from the soil and the first tiny leaves broke through the surface. And because the soil had been prepared with such care, just like you done with my garden, that plant will thrive."

"I'm afraid—"

"Love and fear can't grow in the same garden, and they can't grow in the same heart. You best be weeding fear out of your heart, dear one. Ask the Gardener. He'll know what to do."

I convinced Margaret to go inside while I wandered through her flower beds with my pruners and a large bucket. I deadheaded a purple daylily and removed some dead branches from a flowering almond.

Among the dinner-plate hibiscus, as inspiring as any stained-glass window, I paused to pray. *Lord, weed me. Amen.*

I smacked at a mosquito behind my knee. "Aren't you going to fish?"

Ky threw a stick he'd broken into tiny pieces into the lake. "Wasn't my idea."

"Hey, remember when you'd chase the sticks along the irrigation ditch at Gerry's house?"

"I guess."

I'd brought Ky to Cottonwood Lake because *Befriend Your Child* had encouraged participating in mutually satisfying activities to make communication with a teen less confrontational. Evidently, fishing at Cottonwood Lake wasn't distracting enough for Ky. Even I regretted coming to the lake that was nothing more than a reclaimed quarry edged by a highway and the back side of a warehouse. A home to cranky waterfowl and the world's smallest fish, all the lake had going for it was proximity. The glare off the lake's surface stung my eyes, and a disheveled swan eyed my creel, but there is nothing as tenacious as a mother emotionally severed from her young. I stepped tentatively around Ky's mood, hoping it would dissolve if I pretended it wasn't there.

Blink splashed through the shallows, dunking his head under the water to mouth a rock he'd found.

I cast my line into the lake. "I've been so busy. I wanted to spend some time with you. You're one of my favorite people, you know." *Did I sound convincing?*

Ky slid deeper into his chair and scowled at the horizon. In response to a nibble, I jerked the line to set the hook, but the line was empty—no fish or bait. It was now or never. "I signed you up for the church's softball team."

"You what?"

"Since you won't be spending so much time in front of the computer, I thought you'd like something to do."

He kept his eyes on the distance.

Press on. "Larry's the coach. You know him. He needs a ringer for the team, a pitcher."

"I'm a fielder."

"But you've always wanted—"

"Baseball's different." His words were as flat as the lake.

One summer when my sister and I had laid our heads down on

Grandma's kitchen table and complained that it was too hot and too boring, Grandma gave us the choice of weeding the garden or playing Monopoly. I chose weeding, but Margot insisted we play Monopoly. Since Grandma had handed Margot the game, my sister appointed herself banker and queen of Monopolyland. She declared my hotels a fire hazard and ordered them demolished. Then she fined me for moving my shoe too fast and made me use the thimble instead. When Margot accused me of buying a house with counterfeit money, I complained to Grandma. All my tattling earned me was an afternoon nap. Margot helped Grandma make seven-minute frosting.

And now Ky was changing the rules. If baseball wasn't the fulcrum of his life, what was? I hoped he was bluffing. "Your first practice is tomorrow night at seven. You can ride your bike."

"Tire's flat." He stood, started to say something, then turned to walk along the shore of the lake. I put down my pole and followed him. To match his stride, I had to jog every few steps. "Is there something going on I need to know about?"

"I'll play, all right? If that's what you want, I'll play."

"I thought you'd enjoy it, a chance to play ball, to be with people." A thought I'd been dodging for days reappeared. "Is this about your dad? Are you missing him?"

"No. Well, yeah, I miss him." He stopped and looked down at me. "No, this isn't about Dad. I know I screwed up. But my room's clean now. I just want my modem back."

Ky continued on without me. I wanted to follow him, but instead, I whistled for Blink to join him.

A cruel trick of memory flashed Ky's radiant face before me—at two, at five, and even at seven. He used to light up every time I entered the room. And in playful games of tag, he would look back at me, inviting me into the chase with a glint in his eye. The memory awoke an unfair anticipation in my heart, so I waited, watching him walk the wide arc of the shore, believing he would turn and invite me into his world. When the trail turned into a stand of tamarisk and he disappeared, I packed our gear into the Yukon and prayed.

"There are two things I need, Lord. Walk with Ky through all the places I cannot go, and please, please, please make him turn and wave once in a while."

⁓

A white enamel appliance hunched on the kitchen counter like a rabbit. Out of its spout, a cord of green pulp oozed, soft and glossy, into a cup under its chin. Louise held the stuff under my nose. "Sugar, this is the elixir of life. Give it a little taste. See what you think." Her eyebrows rose in anticipation.

"I don't know, Louise. It's grass water."

"This isn't regular ol' grass. This is wheatgrass, rich in chlorophyll and oxygen to rebuild the blood and increase stamina."

"What does it taste like?"

"Like the very breath of springtime, sweet and refreshin'."

"You haven't tasted it, have you?"

"I thought since you like plants so much, you should have the first taste."

"Pond scum isn't this green."

"Do you have any orange juice? We could mix them together, add a sprig of mint."

When I told Louise I wouldn't even let Blink drink it, she took the cup from me and poured it down the kitchen drain. "I have a whole new respect for cows, eating grass day and night. And come to think of it, I've never seen a cow with more stamina than it could use."

As we worked at washing the appliance's auger and the filters, we talked about anything but juicers. Friends do that when one of them has tried too hard to be something other than what they are and spent too much money doing it. When all of the parts were clean and lying out on towels, I helped Louise put the juicer back in the box, careful to bundle the cord and fasten it with the twist tie. I even offered to return it to the store for her.

"No," she said, "I want to talk to the salesclerk about the healing attributes of chocolate, but you can make some of that powdered lemonade you have. Just lookin' at that electric bunny rabbit puts a bitter taste in my mouth."

We clinked our lemonade glasses, and I gave the toast. "To chemicals."

JULY
28

Of my three tomato plants, two have curly top.
I ripped out the infected plants to save the
remaining plant. Added mulch to help with
blossom end rot, too.

Christopher Stohl glanced nervously behind me, so I looked, too. Through the doors of the Walled Garden sales area, a mother and her toddler son browsed through the annuals like beachcombers collecting seashells. The boy held a flowering pot at arm's length for his mother to admire. Nothing threatening there.

"I hope you left your dog at home," Christopher said.

He bit at his cuticle, and beads of sweat swelled on his forehead. Under his tidy shirt, I was sure his heart beat like a sparrow's.

"Don't worry," I said, softer. "My dog's miles away from here."

His chest rose and fell. "Good."

"You were saying?"

"I will be happy to consider your credit application when it arrives. Not until then."

Self-doubt tapped me on the shoulder. *Ky said he'd mailed the envelope, hadn't he?* "Could you check your inbox? It was mailed last week."

"It's after five o'clock, Mrs. Garrett. My inbox is empty. Now, if you'd like to take another application and fill it out, you can bring it back tomorrow. I trust you have photocopies of your references."

I didn't. The credit report and personal financial report, though puny, were easily reproduced but the references were not. Muriel, the bank manager, had sat down at her computer and written a glowing letter the moment I'd asked, and Louise, well, she had all but nominated me for sainthood in a handwritten letter. I didn't want to ask them to write letters again. Behind Christopher, Kathleen pushed a broom around the sales area.

He picked lint off his shirt. "Once I have the application in my hands, it only takes a few days—"

"A few days? That's too long. The wedding is in two days."

He hiked up his khakis. "I can't make your problems mine, can I?" He gestured toward the double-tiered cart I'd filled with petunias and marigolds. "Be sure you put those back where you got them. It's closing time." Kathleen handed Christopher the cash drawer, and he rushed off to his office.

She stuck her tongue out at his back. "Don't worry. You'll get your flowers. You can bet he didn't graduate at the top of his class in customer service. Let me add this up for you." Kathleen tapped the total key. "Do you have a credit card?"

I did, but the one issued in my name only had a small credit line. I explained that to Kathleen.

She patted my hand. "Okay then, it's time to get creative. You know, think outside the Christopher."

She rummaged under the counter until she emerged with another credit card and scanned it.

"What are you doing?" I asked.

"This is my sky-miles card. I use it for everything. I even pay my daughter's tuition with it. When she graduates, I'm quitting this place and heading for New Zealand. This purchase inches me over the equator. I'm down under at last."

"I can't let you do that."

She pushed her glasses up her nose. "Why not?"

"I'd owe you the money."

Her glasses slipped down her nose again. "Would you rather owe the money to me or Mr. All-Work-and-No-Heart?"

"Kathleen . . ."

"I don't want to hear another word of protest." She lowered her voice and took my hand. "I'll never forget that it was you who sat with me after John's heart attack long after my own mother went home, and it was you who drove us home when he was discharged from the hospital. I've hated not being able to return that particular kindness to you. This is a friend helping a friend. Let's load your purchase up."

~~~

In a book I'd bought at Barnes and Noble, I thumbed through the chapter on adolescent socialization, *Ready! Set! Grow! Independence in the Teen Years*. Everything about Ky's behavior lately had undermined the previous thirteen years of making him acceptable in public places. He'd abandoned niceties like *please* and *thank you,* reverted to eating with his hands, and now he was lying, something he hadn't tried since he'd blamed Blink for scribbling on a newly painted wall.

I sat in Scott's chair and with a prickling dread, watched for Andrea and Ky to come home from softball practice. The credit application I'd given Ky to mail lay on the coffee table in the family room. When he got home, I would sit down with him. That was the easy part. Then what? According to the book, his behavior was completely normal. The starting gun for his race toward independence had fired, only I was still in my warm-up suit. It was time to get into the game. I could see how it worked. Ky turned surly and unresponsive; I prayed for graduation day. Only four more years to go.

When the Yukon rounded the corner, I hurried to the family room and opened the newspaper. I stared at a cell phone ad. This one episode of irresponsibility, I reminded myself, didn't define Ky, nor did it seal his future. It was an experiment. My job was to see that it failed. The book said to do it with empathy. I guessed I was experimenting, too.

Andrea dropped the car keys on the island. "There isn't one spot of shade at the practice diamond—not one." She turned toward the hall and the stairs. "I've got to shower. Aubrey will be here in an hour."

"Aubrey?" I asked.

She smiled over her shoulder. "Gotta go."

Ky collapsed into the chair opposite me. His face was blotched from exertion in the heat. He called after Andrea, "Is he the geek with the orange hair?"

But she was gone, off duty for the night.

"You didn't tell me it was a coed team," he said. "It's a good thing, though. The girls throw better than the guys. And you know that lady that sings in the choir, the one who sings really loud and wears her hair in braids? She's the catcher. She's awesome—when the pitcher gets it in her mitt. Don't even ask me about hitting." He pushed his hair off his forehead. "I'm the youngest, but there's a cool guy who came to practice on his longboard. He goes to college in Wyoming, said he's not sure he wants to play. He just watched. It was his first time, too."

Ky hadn't talked this much in a long time. I asked him if I knew anyone else on the team. He listed all the team members from the first baseman to the left fielder. "I think most of them come because Larry talked them into it. They aren't exactly the athletic types. Man, I could drink a gallon."

While I listened, I prayed for exquisite wisdom. Only the best would do. Ky had so many important lessons to learn, but I was enjoying his banter. Maybe his lapse wasn't that important. Kathleen had saved the day. No harm, no foul.

"Get a drink," I said. "There's some lemonade in the fridge. Then come back and sit down."

"Why? What now?"

I fought to keep my voice light. "Something unexpected happened today. I want to tell you about it."

He balked, studying me. Thirst won over curiosity. He brought his glass back to the family room and sat on the edge of the chair, poised to flee.

I'd revised and rehearsed my opening line over and over. But sitting there, I couldn't remember the first word. It wasn't that my son scared me. With Scott gone, I'd lost his tempering influence, not to mention his first-hand knowledge of the male psyche. I was running blindfolded. I tried to think of Ky as a cross-country runner who had strayed from the course. The job of the race official, that would be me, was to point the runner back to where he'd left the course so he wouldn't be disqualified. I was doing Ky a favor.

I pointed to the envelope. "I found this in your desk drawer."

He fixed his gaze on the envelope. "Mom . . ." He glowered at me. "You went through my desk?"

"Yes, I did. I didn't want to, hated doing it, but I needed to know if my envelope had been mailed."

"That's my stuff. You had no right."

"If you like, we can talk about that when we're done with this." I took a sip of lemonade. "What did you tell me about the envelope when I asked about it?"

"All you want me to do around here is work. This is my vacation. I'm supposed to be relaxing." He flopped back into the chair.

"You're right. You work hard in school. You deserve a break. Now what did you tell me about the envelope?"

"My bike has a flat."

"That's a problem. What did you tell—?"

He covered his face with his hands. "Don't make me say it."

"Can you assure me it won't happen again?"

"*Yes*. Can I go now?"

JULY
29

Will the heat ever end? Maple trees around town are suffering—iron deficiencies and leaf scorch. Deep-watered the birch today. Don't want it to go the way of the maples.

Roseanne gasped when she saw me. "Does it hurt?"

"Only when I breathe."

"Didn't you wear sunscreen?"

"I thought so." I turned to look in the bathroom mirror. At Andrea's insistence, I wore her black sheath—square-necked and sleeveless. Unfortunately, the T-shirt I'd worn all day was a V-neck with capped sleeves. "I used a tube of SPF 30 I borrowed from Gloria. I guess it was pretty old."

I'd gone to Gloria's before the sun rose that morning to plant the petunias and marigolds for her daughter's wedding, but even so, the fence repair guys were already there. I tried working around them, but after they'd stomped on my petunias a couple times, I sat in the shade and waited for them to clear out. Then the caterers showed up and wanted to erect the tent for the reception. The flower beds were baking in the afternoon sun by the time I started planting again. I'd felt better about the delays when Gloria had written a check and padded it with a generous tip.

Roseanne joined me in front of the mirror. "You look great in that dress. It fits like a glove."

"Too tight?"

"Not at all. I've only seen you in overalls. This is better."

I turned for a side view. The fabric pulled a bit at the hips but not too much. "I've been walking with Louise."

"Keep it up."

Roseanne wore a sheath, too, emerald silk, scoop-necked with a slit to mid-thigh, not so daring because of her long legs. A gold chain, as delicate as a promise, followed the contours of her collarbone, and a single diamond rested against her *café au lait* skin. Her hair was swept up into a sleek chignon. So finely defined were her coming-ins and going-outs, she looked as though she'd been shaped on a lathe.

The oversized sunglasses Gloria had insisted I wear had left circles of pale flesh around my eyes to give me a look of perpetual amazement. Like Roseanne, I wore my hair up, but with Andrea's flair for the surreal. She'd gathered my hair and twisted it until the coil buckled. Then she fastened it with a bejeweled chopstick and coated the loose ends with wax so spikes radiated peacock-style from my crown. Andrea had also painted my fingernails red, but my toenails remained *au naturel*. We'd agreed the less attention brought to my feet the better, sunburned as they were from working in my Birkenstocks.

A sudden urge to crawl under the bedcovers overwhelmed me. "I can't go like this, Roseanne."

"Of course you can. You have a sunburn, not the plague. It makes you look adventurous and outdoorsy."

"I wouldn't want to mislead anyone."

"What are you talking about? You're outdoorsy." She slung her evening bag over her shoulder. "Ready?"

~~~

Roseanne did everything to perfection, including transforming a Sunday school classroom into a Moroccan dining salon. Potted plants filled the corners of the room and iron sconces held flickering candles. She'd draped bulletin boards and easels with lengths of gold and red tapestry. Around the lowered table, stacks of tasseled cushions replaced plastic classroom chairs. Platters of lemons and figs and pomegranates nestled in the folds of gold organza, and gold-rimmed goblets sat on painted tiles. All that remained of the Sunday school room was a poster of the Ten Commandments. That seemed fitting.

I whispered in her ear. "It's beautiful."

"Thanks, but don't spill anything on the cushions. They're silk. I borrowed them from Uptown Decorators." She pushed me toward the other dinner guests. "Now mingle."

A woman as slight as a sparrow flitted over. "You look as uncomfortable as I feel. That's some sunburn. Have you ever been to one of these things before?"

"This is my first time."

Within a minute, I knew her name was Karen and she'd been engaged twice but never married. On the Myers-Briggs inventory, she was an ESTJ, she told me, although her extrovert barely dominated. She spoke without elaboration, although I would have said Myers-Briggs was a pharmaceutical company until moments before.

"You can see why I couldn't commit until I was absolutely certain," she said.

I nodded stupidly while she made it clear her mother had reserved her place at the Table of Ten function. Karen wore a black skirt, straight and hemmed at the knee, and a white blouse buttoned to the throat. I couldn't help thinking she wanted to be mistaken for the wait staff and appropriately overlooked. Then she told me about the singles groups she'd attended and how lopsided they'd been.

"As with everything else, men have the advantage in the singles game."

When she took a breath, I introduced myself.

"Nice to meet you." She smiled sadly. "At least I won't be eating alone tonight."

One of the servers fussed over a portable CD player, and exotic music filled the room. The beat roused me, so I tapped my foot and tried to pick out the instruments. Banjo? Bongo drum? Pencil cup?

Karen began to list the ten worst churches for singles, but when three men walked in and were greeted by Roseanne, Karen stopped talking to watch.

I marveled at how quickly old instincts kicked in. In a heartbeat, I had them categorized by occupation. The guy with great hair and a smiling handshake was a salesman, probably cars or large appliances. The man in the middle was a grocery store manager. He seemed coiled, ready to solve the next crisis, like there would be a cleanup in aisle four at any moment. He wore dependable shoes. The third guy, like me, kept the beat to the music with his foot. A middle school band teacher? He smiled too much for that, and his shirt matched his slacks. I guessed construction, some kind of engineer, maybe an architect. None of them were Scott or even Scott-like.

Lord, what am I doing here?

Karen turned her back to the new arrivals and whispered, "I know that guy, the one tapping his foot. He should be nervous. He's married."

"Are you sure?"

"I work with his wife."

"Should we tell someone?"

"I'll spread the word." Karen left to talk to two women admiring the table.

I looked for Roseanne, but she was greeting the next contestant, a man who wore his clothes trim to his muscled body. When he moved, the buttons pulled at their openings. He looked around the room, and before I could avert my glance, he waved and walked over.

Officer Ortiz offered his hand. "Mrs. Garrett, how nice to see a familiar face. I didn't expect to know anyone."

That was what I'd hoped, too.

"You must be staying out of trouble," he said. "I haven't pulled you over in a while."

Say something. Anything. "I've been working a lot."

"Looks like you've been working in the sun." He leaned in. "I'm glad to see you're getting out. It's good for you. As for me, my wife and I split up. She got tired of worrying about me when I was working. It isn't easy being married to a cop."

Something told me there was more to that story.

Roseanne rang a gong. "Time to take your seats. Dinner is ready."

Karen sidled up to me and whispered, "I moved the jerk's place card next to mine so I can keep an eye on him."

I felt a pop as I sat, and my dress was suddenly roomier. I grabbed for the back seam. It had ripped open from below the zipper to the hem. I overlapped the opening to cover my expansive white cotton panties. The other dinner guests were too involved in adjusting their cushions and greeting their neighbors to notice. I committed myself to staying put until everyone but Roseanne had left for the evening. More couscous for me.

A late arrival hurried in and sat next to Roseanne. He wore rumpled khakis and a white polo shirt with an upturned collar, a tennis bum from the looks of him or maybe a trust funder. Either that or he was a Rip Van Winkle from the early eighties just waking from his long nap. When he perused the faces around the table, I had to stifle a laugh. He looked like a radar dish scanning the horizon.

The grocery store manager who sat to my left turned out to be an elementary school principal, so I wasn't too wrong about the air of impending doom about him. Our conversation stalled when he acknowledged his ex was the gardener of the family, and she'd gotten the house. The salesman sat to my right listening intently to a woman explaining the duties of an ostomy nurse.

Before dinner, the caterer, a short man with intense eyes and a pencil-thin mustache, spoke to us in accented English. "It is hoping you will enjoy such hospitality tonight as our guests. As well as we are able, we will accommodate a traditional Moroccan dinner. It is only for you to enjoy the food and for us to be honored in service to you. Never hurry great food or good company. First, we wash the hands."

Two preteen girls as demure as herons carried a brass bowl with an attached soap dish for each guest to wash his or her hands. The younger girl dried my hands with a warmed towel and returned my smile. Her sister nudged her on with a grunt.

Older sisters. They're all the same.

The salesman's face registered surprise, and the next thing I knew, the bowl had overturned in my lap. I started to stand up to save the cushions from the soapy water but thought better of it. Anxious looks, fitful apologies, and blotting towels swarmed around me. "Please forgive my clumsy daughter," said the caterer. Across the room, the girl's face pinched with worry.

"I did it," I said. "I turned and hit the bowl with my elbow. I'm the one who's sorry. Please apologize to your daughter."

Roseanne was at my elbow. "Let's go dry your dress."

"No, it feels good against my sunburn. Please, let's just continue." I met her eyes. "Please."

"Are you all right?"

"Never better," I said and hoped she believed me, at least for now. "I'm sorry about the cushions."

"I was only kidding about borrowing them."

Good friends always tell the truth; excellent friends save it for later.

The sisters refilled their bowl and finished washing the hands of the guests. The first course arrived, a circle of pastry sprinkled with sugar and a crosshatching of cinnamon. The Moroccans had it right—serve dessert first. As I parted the flaky pastry with my fork to find a savory chicken dish, I discovered I'd been wrong about the salesman, too. He was an evangelistic podiatrist, preaching arch support and low heels.

He winced at my Birkenstocks. "I like to see the whole foot protected in work situations."

All I saw of the podiatrist and the principal from then on were the backs of their heads, so I spent the rest of the dinner occupied with my food. Like the colors and designs of their fabrics and tiles, Moroccan food shouted—ginger, lemon, and lots and lots of peppers. I asked the younger sister to leave a pitcher of water on the table.

My plate disappeared the moment I propped the fork on its rim, and another plate of tiny beef kabobs appeared in its place. Then the sisters brought out bowls of lamb and prune stew and couscous with spicy vegetables. The younger sister patted my shoulder as she walked by.

Across from me, Roseanne and Radarman talked and smiled. Their kabobs lay uneaten. She touched his arm when he threw back his head to laugh at something Roseanne had said. The older sister piled empty plates into the younger sister's arms. I waited for the younger sister to turn to me so I could smile encouragingly at her, but she was too busy to look.

Karen was keeping her promise to monopolize the married man's attention. He was leaning toward her. Her chin was propped on her palm. In the amber glow of candlelight, her cheeks bloomed with pleasure. I waited for her to look my way so I could mouth, "What's up?" She never did.

The principal asked me to pass the water. I appreciated the conversation. Officer Ortiz smiled when I looked his way. That was nice, but then he continued his conversation with his neighbor, a doughy woman wearing a tired sundress. I stirred the couscous around my plate to gather courage for another bite of the fiery dish. I mopped my forehead with my damp napkin.

As we drank our mint tea, Roseanne stood up to thank everyone for coming. "I hope you enjoyed yourselves and met some very interesting people. Don't forget to exchange cards before you leave."

The principal offered his hand. "Nice to meet you, Milly. Hope your sunburn heals quickly. You know, you could get cancer from that. You better be careful."

When I turned around to thank the podiatrist, he had already left the table to talk with the loan officer by the door. I watched them exchange cards.

Roseanne tapped me on the shoulder. "Stefan offered to help clean up and drive me home, so you don't have to stay."

"The guy who looks like a radar dish?"

"He does not. He's very nice. You'd like him."

I told Roseanne about my torn dress. She pulled the drape off the easel and tied it around me like a sarong. "Pretty as a picture." She kissed my cheek. "I'll call you tomorrow."

"I'm paying for those cushions."

"We'll talk later."

In the parking lot, Karen and the married guy were exchanging cards. Whether it was the sunburn or the torn dress or eating alone in the company of strangers, I confronted them. "What do you think you're doing? Is nothing sacred, including marriage vows?" The parking lot was dark, but I was aware of a growing audience, so I lowered my voice and spoke to the guy. "Do the honorable thing. Go home to your wife."

"You must have me confused—"

I didn't care who heard me then. "That's what you'd like us to believe. Karen knows you're married."

Karen put her hand on my arm. "I was mistaken. I didn't wear my glasses. When I got closer to him, I realized he wasn't the guy I thought he was. I should have told you. I'm sorry."

~~~

Lights blazed from the house. Inside, I imagined Andrea, Louise, and Ky watching television but really waiting for me. The thought of answering their questions about the evening demoralized me. Where would I start? The torn dress? The ruined cushions? My empty pockets? So I sat in the Yukon to recoup what remained of my self-esteem. Of all things, I remembered the last vacation we'd had as a family.

Scott, Ky, and I had driven to Lake Tahoe in late July. I'd long since learned to appreciate the beauty of the desert, the sculptured rocks and the sincere simplicity of the plant life, but only an incredulous stupor settled over me along Interstate 80 west of Salt Lake City. To the north of the highway is the Great Salt Lake, great only for its largess. The lake is flat and lifeless, save for some algae and bacteria and a few billion brine shrimp, those fluttering creatures sold as sea monkeys on the backs of comic books. The shimmer off the lake smudged the line between sky and water. Mountains rose to the south. Just when I thought it couldn't get worse, we entered the Bonneville Salt Flats. Scott tried to enhance the scenery with history. He told us the area was famous for being the practice bombing range for the Enola Gay crew and for people in rocket cars compelled to go faster than anyone else. Such races of futility were possible on the flats because there was nothing to run into—nothing at all.

My eye searched for something to entertain it. Other travelers had stopped to arrange rocks into messages no one would ever read. They were that desperate to disturb the regularity of the scenery. Even a speed bump would have been a welcome diversion. Just as my brain was about to slip into neutral, a shape rose on the horizon. Scott and Ky saw it, too.

"Is it a truck stop? Can we get some ice cream?"

"No, it's probably a gas well."

Whatever it was, we couldn't take our eyes off of it.

"I bet it's a microwave tower."

"No, more like Doppler Radar, or maybe a cell phone antenna."

It was a sculpture of tennis balls on a giant multi-tined fork. As much as we wanted to make sense of the thing, its only function seemed to be diverting travelers' attention from the great void.

"It's a rest stop." Scott's voice was as lifeless as the scenery. "Does anyone need to stop?"

No one did. We zoomed past the thing. The sculpture loomed weird and conspicuous and more than a little disappointing.

As I reviewed the Table of Ten event, I felt an uncomfortable kinship with the artwork. My eyes burned to cry, but I wouldn't have it. "Come on," I told myself. "I gave the game of life a try. It wasn't as safe as I'd hoped, but I'm still standing." What had I expected?

<center>~~~</center>

I managed to keep my composure until I saw my mother and Margot sitting at my kitchen table with Andrea.

My mother drew me to her chest. "You didn't have a good time, did you?" Her hair held the scent of the ocean, and its familiarity made me cry all the harder. "I'm so sorry, Bré," she said, calling me by the name only she used, the most namelike syllable of my given name, Montbretia.

"You went dressed like that?" Margot asked.

"Hush now, Margot. Your sister's had a rough night."

Being in my mother's arms was like being in my other skin, so familiar were the cushions of her shoulders and the rhythm of her heartbeat. I waited for her grip to lessen, but she held me tighter, like a mother does, hoping to squeeze the pain out. Her hair tickled my nose, but I stayed in her arms, trying to sort the scents of salt and seaweed and incense.

A chair scraped against the floor. "It was so nice to meet you both," Andrea said. "One of you can sleep in my bed. I can go to Louise's." She stroked my hair. "It's going to be all right."

"I tore your dress," I said.

"That's okay. I was going to give it to you anyway. It looks better on you."

I cried harder, not from cruelty or missed opportunities, but from kindness, as unsettling as any homecoming.

Mother opened cupboards until she found the tea. She wore a gathered skirt with tiers of gauzy fabric. It swayed as she filled the teapot with water and adjusted the flame. I'd forgotten how gracefully she moved in her work. She put a steaming mug in front of me. It was all I could do not to grab her hand and pull it to my chest.

Margot whispered, but it sounded more like a hiss. "When, exactly, were you going to tell us about Scott's dark little secret?"

"I . . ."

"Do you have any proof that girl is Scott's daughter? She could be robbing you blind. How many other little surprises did Scott leave behind?"

"Why do you have to be so hateful to your sister?" asked my mother.

Margot blinked. "He's dead. What does it matter?"

"Love doesn't end when a heart stops beating."

"That's a pile of—"

"That will be enough," Mother said.

I marveled at how quickly we'd slipped into our familial roles: Margot, the older sister, driven and critical; me, the vulnerable one; and Mother, the woman with a thousand faces. That night she was Jasmine, a tender of wounds.

Margot glowered at her tea. "Do you have coffee?"

When I rose to make it, my mother stopped me. "I'll do it."

Margot's gloom deepened, which wasn't unusual, but her appearance worried me. She wore a terrycloth jogging set, the kind no one ever wore jogging. The sleek lines and designer label were meant to make the wearer look sporty and relaxed, which had never described Margot. Her hair hung over her shoulders, straight and spiritless.

"Are you all right?" I asked her.

"Let's not get confused about who's the charity case around here."

"You look awful," I pressed.

"Try touring the homeless shelters of Los Angeles County. At least I don't have a tablecloth tied around my waist."

I ignored her dig. "Homeless shelters?"

Margot gestured to Mother with a tilt of her head. "That's where I found dear ol' Mother."

Mother squeezed a long thread of honey into her tea. "Your sister thought I needed rescuing."

"Everything she owns is in that bag," Margot said.

A canvas bag, no bigger than a sack of potatoes, leaned like a dozing Buddha against the wall.

"My needs are simple," Mother said.

Over the years, she'd told us in so many ways that we didn't own her—by the way she walked away with a swift, deliberate stride, and the way she never said she was sorry, and most telling of all, how she'd disdained the discreet living out of our lives.

"Did you want to come here?" I asked. *Please say yes.*

"That shelter was poison," Margot said.

"Do you want to be here, Mother?" I asked again.

"I'm so happy to see you."

"Mother?"

She looked at me, her head cocked to the side, much too girlish for a grandmother. "It's good that I'm here. Maybe I can help."

—⁓—

I stretched the last corner of the fitted sheet over the guest bed Andrea had abandoned. "Mother looks good—older, but good, don't you think?"

"I cleaned her up," Margot said. She snapped the flat sheet open and let it float to the bed. "I hired a private investigator last month. When he came up empty, I got in my car and drove from shelter to shelter. If there's one shelter worse than another, that's where I found her."

"Oh."

"She wouldn't leave until I promised we'd see you. I was afraid she'd change her mind, so I drove straight to the airport. I don't even have a change of underwear." She shook a pillow into its case and folded back the covers. "I'm done with her."

"Done with her? What do you mean?" But I knew. I'd been done with her before, too.

"I've looked for her for the last time. She isn't my problem anymore."

It was one thing for me to voice weariness over my mother; it scared me to hear it from Margot. "Let's get a good night's sleep. We'll round up some fresh clothes for you. You'll feel better; you'll see. Things will be better in the morning."

"I'm leaving in the morning."

"In the morning? I need to talk to her, spend time with you. You have to stay longer."

Margot lay on top of the bed in her clothes and shoes and turned to the wall. "You're in luck. She wants to stay with you."

"Margot . . ."

"I already asked her to stay with me. She wasn't interested, so I brought her here. You can have Mother all to yourself. I don't care anymore."

"She's your mother, too."

"Some mothers eat their young, you know."

"Close your eyes." Mother rubbed the aloe lotion between her hands and spread it over my forehead and across my nose and cheeks. "Better?"

"Much."

Her voice wore the weariness of airport lounges and the disorganized conversations of reacquaintance. "Lie down."

"Aren't you tired?"

"Let me do this for you. Now lie down."

I kicked off my Birkenstocks and lay on the bed. "I'm so glad Margot found you."

She smoothed the lotion down my arm. "How did I have a daughter so hard and bitter?"

"She's protecting herself."

"From what? A meteor couldn't crack her."

She's protecting herself from you, Mother. "She looked and looked for you."

"I wasn't lost."

I pulled my arm from her. "To Margot you were."

"That's nonsense, Bré."

I lay heavily on the bed, too eager to surrender Margot's cause to buy a few tender moments with my mother. She slathered the aloe on my neck and shoulders. A flash of lightning lit the room, but it was too far off to hear its thunder. I supposed that meant another plume of smoke to the north in the morning. I closed my eyes. "That feels good."

Mother sang, "Hush little baby, don't say a word . . ."

AUG

1

Remember this combo of plants for next year: a cool blue plumbago, an orange-yellow gloriosa daisy, moonbeam coreopsis, and blue oat grass. Prettier than any arrangement.

Mother moaned and twisted in her sleep. "No*oo*! Do*oo*n't!"

I rolled over to wake her from the nightmare, but her face had already relaxed and her sticky-throated snores resumed soon after. Outside, the birds called to one another, at first singularly and then together in an indecorous chatter, as if it were the very first day the sun had ever risen.

I studied my mother in the truthful light of morning. She lay on her back with her mouth agape. Her hair, once as deeply grained as lacquered rosewood, lay dull and disorderly across the pillow.

Stepping lightly down the stairs so I wouldn't wake her, I made a pot of coffee and snapped on the light beside Scott's chair. The cool leather raised goose bumps on my arms. I made a mental list of my Monday clients. I would be home by two. My stomach fluttered when I thought of asking my mother to stay to help with Ky and meals and all.

I opened my Bible to Psalm 131. *I have stilled and quieted my soul; like a weaned child with its mother. . . .*

I woke again to hear my mother talking in the kitchen. "You did all of this by yourself? It's the most beautiful kitchen I've ever seen. The tile, too?"

"And the family room," Droop said.

"You're an amazing artist. I dabble in textiles myself." A pause. "Do you ever mix media, Droop?"

A woman recognizes when another woman's words are meant to hook the fleshy underside of a man's ego. "Good morning," I said, walking into the kitchen. "How's the coffee?"

Droop blushed from his dome to the V of chest exposed at the collar. "I best be going. Don't want to disappoint the Morgans. Nope, don't wanna be late." Droop poured the last of his coffee down the drain and stopped at the door. "It was a pleasure to meet you, Elizabeth."

"Elizabeth?"

Droop put his painter's cap on crooked. "I'm off," he said just as the screen door slammed shut.

Mother shrugged her shoulders. "It's an Elizabeth kind of morning." She sauntered to the window to watch Droop walk to the Morgans'.

"Droop's a married man, Mother."

"He's a man, all right. Did you see how muscled his—"

"Did you see his wedding ring? Some people take their promises seriously."

"It's too early in the day for condemnation. . . ." She set her coffee cup on the island. "I'm sorry, Bré. It's so good to see you. Let's not be cross so early in the day. Let's have our coffee in your beautiful garden."

Someone was missing. "Where's Margot?"

"She's gone," she said, wiping up a dribble of coffee on the counter. "A taxi came about five."

We sat on the bench under the honey locust tree. The morning air, saturated with smoke and dust, hung heavily around us, and the papery blossoms of a rose of Sharon watched attentively. Margot's absence made me feel self-conscious.

"I'm sorry Margot had to leave," I said.

"Margot will always do what keeps Margot queen of her life, even if it means chopping off her own head."

"She loves you very much."

A pair of mourning doves cozied up on the rose arbor.

"I'm so happy you're going out again. But darling, you don't have to go to events for desperate people. You're beautiful." Her smile gathered her skin at her eyes. "Even with a sunburn, you're gorgeous. You need to loosen up a little, that's all. Life is a glorious banquet, not a duty. Come to the table, Bré. There are plenty of men to dine with."

A gluttonous bumblebee hovered over one blossom and then the next on a nearby hyssop. Each flower bent under his weight and bounced when he left.

"Ky's a charming young man," she said. "You're doing a wonderful job with him."

"It's been a hard summer." I told her how our summer plans had dissolved and about Ky's best friend moving and the harsh words we'd exchanged. "He still needs someone around to supervise him."

"He's fourteen," she said as if I'd forgotten a decade of birthdays.

"That's the problem."

"Oh, Bré, children need room to—"

"I know he doesn't need a warden, just someone to be here so his friends can come over and to see that things get done." *It would mean so much to me if you volunteered.* With the courage, or desperation, born in a mother's heart, I asked the question I'd never asked of her before, "How long are you planning to stay?" and held my breath.

Her brow creased ever so slightly as she looked down the garden path. "I don't know."

"I could really use your help, just until school starts in about a month."

She looked off. What was she calculating, how quickly she could get to the bus station?

"I'd love to spend time with Ky," she said finally. "Doesn't he like to draw? We could sketch together."

There would be plenty of time to adjust her expectations about teenaged boys. "Thanks, Mother." I left her in the garden while I showered and dressed.

I was surprised to find Ky reading in bed when I knocked and entered his room. "You're up?"

"Been up an hour."

Softball equipment littered the floor, and there were empty glasses on his desk, but I stifled the urge to scold him. He knew how he could earn his modem back. All he needed was the space to succeed or fail.

I sat on his bed. "Listen, I think we may have found the solution for the rest of the summer. Your grandmother has agreed to stay here until school starts."

"I don't need a babysitter. I don't even know her. You said she was a loony moony."

I regretted everything I'd ever said about my mother in his presence. "You'll say the same thing about me to your kids."

"Yeah, but at least you take care of me."

"Is that approval or an accusation?"

"*Mom.*"

"Right, well, the cruel truth is I have to work. Somehow, we have to make that less isolating for you. With your grandmother here, your friends can come over or she can drive you to their houses. And I've instructed her to give you sage advice and to remind you to do your chores."

"When is all of this going to start?"

"Today."

"I don't even know what to call her."

"Ask her. She's always been excellent at coming up with names for herself."

I really should not have said that.

Mickey Greenwell met me in her driveway. "The list is long today. I hope it doesn't take more than your usual time. I don't want to pay extra."

And I wanted to get home. I read the list. "If I put my head down and work steadily, there shouldn't be a problem."

Mrs. Greenwell made a list every time I came and insisted on expanding on each item before I began. I'd hoped over time she would find me trustworthy enough to go about my work without her input, but I'd learned her vigilance had little to do with my competence. If I tried to hurry her, it only took longer.

"If you take a look at the lilacs, you'll see they have powdery mildew like last year. Just the other day, I saw a man on HGTV pruning out the older branches to improve airflow to prevent powdery mildew from even starting. He said the pruning made for a happier plant, so I mixed a bucket of bleach for you to dip your pruners in. I don't want you spreading that nasty stuff to the other plants."

I had uncharitable thoughts about the HGTV gardener. "If we prune the lilacs now, they won't bloom very well next year." I showed her the buds on the new growth.

"Why would that man give such bad advice?" she asked.

"It's good advice for the upper New England states, just not for the Desert Southwest."

She wrung her hands. "What can we do about the powdery mildew? It looks awful."

"Remember how I wanted to spray with horticultural oil after they'd bloomed? That would have helped, but it's too late for that now, too. With the heat, it would be like deep-fat frying the leaves. The powdery mildew won't hurt the plant. I think it's best if we wait until next year."

"If you think that's best." She read the next item on her list. "Let's look at the roses by the patio."

"The ones I sprayed last week?"

"They still look bad."

The spiel for controlling thrips would produce another five minutes of hand-wringing and second-guessing. "Excuse me; I have to make a phone call."

Mrs. Greenwell opened her mouth to protest.

"I won't start the clock until I actually start working," I said, and her shoulders relaxed.

Although the phone was in my pocket, I went to the truck to make the call. "Hello, Mother. How are things going?"

"Do you always call home this much? No wonder Ky's cranky."

"Did he complain?"

"Listen, Bré, everything's fine. Since your last call, he's been outside to water something in pots, and I can hear the vacuum cleaner running upstairs."

"The vacuum cleaner? Really?"

An awkward silence filled the distance between us before she spoke again. "Please give me a chance, Bré. I'm trying so hard. Can the past be the past?"

"Okay." I wished I could have said it stronger.

The whole time Mrs. Greenwell instructed me on how to deadhead her purple coneflowers, I replayed my mother's plea. I wasn't the only one who needed to move on from the past.

I remembered my mother the summer I'd turned sixteen. She had been forty or so, not that much older than I am now. Her skin was as pale as I'd ever seen it, which made her auburn hair startling by contrast. She blamed her pallor on San Francisco.

"The sun never shines here," she said.

I'd tired of my grandmother's rules, so I'd run away to live with my mother. My father hadn't been dead a year, but my mother had been gone much longer, maybe five years. She greeted me at the door of her apartment. "Bré, you're free," she said and we embraced.

She bought a mattress from a thrift store for me to sleep on. We leaned it against the living room wall each morning so we could walk around her small apartment. I borrowed her clothes and stopped using a curling iron. I told Mother's friends I'd inherited my curls from her, but in reality, it was a perm my grandmother had given me. I read all of the books stacked by Mother's bed, even quoted them when her friends dropped by on weekends with crusty bread and bottles of wine. That made my mother smile.

One morning, she asked me, "Shouldn't you be going to school?"

"It's Saturday."

It was always Saturday.

Most days, I went to work with my mother at the Steele Trap Bookstore. I read used books and drank tea all day. It was Lydia, the store manager, who hosted my sixteenth birthday party. Mostly the clerks and customers from the bookstore came. All of them soared on a different orbit than my grandmother. They smelled like the earth, wore knobby fabrics, and hung earrings as intricate as sculptures from their ears, and so did I. The women were sojourners, happy to welcome another traveler. Together we sought balance in a skewed universe with artifacts we warmed in our hands and memories we'd stored in sheltered places. Mother was a part of the circle, yet apart. She played a role, carried the props, but she looked out the window as we talked feverishly about ancient truths rediscovered. The circle enclosed me in their fellowship.

We didn't go home after the birthday party at Lydia's. My mother took me to another party—much louder and with a younger crowd. The energy made me itch. As soon as we walked through the door, I asked Mother if we could leave, but someone pulled her away from me. Over her shoulder, she said, "Be free, Bré."

What kind of mother would say such a thing?

When she came to the kitchen later to refresh the ice in her drink, she found me sitting on the floor between the counter and a sideboard writing in my new journal. "Get up and dance, Bré. You write in the journal after a party, not during." She pulled me into the middle of dancers chanting with the music, "Call me!" When she noticed I wasn't dancing, she smiled knowingly and kissed me on the cheek. "Come on."

Mother found her purse in a pile of coats that had been pushed off a bed onto the floor. "Here's your birthday card. Open it."

I leaned against the doorjamb to watch her cross the room. A group of partiers opened a tight huddle of conversation as she neared. Within a minute, their drinks were held unnoticed as she told a story with broad gestures. They laughed sharply and urged her on with their attention. I'd never seen her more beautiful. Something in her had expanded to fill her skin.

A marijuana joint fell out of the card my mother had signed Zudora, the name that represented the woman and the time that had severed my parents' marriage. I looked around to see if anyone had noticed the joint's inelegant form at my feet. Not one eye met mine as I stooped to pick it off the rug. The people and the place could not have been more dissimilar to the lunchroom at Rancho del Sur High School, but I was still me—invisible, detached, singular. I held the cigarette between my thumb and middle finger for an hour. When someone asked me, finally, if I needed a light, I said yes.

I woke up the next morning in our apartment with a sore hip where my initials had been tattooed in black caps—MIB. I remembered thinking the teddy bear I'd been given by the tattoo artist was the sweetest thing I'd ever seen. In the morning, it was a cheap carnival teddy with scratchy fur and a missing eye. When I woke my mother to tell her how much I regretted getting the tattoo, she said dreamily, "Bré rhymes with free."

That had been the fifty-ninth time I'd given up on my mother and the first and last time I'd used drugs.

I excused myself from Mrs. Greenwell to call home again. "Is there anything you want me to pick up at the store on the way home?"

"Are you checking on me again?" asked my mother.

"No, I thought you might need something."

"I'm fine." She hung up.

~~~

While I ran water for an evening bath, I called Margot. "She's really trying. She was great with Ky today. He actually smiled at dinner tonight."

"He probably had gas."

"Trust me, he doesn't smile when he has gas. Nobody does."

She snorted a laugh, so I asked, pleaded really, for her to come back for the weekend. "She's the only mother we have. We have to try."

"I'm surprised at you. It's one thing for you to fall all over her. Now you're sacrificing your son to the queen of the gypsies?"

After our mother had motored off to Washington, D.C., to lobby for the ERA, Margot caught me crying in my grandmother's garden. She demanded a handful of strawberries for my display of weakness. I should have run to her and clung to her so tightly that no matter how hard she tried to pull away, we would have stood together in our hurt. I like to think I would have done just that if she hadn't hurled a rock at my forehead. Ever since then I've been dodging Margot's rocks. Now it was time to cling.

"Margot, it would mean so much to have you here. We should be helping each other. You're my sister. Please come."

"She doesn't want me."

"We don't know what she wants, and it's pretty clear she doesn't, either."

"You didn't see how angry she was when I found her or how her face lit up when I mentioned coming to see you."

"Oh, Margot—"

"Don't be sorry for me. It's a huge relief to know the truth. I'd asked myself a million times why she wouldn't stay with us. I watched for things in Dad and the house and Grandma. I thought it might be the uneven temperature of the oven or the boat Dad bought without talking with her. I even blamed the cat. Remember? He was always bringing dead lizards home." The phone went quiet. I expected the line to go dead, but Margot spoke again as if each word burned her throat. "It wasn't any of those things. It was me. She left me."

"She left all of us."

"But she's with you now, isn't she?"

"You know that won't last."

"Keep that in mind."

"Margot, I won't leave you."

The dial tone hummed in my ear.

AUG

2

Wasn't going to mention the heat, but it's a bit cooler: 97°. Yahoo! Afternoon thunderstorm sprinkled lightly.

I woke with a start when Louise clicked on the living room lamp and stood over me, hands on hips. "Do I look lopsided to you?"

After-images of light bulbs blinked on and off before me. "Give me a minute."

"How'd you end up on the sofa?"

"My mother yells a lot in her sleep."

Louise turned to the side. "Maybe you can tell better from the side. Look at me this way. And now from the other side. Notice anything?"

Louise wore a chartreuse sport top with matching spandex shorts. A slice of doughy skin bulged a bit at the waist. She didn't want to hear about that. "You are very, very green for this time of the morning."

She faced me again. "Sit up and take a good look. I've lost a bushel of weight since I bought the pros . . . prosthee . . . the rubber thing, you know, the artificial thing. All I need to know, is one side bigger than the other?"

Now that I knew what I was looking at, sure enough Louise was asymmetrical. "Just a little."

"Do you know how much these things cost? You'd think they'd make them adjustable. Maybe if I poked a hole—"

"Hold that thought. I'll be right back."

I didn't want to wake my mother, so I dressed from a pile of dirty clothes by the washer. I checked my sunburn in the hall mirror. My face no longer looked like a tomato. With a fresh crop of freckles, I was more watermelon-like. I roused Blink, our pacesetter, from Ky's room. We joined Louise on the front porch, where she was strapping weights to her wrists.

"You remember the young man at the fitness store, the one with dimples as deep as rain barrels? He told me I was ready to build muscle mass." She shook the extra skin of her upper arms at me. "I'm going to fill my flying-squirrel flaps with rock hard muscle, you just wait and see. My days of waving from both ends of my arm are numbered."

I couldn't think of one thing to say about that. "Lead the way, Blink."

Blink set a killer pace down the block and around the corner. Louise pumped her arms in wide arcs. Thanks to Blink, my upper body workout came from being pulled from one tree to another. I really felt the burn pulling him away from a fire hydrant. He was such a dog sometimes.

By the time we got to Ninth Avenue, Louise was gulping air, but it took more than hypoxia to quiet her. "How's Mama?"

"Okay."

"But?"

"I hate leaving Ky with her. The wind might change and off she'd go."

"Ky's . . . only . . . a phone call . . . away . . . from you . . . and I'm . . . close."

Yes, I had a cell phone, but proximity wasn't the issue. "It hurts when she leaves."

Louise stopped to strip off the wristbands and handed them to me. "I've always . . . loved . . . flying squirrels."

When Louise could walk and talk again, we continued down Ninth, only slower.

"Yes, leaving hurts," she said. "But Ky's not you. His heart is firmly set in love. Your mama can't undo that. And she certainly won't break him."

"I might. He's been so ugly lately."

She laughed. "Ah yes, the testosterone-induced psychosis of teenaged boys. Where do y'all think Robert Louis Stevenson got the idea for Dr. Jekyll and Mr. Hyde?"

"I wouldn't feel good about leaving Dr. Jekyll or Mr. Hyde with my mother."

"But that's the gift of parenting. When we send our babies into the world, we understand in an itsy-bitsy, teeny-tiny way the Father's trepidation when He sent His Son into the world."

I stopped dead in my tracks. "Louise, we crucified Him."

She stopped, too. "Only because He let us."

Only the padding of our footsteps and Blink's panting filled the space between us for several blocks. Louise spoke first. "I've been noodlin' over that meditation verse, the one from Psalm 131. Anything strike you about it?"

"Only how absolutely wonderful being quiet and still would be."

"Honey lamb, I want you to consider something. When a mama weans her infant, and her milk dries up, the relationship between the mama and baby changes. The child grows more and more independent until that glorious day when it contributes as much to the relationship as she does—right around the child's fortieth birthday or there 'bouts. You, my sweet, deserving friend, are still rooting at your mother's breast. You need to be weaned."

"You can't be serious."

"I'm as serious as a hungry cat watchin' a mouse hole. You might want to read that psalm again."

The thought of adding one more thing to my to-do list slipped my clutch. "I'll try."

"You won't be sorry."

We turned the corner to Louise's house, and Blink pulled harder. My heart sank. Larry leaned against the Sweet Suzy truck parked at the curb. The object of Blink's desire, Goliath, sat preening herself at Larry's feet. Larry looked up and waved.

Louise waved back. "Maybe you can get Larry to drive you home again. I know he's been slipping you goodies from his truck."

I started to protest, but she raised her hand to stop me. "I know you too well, sugar. You can't hide anything from me."

Since my last encounter with Larry, I'd decided he was harmless. He loved riling me and seeing my face turn red, but when the chips were down, Larry was a friend. He'd proven he could be a white knight and a boy's best friend. In short, Larry was a cliché, a sidekick, a buddy.

"Louise, I'm feeling strong. I think I'll cross the street here and walk a couple more blocks, really get the old ticker beating."

Blink wasn't interested in getting my ticker beating. He only had eyes for Goliath. After three failed attempts at course correction, I surrendered to Blink's leadership. I had no choice. The leash was wound tightly around my wrist.

"Hey there, gorgeous!" Larry called as I got closer.

"You better pick up your cat," I said. "I don't think we're stopping."

Goliath licked her paws, oblivious to Blink's charge.

"Blink, sit!" Larry said.

One inch from Goliath's nose, Blink lowered his haunches to the pavement. His muscles quivered and his nose twitched, but he stayed put. As for me, I'd decided long ago never to trust anyone or anything that could lick its own neck. I kept my distance from Goliath.

Larry bent to scratch Blink's ears. "It's hard to resist a pretty lady, isn't it, boy?" Then Larry winked at me and my face burned with embarrassment.

Louise caught up. "Is Connie inside?"

"As snug as a bug in a rug."

"That's what I like to hear."

Larry brushed Blink's fur off his hands. "I can tell Ma's getting better. She's telling me what to do. I think she's about ready to stay home."

I excused myself before Larry had a chance to get personal.

"Wait a minute, sweet pea," Louise called, heading up her walk. "I'll be right back. I've got a surprise for you."

"I'll come back later," I said.

She spoke with rare authority. "Don't move."

Louise disappeared into her house, and Blink lay down in front of Goliath, so I relaxed the leash.

Larry leaned against the truck and crossed his arms. "Ky's a good ball

player. He's smart. He knows how to read the other players. He antici-
pates their moves. He'll be a real asset to the team."

"He's been a little moody lately."

"Only until you drive around the corner."

"What's that supposed to mean?"

He laughed. "Don't get your hackles up, now. It's a tough time for a
kid. He's not a child anymore and his mama is there to remind him he's
not a man, either. He'll get past it and so will you."

"And how many parenting books have you read lately?"

"Only weak-minded people consult parenting books."

"Really?"

"Parenting is common sense, pure and simple."

"Someday, you're going to eat those words, bones and all."

"Not me. When I'm a father—"

Louise's screen door slammed. "Yoo-hoo! Here's your surprise!"

Larry scooped up Goliath. "You ladies have a nice day." He paused at
the door of the truck. "What tasty treat would you like me to bring to the
game on Saturday?"

"I saw a commercial for Sweet Suzy Double Chocolate Chip Cookies
on TV last night," I said.

"Done." He climbed into the driver's seat and yelled over the idling
engine. "If you're not doing anything later, we could go to a beach town
I know in central California! Great clam chowder! Lots of fog!"

Fog sounded wonderful. "Sorry, I'm doing the laundry this afternoon.
Another time, perhaps!"

"Hope springs eternal!"

I watched him pull away from the curb and drive down the street.

Louise whispered in my ear. "He's gotten under your skin, hasn't he?

"He most certainly has not."

When I told her I had to get to work, she handed me the Too Cute
bag. The store specialized in ensembles embroidered with cutesy carica-
tures of woodland creatures. Louise supported the store single-handedly.
I'd only been inside once and quickly turned around to leave.

"I bought a little something for you to wear tonight." Louise cocked her head and batted her fake eyelashes, which meant she knew something I would soon regret.

"Tell me," I said.

"I've nearly exploded from holding the news in. I got the call yesterday afternoon. Manley took a message, but I called them back as soon as I could. It didn't even bother me that I broke a nail punchin' the phone keys. Virginia got me right in to get the nail fixed. Do y'all like the color—"

"Louise!"

"Oh, goodness me. We've gotten our first response from the press releases I sent out to the television stations. Channel Two wants to interview you at five thirty tonight. They need a garden expert to talk about the drought." Louise kissed my cheek and turned to leave. She waved but didn't turn around. "I'll be over at five to help you get ready."

"Louise?"

"You're welcome, sugar."

The sense of touch burnishes our memories. Pragmatists remember an old quilt with its puckered seams and gauzy cotton, while the more adventurous recall the slide of silk against their skin. A kiss planted on a puppy's ear brings a smile to the guileless. For gardeners like me, it's the first timid days of spring, when the temperature teeters—one minute warm, the next icy. But a child heavy with sleep against our chests trumps the sweetness of every memory.

Phoebe got heavier in my arms. "I think she's asleep," I said.

"Let's try to put her down," Roseanne whispered.

"Maybe I should walk her awhile longer." I walked around the kitchen table while Roseanne studied the revisions I'd made to her garden plan. "Take your time. Make sure it's exactly what you want."

"She gets so heavy."

"I'm fine. Don't worry." Phoebe's body was a warm compress on my chest, restorative and soothing. *Thanks, Lord.*

"What's a penstemon again?" Roseanne asked.

"They're beardtongues."

Her frown deepened. I could have opened a plant book to show her a picture of the flowers, but that meant putting Phoebe down. "Pustemons are nectar factories on a stem, totally irresistible to hummingbirds and butterflies, and they have the sweetest funnel-shaped flowers." I pointed to the Husker Red penstemon on the plan. "This one's my favorite. The flowers are nice, white, not particularly spectacular in themselves, but the foliage is red to purple, so the plant adds color to the flower bed long after the flower has bloomed. I've planned a couple by the birdbath, sort of a one-stop shop for the hummingbirds."

"And they're xeric?"

"They're tough little buggers, all right. I've seen native varieties growing out of rocks. When they're blooming along with the gaura and the hyssops, you'll need a control tower to keep the hummingbirds in line."

"Phoebe will love it. Now let me take her from you. You look so tired."

Roseanne transferred Phoebe to her shoulder, and a resident ache settled into a cubby just below my heart. When she returned, Roseanne offered me a Diet Pepsi and a comfortable chair, as I'd hoped she would. My mother had walked with me out to the Daisy Mobile that morning to ask me to trust her. I'd promised her I wouldn't be home before four to give her and Ky a chance to get acquainted. I told Roseanne about my mother's visit.

"How in the world did you get the plan finished with all that going on?" When I didn't answer, she asked, "How much sleep did you get last night?"

"I slept on the sofa."

"Why don't you lie down on my bed? My house has to be quieter than yours. I'll wake you in an hour, I promise."

The doorbell rang. Roseanne looked at her watch and sighed. "I wondered if he'd forgotten about me."

"Who?" I asked, but she was already at the door.

Roseanne came back to the living room smiling. "He's sent something every day since the Table of Ten party."

That explained why she hadn't called. "Not Radarman, I hope."

"His name is Stefan."

"Yes, but does he get good reception?"

"You can be so mean," Roseanne said, but she was smiling and playing with the bag's tulle bow.

"Do you want me to leave so you can open it alone?"

"Don't be silly. Stefan and I have just talked on the phone a few times."

A few times? "You better open it. It might be his television remote. Or is it too soon for that kind of commitment?"

"Very funny." She tore through the tissue paper to lift out a long, flat box, a velvety one, the kind that held expensive jewelry. She paused before opening it. "He wouldn't. Would he?"

"Open it."

Roseanne took a small parchment scroll out of the box. She read the message silently and then out loud. "Roses are red. Carnivals are thrilling. I want to eat corn dogs with you and your offspring. Call me. Stefan." She pulled three plastic wristbands from the bag. "I guess we're going to the carnival tonight. I better call him."

I was embarrassed to admit it, but a hot dog on a stick and a pitiful poem had brought me to the precipice of self-pity.

Roseanne saw the struggle on my face. She sat again and took my hand. "Forgive my selfishness. You were telling me about your mother and Ky and how tired you are. Please stay for a rest. I'll put some lovely music on. You'll be to sleep in no time."

"Don't be silly. I can't take a nap. I'm too excited for you." I returned to the kitchen table to repack my portfolio. "Besides, Louise has some promotional thing for me to do tonight. She even bought me a new outfit."

Roseanne stacked my plant books. "I'm sorry the Table of Ten dinner didn't work out for you."

"You shouldn't be apologizing. It's not your fault."

"Don't let it get you down. There'll be another event, something different this month. I'll make sure you get an invitation. You never know, your prince might show up. You wouldn't want to miss him."

"If my prince shows up with a glass Birkenstock, send him over."

"You won't come?"

I zipped the portfolio case. "I don't think so. With Ky being so teenagerish and my mother being so motherish, my Prince Charming is going to have to take a number."

~~~

Ky lay reading on the family room sofa with a jar of peanut butter, a spoon, and a jug of milk.

A tiny bubble of alarm popped. "Where's your grandmother?"

"I dunno."

"Is she home?"

"I dunno."

"Ky."

"What?"

"Is your grandmother home?"

"I said I don't know."

I repressed the urge to growl and headed up the stairs two at a time. The bed in Andrea's room was made. I smelled the pillows. Tide. I looked for her bag in the closet and under the bed. When I saw that her toothbrush was gone from the bathroom, I returned to Ky.

"When was the last time you saw your grandmother?"

"About ten, I think."

"You *think*? Ky, this is important. When was the last time you saw your grandmother today?"

As if finally hearing me, he asked, "Did something happen to Grandma?"

"No, but her bag's gone. She's probably on her way back to California."

"Oh."

He reloaded his spoon with peanut butter and turned a page.

~~~

"Trust me?" Louise stood over me with a jumbo curling iron. "Despite my head's present resemblance to a tennis ball, I've curled my own hair since I was knee high to a plow mule."

I didn't want Louise pouting with a hot appliance so close to my face. "Of course I do. When have you ever let me down?"

Our eyes met in the mirror. "This will be different," she said. "I promise."

I sat on a stool in front of my bathroom mirror while Louise twisted sections of my hair and attached them to my head with clips, just like a real hairdresser. I relaxed a little.

"Are you going fishing tonight?" I asked.

Louise wore khaki pants and a fly-fishing vest over a Hawaiian blouse. "I assume you're referring to my vest. I'll have you know all the great directors wear them—even Steven Spielberg. The pockets come in handy for notes and lenses, important director stuff."

She'd dressed for her part and I'd dressed for mine, thanks, once again, to Louise. The Too Cute bag had held a linen robin's-egg blazer with tone-on-tone embroidery at the cuff and hem. She'd found the blazer on the clearance rack but got there too late to purchase the matching pair of slacks. I didn't mind. I had slipped on a pair of denim shorts with my dress Birkenstocks. Louise had protested, but when she saw I wouldn't change, she'd promised to talk to the cameraman about keeping the shot close in.

Louise pulled the curling iron through my hair, held it in place briefly, and released a perfect flip that brushed my shoulder. "See?" she asked.

"You've been moonlighting at Virginia's, haven't you?"

"I should. I can't seem to stop playing with people's hair. Be sure you see Connie today."

"Dreadlocks?"

"Nope. I braided every hair on her head and finished off each braid with a bead. She looks positively tropical." Louise rolled another strand of hair around the curling iron and released it. "Listen up. The camera crew will be here any minute. I e-mailed the reporter the same questions I gave you, so there shouldn't be any surprises." She dug three marbles out of her vest pocket and handed them to me. "I want you to carry these during the interview. They'll remind you to say Perennially Yours three times. The marketing book said—"

"You read a marketing book?"

"There were a lot of pictures." She loosened a clip and pulled another section of hair through the curling iron. "Now where was I?"

"The marketing book you read . . ."

"Marketing book?"

"You read a marketing book . . ."

She fanned herself with her hand. "Do you have the cooler on? It's hotter than blazes in here."

I assured her the cooler was turned to high.

Louise's face glowed with sweat. "Give me a minute. I'm having a power surge. You better move that box of tissues to a safe distance. Magazines have spontaneously combusted during my surges." She removed the vest and mopped her face with a tissue. "Anyway, name-dropping is the whole purpose of the interview. Say Perennially Yours at least three times. More is better. According to the book, being on television instantly qualifies you as an expert, even if you tell folks to eat their lawn and mow their vegetables."

Louise worked silently as she finished the back of my hair and moved on to the side. She rolled another length of hair and held the curling iron in place. Within moments the heat got uncomfortable against my scalp. Oblivious to my discomfort, she squinted on a thought.

"Louise?"

She didn't move.

"Louise!"

She released the curl. "Oh, sugar, I'm sorry. Did I burn you?"

I winced at her touch. "It's a little tender."

She sat on the edge of the tub with her face in her hands.

I went to her. "It's no big deal. It's a teensy bit scorched is all. Look, I've fanned the smoke away so you can see the blisters."

"You can always make me laugh." She blew her nose, and a tear spilled over her cheek when she said, "Remember that little gal who came to the house last week, the one riddled with cancer? I got a call today."

Death, expected or not, always gut-punched me. Whammy. "Oh."

"There won't be a funeral. The mama's a hornet's nest of anger. It's so very hard to be left behind."

We embraced and bowed our heads, forehead to forehead, on the side of the tub.

"Don't you dare cry and mess up your makeup," she warned.

"I won't if you won't."

"We need to pray. You do it or I'll start crying again."

"I don't think I can."

Louise was quiet for a while, so I waited, knowing she was composing her thoughts. She finally prayed, "We want to be happy for you and your newest resident. You've waited a long time for this homecoming. But it's hard for us, Lord. Heaven seems so far away, and it's harder still when we see the brokenness of the mama. She's so scared and lonely. We entrust her shattered heart to you. Wrap her in your strong arms until she's ready for the new heart you've made for her."

Ky called up the stairs. "Mom, the camera dude is here!"

"Oh dear, we didn't finish your hair," Louise said.

One side of my hairdo lay tame and sleek; the other side exerted its fiery personality with one overzealous curl. "Nothing a butterfly clip can't fix," I said.

~⁓

A tumble of cables snaked their way from the Channel Two van to the front yard, where a cameraman fussed with his equipment. Behind the van, a Focus painted with the station's logo screeched to a stop and a young woman in a red blazer stepped out. She ran her fingers through her hair and applied fresh lipstick using the car's side mirror. A technician handed her a microphone. She looked familiar.

"Give me the countdown," she said to the cameraman.

"One twenty. Mark."

My tummy jumped. I introduced myself to the woman, who looked fresh out of journalism school, or at least I hoped she was out of journalism school. "Should we talk a little before the interview?" I asked.

"No time for that. I read your bio. Follow my lead."

My bio?

"Can she stand on the other side?" Louise asked. "We had a little trouble with her hair." But the woman put her hand to her ear and waved Louise off.

Louise tucked the rebellious side of my hair into the collar of my jacket. "Don't move. Don't look at the camera. And don't forget to say Perennially Yours three times."

Andrea stepped up with a makeup sponge. "Just a dab around the eyes. There. Perfect. Good luck."

Louise kissed my cheek. "You look gorgeous. Remember, *three* times."

I scanned the crowd of neighbors and curious children on bicycles that gathered behind the cameraman. Ky smiled and shrugged. The place where my mother should have stood beside him was taken by my neighbor, Sarah, and her little girl.

"Okay, okay, we're going live." The cameraman counted, "Three . . . two . . ." A bright light flashed on.

"Thank you, Justin. This is Candy Conroy. I'm here live with Miffy Gardner, noted author and lecturer. Her latest book on the life and times of Tommy Blair, *The Parliamentary Years*, is hitting bookstore shelves this week. Tell me, Ms. Gardner, knowing the man like you do, what made Mr. Blair reinstitute the draft?"

"The draft?"

I heard Ky whisper, "Mom didn't write a book."

I felt a tap on my shoe. Louise looked up from her position at my feet. "Say something."

Candy cleared her throat. "We're live, Ms. Gardner. You must be very excited about your new book. I couldn't put it down—an absolutely scintillating read. It was pretty thick, too. How long did it take to write?"

I took a breath and affected a sense of calm authority I didn't possess. "We're facing something more important than the release of my book, Candy. We've just lived through the hottest month in recorded history for western Colorado. If that wasn't hard enough, the five-year drought has depleted our water reserves while growth has increased our water demand. You may not know it, Candy, but I wear another hat as owner of Perennially Yours Garden Designs and Maintenance." *That's one.* "If you don't mind, I'd like to give your listeners some pointers on keeping their gardens healthy while using Colorado water resources responsibly."

Candy pushed away a celebratory peach smoothie from Louise. "Next time, don't mail a press release until your client is prepared for the interview you've booked."

"Now haven't you gone and nailed the problem right on its pointy little head. Preparation. That's advice we could all use." I thought Louise demonstrated amazing constraint.

I changed my clothes and joined the party as Louise uncovered a tray of lemon scones. My mouth got all juicy inside. The phone rang as I reached for the largest scone. It was Harlan Chandler.

"I saw you on the news," he said. "When can you come back? My yard's looking worse than ever."

I booked him for early the next week.

"I'll try to get your book read before you come," he said and hung up.

Ky picked up the last scone and shoved the whole thing into his mouth.

I lay on the bed trying to keep any part of my body from touching another part. I kicked off the sheet and got up to pace the room. The curtains hung unmoving over the window. Blink plodded out of the room and down the stairs. I scanned the street, looking for my mother.

"Forget it," I said, surrendering to the futility of sleep. I opened my Bible and read the verses Louise had told me to reread in Psalm 131.

My heart is not proud, O Lord,

No, it's scared to death.

my eyes are not haughty;

I do not concern myself with great matters

Only the mortgage and the utility bill.

or things too wonderful for me.

Like Ben? That door is closed—very, very closed. It's time to move on, sister.

But I have stilled and quieted my soul;

like a weaned child with its mother,

like a weaned child is my soul within me.

Weaning is an awfully nice word for something that feels like having your heart wrenched out of your chest. Just after Ky's first birthday, I knew the time had come to wean him. He was ready. Even if I turned the radio and the television off and took the phone off the hook while he was nursing, he stopped to look toward the door every time a car drove by, which happened every forty-five seconds. Weaning Ky should have been a piece of cake. It wasn't.

Every time I picked him up, he rooted around for my breast, and when Scott offered him a bottle, his face puckered red with indignation. He screamed long into the night. Not being able to satisfy his hunger burned a hole in me, so it was Scott who walked him in a circuitous path through the living room and kitchen and dining room that first night. As dawn neared, Scott sent me to soak in the tub to soothe my sore breasts. I cranked up the radio and closed the door to mourn the end of my physical bond to my son. Within hours, Ky's hunger had overwhelmed his preference, and he took the bottle eagerly. That was that.

"Lord, I'm tired of rooting at my mother for what she cannot give me, but I'm so good at it, I don't know how to stop. Satisfy me as I rest in your everlasting arms. You know where she is tonight. Protect her with your strong arms. Amen."

I waved a dismissive hand at the window, but it was really my mother I waved away. I lay down on my pillow, the one my mother had slept on the first night she was here. The warmth of my head released her scent from the pillow, and I wept. The first night of weaning is always the hardest.

AUG
6

I'm wilting, but the Cupid's dart comes back bright-eyed every morning after a summer night's rest. And they are startlingly (is that a word?) blue! What charmers.

Ky scratched at the mound with his cleat and threw several warm-up pitches until the batter stepped up to the plate. The catcher, the chubby alto from the choir, jumped to catch a high pitch and missed. "Hey, remember my old knees!"

"Sorry!" Ky called back to her.

I sat hip to hip on a plank with Louise and Andrea under a golf umbrella Louise had bought at a yard sale. Although it was emblazoned with a pharmaceutical logo too personal to mention, I didn't care. Our bare arms were slick with sweat where they touched. We each held a Big Gulp.

The field was an expanse of weed stubble and dust. Every time a batter got a hit, the crowd cowered from the dust that was kicked up on the infield. I sucked on the straw to wash the taste of dirt from my mouth, and I was about to ask Louise to spit in my eye. It was that dry.

"Hey, batta, batta, batta," Louise shouted, but her drawl made it sound more flirtatious than distracting.

"Save your energy," I said. "The batter hasn't even gotten to the plate yet."

"I recognize that player. She tried to sell me queen-size panty hose a few years back."

"'Vengeance is mine; I will repay, saith the Lord.'" I recited the verse I'd memorized as a child to vex Margot.

"Nothing vengeful about it. I'm just doing my part."

Ky massaged dirt into the ball and stared down his opponent. He swung his throwing arm back and stepped into the pitch. The slow, steeply arced pitch of a softball looks deceptively easy to throw. Ky's pitch should have crossed home plate on the downside of its arc and just inside the batter's strike zone, but instead, it sailed over the catcher's head. Three similar pitches followed.

"Ball four. Take a base."

Francey Houge, the church librarian and centerfielder, sat down among the weeds. No amount of cajoling from her teammates, or Larry, could make her stand.

"And you thought this would be good for him?" Andrea asked.

I'd also thought fat-free salad dressing was a good idea—until I tasted it.

"Whoever scheduled a two-o'clock game when it's ninety-nine in the shade is off my Christmas card list," Louise said.

Larry made the timeout sign with his hands and walked to the mound.

"Maybe he'll send him to the benchy-thing," Louise said.

"The dugout," I corrected.

"But it's only a board."

"It's still the dugout."

"Fine, the dugout. Could we go home if he gets to sit on it?" Louise asked.

I took a sip of my Big Gulp to wet my vocal chords. "Only three innings to go, unless, of course, by some miracle, Ky's team gets a turn at bat and they score four runs. Then we're looking at five more innings."

"Oh."

Ky's chin almost touched his chest as Larry talked to him. Although I couldn't hear the conversation, it looked like every other midbattle motivational talk since the dawn of man. Heads nodded and spit flew and equipment got tugged back into place. Larry returned to the dugout without Ky.

I've always said that I believed in miracles, and what happened next proved they exist. Ky's team managed to sharpen their defense enough to hold their opponents' score to eleven, and they scored enough runs to drag the game to seven innings, but Ky still spent more time looking at the dirt than pitching. I sent a silent promise to him that he didn't have to play on the team anymore. Then I told Andrea and Louise.

"He'll learn more from losing than winning," Louise said.

"He has plenty of opportunities to lose without going out and looking for them." My chest tightened when I thought of how I'd trusted Larry. "Can't Larry see how defeated Ky is? Why doesn't he take him out?"

"Guys thrive on this kind of agony," Andrea said.

"Not Ky. He's too conscientious. It's killing him to be pitching so poorly."

"You're the one who's squirmin' like a sinner on Sunday," Louise said.

I bumped my head on the umbrella as I stood. "I'm going to talk to Larry."

Despite Louise's protests, I headed for the dugout. Ky pitched short of the plate.

"Much better, Ky," Larry called. "Remember, complete your follow-through."

When an artist's eye comes across an intriguing play of line and proportion and light, her fingers itch to record the interaction with a sketch, even if a pencil and paper aren't handy. Larry, watching his team with the intensity of a general at war, provided such a challenge. I outlined his strong, broad forehead and the curve between his eyes that leveled into an unremarkable yet honest nose, the kind you wouldn't mind staring at while getting a tooth filled. The tip of his nose rounded into the bush of hair on his upper lip, and the rest of his face was lost to me inside his beard. I finished his face myself. Since men with skinny lips are hard to read, I made Larry's upper lip full to match his bottom lip. He needed a cleft in his chin, deep enough to underscore his brashness but not so deep as to make him heroic, say like a Dudley Do-Right. I changed my mind. After all, the man sewed Barbie doll dresses. A cleft was out of the question. I reworked the chin, made it round and indistinct with a jaw-line to match. When the umpire called ball three, I remembered why I was standing there.

"Larry?"

He turned to flash a smile and went immediately back to the game. "Did you see that last pitch? He's improving with each throw."

"Ky's miserable out there. He can't even look at the batter."

"He's visualizing—"

"His *escape*. Can't you relieve him?"

He looked at me. "Relieve him? He's the best pitcher I have."

"Larry, please take him out."

Crack! Wood connected with rawhide. We watched as the left fielder hobbled back to the fence to pick the ball out of the dust. She need not have bothered. Four runners touched home plate, and the umpire blew his whistle to stop the game.

Ky trotted toward us smiling. "It worked!"

Larry and Ky exchanged a series of jabs and playful punches before they finally shook hands. "Awesome game, dude!" Larry said.

The team gathered around Larry and bowed their heads. "Caps off, ladies and gentlemen," he said. "Dear Lord, thanks for an injury-free game, worthy opponents, and a lot of fun today. Humble any proud hearts. Bolster weak ones. Amen."

Larry leaned into me. "You'll find something sweet in Ky's gear bag."

While Andrea showered and Ky checked his e-mail, I took the phone into the basement to call Margot. The phone rang and rang as I plucked the whites out of a mountain of laundry and measured the detergent.

"You honestly thought she'd show up here?" she asked, breathless from her dash to the phone.

"She could. She has before."

"Only when she was stoned." Margot sighed heavily. "Let her go,

Mibby. That's all we can do. She's not going to be Mrs. Cleaver no matter how badly we want it."

"I know." I told Margot how I'd decided to wean myself from Mother. "It's a pretty good illustration, isn't it? I mean, she can only be the person she is. It isn't fair to expect more, and I'm tired of being disappointed." The phone was silent. I checked to see if I had accidentally hit the mute button. "Hello? Margot? Are you there?"

"Are you in therapy?"

"Do I sound like I need it?"

"It took five years of yakking my brains out and about fifty thousand dollars to understand that this mess was about her and not me. Seeing how she responded to you undid it all. When my therapist heard how upset I was, she bumped another patient to see me. It was that or check myself into the loony bin. My therapist wants me to surrender the whole Madonna-as-mother myth. Weaning yourself sounds a bit incestuous, sister dear. Where'd you get such an idea?"

The last time I'd told Margot I read the Bible, she hung up on me. A few days later, I'd received a two-book set from her: *The Lonely Universe: How Science has Erased God From the Human Experience* and *The Mythology of the Bible and Other Comic Books*. I prepared for the dial tone. "I came across a passage in the Bible."

"And that makes moving on easier?"

"Sometimes, but not always. It's all pretty new to me."

"My therapist says that Mother's disappearing act imprinted my brain with distrust. To rebuild the ability to trust, Dr. Fleisher wants me to mother myself. Imagine that. I finally have a kid, and it's me. I would have preferred one that was a little less messed up."

"You're not messed up."

"It's hard to say that with a straight face, isn't it?"

"Being the oldest made Mother's leaving harder on you. I always had you. I'm so grateful, Margot. I really am."

When she spoke again, her voice was taut. "I'll call. Good-bye."

I sprinkled the load of laundry with detergent and pushed the start button. The rush of water against the tub and the mustiness of the basement reassured me with their humble familiarity. Clothes will get dirty. I will wash them. Only if I was grounded in the ordinary could I consider what had just happened between Margot and me. She'd exposed her heart and admitted to having a weak moment. She'd even said good-bye. But it was more than that. Margot was my sister again.

I almost spilled the bleach when the phone rang.

"I didn't—" cough, cough—"call at a bad time, did I?"

The washer shifted into its agitation cycle with a clunk.

"Sounds like your washer could use a new belt."

"Maybe next month."

There was a new energy in Crenshaw's voice. "I've been talking to Brenda, the gal I work with, just like you said. And you won't believe this, she loves to bowl. She's in a league and everything. I guess she's pretty good, too, 'cause she has an impressive handicap. And get this, she asks me every day how my bowling arm is doing. Then she told me something very sad. One of her teammates is moving. I think I'm going to ask her—" cough, cough—"out tomorrow." Cough. "I was hoping you had some ideas about where to take her."

Hello? "Why not take her bowling?"

"Nah, I want to do something special. She bowls three nights a week already."

My stomach growled, so I checked my watch. I headed up the stairs to the kitchen to fix dinner. "It's nice you want to do something special with Brenda, but you'd be jumping the gun. Remember, you're still trying to get to know her. You'll see the real Brenda if she feels comfortable in her surroundings. She likes to bowl. You like to bowl. I'd take her bowling."

"There's another problem. We don't bowl at the same alley."

"You want Brenda to feel comfortable, don't you?"

"Are you sure women like that kind of stuff?"

"Oh yes."

"Let me write that down."

While Crenshaw wrote, I stared into the refrigerator, hoping to find inspiration for a quick meal. I moved to the pantry.

"Are you still praying for me?" he asked.

"Yep." And I was, too. I'd written his name on masking tape and stuck it to the dashboard of the Daisy Mobile.

"That's good. Keep it up."

Someday I'll open the newspaper and read the headline "Sleep Deprivation and Parenting Adolescents Linked." The story, based on research funded by the American Pediatric Association, will support what mothers have known for centuries: adolescent males emerge from their testosterone stupor around midnight. During a brief window of time, rational thought returns; the relationship between cause and effect crystallizes; the ability to communicate in complete sentences re-engages. Most importantly, the invisible audience that second-guesses every movement a teenager makes disperses for the night. In short, if you want to keep in touch with your teenage male, don't plan on going to bed early.

In the waning hours of the day, Ky laid down the mask of angst he'd worn since I'd confiscated his cable modem. He even sat up straighter when he reported how well Margaret's pots were doing, and his eyes glinted as he told me how easy it had been to find his Calvin and Hobbes books in the bookcase. Best of all, the welcome light stayed on when I asked him about his scraped knees.

"Oh that. I fell when Blink and I were racing to the back door."

That response gave me courage to ask him a favor. "Could I hold you for a minute, maybe two?"

He made a three-note complaint out of my name, but he scooted over and leaned into my arms. Then he turned up the volume in time to watch the Rockies highlights on *SportsCenter*.

I rested my cheek on his head. He smelled like an old duffel bag that had been dragged through a swamp, so boyish and so familiar. The ache in my chest receded.

"Hey, Mom. Is there any chance I could get the latest Macabre Pit game?"

"Things are pretty tight right now."

"It didn't hurt to ask."

I assured him it didn't and that I appreciated his good attitude about it.

Ky woke me when he sat up abruptly. "Gross! You're drooling in my hair!"

I swiped my chin with the back of my hand. "I guess I fell asleep."

"Hey," he said sheepishly, "I kinda forgot to tell you Ben called while you were at Louise's."

"He's here? In Orchard City?"

"Yeah, but he's leaving tomorrow." He checked his watch. "Oops. Make that today."

The mantel clock read twelve-thirty, too late to call. Just as well. I mean, the door was closed, right?

Ky bent to kiss my cheek. "He said it was important. He wanted you to call whenever you got home. Sorry."

The picture I'd constructed of Ben skimming the top of a jungle canopy toward the Andes faded into Ben packing mosquito repellent and khaki clothes only ten minutes away. I stared at the phone a long time. What would be the point of calling him? *We're still friends.* But every time we talked, I acted like a lovesick middle schooler. *Maybe he's ill. Maybe he did leave for Ecuador, and he contracted dengue fever.* He had Claire. *She seems a little fussy.* Ben needed someone with grit, someone earthy. *There's nobody earthier than me.*

The phone rang five times before the message machine answered. I hadn't planned on leaving a message. I was considering hanging up when Ben spoke over the recording. "Hello? Hang on a minute." The phone beeped and the recorded message stopped.

Ben cleared his throat. "Hello? Mibby?"

I apologized for calling so late. I blamed Ky. "I just got the message."

"No problem. I wanted to hear your voice before I left."

My voice?

"I guess I finally realized how far Ecuador is from Orchard City."

My heart hiccupped, but I ignored it. I asked him how his training had gone.

"Excellent. I got a lot of fly time on their equipment doing short takeoffs and landings. I'm feeling good about the flying."

"Are you sick or anything?"

"I don't think so."

"That's good."

The phone went quiet. I imagined him rubbing his eyes and checking his watch. He didn't have a shirt on. *Stop that!*

"And you? How are you doing?" he asked.

I was seriously discombobulated. "Okay, mostly."

"I saw you on the news the other night. You were too nice to that airhead reporter, but that's you. You sure looked great."

I paced around the kitchen island, and honestly, I couldn't name my apprehension. One part of me screamed, *Run to him!* The other part cowered for the next blow.

"I've been doing some thinking," he said, and if at all possible, his voice had dropped an octave. I leaned against the doorjamb, figuring it would be the safest place if the earth moved under my feet.

"I've been a real jerk, Mibby, and I know it, but I'm a desperate jerk, so I hope you'll go easy on me."

"Ben, I'm fine with—"

"I better say this before I chicken out. I was wondering if I could e-mail you while I'm gone. I regret letting you slip away. It would make leaving so much easier if I knew we'd be in touch."

"What about Claire?"

"Yeah, well, Claire and I . . . we agreed to go our separate ways. She . . . we value different things."

Yelling *hot diggity dog* into the receiver didn't seem appropriate, so I concentrated on breathing. It wasn't easy.

"I can't blame you for being mad," he said. "You have someone else in your life, don't you? I'm not surprised. I had to try, is all. I would have always wondered if I'd given up too soon."

"Ben?"

"Yes?"

"What's your e-mail address?"

~⌒~

I started the Yukon not knowing where I was headed. When I got to Independence Avenue, where a right turn would take me to Ben's front door, I remembered another night when I'd thought running to Ben was the antidote to my problems. I needed time to think. I turned left and followed Talbott Drive to the interstate. Once I was cruising at seventy-five miles an hour in the opposite direction from Ben, I let myself consider what he had offered me.

Not much.

I was the safe one for him to return to, no doubt about it, but when would the call of the wild sound again and off he'd go? Or would he run into Claire at the grocery store, tucking her hair behind her ear, and go running back to her? And truthfully, Ben hadn't shown that much interest in getting to know Ky. He'd thrown a ball with him a couple times and asked Ky questions about his Little League team. But he'd never gone to one of Ky's games.

What was Ben's pull on me? As I zoomed past the last exit for Orchard City, the answer came to me. Ben was a hottie—and smooth as silk, confident, yet vulnerable, and a pilot, for crying out loud.

The highway mirrored the Colorado River's graceful slide through the canyon. Moonlight glinted off the river, and the running lights of a semi shone in the distance. I exited the highway where the canyon widened enough for a truck stop, and I backtracked toward the city. I knew what I had to do. I pulled into the Taco Bell parking lot and punched Ben's phone number into my cell phone.

"What's up?" he asked groggily.

"I think we should talk."

"Okay."

The way he said okay, so eager and indulgent, I almost allowed myself to second-guess my decision.

"Are you there?" he asked.

"I have a question for you." I just wasn't sure I wanted to hear the answer. "Am I the one?"

"What do you mean?"

"I'm not asking you to commit to forever, but I need to know if . . . if that's what you're thinking, that we have a better-than-average chance at . . . forever."

"You're catching me off guard here."

"Take your time."

"What is it you want to know exactly?"

He's stalling.

"I have a son," I said, "and I'm realizing how being a mother makes the whole dating thing different. I figure it will take at least another year for us to know if marriage is an option, and since any time I commit to knowing you includes Ky, I have to be sure we're moving toward the same goal. I don't mean to make this sound like joining a health club, but you understand, don't you?"

The phone was quiet for a very long time.

"I'm not comfortable saying the word *marriage*," he said.

It was my turn to be quiet. Maybe Ben hadn't understood the question. "I'm not asking you to commit to marriage, just to the goal of marriage. That doesn't mean we're *going* to get married, it just means we're going to *work* toward marriage, unless, of course, we find out we're not a good match. Then it would be stupid to continue dating, because it wouldn't get us where we want to go, which is marriage." I couldn't even hear background noise. "Are you there?"

"Yeah."

Time for a metaphor. "I guess it's like saying I want to go to San Francisco, so I get on a bus to San Francisco. If the bus turns out to be going to Dallas, I'd have to disembark to find another bus that's going to San Francisco. Dating is like taking the bus to marriage. I want to go to marriage, because that's the best place for me and for Ky. If the bus isn't going to marriage, I need to disembark."

"Are you asking me if I want to get married?"

Maybe I should have used a metaphor with airplanes. "I'm asking if, in general, you want to get married."

"Sure."

Good. "But I also need to know if I'm a better-than-average contender."

A Sun Western tour bus pulled into the parking lot. Within seconds of coming to a stop, the door opened and a stream of teenagers in matching T-shirts bolted for the restaurant.

"That's hard to say," said Ben.

It is?

"This is a big decision."

No kidding.

"I'm not even sure I'm going to stay in Orchard City."

You're not?

The bus driver stepped off the bus, hitched up his pants, and wiped the sweat off his forehead with his sleeve.

"Mibby?"

"I guess I'll be disembarking, then," I said. I wished Ben a happy life and pushed the end button.

I waited for the first tremors of a blubberfest. I breathed easily. I felt buoyant. Teenagers sauntered back to the bus in loose sets of twos and threes with oversized drinks and bags of food. A seven-layer burrito sounded good.

AUG

8

Saw a hyssop out by Margaret's I want to add to my garden. Where? I already have sunset hyssop. This must've been a Sonoran Sunset— purplish, magenta, almost neon. Wow!

I knew my mother was in the kitchen before I opened my eyes. The scent of French toast, opulent with real cream, cinnamon, and vanilla, plus her secret ingredient, made my mouth water. But I didn't jump out of bed. I lay there until my heart settled back to its natural pace. I joggled my expectations like skipping stones in my mind to see if they would skim across the water or kerplunk to the bottom. I went to the bathroom to shower.

I arrived in the kitchen in time to see Mother slide thick slices of French toast onto a platter in the oven. I don't know what I'd expected— I guess that she would move around the kitchen self-consciously. Wouldn't most people after disappearing for days?

She peeked under a corner of French toast and flipped it over. "I love your stove, Bré. The heat under the griddle is so even. I'd be cooking all day with a stove like this. How much did it cost?"

I tried to picture Mother flipping French toast on the Santa Monica Pier. "I almost called the police."

"What in heaven for?"

The question revealed the tight orbit of my mother's heart. I watched her closely, hoping to see it swing wider. "I was worried about you."

"Should we get Ky up for breakfast?"

"People who care about each other say something before they leave for a couple days."

"People who care about each other love with an open hand, Bré."

"People who care about each other practice basic courtesy, Mother—things like hello and good-bye, please and thank you, and, oh yes, the ever popular I'm sorry."

She arranged the French toast on a platter. "How many pieces do you want?"

"You promised you'd help with Ky."

"I don't get the weekend off?"

Had it even been thirty-six hours since I'd decided to wean myself from my mother?

"Hey, Grandma. What smells so good?" Ky entered the kitchen grinning.

I checked the clock on the microwave. "Ky, it's seven thirty."

"I got hungry."

Ky hated French toast, so I offered to whip up some pancakes.

"No, thanks. This smells good."

When he asked for seconds, I poured my coffee into a travel mug. I made my voice as light as possible. "What are you two doing today?"

Mother and Ky looked at each other. "I don't know," she said. "We'll have to give it some thought."

It was clear they weren't looking for suggestions. I headed for the door, but a trill of worry sounded in my head. "So you'll be here all day?"

"That's what I promised."

I invited Blink into the cab of the Daisy Mobile, but he wagged his tail and headed for the kitchen.

Expectations are funny things. Aim too high and you're dubbed an incurable optimist. Expect too little, and your pessimism leaves you red-faced. I asked myself again, *What can I realistically expect from my mother?*

French toast and, hopefully, one whole day of staying put.

Margaret fanned herself with the mail. "Farewell."

I pressed the shovel blade under the last tomato plant and pushed on the handle to lift the root ball out of the ground. With a popping of roots, the plant lay mortally wounded in the dirt, another victim of heat and curly top. My effort released the pungent scent of the tomato vine.

Margaret spoke sullenly. "No salsa. No tomato juice. No spaghetti sauce. I predict a long winter without tomatoes to bring out of the pantry."

"The peaches look good this year," I said, hoping to boost her mood.

"Sure will miss Monday night spaghetti."

"They sell sauce in the stores. It's pretty good, too."

"Pfft. I might as well eat roadkill." She turned to shuffle toward the door and gestured for me to follow. "Let's get out of this heat before we're the ones lying in the dirt all shriveled and worthless."

It seemed undignified to leave the sickly plants to die out in the open. "I'll be in as soon as I tidy up the garden."

She shielded her eyes to look at the plot. "It won't bother nothing to leave them be for a couple weeks."

Margaret's nature did not allow for anything to be left undone for more than three minutes.

"I want the garden to look nice for your wedding."

"The neighbors will think you're daft if you don't get out of this heat."

I had to agree.

Inside, Margaret busied herself coaxing ice cubes out of an aluminum tray. "Seems like we can't count on much of anything anymore. Even the weather don't behave itself. Bitter cold in the winter with no snow to cover the deadness. And we can't even see the sky this summer for all the blasted smoke. It's all heat and smoke, smoke and heat. What I wouldn't do for a humdinger of an afternoon thunderstorm to break the monotony." She sighed. "And now the tomatoes . . . nope, there's not much an old gal like me recognizes anymore. I can't drive nowhere without seeing another new subdivision or bank being built. Who has all the money to go in them banks, anyhow?"

Like a child waiting for the merry-go-round to slow so she can jump on, I waited for Margaret to lose momentum before I tried to join the conversation. She bemoaned the cost of gasoline and the increase in traffic and the laziness of grocery baggers as she ran water over the tray and pulled up the lever. The divider popped out of the tray and ice cubes scattered across the floor. As I gathered the fugitive cubes in my T-shirt, I counted the weeks to the wedding in my head. Maybe talking about the wedding would cheer her.

"This is the week you send out the invitations, isn't it?"

Margaret expelled a pitiful moan and slumped into a kitchen chair. "I'm not sure I'll be sending them out at all." Her bottom lip quivered, and tears rolled down her cheeks.

I dumped the ice cubes in the sink and knelt to embrace her. When her cries stilled, I asked, "Has Walter gotten cold feet?"

She blew her nose. "Only because I poured ice water all over them. Walter acted so strangely at supper the other night. He barely ate a bite and he fidgeted so, just like my son done when he tried to hide something from me. I finally told Walter to spit it out, whatever it was, and he did all right." She shook her head. "Explain to me why a man holds a worry in his gut until it's eaten a hole clean through him."

I told her being the mother of a teenage son disqualified me as an expert on males, and that made her smile, if only briefly.

"You best be teaching him to talk to the people who love him."

There weren't enough books in the world to help me do that, but I smiled and said I'd try, because I knew I would.

Margaret insisted on pouring my iced tea before she told the story. "Walter confessed about his assault on my Don Juan roses. Told me all about how you and the girls nabbed him in the act."

Walter had poisoned and killed two of Margaret's Don Juan roses, a gift from her late husband, all in a clumsy attempt to attract Margaret's attention. Oddly, his plan worked, thanks to Louise. I'd wanted to tell Margaret all along.

"We should have told—"

"That wasn't your place. He done it. He should have come clean long ago. As you might imagine, I wasn't none too happy about what he done and felt obliged to tell him so."

She reached for a tin on the refrigerator, the one with the Scottie dogs dancing around the top.

"Molasses cookies?" I asked.

She smiled and light flickered in her eyes. "Your favorite."

Margaret filled a plate with the chewy cookies and sat down across from me. She rubbed the worn tabletop the way people do when their thoughts won't associate with one another. It was the only time I could ever remember seeing her without fingernail polish.

"Tell me all about it," I said.

"I called him every name in the book, names a good Christian woman has no right knowing, let alone hurling them at the man she loves."

"You still love him?"

"For all his high jinx and grumblings, he's a sweet man. Oh yes, I love him, but he don't . . ."

Her shoulders heaved and the tears came again, only freer now that she'd almost uttered the dreaded words. At my touch, her papery skin slid over the dainty bones of her hand.

"Have you talked to him?" I asked.

"I tried. I called and called. He wouldn't answer the phone, so I waited for him to get home from his morning coffee club, even saw him walk in the door. The phone rang and rang. He ignored it. Guess he got himself one of them ID things." Margaret raised her glass but lowered it before she took a sip. "He don't want nothing to do with me. And before you ask, yes, I went over there lots of times. I knocked on the door until my knuckles ached, and I left notes clipped to his mailbox, too."

"Margaret, think about it. Walter has demonstrated some rather unusual courting behavior. If he's that much of a beginner in matters of love, it's possible he knows even less about the power of forgiveness."

As I talked, she blotted her eyes with an embroidered hanky. "Go on."

"You lived next door to Walter and Agatha most of their married life. I imagine you could hear them arguing every once in a while."

"But I didn't listen."

"Of course not. You wouldn't, but you couldn't help seeing how they treated one another afterward, could you?"

Margaret chewed on a cookie and looked out the window to a distant memory. "You can see how me and Quentin could watch what went on over there without trying. We seen Walter come out of the house more than once looking like a whipped puppy. One time, we was sitting here eating our breakfast when he came out of the garage rubbing his eyes and yawning. He looked around to see if anyone was watching while he ran his hands through his hair—and oh, what thick, dark hair he had in those days—and tried to smooth the wrinkles out of his shirt. When he opened the kitchen door, his work boots flew past his head into the back-yard. Agatha had a good throwing arm, but she didn't make him no breakfast that morning. Later, Quentin slipped out of the house with some of my cinnamon rolls and took them to the power station where Walter worked."

The cat clock ticked with every swish of its tail while Margaret chewed her bottom lip. Louise would have sat there as silent as a stone until Margaret nibbled on her dilemma and came to her own conclusion. I had other clients to see that day.

"Desperate times call for desperate measures, Margaret. How badly do you want to get your wedding back on track?"

"You got an idea?"

"How badly?"

"Real bad."

"Then send him flowers."

Margaret rolled her eyes. "I sure am glad they didn't put you in charge of the Rough Riders."

"Sorry."

Margaret stood abruptly. "Let me package some of these cookies for Ky. I might even have something for that dog of yours." Had mentioning the Rough Riders sounded the charge in Margaret's heart? She looked at her fingernails. "I really must get some polish on these nails."

On the way out the door, Margaret thrust the pile of invitations into my empty hand. "Mail these for me."

The teller squinted and wagged a knowing finger. "You're the gardening gal that was on the news last week, aren't you? I told Frank you're the lady I want to fix the mess he made of the flowerbeds by the patio, but we were laughing so hard at the dingbat reporter, neither one of us caught your name. Do you have a card?"

I'd long since stopped filling my pockets with business cards, so I tore a deposit slip out of my checkbook and wrote *Perennially Yours Garden Designs* above my name and address.

She frowned. "You really shouldn't give your account number out like that. Identity theft is a real problem."

I assured her I would remember business cards from then on and gave her the check I'd written for cash.

"Do you want a twenty or a ten and two fives?"

I took the twenty and folded it into the zippered pocket of my purse. That was my pop and incidental money for the week. I thanked the teller and started to walk away but decided to encourage her to call sooner rather than later.

"Because you've been so helpful, I'd be happy to design your garden for a ten—make that a fifteen percent discount off my fees."

"I'll call tomorrow."

I walked to the Daisy Mobile humming "He Has Made Me Glad." Sometimes the veil between time and eternity is very sheer indeed.

Louise and Andrea greeted me in the entry. They held a poster board between them. One of them had written in loopy letters "Birds and Bees and Babies." Louise struggled to keep a straight face, and Andrea huffed impatiently. I was pleased someone besides me had been sucked into the vortex of Louise's indomitable spirit. Louise hadn't been elected captain of her high school cheer squad three years in a row for being phlegmatic. It was perfectly normal for her to be standing in my living room wearing a yellow-and-black striped T-shirt with leggings and bobbing antennae. So when she turned around to waggle her stinger—a well-worn funnel—and her wire-and-tulle wings fell off, it was just another scene from so many others of our unlikely friendship. But now Louise had Andrea to wrangle into her productions. Dressed for work in her Holstein T-shirt, Andrea wore another funnel over her nose and mouth and swept an iridescent scarf languidly with her free arm.

My head throbbed and I could smell myself. "What's this all about?"

"Birds and bees and babies," sang Louise.

"I see a bird and a bee. Where's the baby?"

"Your mother and Ky are off gallivantin' somewhere, and we finally gave up putting a diaper on Blink," Louise said. "Use your imagination."

My imagination had been scorched out of existence by two thirty.

"Before this goes any further," Andrea said, removing the funnel beak, "I want you to know this wasn't my idea."

"I already knew that," I said.

"I gotta get to work," she said and kissed my cheek. "Good luck, talented lady."

Louise started to sit down but thought better of it. She called after Andrea. "You'll wish it had been your idea when Mibby brings home the grand prize."

That's how I learned Louise had entered me in the New Garden division of the sixth annual Dos Rios Garden Club design contest with Roseanne's design.

"It hasn't even been installed yet," I said.

"The judging isn't for another few weeks."

"When, exactly?"

"August twenty-ninth."

"I can't—"

"Before you throw the baby out with the birds and the bees, give a listen to this. The winner of each category will be featured in the *Orchard City Gazette*. But here's the most excitin' part—*Sunset* magazine, the premier magazine of the whole western United States, will be sending a photographer to do a story." Louise's antennae bounced wildly. "Baby girl, you knew you could count on me. Once your design is featured in *Sunset*, the phone will ring off the hook."

She had no idea what she'd suggested. All I'd completed was the design and plant list. Before one shrub could be planted, the sprinkler system had to be designed and installed, but only after the patio had been formed and poured, which could only happen after the old sidewalk and patio had been ripped out. And before any of that could happen, four truckloads of compost had to be Rototilled into the depleted soil so it could be graded and smoothed. Where would I find a cement contractor on such short notice? And most formidable of all was the keeper of the plant crypt, Christopher Stohl. How could I convince him to open an account for me?

Louise studied me through narrowed eyes. "I know that look. You're making a list of all the things you can't control."

"It's been a long day, Louise."

"I'm not asking you to do it tonight. Tomorrow will be fresh with God's mercy and loving-kindness. You can start then."

I headed toward the kitchen for something cold to drink. I stopped abruptly to stand nose to nose with Louise. "I'm going to be completely honest with you. My throat feels like it's been bound with dental floss. I have no idea how I'm going to get done what's already on my plate. I can't go heaping an impossible deadline on top of all that."

"Sugar . . ."

I continued on to the kitchen. *"Louise . . ."*

She followed close behind. "Don't you 'Louise' me. This is a golden opportunity. I've seen Roseanne's plan. It's gorgeous. Oh, baby, I'm so proud of you. A neglected and pitiful garden will be reborn into a sanctuary for birds and bees and babies."

"Actually, the design is meant to attract birds and *butterflies* and one baby, Phoebe."

She shimmied her stinger. "Bees give the title more pizzazzzzz."

I wanted to contradict her, but even the thought of saying the word *pizzazz* threatened to drain my reserves. I handed Louise a can of Pepsi, which she refused with a roll of her shoulder.

"Sweet pea, sit down and close those glorious brown eyes of yours. And no peeking." I heard the water run, and she returned to cover my eyes and forehead with a cool cloth. I slumped back in the chair. Another chair scraped against the floor, and Louise's hand, as soft as a sigh, rested on my knee. "As long as you're being completely honest, let's talk about that list of yours. Have you, or have you not, decided there are things too big for God to handle, specifically, but not exclusively, completing Roseanne's backyard paradise before the contest deadline?"

The cloth dropped and my eyes popped open.

"Close 'em," she warned.

I obeyed even though it stung more to have my eyes closed than open.

"I have my answer. Now we're going to do a little ol' revision of that list of yours. Picture the list with the title 'Things Too Big for God to Manage.' Take the pink eraser out of your pocket and rub that bit of heresy right off the page. Be sure to brush all the pink crumbs off the paper."

I opened my eyes to find Louise's lake-blue eyes on me. "Is this going to take much longer? I need a shower."

"That depends on you." A hint of sadness tainted her voice.

"I'm sorry. What's next?"

"Your list needs a new title."

Louise had no way of knowing I was standing on tiptoe in a glutinous pool of miry clay—and the goo kept rising.

"Maybe I should pray for you." She knelt before me and bowed her head. With her antennae tapping my forehead, she prayed, "Your love is as big as your might, Father. That's why we can ask you to do big things for us. We ask you to help Mibby every step of the way as she follows your example and makes a Garden of Eden for Roseanne and her sweet baby girl. Amen."

Before she'd stopped praying, a cement contractor came to mind and I'd decided to take a Frappuccino peace offering to Christopher Stohl. Yuppies love Starbucks. "I'll try."

"Now that's the brave girl I've always known." Louise raised my hands to her lips and kissed them. She wrinkled her nose. "You best be taking that shower now. Don't you ever forget, Jesus loves you." She buzzed through the kitchen and out the back door. I leaned back into the chair, enjoying the quiet of the house.

Ky burst through the door loaded with grocery bags and his skateboard. He frowned when he saw me. "Hey, you're home early."

"Where's your—"

He dropped the bags and the skateboard on the island. "She's coming. When's dinner? I have practice at seven."

"Isn't today Monday? I thought practices were on Tuesdays and Thursdays."

"Coach has an old-guy meeting at church tomorrow night."

"An elders' meeting?"

"That's it. I'm starved."

Mother entered with more bags. "How do you stand this heat? It sucks the life right out of me."

I closed and locked the door behind her.

"How was your day?" she asked. She wore my favorite denim skirt, the soft one with the flared flounce, and one of Andrea's peasant blouses. My stomach tightened thinking about her borrowing our clothes without asking, but as quickly as the knot came, it loosened. I should have offered my closet to her sooner.

"Okay, and yours?" But she didn't hear me over the rustling of bags and telling Ky to make a sandwich.

"I can do it," I said.

"You look like you could use a shower," she said. "Larry's picking Ky up, so you might as well get yourself cooled down. I'll call you when dinner's ready."

Ky balanced a knife on his finger. "Before you go, can I have the modem?"

"You won't have time to play a game."

"I need to check my e-mail."

Then it dawned on me. "What are you doing with your skateboard?"

Ky collected the ingredients for his sandwich without looking at me. "I wasn't riding it. Grandma took me to the mall to get new bearings. They had the coolest longboard."

"Put the skateboard back in the closet *now*."

He looked at me. "I told you. I wasn't riding it."

"Now."

Mother put the last peach in a bowl. "Bré, he's so proud of that board."

"And I'm so very proud of his nice round head, and I want to keep it

213

that way." Our eyes held for a moment, and then Mother added a bunch of bananas to the bowl.

❦

After my shower, I stared at my unmade bed. By default, making the bed had been Scott's job. The orderliness of a smooth quilt and plumped pillows had greeted me each morning after my shower. I wasn't as grateful as I was relieved that someone out of my seeing had ordered the universe, if only the universe of my bedroom. I missed that.

I straightened the covers of the bed, clicked the fan chain to high, and lay on top of the quilt. The only light in the room bled from around the room-darkening shade. The fan made a slight clicking noise that I found reassuring and Scott had found aggravating. Sleep tugged at me. Maybe God would slip into my universe and set things right as I slept.

But I didn't sleep. I lay there contemplating a paradox of the ages. Was it faith that compelled me to storm into a seemingly impossible plan, or was it merely pig-headed self-determination that demanded God's cooperation in my enterprises? By accepting Louise's challenge, was I testing Him like Gideon, only with plant materials and subcontractors rather than a ram's fleece? There was no denying that the exposure from the contest would be great, but how much would it cost in, say, my sanity or Ky feeling neglected or Mother spinning off to another solar system? Still, some recognition for the design appealed to me more than I liked to admit. I knew I'd try it.

I retrieved the modem from the side pocket of Scott's golf bag and went downstairs. The doorbell rang. It was Larry smiling down at me. He wore his coaching garb: a T-shirt with the numbers 01 appliquéd on the front and running shorts. His legs were long and muscled, like Santa Claus in his university days. And maybe he wasn't as soft in the middle as I'd remembered.

Ky saw the modem in my hand. "What took you so long?" He reached for it.

Larry put a hand out to stop him, still smiling. "Hey, bud. Is this the woman who went through extreme physical pain to birth you?"

Ky looked at me. "I guess so."

"Is this the woman who read *Fox in Socks* until her brain was a poodle in a puddle and taught you how to eat with your mouth closed?" You would have thought Larry had asked Ky to confess to murder. "Well?" Larry pressed.

"Yeah."

"Is this the woman who buys the groceries, cleans the house, and cooks the meals?"

"Grandma helps, and I take out the trash."

"Do you do more than your mother around here?"

Ky looked at me, pleading to be rescued from the inquisition. When I smiled back at him, he finally answered. "No."

"Do you have a paying job?"

"No."

"So you won't be paying for the electricity to power your computer, will you?"

"No."

"She does a lot for you. Wouldn't you agree?"

"I guess."

"So . . ."

"So?"

"So why don't you give your mom a nice hug? You should never leave the house without laying a little sugar on her, and if you have any questions for her, you can ask them respectfully."

Ky's gear bag thudded to the floor and he wrapped his arms around me. It was like hugging a fence post, but it was a hug.

"Was there something you wanted to ask me?" I asked Ky.

He looked down, shook his head.

"Then you guys have a good practice," I said.

Larry and Ky stopped by the car to talk out of my hearing. Ky ran back to the porch and lifted me in a bear hug. "That's from Larry."

Before I could fully commit myself to entering the contest, I needed to talk to Roseanne. "And besides all that, if we win, hundreds of people will tromp through your yard during the tour of the winning entries. I'll completely understand if you hate the idea."

"Are you kidding? Looking out my kitchen window is so depressing. This is great. Go for it, Mibby. Let me know what I can do to help."

"You're sure?"

"Let's just say that I've been picturing a romantic dinner on the patio with a certain someone ever since I saw the finished plan."

"Not Stefan?"

"Yes, I mean Stefan." The emphasis she gave his name told me it sounded sweet to her ears. "I can't believe how lucky, I mean blessed, I am, because I truly am blessed to have met him. We haven't been together that long, but it seems so right. He's nothing like Daniel."

I winced at her giddiness, and I prayed I wasn't jealous. I didn't think so. Any man who worked at being cool was too affected for me. "Roseanne," I said as if stepping onto a newly frozen pond, "it seems a little early to be speaking of together. You've only known him a couple weeks."

"I know, and usually I'd have to agree, but you don't know Stefan. He has me believing in soulmates again."

Bleh.

"I hope I'm not hiring you to put in the new garden, just to turn around and sell the house," she said.

I hoped she didn't mean what I thought she meant.

"I wouldn't be surprised if . . ."

"Roseanne!"

"You're right. What am I saying? That would be stupid, and I'm not stupid, right?"

"You just had a spell is all," I said.

"Whoa, that was scary. I think I'll clean the bathroom. That always brings me back to earth."

"So you want me to go ahead with the installation, and the contest is okay with you?"

"Absolutely."

AUG
9

Though she's a southern belle, my Zuni crape myrtle is thriving, even this summer, with spectacular spikes of delicate purple flowers. They remind me of a sunbonnet Scarlett O'Hara would have worn.

During the last weeks of Louise's chemotherapy, the poison had completely doused her light. She'd receded deep within herself, too tired to think or move or smile. I thought I'd lost her.

So when Louise didn't show up for our walk, I went looking for her. I found her loading a picnic basket into the trunk of her Cadillac. She wore an orange-and-yellow polka-dotted blouse with matching capris fringed with beads. The rhinestones of her yellow cat-eye sunglasses winked in the soft light of morning. Her earrings, as big as Hula-Hoops, pulled at her earlobes. Spots danced before my eyes just looking at her. But even under all of that dazzle, her face seemed thinner. I asked her where she was going.

"I should've called. Everything's just so . . . crazy." I followed her into her house. Manley sat at the kitchen table behind the newspaper. He grunted a greeting and turned the page.

"Let's go upstairs," Louise whispered.

She closed the door of the Geranium Room and patted the bench at the foot of the bed. "Sit with me a minute."

Louise pushed her sunglasses to the top of her head. Her eyes shimmered with tears. "I swear I'm as single-minded as a hound dog huntin' a wounded bear. It's all been about me—how I'm feeling, how I'm healing, how I'm dealing with the awesome reality of cancer. Goodness gracious, I plumb forgot about Manley. He has all but held his breath since the diagnosis, thinking he was about to lose another loved one to the vile C-monster. Well, that sweet darlin' woke me with a cup of coffee and a rose this morning. You know the rose out by the birdbath, the one you said reminded you of my peachy complexion?"

"Tamora?"

"That's the one. It's the most romantic rose in the whole wide world. I just love it. Anyway, he sat with me all quiet and all, and then he asked me a favor, said it just like that. 'I have a favor to ask you, Louisey,' he said. His eyes filled with tears, and then he said, 'Honey, now that Connie's strong enough to be on her own, could we take a rest from cancer? There's just no getting away from it. Maybe I'm being selfish,' he said, 'but I don't want to share you with that awful disease one more day, at least for a while.' How could I say no to that?"

Louise went to the dresser's mirror to blot her eyes. "He's asked me to take a hiatus from taking in guests. He said even Jesus got on a boat and sailed away when He was tired from a day of healing and preaching."

Dry-eyed, she turned from the mirror. "Manley arranged to take the day off, so I've packed a lovely picnic. We're taking it to Redstone to eat along the Crystal River. Manley loves it there. And of course he's packed his fishing gear. I'll read a book in that darlin' gazebo in the park."

"Sounds great."

"I have a little ol' favor to ask of you, too." Louise squared her shoulders and smoothed her top over her chest. "Check me out. Am I even?"

I assured her she was.

She turned back to the mirror to verify my answer. "I ordered a new thingy over the Internet. It's adjustable. I can add or remove tiny beanie bags to change the size. Leave it to another woman to invent something that's practical and comfortable. Do you want to see it?"

"Isn't Manley waiting for you?"

"We can't go anywhere until he's read every word of the sports page."

I rose to leave. "I'm sure he wants his day with you to start as soon as possible."

"I have a minute. What's up?" She pulled me back to the bench and patted the tight place between my shoulders. "Nothing is worth ruining your posture over, sweet pea. Now, tell me what's buzzin' under your bonnet."

"Mother came back."

"That's wonderful."

"But I have no idea where she went or what she was doing."

"She came back. That means something."

"It's never that easy. I asked her to tell me when she was going to take off. She got sanctimonious, and I got snippy. I thought I'd had her disappearing act settled in my head. I was weaned, right? But she's gone two days and I'm grasping at her like a drowning sailor."

"Sweet pea, how long have you been waiting for your mama to move home? And you know by home, I don't mean four walls and a roof. I mean, how long have you waited for your mother to be your mother, not a flower child, not a political activist, and not a devotee of the latest charlatan?"

"Forever." The word burned in my throat.

"What would you tell someone who planted a seed one day and called you the next day to complain they didn't have any flowers yet?"

"Be patient?"

"That's right, be patient. You need to be patient with yourself. It takes a lifetime for us to learn to love the Father, and He's perfect and unchanging. You might want to give yourself a month or two to learn how to love your mother as a grown woman." Louise held me with her blue eyes. "There's something else, isn't there?"

"It's Ky." I told her how he'd gotten up early and eaten my mother's French toast. "I really hate to admit this, but things seem better with Ky since she came. He's eating better and smiling more. Am I jealous of my mother? I don't know."

I fell back on the bed. "And then there's the contest. One minute, I'm sure it's the best thing to do. The next, I'm thinking I should be looking for a real job, maybe even McDonald's."

"You poor thing. Your mind's as busy as a beaver in a lumberyard. Let's sort this out. As for Ky, it's simple. Be alert and keep lovin' the dickens out of him."

"And the contest?"

"What's the worst that could happen if you entered that ol' contest?"

I pictured Christopher sneering, and Judith rolling her eyes, and Roseanne searching for a competent designer in the phone book. "Just that the whole horticulture industry from the Mississippi to the Pacific Ocean would know I'm a hopeless pretender at garden design."

"A little egg on the face never hurt anyone. The important thing to remember is this: nothing can separate you from the love of God. Not even an egg-stained face. Faith is risk, my darlin' girl."

A soft knock on the door startled us. Andrea stepped into the room wearing her work clothes or her pajamas. It was hard to tell which. "Manley's revving the Cadillac under my window."

Louise jumped up. "Sorry, sugar. Go on back to bed."

"See you later," Andrea said sleepily and disappeared.

When I hugged Louise, I felt the hardness of her shoulders. "How much weight have you lost?"

"Too much, according to Manley."

"I agree."

"I'll have a dish of ice cream after lunch, I promise."

In the kitchen, Louise hung her straw purse over her shoulder and turned to wrap her arms around me again. "Good Father, surprise Mibby with your love today. Amen."

The sun glowed pink through the smoky horizon as the Cadillac backed down the driveway and stopped. The tinted window lowered and Louise leaned out the window. "Sugar, could you look in on Connie today, since it's her first day at home alone and all?"

I promised Louise I would.

～✺

I changed out of my walking clothes and into a polo shirt and khaki shorts I'd bought on clearance but never worn. I hardly recognized myself. Hopefully, Christopher Stohl would think I looked reliable enough for a speedy credit application approval. I unbuttoned and buttoned the top button. Either way, my throat felt choky.

I'd spent the last hour revising the credit application and preparing myself to meet with Christopher. With forty minutes remaining until I had to leave for my appointment, I read the first chapter of *Breaking the Teen Code: Loving Your Teen Means Understanding Your Teen*. According to the author, open-ended questions encouraged meaningful dialogue. It was worth a try.

"Hey," I said, sitting in Ky's desk chair. "How are things going? Wait a minute. I mean, what's going on . . . in your life . . . this morning?"

"Nuthin."

"What I meant was, what did you do this morning?"

"Nuthin."

I needed a battering ram and I needed one fast. "You're reading a book, Ky."

"Oh yeah."

"What's it about?"

"Space."

"And?"

"And war stuff. You wouldn't like it."

"So it's science fiction?"

He looked at me over his book. "I guess it would have to be, right?"

It was obvious the author of the parenting book had never actually tried to engage a bona fide teenage male in conversation. I scanned Ky's room for something, anything, besides the peanut shells spilling out of his trash can, to talk about.

I straightened a baseball trophy. "What have you heard from Salvador?"

Ky sat up. A shaft of light reflected off his oily skin. How long had it been since he'd showered? "Oh yeah," he said, and my stomach muscles tightened.

Oh yeah preceded requirements for large sums of money and frantic searches for life-or-death supplies, like quick-drying plaster of Paris for a school project or a subzero sleeping bag for a youth group backpacking trip. I braced myself.

"Salvador's coming tomorrow."

I exhaled. "Here? Is he staying with us?"

"I dunno."

"How's he getting here?"

"I dunno."

"Are his parents coming?"

"I dun—"

"It doesn't matter." A visit from Salvador was a positive thing. It would get Ky out of his room. "He can stay with us if he wants."

"Oh yeah," he said, and I checked my watch. Light danced behind Ky's eyes. The wall had finally been breached. "There's a new computer game, and I promise to limit how much I play it. You'll like the game. No monsters or dead people in this one. It's a problem-solving game. Salvador has it, and his parents are even stricter than you. But I'm a little short."

"What are you asking me?"

"Could you make up the difference and take it out of my allowance next week?"

"I thought we already talked about this."

"That was another game."

"In any case, you know we don't advance allowance around here."

"Just this once," he pleaded.

"How much?"

"Fifty dollars?"

I said no as a reflex more than out of rational thought. Fifty dollars? It sure was expensive to love and understand a teenager—and I lamented his math skills. For a student who could solve for x and y, he sure had miscalculated his loan repayment schedule. It would require several months of allowance, not a week.

"But, Mom, I won't ask for anything else all summer. It can be my birthday present."

His birthday was nine months off. "I have to get going."

He followed me down the stairs and through the kitchen to the side door. My mother sat at the kitchen table knotting her macramé necklaces.

Only her hands moved as we walked in.

"I haven't done anything this summer," Ky said, "not even a movie. No boarding, either. I've only been to the pool once. All I want is one lousy computer game."

He had no way of knowing I was too tired to feel guilty. "Fifty dollars is too much for us right now, Ky."

"Wasn't there life insurance money?"

"Ky!"

"What? Did you spend it all on this stupid kitchen? Some of that was for me, wasn't it?"

I couldn't remember why I'd wanted to talk to him so badly. "Just so you know, the kitchen was paid for long before your father . . . left us. That's how we do things around here. We only buy what we have the money for. You know that. If you want to buy something, you're going to have to save your money."

I checked my watch again. "I have to go, Ky. We'll talk later." My purse wasn't hanging on the doorknob. "Ky, would you mind getting my purse? I think I left it on the bed . . . or maybe on the bathroom counter."

He considered my request longer than necessary before plodding up the stairs. I bit my tongue and flipped the pages of the credit application to check for typos. I felt my mother's eyes on my back. "What?"

"You're awfully hard on him. He's just a boy, and a good boy at that."

The last thing I needed was parenting advice from an aging gypsy. I answered without turning. "He's being a brat."

Upstairs, doors slammed and the floor creaked under the weight of Ky's search. Finally, he thumped down the stairs and into the kitchen. He handed me the purse. "Here, good luck," he said and kissed my cheek. Add that to a long list of aggravating things about teens. Just when you're ready to duke it out with Mr. Hyde, Dr. Jekyll makes an appearance. I grabbed my portfolio and left.

~⌒~

It was only eleven o'clock in the morning and my golf shirt was soaked with sweat. I was sure it had nothing to do with being in Christopher Stohl's office. "I have the credit application ready for your approval. I've also included a résumé of design work I've done for both commercial and residential properties. Feel free to call any of my clients or drive by to see my work."

Christopher gestured at my portfolio case. "Do you have a sample of your work?" He sucked on the Frappuccino I'd brought from Starbucks as he studied the design I'd done for Roseanne.

"It's an exciting project," I said. "The homeowner has given me carte blanche to design a backyard garden that's visually stimulating and water responsible. As you can see, I've eliminated the lawn but maintained interest with texture and color through the use of drought-tolerant ornamental grasses, flowering shrubs, and perennials. The rendering might make that easier to see."

I propped the rendering I'd painted of Roseanne's backyard on Christopher's desk. "I designed the garden with your inventory in mind. You have a great selection."

"I'm impressed, Mrs. Garrett. I had no idea you were so talented."

"I'm only as good as the plant materials I use," I said, hoping I didn't sound as desperate as I was.

He nodded his agreement. "I suppose there's a reason you brought this to show me?"

I tried not to sound too eager. "I've entered the Dos Rios design contest. I think this design has a good chance to win, especially with the emphasis on water conservation. But I need to begin the installation as soon as possible."

"If I'm not mistaken, that contest is judged at the end of the month. That doesn't give you much time."

I swallowed hard, but my voice sounded pinched anyway. "There's plenty of time. It's a matter of coordinating the subcontractors and gathering my supplies, like your beautiful plants."

"Mrs. Garrett—"

"I'm not asking for anything unreasonable. I only need you to approve my credit application quickly, so—"

"It will take a long time to contact all these references."

Breathe. "How long?"

"Lots of people are vacationing. It's hard to get calls returned in a timely manner. I can't do any better than two weeks."

"Did I mention that I plan on posting a sign saying all of the plants are from Walled Garden?"

"If I were to expedite the process for you—"

"Chris . . . Christopher, this is an important opportunity for me, and it could be a help to you, too."

"What are you implying?"

"Business drops off during the heat of summer—"

"That may have been true with the previous owner." He slurped the last of his Frappuccino. "Two weeks. Take it or leave it."

The shuttle driver from Out West Used Car Emporium dropped me off in front of the house. I lugged a box full of Scott's personal belongings I'd emptied from the Yukon into the house. A check for fifteen thousand dollars was tucked behind the register in my checkbook. I should've been wondering how we were going to get around with the Daisy Mobile as our only transportation, but my own recklessness intoxicated me. Practical issues would come later.

A note from Ky and Mother said they'd walked to the library and would be back by four. I scribbled a reply at the bottom to tell them I had an appointment at four and needed to stop by Walled Garden to buy supplies for Roseanne's garden. I would be home by six or six thirty.

On the way to my bedroom to change out of my yuppie uniform, I stepped into Ky's bedroom. The peanut shells had been picked up off the floor, and the trash can had been emptied. I left a thank-you note on his pillow. But still, there was that smell of dead things, so I opened the window. That was when I saw Andrea in the garden. She held an umbrella against the sun and dangled her feet in the pond. I couldn't see her face, but she was reading the Gospel of John Louise had given her. She lowered the booklet to her lap.

I turned from the window to lean against Ky's wall. "Holy Spirit, you are so mysterious to me, but I know it is your work that sparks our faith.

Do that for Andrea, please, so she'll know the love of her eternal Father."

When I looked back out the window, Andrea was reading again.

"Amen."

The first twang of regret about selling the Yukon hit the moment I reached for the Daisy Mobile's air-conditioner controls. It didn't have any. Blink jumped up to my opened window to whine.

"Blink, you know it's too hot to be toting a dog all over town."

He dropped his chin to the window and heaved a sigh that trembled his jowls. "Can you be a good dog?"

He answered by running to the passenger side of the truck and barking at the door.

At Rocky Mountain Irrigation Supply, Blink visited his old pal Wendy the prehistoric basset while I discussed Roseanne's sprinkler plan with the head designer. John had coached me through the many permutations of our sprinkler system, so I knew he was up to the task.

I laid Roseanne's plan on John's drafting table and gave him my best stranded-kitty look. "John, I've entered this design in the Dos Rios contest. I needed the sprinkler plan yesterday."

John counted out loud as he pointed to each area of the plan. "Looks like eight to ten zones." He looked up and smiled. "I'm helpless when you turn those beautiful brown eyes on me. The plan will be ready by closing."

"Today?"

"No problem."

I pulled onto the highway heading toward Walled Garden and humming "What a Friend I Have in Jesus." I remembered Louise's prayer. That little bit of grace warmed my heart and reminded me of my promise to check on Connie. I turned around to head east.

Connie lived in one of those low-slung clapboard farmhouses with a sloping roof that looked like the jaunty tip of a hat over the brow. A blue spruce squatted by the driveway that arced across the front yard. Petunias and sweet-potato vines filled an ore car, a rusty bucket, and a wheel-less wheelbarrow. A ceramic sign read, *Love grown here.*

Not so long ago, I knew, Connie and her husband had grown alfalfa and onions on their farm east of Orchard City. She had sold off all but two acres after her husband died. Soon after that, the two-lane road in front of her house had become a four-lane east-west artery. A sea of identical rooflines surrounded her property. I parked the Daisy Mobile in the shade of a cottonwood.

Connie filled a plate with homemade shortbread cookies. "There's something about being in your own home. I didn't even take a nap this morning. I did a couple loads of laundry and got them hung out to dry. By the time I finished hanging the sheets, the pillowcases were dry. Guess this heat's good for something."

"Louise would say, 'Don't y'all get yourself plumb tuckered, now.'"

Connie laughed. "You tell her I'll sit down if she brings some lemon scones over."

I pulled a check for Larry out of my pocket. "Could you make sure Larry gets this?"

"Just leave it on the table. Now bring your cookies with you. I'll show you my Barbie room."

Outside the back door, Blink lapped water from the large bowl Connie had filled for him.

"Will Blink bother Goliath?" I asked.

"I hope so." She winked and gestured for me to follow her down a hall. Floor-to-ceiling bookshelves lined two walls of the converted bedroom that was now Connie's workroom. One shelf held a bevy of Barbie brides complete with veils and bouquets. Another shelf looked like the lobby of the United Nations for Barbie world. Hardworking Barbies filled another shelf. A doctor. A jockey. A chef. But no gardeners. Barbies in evening gowns filled several shelves of the bookcase and more posed on an adjacent tabletop. Despite Connie's practical approach to life and fashion, the heart of a romantic beat in her chest.

"I love anything that sparkles." She lifted the skirt of a Barbie evening gown made of cappuccino-colored silk to show the inside detail of the gown. "I line everything to make the clothes more durable, and they just lie nicer, don't you think?"

I agreed with her and admired one of her international dolls, a Barbie in traditional Japanese dress.

"Isn't she pretty?" Connie handed me a postcard from the shelf. Under a thin layer of dust, the glossy picture showed a Japanese woman strolling in a park under a paper parasol. "Larry sent that postcard along with a book on traditional Japanese dress *and* a length of the fabric. He knew I'd have to make a Barbie to look just like the picture. I read the book from cover to cover the very day it came. This is a yukato, or is it a yukata, kimono?"

Larry didn't fit my profile of an international traveler. "When did he go to Japan?"

The smile faded from Connie's face. She wiped the dust from the postcard. "Has it been ten years? Yes, I believe it has. He told us he was going over there to visit a friend, but between you and me, he went there to hide. Can you imagine Larry hiding in Japan?"

I couldn't, but before I had a chance to ask her about why he would even try, Connie told me the whole story.

"Not too many folks know this, but Larry was engaged, even had a date picked and the church booked. I helped him decide on a Hawaiian honeymoon. He wanted to surprise Melissa. She was such a sweet little thing. Looking back now, I should have seen it coming. That George— have you ever met George, Larry's brother?"

I shook my head.

"No, you wouldn't have, I guess." Connie fingered the collar of her blouse. "Larry and George were inseparable. George even followed Larry to Colorado State when Larry got out of the service. We felt so much better knowing Larry was keeping an eye on his brother. George could be such a rascal. I had no idea."

She sighed. "Long story short, while Larry was working two jobs and taking summer classes so he and Melissa could get married that fall like Melissa wanted, George was in Kentucky making sweet on Larry's fiancée. We all thought George was taking a semester abroad. Hmph. I guess Larry cashed in the honeymoon tickets. I've never had the heart to ask. George married Melissa, and they settled in Kentucky. They both sell real estate in the Louisville area near her parents. They send me cards for Christmas and my birthday."

Ten years had done little to soften Connie's pain. "I'm so sorry," I said.

She straightened the folds of the doll's kimono and set the postcard back in its place. "I've overheard Larry leaving a message on George's phone machine to say he loves his brother and forgives him. I don't think George returns Larry's calls. If he has, Larry's never told me about it."

"George must be doing pretty good. He sent a big check to buy his father's tombstone. Larry told me to use it, but I couldn't. It's still in my dainties drawer. I grieve more for George than my very own husband." Connie shook her head as if refusing a thought. "George is in the Lord's hands. In His time, George will accept his brother's and his Lord's forgiveness and come back to us."

A screen door slammed somewhere. "Hey, Ma! Mibby!"

It was Larry.

Connie gasped and whispered, "You must never tell him I told you about George and Melissa."

Larry walked into Connie's workroom before I had a chance to reassure her that the story was safe with me. He held his hands behind his back. My stomach growled again, only this time I was thinking about Coconut Dream Cakes.

"Hello, ladies. How are you on this fine summer afternoon?" Larry's face was flush and glistened with sweat. He presented two bouquets of dahlias—one for Connie and one for me. "Beauties for the beauties." He kissed his mother's cheek.

The dahlias were a jewel box of color in my hands. A giant red dahlia with white-tipped petals, about eight inches across, dominated the bouquet. A yellow dahlia with broad tongues of color resembled a water lily, and a deep burgundy with compact petals almost formed a perfect sphere. There were vibrant magentas and oranges and a lemony blossom with red-striped petals. A fuchsia-colored anemone-shaped flower budded up to another flower the size of a grapefruit with the graduated hues of a winter sunset. It took both hands to hold the fat bundle of stems.

"Wow, this one looks like a water lily," I said.

"That's an Olympic Flame."

"*You* grow these?"

"Kind of hard to believe, isn't it?"

"Don't let him fool you," Connie said. "He took first prize at the fair last year and came in second the year before. He just hasn't broken any world records for size."

Larry's eyes grew wider. "I like the big ones."

"Take Mibby out to see your dahlias," Connie said. "She'd rather see your flowers than my dolls."

I looked at my watch. "I have to get to Walled Garden before they close."

"This won't take long," he said.

"I think I'll sit in my rocking chair and close my eyes for a minute," Connie said. "You two go on."

We walked down a path through the shady lawn behind the house. Connie's laundry hung as still as tombstones in the afternoon heat. As soon as we stepped onto the gravel driveway, I regretted leaving the cool house. I pulled my hat down to my eyebrows and followed Larry past a windowless building on one side and a tidy vegetable garden on the other. Beyond the building stood two metal-framed shade structures, each about fifteen feet long—maybe twenty—and about ten feet across. Three rows of dahlia bushes, shoulder-high to me, grew the length of each structure.

"I'm experimenting with a denser shade cloth this season," he said. "I'm hoping to encourage longer stems."

We walked between the first two rows of bushes. Everything about the garden demonstrated great care. The maturing bushes were supported by three rows of twine, evenly spaced and tight, strung from end posts to reach the full length of the growing beds, and irrigation furrows ran in straight lines along both sides of each row. Not one weed grew.

The care Larry gave his garden showed even more in the health of the plants. Leathery leaves, deep green and free of scorch or insect damage, alternated up stalks as large around as my thumb and bigger. Round buds, taut from the pressure of the maturing flowers within, awaited their appointed time to bloom. And blossoms, some as round as balls, others as broad as dinner plates, some with petals like spoons, but all intensely colorful, held their heads proudly above the foliage. Not one shy flower grew among them. My pulse quickened.

"The dahlias in this first row," he said, "are the varieties my father grew for my mom. She liked the small to medium heads for arrangements. I suspect if you've ever had the sniffles, you've gotten one of Mom's bouquets."

Connie had brought a bouquet when Ky had strep throat just after school started last fall. The colors and variety had taken my breath away. She'd even told me then that Larry grew the dahlias in his father's garden, but I'd let that piece of wonderment go forgotten until now.

"This pink's a Gay Princess, and this purple with white tips is Rothsay Reveller. Mom likes those. And this is the water lily dahlia I put in your bouquet, Olympic Flame. It's hard to grow a good orange."

Dahlias require regular deadheading and disbudding, plus the tubers have to be dug up in late fall to be washed and divided and trimmed before they're labeled and stored. The routine starts all over again when the tubers are planted in the spring. In my own garden, I treated the dahlias as annuals and didn't plant them every year. Larry grew at least thirty different varieties.

"Geez, Larry. This is a lot of work."

"You don't know the half of it. I've spent more time in this flower garden than I have eating, and that's saying a lot. Of course, Dad saw to it that I didn't eat unless I spent a lot of time in the garden."

"They're beautiful, Larry, just beautiful."

"When I left home for the army, I never wanted to see another dahlia as long as I lived. I'd spent every Saturday from March to November doing something in this garden with my dad. And in the winter, just when I wanted to flop in front of the TV to watch *The Dukes of Hazzard,* in came Dad with his seed capsules. More than once I made the mistake of complaining, and then I'd have to hear the whole speech."

Larry imitated his father. "Son, when God created a place to be with man, he created a garden. That's why there's no finer place to view the power and restraint of God's hand. Now look at this petal, son. Can't you see the stroke of the Father's finger in the way it curves just so?"

Larry stooped to pick a withered leaf from a firecracker-red dahlia.

When he spoke again, emotion tempered his voice. "I'd give just about anything to walk these rows with him again."

We walked the length of the shade structure and stopped and looked at each variety. Larry cradled the flowers in his hand and stroked the petals with his thumb. "I think the heat's slowed the blooming a bit. I'm hoping things start popping when it cools down."

I looked at my watch again. More time had passed than I realized.

"You have to see the big boys before you go." He led me to the last row. "They're just starting to come on. There's a yellow and a white that will bloom first, but real soon, the Zorros will start blooming. They're big ol' red guys, real flashy."

I had a million questions for him. When did he dig the tubers? Where did he store them? How did he propagate the plants? But my questions would have started a conversation I didn't have time to finish. Then I noticed another dense line of dahlias growing along the back fence. Some were shaded by umbrellas fastened to long stakes. I had a few more minutes to spare.

"What's with the umbrellas?" I asked.

"Those are my babies," he said, walking toward the fence.

I looked at my watch. If I took Blink with me to Walled Garden, I'd have plenty of time to select the plants for Roseanne's yard. I stretched my stride to keep up with Larry.

"I collected the seeds last winter," he said. "And the dahlias weren't exactly generous. Some flowers only had a few seeds, but none of them had more than a dozen. And of those, less than half germinated. I'm still learning. There are a couple varieties that haven't bloomed yet. I'm like Forrest Gump and his box of chocolates. I never know what I'll get."

"And the umbrellas?"

"They keep the flowers from fading in the bright sunlight." We walked down the row with Larry commenting on the progress and potential of each plant. He cupped a blossom in his hand. "This is a keeper. The head is at a good forty-five-degree angle, and gold is a popular color right now. I'm thinking about taking number four, here, to the fair next year."

"Number four?"

"I haven't come up with a name yet."

The color reminded me of the eastern sky when the sun seems to pause below the horizon at dawn. "How about Colorado Morning?"

Larry looked at me hard. I looked right back at him, trying to see the Larry who'd been betrayed by his brother, but I flinched under his gaze.

"What?" I asked, angered at being flustered.

"You have flecks of gold around your pupils."

"I do not."

"Yes you do. I'm going to call this one Mibby's Light."

The intimacy of the gesture warmed my face. It was time to put an end to the flirting, once and for all. "Don't do that anymore, Larry."

"Don't do what?"

"Don't . . . just don't."

"I named a flower after you. You should be flattered. I meant it as a compliment."

"But you're always doing things like that and saying things that aren't true."

His eyes softened. "What have I ever said that wasn't true?"

I wasn't about to catalog out loud all the times he'd told me I was pretty or a great mom or whatever. I stood there, silent as a post, trying to think of something to say, something about the weather or the price of gas or how frustrating it was to drive down Peach Farm Road with all the road construction.

It was then I learned that the earnestness of a man's voice can tap on a heart and ask it to dance and never say a word to the thinking part of a woman. I'd seen it in the movies but never in real life, not until Larry said, "If we ate breakfast at the same table, I'd tell you every day how beautiful you are, and pretty soon, you'd believe it as much as I do."

My heart leapt into a one-legged happy dance. I didn't dare make eye contact with Larry. He would see that his voice had ricocheted within me. Instead, I watched a bee collect nectar from one of his giant dahlias and wondered if it had inadvertently created a new species just by stopping by.

Oh brother.

"Look at me." His voice tumbled like stones in a creek.

"What?" My question seethed with contempt, but the answer was written right there in his eyes. For all his bravado, he had always said what he'd meant. My face burned hotter.

"Mibby?"

I stared at the ground between his boots. "I'm so sorry. I just can't . . . I mean, I don't . . ."

"I've meant every word I said."

"I'm sorry. I thought you were kidding. I should have said something sooner."

Rather than look at his face, I looked at my watch again, but I didn't have to read the numbers to know it was time to leave. "I have to go."

He said my name again as if he were asking me a hundred questions at once. I couldn't help looking at him to see what he meant. His eyes, as cool as a mountain meadow, held my gaze. Whatever he was looking for in my eyes wasn't there.

"Let me put those flowers in a bucket of water. They'll last longer." He disappeared into the windowless building.

I hollered for Blink and, contrary to type, he trotted to the Daisy Mobile and hopped in. I gave him an appreciatory scratch behind his ears. "Thanks, bud. We're outta here."

Larry delivered the flowers and stepped back as I settled the bucket on the seat beside me and started the truck. When I turned to thank him for the flowers, he looked like a basketball that had been left on the playground all winter.

I pounded on the steering wheel from Sixteenth to Tenth. "How could I be so stupid? Oh man, I didn't mean to hurt him. But he's the one who invites women to pink tomato festivals and for walks on Waikiki Beach. Oh man. I can't believe he actually thought . . ." But even for me, that thought was too condescending to say out loud.

Maybe being direct would have been the kindest thing. "Larry, you're nice and smart and a very good gardener, but I will never love you. You're not my type."

I wanted to be a woman with a spine and a heart, not a shield and a spear.

Then why did your heart do a one-legged happy dance?

"I don't know!"

A construction truck drove by with two German shepherds in the back. Blink stood to squeeze his head out the window to return their greetings and toppled the bucket of flowers into my lap. Water soaked my overalls, and my feet slid in a muddy puddle on the floorboard.

"Sit down!" I slapped Blink's hind end. "Sit down, now!"

He pulled his head into the cab and looked at me over his shoulder. He must have decided I meant business because he leaned against the door and stared forward.

I turned off Peach Farm Road and onto Jefferson Avenue toward Walled Garden. Once I passed the subdivisions and entered the green expanse of gentleman farms, I parked by a pasture of grazing sheep to collect the scattered bouquet. I forgot to shift out of gear, so the truck lurched and died. Like choreographed dancers, the sheep raised their heads, turned their backs on me, and resumed grazing. Blink's eyes flitted from me to the sheep, but he didn't move.

"Lord, I don't know how to pray, and I don't know what just happened back there. Larry is *not* my type. That little electrical something or other that zipped through me was an anomaly, an emotional backfire, and that's all, *not* love and certainly not attraction. Larry? I don't think so."

I stopped ranting long enough to swig some lukewarm water. Mid-gulp, a thought closed my throat and redoubled my prayers. "He thinks he knows everything, Lord, and he's a Sweet Suzy delivery man, a noble profession but not, you know, considered upwardly mobile. A gal has to consider her future. And the beard . . . I wanted to ask Connie what he was hiding under there, but that's not a question you ask a mother. And there's another thing. The man lives with his mother."

So do you.

"It's not the same thing." I didn't have to be on the debate team to know my arguments were shallow. I changed tactics. "I'd be nothing but trouble for him. There are so many nice girls—lots younger, no excess baggage—who'd love a guy like Larry. He's a good guy and a great dahlia grower, but definitely not a guy to date, and certainly not marriage material. He deserves someone really, really special. Won't you do that for Larry? Amen."

Congratulating myself on my selflessness, I jiggled the gearshift to make sure I was in neutral and turned the key. The engine groaned, caught, and died. Nothing unusual. I repeated the start-up ritual by holding the key in the start position and pumping the gas pedal. Same result.

Uh-oh.

On the third try, the ignition clicked, period.

I counted to ten and turned the key. I counted to twenty and turned the key. While I counted to a hundred, I watched the grazing sheep. One ragtag ewe stood at attention, staring at the truck, and most assuredly, at Blink drooling all over the passenger window. The ewe stood undaunted by the afternoon heat, even wearing her dilapidated woolen coat. Just looking at her made my armpits sticky.

"Sheep sure are dumb," I said out loud, not to Blink or anyone, just because it seemed to be the truest thing I knew at the moment, and knowing something true deserved some recognition.

My sheep listen to my voice.

"I didn't mean to disparage—"

My sheep listen to my voice.

"I need to get to Walled Garden before it closes."

My sheep listen to my voice.

A car zoomed by. The sheep bleated. A bee buzzed in and out of the cab. I let myself breathe deeply of the freshly cut alfalfa in a nearby field. A bead of sweat rolled down the side of my face. Blink sighed.

I turned the key again, and only after the engine roared to life did I think to press the gas pedal.

～◞

I looped the last sold tag onto a hummingbird trumpet vine and headed for the sales area. Across the parking lot, Christopher parked his Audi and strode up the walk at a quick clip toward the sales area, where Kathleen and Blink waited for me.

I hurried to catch up with him. "Hey, Christopher, how was racquetball?"

"Terrible." He frowned. "How did you know I was playing?"

Uh-oh. "Kathleen."

"I'm not even close to approving your application. I hope you won't be coming in every day—"

"No problem. I'm a cash-paying customer today."

He stopped and folded his arms over his chest. "Good. That's very good. Have you found everything you need? Kathleen should be out here helping you."

"She's been a tremendous help. She's writing up the invoice while I finish tagging the shrubs."

"Shrubs?"

"Sure, and perennials and several trees. The plants are for the garden job I told you about this morning." His face didn't register the recognition I'd hoped for, so I told him what he wanted to hear. "There must be over a hundred plants in all."

"Really?"

"And since the homeowner is eager for the garden to look established, I've upsized all the perennials."

His hands were in his pockets now, the picture of relaxed camaraderie. He leaned forward enough to make me uncomfortable. Finally, I knew what motivated him. Money.

"Is there anything else you'll need, Mrs. Garrett?"

"It's all on the invoice. Half a dozen large boulders. Twenty cubic yards of cedar mulch. And the fountain supplies. The client will be out to select several pieces of statuary and garden lighting later this week."

"Sounds charming, Mrs. Garrett. I can't wait to see it."

"And I can't wait for you to see it." I loathed myself at that moment, baiting him with promised sales to avoid a call to animal control over Blink's presence. "I better get in there and pay Kathleen so she can go home."

Christopher checked his watch. "Don't worry. She'll stay as long as you need her."

❧

Louise worked to attach a ceramic lamb pin to the strap of my denim overalls. "I found this little lamby pin in a gift shop in Glenwood Springs.

Manley wanted to soak in the hot springs, but I'm not quite ready to wear a bathing suit in public yet, so I went shoppin'. The instant I saw the sweet face on this pin, I thought of you. Did you see his little heart nose?" She patted my cheek. "I hope you enjoy wearing him."

"Thanks, Louise. It's really cute."

"I want you to remember your Good Shepherd is lookin' after you every time you look at it."

"I know I will."

"Now, didn't I pray you'd be surprised by love this morning? Well?"

I thought of my heart's one-legged happy dance and swallowed, but I didn't know how to answer Louise. "The day's not over."

"This isn't a good time for me, Crenshaw."

That was an understatement. I'd just told Ky that I sold the Yukon and braced myself for the backlash. It didn't come. Instead, he suggested an acceptable replacement vehicle, namely a Jeep Wrangler. He said he would be happy to drive a Jeep to school when he got his license in 518 days. He considered the Yukon too middle class for cruising. He never mentioned his father or the memories we'd collected traveling in the Yukon. However inevitable or temporary his self-centeredness proved to be, at that moment, I ached with disappointment in him. I'd gone to my bedroom, because the sight of him scouring the auto classifieds had broken my heart.

Now I had Crenshaw on the phone. Maybe he wasn't mooning over a Jeep, but his preoccupation with Brenda was just as adolescent.

"I don't know what to do the next time I see Brenda, and she's scheduled to work tomorrow. She's a great little bowler . . . and funny. Oh man, can she tell a great story. And get this—she likes mustard on her French fries, just like me."

I remembered when Scott had told me banana ice cream was his favorite flavor. I'd never met another living soul who'd named banana ice cream as his favorite. Knowing that had only made me love him more.

"Common tastes are good. Now she needs to know she's important to you."

"I'll buy her a ring."

"Whoa there, big fella. You'll scare her off. You show her she's important by meeting her needs."

"She don't need nothing. She's perfect."

"Everybody needs something. Listen to her. She'll tell you what she needs."

"Should I have her make a list?"

Extrapolation sure wasn't Crenshaw's strong point. "It's not like that. If she says she's tired, offer her a chair. If she says she's thirsty, get her a drink. If she says she's had a bad day, try to make it better. Send a pizza to her house so she won't have to cook. Dedicate a song to her on the radio. Mow her lawn. Sweep her steps. Send her a dozen roses, one rose at a time."

"This sounds like a lot of work."

"It isn't rocket science, Crenshaw. It's just paying attention."

"Let me get this straight. I listen to her and get her a chair, and then I can ask her to marry me?"

"You can't just offer a girl a seat and ask for a death-do-us-part commitment. Building love is a marathon, not a sprint. Brenda has to be convinced her needs are your top priority for at least a year, maybe two."

"Two *years?*"

"And if you're lucky, she'll make it her life's devotion to put your needs above her own with the same passion."

"I like passion."

"I knew you would."

There was a long silence. "I think you better keep praying for me."

After I hung up, I couldn't remember hearing Crenshaw cough. Not even once.

AUG

10

Droop stuck his head in the kitchen door. "Is it safe to come in? I mean, your mother ain't around, is she?"

"She's in the tub."

"Do I have time for a cup of coffee?"

I slipped a peanut-butter-and-jelly sandwich into a Baggie. "Enter at your own risk."

Droop opened the cupboard to find a mug. "You're getting an early start."

My goal was to arrive at Margaret's, my first client of the day, by seven. "The sooner I start, the sooner I'll get to Roseanne's. Today, I clear the junk that's accumulated between the garage and the fence. And I'm hoping to dig out a dead lilac shrub. After that, I'm stuck until I find someone to demolish the existing patio and sidewalk."

"You ain't looking at me, are you?"

A girl can dream.

"Them cement guys have crews to do that," he said.

"And they all have excuses why they can't get to my job before the contest."

"Have you asked Larry?"

Droop was the thirty-ninth person to suggest I ask Larry to help me. Or had it just seemed that way?

"Well?" he pressed.

No question, Larry possessed the brawn, the brains, and the horticultural sensibilities to be my most likely candidate. But I didn't feel right about asking him after I'd deflated his ego. Besides, Larry tousled my thoughts. One minute he was a gentle giant, rich in faith and wisdom, humble even. The next minute, he oozed cocky self-assurance. I needed my wits about me. The assistant I dreamed of jumped to grunted orders with a tail wag and kept coming back for more. And if he worked for kibble, all the better.

Droop held the coffeepot over my mug. "I *said,* more coffee?".

"Sure." That was exactly the problem with Larry. He was distracting.

"Do you want to get this here job done or not?"

"Larry's mother depends on him."

"Funny you should say that. Get that boy of yours out there working with you. Sweatin' in the hot sun sweetens the attitude just like that." Droop snapped his fingers.

"I tried that once. He's more trouble than he's worth."

"Bingo! There's 'nother reason to get Larry on board. No matter how smart and capable a mother is, a man's got to teach a boy how to be a man."

How had a simple garden installation become summer quarter at Masculinity University? Besides, Larry wasn't the only man in Ky's life. "You're a good role model."

"Now you're just sweet-talkin' an old man." He removed his cap to rub his head, a sign he had something unpleasant to say. "Even though I thought I'd die trying to please your neighbors, I'm putting the last coat of varnish on the window seat today. I'm outta here. I'm heading for the mountains first thing tomorrow. I've been contracted to renovate a cabin at Trout Lake for a glad-handin' Texan, and thanks to Mr. and Mrs. Born-to-Argue next door, I'm five weeks behind before I even get started." Droop lowered his head and his voice. "You know, don't you, there's nothing I'd like better than to be the one to teach Ky how to work like a man, but Larry's the better man by far."

"Stop right there," I said, tired of hearing how perfect Larry was. "All I need is some brawn and smarts to help me get one solitary garden installed. It's hard enough raising a son alone and putting food on the table and holding my head above water financially. Did I say above water? If only it would rain. I've got enough on my mind without Larry teasing me all the—" Droop's eyes widened. I'd overloaded him that easily. "Keep your ears open for me. If you hear of anyone needing work or—"

Footsteps creaked on the stairs and we both looked toward the hall.

Droop gulped the last of his coffee. "I best be gettin' to work. I know which side of the biscuit the honey's on, if you know what I mean." And he was gone.

I added a bunch of grapes and two peaches to my insulated lunch box. I was filling a water jug when Ky shuffled into the kitchen ahead of his grandmother. She headed for the teapot. Ky headed for the computer in the family room.

She patted my shoulder as she walked to the stove, and the scent of chamomile *Pré de Provence* soap, a preference we shared, followed her. "Good morning, Bré. How'd you sleep?"

Before I could answer her, Ky stopped short of the computer. He all but stomped his foot. "I hate this."

The *Loving Your Teen* book said to ignore the attitude and speak to the words. "That's interesting." It was the best I could do.

He shifted his weight and huffed. "May I *please* have the modem?"

The book also said not to let yourself be bullied. I fought to keep my voice from wavering when I said, "I don't have time right now."

He slammed the computer chair back into place and collapsed onto the sofa. My stomach cramped into a hard ball. The back of his head would have made a perfect target to throw it at.

Mother stepped between us. "Since you're trying to get off to work, tell me where the modem is, and I'll be sure to confiscate it and return it to its secret hiding place when his time is up."

Is she mocking me?

"Pleeease," Ky moaned.

The night before, I'd read, "In the heat of negotiating positive behaviors, don't stoop to the teen's level." I stood mute.

"He needs to keep in touch with his friend, Bré."

I looked from my mother to Ky. I'd seen happier faces on gargoyles. "I'll give you the modem when I come home. Ky, you should have your chores done by then. Don't forget to—"

"I *know*. Water the pots and feed the dog." He scuffed down the hall toward the stairs, and most probably, his bed.

Maybe Droop had been right. A day of hard work in the sun would soften Ky's attitude, or would it? Then I remembered the contest deadline. The schedule was too tight to wangle Ky into a day's work and get my own work done, too.

In the driveway, Mother came to the window of the Daisy Mobile. "Ky's too old to be babysat by his grandmother all day. Let him go to the skate park, or at least give him what he needs to play on the computer. You don't want a frustrated teenage boy on your hands."

I stared out the windshield. Everything I thought to say sounded churlish, even to me. "I'm running late." I ground the gearshift into reverse and backed down the driveway. Somewhere between *Loving Your Teen's* do-or-die philosophy and my mother's permissiveness, the balance of power, at least for Ky and me, lay undiscovered. When I stopped to wait for traffic at the sidewalk, I actually considered returning to the house to give Ky the modem. Mother stood cross-armed in the driveway watching me. I backed into the street and headed for Margaret's.

"What's he doing now?" Margaret whispered, even though Walter's car sat parked in front of his detached garage, and we were in her kitchen. I watched him through a narrow gap in the curtains.

"He's pounding the steering wheel," I said.

"Like that would help." She clicked her tongue. "What's he doing now?"

"He's getting out of the car."

"Is he opening the hood?"

"No, he's going inside."

"Inside? The house?" Margaret parted the curtains. "He can't do that. He won't find the notes."

"Here he comes again."

"I hope he didn't call a mechanic."

"What's this all about?"

"I stole his distributor cap."

I straightened and took a good look at Margaret. Loose strands of hair had escaped her tightly wound braids, and her blouse puckered where she'd skipped a buttonhole. "You stole it? Why?"

Margaret explained how she'd sneaked into Walter's garage and stolen his distributor cap during the night. "One good turn of vandalism deserves another."

"I don't think—"

"Don't worry none. I done it to get his attention is all. I left something better in its place."

"Like what?"

"See what he's doing first."

I put my eye to the opening again. "He's lifting the hood."

Margaret put her cheek to mine to sneak a peek. "I wish I could find my glasses. I can't see a thing."

"He has the hood up, so there's nothing to see."

"He knows something's up now. There's a little basket of cinnamon rolls under the hood. I put them there myself."

"He's lowering the hood . . . he has a basket." I jumped back from the window. "He's looking over here!"

"You bet he is. He can't ignore me now. What's he doing?"

I stood on my tiptoes to look through a break in the curtains. "He's sitting on the back steps reading a note."

"What's he doing now?"

"He's . . . blowing his nose."

"Oh, for goodness' sake. How can he blow his nose at a time like this?"

"He's taking a bite of cinnamon roll . . . he's chewing . . . chewing . . . chewing."

"Take another bite, Walter."

"You didn't poison him, did you?"

"Of course not. Ruth had her cloak. I have my cinnamon rolls. I rolled notes into each one. I know Walter. He won't stop till he's eaten all of them cinnamon rolls."

He took another bite, and a coil of paper hung from his mouth.

"He's reading a strip of paper," I said.

"What color is it?"

"White."

"That one says I will never throw his boots at him."

"He's pulling a pink strip out of another roll."

"He isn't eating the cinnamon roll?"

"Nope. He's reading the note."

"Pink, huh? I think that one says I won't never make him sleep in the garage."

"He's looking over here. . . . Now he's pulling out another strip. . . . It's green . . . he's reading . . . reading . . . reading." My calf knotted in pain, so I limped around the kitchen table. "Give me a minute to walk out this cramp."

"Never mind that. What's he doing now?"

"It really hurts."

"You have to watch him."

I went back to the window.

"What's he doing?"

"He's coming over here!"

Margaret pulled on my arm. "You have to leave."

At the front door, I planted my feet. "What did you write on the green paper?"

"Never you mind. Now, get!"

I swung the pickax over my head and let it fall to the ground. The point bounced off the hard-packed clay and jarred my joints. I wiped my sweaty palms on my overalls and swung again.

"Would it help to soak the area with water?" Roseanne asked.

Softening the soil with water would cost me time I didn't have, but I saw no other way to get the lilac stump out of the ground. Roseanne, dressed in a T-shirt and short overalls like mine, helped me scratch enough soil together to build an earthen basin around the stump.

I gave her marching orders. "Keep the basin full of water until you go to bed tonight. That should make the ground easier to dig by morning."

"Listen, Mibby, I don't want you to hurt yourself trying to get the garden done in time for the contest. Take your time, okay?"

I ticked off the things I'd accomplished in Roseanne's garden that afternoon. I'd sawed all the limbs from a dead lilac bush and loaded its remains into the Daisy Mobile's bed. Then I'd piled on a mishmash of broken furniture and wood scraps from the side of the garage. That sent a large colony of spiders looking for new residences. *Good riddance.* I'd felt smug about my progress until I came across two metal clothesline poles still wearing their concrete booties at the bottom of the heap. No amount of pulling, even with Roseanne's help, budged the behemoths. I planned to try pulling them out with the Daisy Mobile the next day, that is if I could shake the image of pulling the garage to the ground in the process.

"The schedule's pretty tight," I told her, "but I can do it if I don't have too many more days like today." My optimism surprised me.

"You mean more to me than the contest," she said.

I reassured her that meeting the deadline was all a matter of pacing and planning and more than a little grace. Never mind that my pace had screeched to a halt and my planning had flitted out the window on the first day, which was nothing unusual for any kind of contractor. There were always surprises, and surprises meant setbacks, so I'd put a fudge factor, two free days, into the schedule. One down. One to go.

"I'm so happy to be doing this for you," I said. "Please don't worry about me."

"I don't want you to think I'd be disappointed if you decided to drop out of the contest."

"I know, and I'm grateful." I didn't know how long I could exude confidence, so I changed the subject. "How's Stefan?"

Roseanne watched the earthen basin fill with water. "I don't know. I haven't heard from him in a while. We usually talk several times every day, but it's like he's disappeared from the face of the earth. He doesn't even return my messages. The notes have stopped, too. The daily gifts . . . they weren't that important to me. I hope I didn't say anything . . ."

"Maybe he had to go out of town for a few days," I said.

"He just got back from Dallas. He told me how glad he was to stay home for the rest of the month."

To Roseanne, I said, "Something important came up. I'm sure of it." But on the inside, I was thinking, *Listen, bub, you better call, and I mean today.*

The water spilled over the basin, but Roseanne didn't move. "I was going to go to church tonight, but I think I'll stay home in case he calls."

I took the hose from her hand and closed the valve to stop the water. "He can always leave a message."

"I suppose . . ."

~

The counter girl at Dairy Queen held out her hand. "That'll be $8.28."

I unzipped the inside pocket of my purse to retrieve the twenty-dollar bill I'd withdrawn from my checking account for the week's incidentals. It wasn't there. I raked through the bottom of my purse and checked my wallet. The counter girl's palm hovered above the counter waiting for the money. I flashed a smile before I checked my purse again. Empty. And the checkbook, I knew, lay in the drawer with the bills. I offered the girl a credit card.

"Actually, we don't do credit cards."

In desperation, I dumped the contents of my purse on the counter. Behind me, someone said, "That's just great."

Bank receipts. Dog bone. Zinc oxide. *Where's the cap?* Mechanical pencil. Band-Aid wrapper. Hot-sauce packet. Plant stakes. Watch battery. *Is this the new one or the dead one?* Notebook. Carmex. Cough drops. But no money. Not one red cent.

"Is this gonna take much longer?" asked a girl behind me.

Next to me, a credit card machine blinked the message *Swipe card*. I gestured at the machine with my credit card. "I thought you said you didn't take credit cards."

"Actually, we only take credit cards for purchases over ten dollars."

"Great. Ring up $10.01 and take my credit card."

"Actually, I can't do that."

"Why not?"

"I have touch pads on the register for a DQ cone and a DQ sundae and a Pecan Mudslide and a double cheeseburger and a—"

Behind her, a fluorescent sign with a picture of an ice cream cake flickered. "How about a frozen cake?"

"What flavor?"

"Whatever's on top."

The girl barely turned to look through the glass doors of the freezer case. "Actually, you can't have that one. It's a special order."

"Then I'll take the first one you come to that's not a special order."

"Actually, there's nobody actually here to write on the cake for you."

"Listen, it actually doesn't bother me to buy a blank cake. Just grab any cake so I can get out of here."

The crowd behind me grunted its approval.

"Chocolate or vanilla?" she asked, and I knew I'd have to play along to get out of the ice cream parlor alive.

"Chocolate."

"Well, actually, we don't have any chocolate left."

"Vanilla would be fine."

"Winnie the Pooh or Buzz Lightyear?"

"Winnie the Pooh?"

"Cool, we actually have one."

The crowd cheered as I signed the charge receipt.

My family sat around a concrete table on the Dairy Queen patio. Heat seeped from the pavement as the sun held its position on the horizon. Andrea sipped her water, the only thing on the menu board that was organic. All that remained of Ky's sundae were smudges of chocolate on his sleeve where he had wiped his mouth. Louise stirred her ice cream lazily. My mother had stayed home and refused my offers to bring her a treat home, mumbling something about hydrogenated chicken fat. My chocolate sundae resembled a Rorschach inkblot test—a chocolate Smurf poised to swallow a four-fingered starfish. I hated to think what that could mean.

Ky gouged a hunk of Winnie the Pooh and filled his mouth. "Wha dook ooh so wong?"

"It's the weirdest thing," I said. "I had a twenty-dollar bill in my purse this morning, and now it's gone."

"Did you check the truck?" Andrea asked. "There's a pile of stuff on the seat."

That pile of stuff was my mobile office. "I know for certain I put it in my purse. I keep my incidental money separate." On the very edge of my sight, Ky bit his lip. "Ky, did you see a twenty anywhere?"

He grabbed a napkin to wipe ice cream off his fingers. "Um . . ." He looked over our heads furtively. "I need a fork." With that, he went back inside the restaurant.

I didn't have to read a book to know my son had squirmed under my question, but squirming wasn't unusual these days. He squirmed, fidgeted, and bounced most of the day. Besides, he wouldn't take money without asking. I knew he wouldn't. I stirred my sundae into chocolate soup.

"You're not thinking Ky took it, are you?" asked Andrea.

I assured her as convincingly as I could that I wasn't.

"Funny," she said. "He looked guilty to me."

I waved off her comment. "Fourteen-year-old boys always look guilty. Did he tell you Salvador canceled his visit? He got a better offer from one of his new friends. Kids can sure be creepy."

"Bummer," Andrea said, and I knew she understood Ky's disappointment.

Andrea and Ky walked ahead of Louise and me like they had somewhere to go. Louise had gone to Virginia that day for her first real haircut since she'd lost her hair. Since it was still too short to flip or curl, Virginia had given Louise a just-out-of-bed do. Imagine Medusa with baby snakes. Her eyes glinted in the late day's light, and her cheeks flushed with color. Louise definitely liked the way she looked. Maybe that explained why she'd dressed without a hint of theme in a knobby silk outfit the color of sea glass, and in sandals, footwear I'd never seen her wear. Feet, she'd told me our first summer as friends, were too undignified to flash about before cousins and strangers. But that evening, she wore broad-banded sandals that revealed her carnation-pink toenails. In the middle of her chest, a slice of aqua-blue agate, as big as a pocket watch, lay against her creamy skin. I decided she looked sturdy enough to answer a weighty theological question.

"Louise," I said cautiously, stepping carefully into the question that had dogged me since I'd left the grazing sheep. When the conversational shoehorn I needed wouldn't form, I blurted, "You know how sometimes you don't want God to say something so badly, it's all you really hear? How in the world do you know when it's God talking or you're just projecting what you think God would say if He was, say, an ogre or something?"

"Say that again, sweet pea, only slower this time."

She needed an example. "Let's say, for instance, you . . . I don't know . . . let's say you've been asked to serve on a certain committee at church. Say it's the grounds and maintenance committee, and you would rather be on the worship committee, because you know nothing about air-conditioners or the life expectancy of upholstery; and besides, the grounds and maintenance committee has workdays every other Saturday. And even though you've told the nominating committee you don't feel gifted in maintenance, they ask you to pray about it. So you say you will, because you don't want anyone to think you're not willing to be on the grounds and maintenance committee, but you also know that praying will give God a chance to say you should be on the grounds and maintenance committee. He might even insist you *chair* the committee as an opportunity to grow and depend on Him. Here's my question."

"I didn't know the grounds and maintenance committee has workdays every other Saturday."

"They do, but that doesn't have anything to do with my question. So here it goes—"

"God is not an ogre," she said.

I had to promise Louise I would read the fifth chapter of Matthew before she'd let me ask my question. "How do you know when it's guilt talking or God talking?"

"Wait a minute. Who's leaving the grounds and maintenance committee?"

"No one, Louise."

She stopped walking. "You just said—"

"It was an illustration."

"Oh."

We walked in silence for a block. I wondered if telling Louise the real reason for my question was worth the chance she would side with the sheep and send me running to Larry. *She would never* . . . "Forget the illustration, Louise."

"Does that mean you're going to tell me what really happened when you went to see Connie and Larry yesterday?"

"When I went to see Connie, Larry was there. The end."

"If you say so."

"We both know Larry is not my type, right? Of course he's not. I mean, is there another man more unlike Scott? Not hardly, and Scott was certainly my type—steady, thoughtful, athletic, a professional, and well respected in the community. I could go on and on. Scott was perfect, or almost perfect, at least for me. Larry? I don't know. Something weird happened in his dahlia garden." I checked to see if her eyebrows were dancing with innuendo. They weren't, so I trudged on. "Larry did something funny with his voice. My heart almost jumped out of my chest. I've been trying to figure it out all day. I'm thinking he spoke in the same key as Scott, only I wouldn't know it, because I'm not a musician, but my subconscious would know, wouldn't it? Of course it would, so that explains why my heart fluttered. It was a false alarm, that's all. Phew! It's funny to think about now, but I thought it was an attraction to Larry, which it couldn't be, because Larry is not my type . . . at all.

"Anyway, I told God He needed to find someone else, a nice young woman more worthy of a man like Larry." I felt funny fibbing about my talk with God. "Actually, I asked God *not* to make me love him, and then I thought I heard a quiet whispering in my heart to listen to the Shepherd. I'm sure it was just looking at that stupid sheep and thinking I heard God.

"Think about it. God can't make me, or anyone, love a person, or even His own Son, for goodness' sake, so what am I afraid of? Of course, as a believer, I'm called to love my friends and enemies. What was I worried about? Of course, I'm supposed to love Larry—like a *brother*. Here I am all twittered about God making me love him, and He just wants me to love him, not *love* him. I can do that."

"Is this the part where I'm supposed to jump in?"

I felt so much better after I'd had the little talk with myself. "Sure."

"If you heard the Shepherd telling you to love, you heard correctly."

That's what I thought.

*Cooler? Really? Hardly seems like it
when I'm out in the heat all day.
Still, Margaret and Walter's wedding pots
look great. Must fertilize.*

Larry removed his ear protectors and shouted over the air compressor, "Louise called! Said you needed help! I can get the stoop out today and the sidewalk tomorrow!" Sweat ran off his forehead and into his beard. He must have seen me weighing his offer. "Just until you find someone else!"

Beckoned or not, Larry was my knight. "Okay! Thanks!"

He adjusted his protective goggles, hefted the jackhammer into place, and pressed the trigger. In the time it took me to ask myself if I'd made the right decision, a piece of concrete fissured and broke away from the stoop. That answered my question. While Larry chipped away at the stoop, I loaded the concrete pieces into the wheelbarrow and took them to the alley. We started just after two and worked that way until the stoop and the sidewalk were only memories.

"That went better than I thought," Larry said. "What's next?"

"Look, Larry, I'm not going to hold you to your offer. This is a lot of work for a man who's put in a full day of work already."

"You're doing me a favor. After a day in the delivery truck, I'm as stiff as a board. There's nothing like some heave-ho to get the kinks out. That reminds me, I have some Strawberry Cream Balls in the car."

Larry and I sat in a narrow wedge of shade cast by the garage and ate our Sweet Suzy treats. My muscles throbbed from the effort of hauling all that concrete to the alley, although truthfully, Larry had carried more than I had. I was so tired I could have lain among the weeds to sleep through the night.

"So what are you using to amend the soil?" he asked.

I talked around the cream ball in my mouth. "Compost and more compost."

We compared the attributes of different soil amendments until the wedge of shadow melded with the shadow of the house, and Larry could stretch out his legs. "You have to be so careful with manure," he said. "I learned the hard way to get it tested for salts. I nearly lost my garden one year."

Once we'd exhausted the topic of manure, we lamented the curly top infestation of the valley's plants while we ate through another package of cream balls. "Margaret had me rip out her tomato plants this week. She nearly cried imagining a winter without tomato juice," I said. That comment started a conversation on salsa recipes and the heat index of peppers. Larry liked serranos. I preferred poblanos.

I asked him about his work at the University of Virginia.

"While I was going to school, I worked for the university in janitorial services. By the time I graduated, it was clear I wasn't made for academic politicking, so the pursuit of a doctorate lost its appeal. And teaching American History to a room full of ninth graders appealed even less." He shrugged. "When a full-time position came up, I grabbed it."

"So you were a janitor?"

"It was great work. Being a janitor taught me the secret to a happy life—work at a job you can finish by the end of the day, so you'll have time and energy to do what really matters."

"And what really matters?"

"Lots of stuff—reading a good book, spending time with friends, hearing a lecture on the race to seize Berchtesgarden—stuff like that."

"And Sweet Suzy?"

"It's a good company. I go to work early, but there's plenty of daylight to play in the garden when I get home. What could be better?"

It wasn't until he told me about a newly opened dahlia among his hybrids that I even considered, and then dismissed, being uncomfortable around him. I'd made too much of a simple give-and-take between friends in his dahlia garden, and I knew it then. Of course, I was to love Larry as a brother. No problem. He was a nice guy and a nice friend to have around. All through the blistering heat of the afternoon, Larry had worked steadily at breaking up the concrete. We'd talked as gardeners do about living things and how to entice them to thrive under our care. Recipes were exchanged and a piece of shade was shared. Nothing more.

"You worked hard today," he said.

"Not as hard as you."

He handed me an unopened box of cream balls. "Take these home for Ky and Andrea. I have some more in the trunk if you think you need more."

I was about to ask Larry a question about dahlia propagation when Roseanne honked her horn from the driveway. By the time she'd freed Phoebe from her car seat, Larry had gotten into his car and left.

"Who was that?" Roseanne asked.

"A friend."

"Do you think he'd like to go to speed dating night?"

"No way."

"I'll fertilize you tomorrow, I promise," I told the last of Walter and Margaret's wedding pots as I filled the last container with water. I'd collected a fistful of spent blossoms and scorched leaves as I watered. Rather than walk all the way to the compost pile on my rubbery legs, I tossed the scraps into our household trash can and missed. I considered leaving the mess where it lay. A few geranium leaves and shriveled *Bacopa* flowers wouldn't hurt anything. Then I heard my grandmother's voice, *"Don't think you're going to leave that there for me to pick up."*

I won't, Grandma.

Inside the trash can, I found a glossy box covered with a camouflage design. It had been wedged between the plastic bags and the wall of the trash can as if someone—Ky—had hidden it. Red letters boasted *Commandos From the Dark Lair!* A cross between a horned dragon and a swamp creature brandished a futuristic gun—a dark lair commando, no doubt. Captions promised adventure and immortality.

Ky? You little . . . Wait a minute. Don't jump to conclusions.

Ky could have picked up the game in any manner of ways. He could have bought it on sale for half price or traded something of equal value in boy world, like a fistful of baseball cards. But no, Ky loved his baseball cards. Over half of them had belonged to Scott when he was a boy. But I'd also thought Ky would never take money from my purse. . . .

Why do I have a bad feeling about this?

～

Ky spoke without taking his eyes off the monitor. "Hey, you missed a great dinner. Grandma made veggie lasagna and it was really good. Even Andrea liked it." On the screen, a tank vaporized. "Yeah!"

"I have a question for you."

He blew up a car and a hot dog stand.

"Ky, I'm really tired. Could you stop to talk with me for a minute?"

A policeman jumped into the picture, gun drawn, and crouched down for a shot at Ky. Blood spurted from the man's chest when Ky rapid-fired the mouse.

"That's enough!"

"What? It's a game. I'll turn it off."

"No, uninstall it now."

"I'll turn it off." He closed down the program with a few clicks of the mouse. White clouds on a blue sky appeared on the screen. "See, it's gone."

"That's not good enough. I want that vile stuff out of my house, now. If you don't uninstall it this minute, I will. Where's the CD?"

"Mom, it's not my game. I borrowed it from . . . Dustin."

"Then why did you throw the box away? Better yet, why did you push it down the side of the trash can? I don't ask much of you, Ky, but I do want the truth from you. Where did you get this game?"

"I told you."

"That's why I'm giving you another chance to answer the question. Where did you get the game?"

"I said, Dustin."

My anger was a giant boulder tumbling downhill. If I tried to stop it, I was sure it would crush me. "Who's Dustin? Was he over here? Is he in your class? How do you know him?"

"Do you want me to answer the questions or not?"

We were both screaming now. I punched the CD-ROM eject button. Ky reached for the CD. I clenched his wrist. The CD slid back into the computer. Ky shook me free.

"Go to your room!" I screamed. "Now! I don't want to see you again until you can be straight with me."

He stepped between me and the computer. "What are you going to do?"

"Get up to your room."

"What are you going to do?"

"I'm going to put the CD somewhere safe until Dustin can come over with his parents to get it. Then I'll uninstall the program."

"That's stupid. It's just a game. The characters are made up. Don't you get that?"

I hit the eject button again and reached for the CD. Ky grabbed it first and held the CD out of my reach. I stepped on the chair to extend my grasp, but the chair rolled out from under me, and I fell into Ky. He hit the coffee table with the bony rise of his cheek. I heard the thud of contact, but Ky wouldn't show me his wound. He was crying quietly now, taking long, deep breaths. My chest sagged with regret.

"I'm sorry. I'm so sorry. Oh, please forgive me, Ky. I'm so sorry." I reached for his hand, but he pulled it away and started down the hall.

"Never mind. I'm fine."

I followed him. "Let me see your face."

"I'll take care of it. I don't need you."

I stood at the bottom of the stairs watching my son walk away. Regret had doused my anger like a cold bucket of water. I started to follow him.

A hand on my arm held me in place. It was my mother.

"Bré, let him go. You both need to calm down."

The only thing more potent than regret is shame. Rather than admit it, I turned on my mother. "I am not Bré. I hate that name. I'm Mibby. This is my house. Ky is my son. Don't forget that."

"Do you want me to go?"

Of all the times I had wished she would ask me that very question . . . .

AUG
23

So this is our monsoon month. Finally,
a thunderstorm came through the valley.
Sounded great, smelled great, felt great—
but barely enough rain to wet the sidewalk.

All through the first week of installing Roseanne's garden and into the next, Larry showed up at Roseanne's, usually before me but always by two in the afternoon. We settled into a routine of working for an hour and then breaking for a snack. Larry brought the Sweet Suzy products, and I supplied the homemade iced tea and sometimes something from the coffee shop. Roseanne joined us for a snack on the days when Phoebe napped. After a few days, Larry began stopping by the house to pick up Ky on his way to Roseanne's, knowing better than me, I supposed, that Ky needed to be there. Droop had been right. Under Larry's supervision, Ky learned how to run a Rototiller, smooth an expanse of soil into a level grade, and read a sprinkler plan. Ky even suggested I add a hose bib near the fountain to make it easy for Roseanne to refill the catch basin. For that, he'd earned a bonus of two hours of modem use.

Ky remained distant, but I couldn't really blame him. In our silent agreement, we had vowed not to talk about the incident over the CD. When Larry asked him about the bruise on his face, Ky told him he'd slipped in his socks on the hardwood floors. I couldn't bring myself to thank Ky for not elaborating. I still winced every time I saw the bruise under his eye, now fainter but a ghastly shade of green. The tension between us had dissipated rather than been resolved, which only fueled my shame.

I'd spent the morning pruning Mrs. Bridgewater's overgrown junipers so she could see out her living room windows. In the process, I was poked and scratched and experienced too much one-on-one time with a herd of spiders.

Working in the sun at Roseanne's held no appeal, but any thoughts of playing hooky were dismissed when I thought of Larry and Ky setting the sandstone path without my help. I need not have worried. When I got there, Larry and Phoebe were playing under the patio umbrella. Phoebe squealed and grabbed for his beard. Larry made a big show of howling in pain, which only made Phoebe squeal louder. Ky sat slumped in a chair listening to his MP3 player. He roused himself enough to thank me convincingly for the Big Gulp I handed him.

"Where's the sandstone?" I asked Larry.

He held Phoebe over his head. When he said "Whoops," her eyes widened in anticipation of a daisy plunge to his knee. Only when Phoebe was happily riding his bouncing knee did Larry look at me. "Sorry, I couldn't stop mid-whoops-a-daisy."

"The sandstone is sitting on a truck beside the road between here and Glenwood Springs. The truck broke its axle. The yard foreman is sending a forklift and another truck, but the stone won't be here until tomorrow."

Maybe Roseanne needed company under the air-conditioner vent. "Where's Roseanne?"

"She seemed a little ragged around the edges when we got here, so I sent her inside to cool off."

I'm ragged around my edges.

But before I felt free to join her, I looked around the garden. Where weeds and broken concrete had dominated the yard, tiny plastic flags marked sprinkler heads in the freshly tilled and smoothed soil. I'd spray-painted lines in the dirt to show where the sandstone paths were to wind through the shrub beds to the strawberry patch and on to the playhouse and the garage. With Larry and Ky's help, the new garden was ahead of schedule. All that remained before planting was to lay the sandstone paths and sitting areas, assemble the fountain, and if time allowed, build the playhouse.

Larry interrupted my thinking. "The way I see it, there isn't a whole lot we can do around here until the sandstone arrives. We might as well go fishing, unless, of course, the boss lady has other plans."

"You mean now?"

"The trout are calling my name," he said with his hand to his ear. "And, wait a minute. Yes, they're calling Ky's name, too."

"Mom, can we?"

Larry held Phoebe to his chest. "We can be on top of the Mesa in forty minutes."

"We haven't been up there all summer," Ky said.

The thin air of the Mesa would be as cool as any air-conditioned room, maybe cooler. "Okay."

"We'll stop by and get your mother and Andrea," Larry said.

Ky told Larry that Andrea was working and his grandmother didn't believe in killing fish.

Larry rolled his eyes. "No Gummi Worms for her. How about you, Ky? You got any aversion to spending the afternoon tossing a line into a crystal-blue lake and waiting for a fish to bite your hook?"

Ky actually managed a smile. "Maybe Roseanne would like to go, too."

~~

Larry drove Roseanne's minivan on a narrow shelf of road that hugged the canyon wall. In Colorado it was called a highway. We passed small ranches and vacation homes tucked among the scrub oak and mountain mahogany. I touched the glass of my window. It was cooler, but not cool. The temperature readout on the overhead console read 87°, kind of disappointing.

"Let's get some of that fresh mountain air in here," Larry said, switching off the air-conditioner and lowering the windows.

We drove past Forest Ridge Ski Resort and into the aspen and spruce forests of the steeper slopes. Goliath sat on Larry's lap to enjoy the fresh air. Blink and I sat in the very back. The sight of a cat sitting in front of an opened window activated Blink's salivary glands. To keep Roseanne's car seat from getting drenched, I let him drool in my lap. In front of me, Phoebe giggled every time she turned to see Blink in the back seat.

The road rose steeper to zigzag through boulders and stands of aspens and narrow fingers of meadows formed by winter avalanches. Only red gilia and mule ears spotted the roadside. My stomach churned with every curve. I'd traveled the road countless times, so when we rode through a slope covered by lava boulders, I sighed with relief. Soon the curves would soften and my stomach would return to its assigned place.

Larry shifted the van into low. "Lean forward," he said, and Ky groaned, but we all laughed.

Nearing the summit—if you could call the flat top of a mesa a summit—the incline eased. The van traveled easily on the gentle rise and fall of the road through alpine meadows and boggy bottoms. Ky rode the wave of air with the palm of his hand. At ten thousand feet, we finally outdistanced the haze of smoke and dust. The sky was startlingly blue again. Only two clouds, as lonely as life rafts in an ocean, sailed across the sky.

"Think the fish are biting at Kearn Lake?" Larry asked Ky.

"Can we go to Willard?"

I almost protested. Willard Lake had been Scott's favorite fishing spot.

"Sure. My dad had a sacred fishing spot at Willard. If my brother or I dared to cast too close to the hole, we sure heard about it." Larry laughed. "I don't think Dad pulled one solitary fish out of that hole."

"Maybe he didn't like fish," Roseanne said.

"It had nothing to do with fish. He took the Sunday crossword puzzle with him. We didn't leave the lake until the last letter was written in the last square. I can remember him finishing by the light of a lantern."

Conversation stopped when we rounded the last broad curve to the parking lot at Willard Lake. What should have been a sapphire-blue lake was an empty platter of cracked mud. Only a few puddles of water reflected the sky in the deepest depressions of the lake bottom. I'd seen the water level drop in late summer to expose a raw edge of shoreline like a boy's pale skin after a haircut, but the drop had only meant school and Thanksgiving and Christmas were on their way. All the lake spoke of now was another year of drought and the uncertainty that came with it.

"Cool, I can walk on the lake," Ky said, running with Blink toward the lake bottom.

Roseanne hefted Phoebe in a baby carrier to her back. "Phoebe and I'll go with Ky and Blink. She loves that dog."

Larry stepped onto the lake bottom to help Roseanne down the steep bank. "I could carry the baby for you," he said.

"She's not so heavy."

When he extended his hand to me, I sat on a stump and covered my eyes. A wave of despair washed over me, just as it had the time Margot had carelessly walked on our father's grave.

"I've got just the thing in my creel," Larry said.

As long as I'd been able to imagine the reservoir's sparkling blue, I was hopeful cooler days would come and that juicy storms would ride the shoulders of the jet stream to drop silver-dollar snowflakes on the mountains. I couldn't even imagine the amount of snow it would take to fill Willard Lake. The summer heat had burned the silence and coolness of snow right out of me and left a lakebed as dry and bland as a paper bag.

Ugh.

Larry patted my knee. "Here, have a Coconut Dream Cake. The drought won't go on forever. No drought ever has."

No need to hoard the misery for myself. "Maybe all the doom and gloom about global warming is right after all," I said, stuffing my cheeks with cake, but my mouth was almost too dry to swallow. I returned the remaining cake to its wrapper.

Larry rested his hand on my knee again, and I didn't mind. It was warm and strong, and most of all, reassuring.

"I'm sorry I brought you up here," he said.

"You had no way of knowing the lake was dry."

"There's over three hundred lakes to choose from. We'll find another."

Ky pried tiles of dried mud off the lake bottom and threw the clods at the puddles. The sky reflected in the pools shimmied with each direct hit.

"Nah, this is good for me to see. There's nothing like a smack of reality to upend your business plan."

"You're taking the drought awfully personally."

"I'm taking it *very* personally. It's not like I haven't tried trusting God, but really, the thought of taking a nap on a sinking ship . . . I'm not made that way."

Larry raised his eyebrows, but I ignored their question.

Roseanne had Phoebe out of the pack and toddling toward the far shore. Ky had given up on displacing the last of the puddles and was overturning rocks. There was nothing like a little mountain air to neutralize the effects of testosterone on a growing boy. He found something to pick up and show Phoebe. Her squeal echoed off the ridge above the lake.

I was in full self-pity mode. "I trusted God to bring the rain. It didn't come. I trusted God to provide clients. The drought scared them off. I asked God to be my son's father and provide him with good friends. I'm thinking God's parenting skills leave a lot to be desired."

We sat in silence for a long time. I figured my blasphemy had finally sucked all of the bluster out of Larry. Even if I won the garden design competition, there was no guarantee the snow and the rain would come, so what good was a blue ribbon? I pictured myself and Ky loading the Daisy Mobile with our belongings and moving out of town.

"Let's go for a walk," Larry offered.

I can't feel sorry for myself and walk at the same time, so I declined his invitation. "I don't—"

"Sure you do." He pulled me up by the elbows and turned me toward a stand of spruce. "Let's go."

The trees stood so tall and straight, it didn't take much imagination to think of them as a disapproving mob. Below the trees, the wild flowers and grasses grew in sparse clumps. The foliage looked ragged, and the brittle cushion of needles under our feet snapped as we walked. If a walk in the woods was supposed to make me feel better, it had failed.

After walking in silence for a time, Larry stooped to look at the forest floor. "It's really dry." He retraced his steps, and I followed him until we left the trees again. On the far ridge across the lake, swaths of deep green spruce, interrupted only by the fresh green of the aspens, seemed more like a tapestry than a forest.

"I don't think trust is the starting point for blessing," he said.

I looked at the ridge more closely.

"You'd think the trees would show the effects of the drought," he said, "but there they are, in front of God and everybody, looking like it's been raining every day."

Larry needed a lesson in Botany 101. "Trees have amazing tap roots. They can reach the saturated ground below the lake. That's why the trees are thriving."

"Would you say the trees have an advantage for survival because they're near the lake?" he asked.

"Yes, and being near the lake—even a dry lake—only gets more important as the drought drags on."

"This reminds me of a passage in Jeremiah," he said, and then he quoted the verses from memory. "'Blessed is the *woman* who trusts in the Lord, whose confidence is in him. He'—excuse me—*she* 'will be like a tree planted by the water that sends out its roots by the stream. It does not fear when heat comes; its leaves are always green. It has no worries in a year of drought and never fails to bear fruit.'"

"I was green in the car coming up here."

He laughed and turned toward the lake. "That's a start."

"What are you trying to say?"

"Answer this: Where is the starting place for blessing?"

"It's where you plant yourself?"

"You got it."

～⌒

"You and Larry sure had a lot to talk about today," Roseanne said, scraping the last of the enchilada casserole into a plastic bowl.

"He's a good friend," I said.

She submerged the pan into a sink full of sudsy water. "Nothing more?"

"What else would we be?"

"I don't know. He sure has a way with kids."

She meant Phoebe. I could hear it in her voice.

"He brought Phoebe a book about lambs today," she said.

Lambs?

"He can sure make her laugh."

Something itched in me like a wool sweater on a cotton-sweater day. "What about Stefan?"

She sighed and scrubbed the dish harder. "He had me fooled. I thought I was special, but it turns out, he has a whole harem of needy women he shuffles through. I guess I got too possessive, because he hasn't called in a while."

"I'm sorry."

"There's nothing to be sorry about, but I'm sure embarrassed I was so flattered by his attention. From now on, I'm only dating guys after I get to know them."

"Really?"

"Go ahead and say it. I deserve it."

"I told you so?"

"Ouch."

My mother had washed the sheets and hung them out to dry before she'd made the bed. I pulled the sheet over my face and breathed in the hot sun and let the rough sheet rest on my cheeks, just the way I had the summer I was almost eleven, only it was Grandma who had hung out the sheets. I was still mostly child that year. I played with dolls and collected snails in Grandma's sun-tea jar and chewed on sour grass until my jaws ached. But there was a new part of me who was a stranger. She studied with rapt wonder the way sweat streamed down a boy's face right before she kicked him in the shins. Maybe it was the sheets that coaxed a dream about Bradley.

In my dream, it was Valentine's Day, and I was out to recess with my classmates, only we were too excited about the coming party to play an organized game. The wind blew, and the clouds hung heavy with rain.

The girls huddled in twos and threes. I clung to Ginny, my best friend of the week. The boys circled us like predators, gathering their courage to put their arms around our shoulders, and then the couples walked that way until the girls batted them off or the suspense got too great and the boy had to walk away before he exploded. Each girl giggled and taunted, afraid a boy would choose her and terrified he wouldn't. In my dream, the feelings were as fresh as they had been on a long-ago day, but everything about Bradley was different.

On the real Valentine's Day of fifth grade, Bradley had presented me with an oversized valentine with a flocked shaggy dog holding a heart that said *Be mine, forever!* I looked around to see if anyone had seen Bradley give me the card. I checked the price. He'd paid $1.29. *What a geek!* Moles were Bradley's most outstanding feature. In my dream, none of that mattered. I was smitten. He was my sun, my moon, and my stars. My heart had been won by his kindness alone. *I'll follow you anywhere, Bradley!* The recess bell interrupted my declaration of love. And then it rang again.

Brrring!

"Hello?"

"Did I wake you up?"

"Who is this?"

"Hollis, I mean Crenshaw, only I don't go by Crenshaw no more. Brenda likes Hollis better, except she calls me Holly. I . . . I kind of like it."

Holly?

"Are you there?" he asked.

For a split second, I wondered if I was still in a dreamland recess. "I'm here."

"Are you awake? I could really use your help."

I sat up and clicked on the lamp. The clock read nine-twenty. I'd been asleep ten minutes. "Well?"

"I really like Brenda."

"Good."

"No, that's bad."

"Bad?"

"I don't like the way I'm feeling."

"How's that?"

"Like if I don't see her for an hour, I might go crazy. I'm forgetting to order pancake syrup; I'm drawing little hearts on the timecards; I gave a stupid, good-for-nothing, lazy busboy Saturday night off. I only want to be with Brenda, and she's all I want to think about when she ain't around. The district manager wrote me up for writing her name all over my order sheets. I can't go on like this."

"Cren . . . Hollis, have you ever felt like this before?"

"Never."

"Not even when you and your wife were dating?"

"You have to believe me. I've never drawn a heart in my whole life."

I was tempted to tell him to take two aspirin and call me in the morning. The love doctor needed her shut-eye. But there was something pitiful about a man who had never been tempted to draw one pudgy red heart.

"Don't worry. It's nothing terminal," I said.

"Huh?"

"You won't die from infatuation, but the only antidote is to move on to loving Brenda."

"I already do."

"You can't. It takes a lot longer than a couple weeks to love somebody."

"I don't have too much time. At this rate, I'll be out of work in a day or two."

"Once you decide to love someone, the symptoms of infatuation start diminishing almost immediately."

"Really? I'm about to crawl out of my skin. You gotta help me."

I folded the hem of the sheet over the blanket and plumped my pillow against the headboard. "The first step is to start thinking in the long term."

"Like ordering enough bacon for Sunday on Wednesday?"

"It's more like planning for a vacation. Let's say you want to go to Cozumel next February."

"Where's that?"

"Mexico."

"I like tacos."

"Good, because once you'd made the decision to go, you'd be very excited. All you'd think about are sandy beaches and warm Caribbean seas and—"

"Do they have a swimming pool with a slide?"

"Sure, now listen up. No amount of dreaming about beaches and snorkeling is going to get you to Cozumel. You're going to have to . . . what?"

"Buy a plane ticket?"

"Yes, exactly, and what else?"

"Rent a motel room?"

"Yes."

"And get some new swim trunks? Mine don't fit so well anymore. Too many pancakes."

"That's the spirit. Once you start preparing for the trip, you go from being giddy with excitement to carefully working toward having what you need to get to Cozumel to have a good time."

"Why am I going to Mexico again?"

"Deciding to take an exciting trip is like the early days of a relationship. You can hardly think of anything else. Once you decide on a destination, you settle into the job of being prepared for the trip, just like a relationship."

"So a relationship is like a vacation." The phone went quiet for a long moment. "Where are we going?" he asked.

"Marriage."

"Oh boy."

"That means you and Brenda have a lot of preparation to do. You have to talk about all the tough issues, like children and religion and . . . some other stuff."

"Religion's tough, all right. Brenda keeps asking me to go to church with her."

"There you go. Faith is important to Brenda. If it isn't important to you, the gentlemanly thing to do would be to let her know."

"Do you think she might tell me to take a hike if I do?"

"She might."

"What if I'm not sure about religion but I'm willing to find out?"

"Tell her what you just told me, and then give getting to know God your best effort."

"Are you still praying for me?"

"Whenever I get in my truck."

"Do you get in your truck a lot?"

"About a hundred times a day."

He laughed and snorted. "Keep truckin'."

It was the first time I'd ever heard Crenshaw laugh.

As I was falling asleep for the second time that night, I remembered my walk in the woods with Larry and his answer to my question "Where is the starting place for blessing?"

I snapped the bedside lamp back on and reset my alarm for half an hour earlier. If I was going to plant myself close to God, I'd need more than five minutes of prayer and Bible reading to do it.

AUG
24

Last tomato plant has succumbed to curly top virus. Thank goodness for farmers' market, but even their tomatoes are puny. Morning glories have grown inside one of the birdhouses and lifted the roof. Closer supervision necessary!

Louise scooped flour into a measuring cup, leveled it with a knife, and added it to a mixing bowl, the kind you use to bake for a hundred of your closest friends. Her Double or Nuttin' Brownies were baking in the oven. Louise's philosophy of life and baking melded perfectly: double the good stuff. The brownies had chocolate chips and twice the nuts. When they cooled she would slather them with chocolate frosting and drizzle them with caramel. My mouth got watery just thinking about them.

Her measuring spoons clanked as she added baking powder and salt. "I feared I'd forgotten the recipe, but makin' scones is like riding a bicycle, only a lot less work and a much better payoff."

Louise grated the rind of a lemon into the bowl. "It's funny how something as ordinary as baking can be like slippin' the last piece of a jigsaw puzzle into place. Every cell in my body is sighin' with relief. What's next, sweet pea, Gone to Heaven Chocolate Pie or Chocolate Mini Kisses Truffle Cake? Or maybe with the brownies, that would be too much chocolate?"

My eyes met hers. "Too much chocolate?" she asked. "Glory be, what am I thinking?"

"How are you feeling?" I asked.

"Never better." Louise looked up from cutting the butter into the flour. "What?"

"You're actually touching refined flour."

"Ain't it grand?"

The timer buzzed, and she asked me to get the brownies out of the oven. "I haven't abandoned healthy eating altogether, but it's time to get reasonable. I watched Manley chew his tofu crab at dinner last night for five whole minutes. Then he had to wash it down with a big ol' swig of milk. I think that man would eat cardboard if he thought it would make me happy. Well, it's time I made him happy for a change. Tonight, it's lasagna with real Italian sausage and processed cheese. I get goose bumps just thinking about all that flavorful fat swirling around in my mouth. For dessert, I'll make a heart-shaped tiramisu."

"Why are you baking all this other stuff?"

"Roseanne was as twittery as a songbird over her caterer canceling for her speed-dating event, so I offered to help her out. By the way, do you think folks would like those adorable tuxedo strawberries I made a couple New Year's ago, the ones with chocolate buttons? I saw some luscious strawberries in the market this morning."

"When exactly is the speed-dating event?"

"I'm supposed to have the goodies at the skating rink by five."

"Tonight?"

Finally, a setting in which I felt comfortable—a roller skating rink. I skated in and out of the small tables on the rink floor to light the floating gardenia candles. The lights dimmed. A spotlight hit the mirrored ball. Over the speakers, "Only You" played. Instant mood. When a shaft of light pierced the darkness, I spun to skate backward to see who came through the door. It was Stefan. Roseanne walked toward him. We'd feared he would make an appearance, so we'd made a plan. I skated to Roseanne. Her hand trembled in mine, but when she spoke, her voice was strong. "You're not welcome at this event."

Stefan was all confidence with his wide smile and bobblehead cockiness. Roseanne held his gaze but didn't return his smile.

He looked at me and back to Roseanne. "What's this all about?" he finally asked.

"I have five new friends—Sally, Linda, Judi, Robin, and Polly," Roseanne said. "I think you know them, too."

"We never agreed to an exclusive relationship, Roseanne. I don't see what the problem is."

"You may never have explicitly said our relationship was exclusive, but you implied it."

"I'm sorry if desperation has colored your perceptions, but you can't blame me for that."

"You're right, I can't, but I can save the nine women I invited here tonight from being treated disrespectfully by you. I've invited a gentleman of character and dignity to take your place. You're free to go."

"That's ridiculous." He made a move toward the registration table. Roseanne stopped him with a hand to his chest.

"There is no longer a place for you at this event. It's time for you to go," she said without a hint of malice. She was good.

He held her gaze longer than necessary before turning and leaving the building.

Roseanne squeezed my hand before she let go. "I've been dreading that encounter all afternoon."

"You did good, girl friend. So who's the Mr. Wonderful you got to replace Stefan?"

"Who else? Larry."

Roseanne stood in the center of the rink with a microphone. "We have a few rules to keep this speed-dating event positive and pleasant for everyone. Please share first names only and refrain from giving your home address. You're all adults, so I'll leave it up to you when you want to disclose this information in the future, but it's prudent to take small steps at first. You have ten minutes to get to know the person across from you.

Mibby helped me come up with a few get-to-know-you questions that I've copied and set at each place. The ladies will stay in their seats, and the gentlemen will rotate from table to table when the disc jockey sounds the horn." She chewed on her lip for a while before she raised the microphone to her mouth again. "If you are here for any reason other than to pursue a relationship that is honoring to God and mutually beneficial, please leave now. Those remaining will applaud your honesty."

A few people coughed into their hands, but no one moved. "Good," she said. "Let's have a great time. Larry, will you pray for us?"

Larry left the pack of men and skated with long, easy strokes to where Roseanne stood. "Let's bow our heads. Father God, each person here is wondering right now why in the world they agreed to be here tonight. You know, don't you? We're lonely enough to put roller skates on and risk looking totally stupid for the chance of meeting that special someone. Lord, we vow to be honest and trusting, so any relationship started here tonight will have a good foundation. Bless us with fun and your presence. In Jesus' name, amen."

It was clear Don hadn't tried to roller skate in a long time. Two men flanked him to help him to my table. He looked to be about my height and wore a plaid button-down shirt of safe and masculine colors with Wrangler jeans. It was a lot of blue. He had almond-shaped eyes that could have been blue or brown. It was hard to tell in the low light. His nose, a perfect right triangle, overwhelmed his face.

"Are you a nurse?" he asked.

"No, I'm a garden designer."

"Oh. We might as well get this over with. Do you want to go first, or should I?"

"Go ahead."

"Okay then. My name is Don. I'm forty years old. My occupation is orthopedic shoe fitter. I only have one hobby, ham radio. I don't have any children. My marital status is divorced. It's been twelve years. Meatloaf is my favorite food, as long as it isn't too spicy."

Spicy meatloaf?

The more I looked at Don, the more he looked like Bradley. "Did you ever live in San Diego?" I asked.

"That isn't one of the questions."

"Sorry."

He ran a finger down the list of questions. "Let's see, where was I? What do I do for fun? I spend a lot of time on my ham radio. My last vacation was to the Rocky Mountain Ham Radio Association conference in Twin Falls. That's in Idaho. It's your turn."

Following Don's lead, I answered the get-to-know-you questions in order.

"It's too bad you're not a nurse," he said. "I'm a diabetic, and it would sure be nice to find someone who understood all about blood sugar." While Don explained the long-term health risks associated with diabetes, I watched Larry laugh across the rink at something a lady with big hair and expressive hands had said. He looked pretty good with his hair and beard newly trimmed.

"Do you eat sweets?" Don asked. "I have a hard time controlling my sugar levels if I don't eat correctly. You do cook, don't you? And some- times things go bad. Then I need someone to call 9-1-1."

A primordial scream welled up inside me. I prayed the horn would sound soon.

When Derek sat across from me, I was tempted to ask him if his mother knew where he was that night. He looked that young. Ky would have loved him—for a brother. In the summer, he was a river guide, and he lived in Telluride every winter to teach snowboarding. He hoped to qualify for the winter X Games in two events: slopestyle and superpipe. I had no idea what he was talking about, but it sounded painful.

"How old are you?" I asked.

"Thirty, man."

Have you ever sat still for three minutes? "Have you ever been married?"

"No way, but I have a kid."

Long before we reached this part of the conversation, I'd eliminated him as a prospect. We needed something neutral to talk about and fast. "Tell me about your kid."

"He's a cool little dude."

Next came Steve, age thirty-nine, whose idea of a great time was watching *Star Trek* reruns and eating Hungry Man dinners. He told me about his six children, none of whom lived with him: a seventeen-year-old girl living with his ex-girlfriend and her second husband in Maine, twin girls from his first marriage, and two boys and a girl from his third marriage.

Steve reached across the table to touch my hand. "As you can see, I haven't been the most successful husband in the world, but I'd love to try the kind of marriage God intended. I'd even like to try my hand at being a father again."

Run! "I wish you all the luck in the world."

Only one more contestant to go before the break and Louise's lemon scones.

"Hello, Mibby." Bill shook my hand. His hair was mostly gray but full, and his eyes were burnt-butter brown. "If you don't want to waste your time with an old geezer like me, I'd sure understand. I'm beginning to think my daughter lied about my age to get me into this thing. She's always hounding me to join the land of the living."

"That sounds familiar." His manner was so forthright, I felt comfortable asking his age.

"I'm fifty-six and a grandfather. Want to see some pictures?" He opened his wallet. "Here's Chloe; she's two and a spittin' image of her mother, my eldest daughter, Angela. This wrinkly thing is my newest grandson, Chad. I took this photograph just minutes after he was born. What an amazing experience. I call my daughter every day to thank her for including me in his birth. He's five months old now." Bill flipped the plastic sleeves of his wallet, stopping at each picture to share a name and a tidbit. "And last but not least, this is Sophie. At a mere eighteen months, she has stolen her grandpa's heart. She looks so much like my wife. Sometimes she'll look over her shoulder at me and smile like a little vixen. It's as if Janet is in the room with me." Bill slipped away to visit his memory for a moment. "I took my three kids and their families to Hawaii last winter. Sophie always had time for Grandpa's fishing stories and a nap in the hammock."

When the horn blew, Bill had just started to tell me about his wife's tragic stroke. "I guess you're saved by the bell, Mibby."

I held out one of my cards to Bill, the only card I'd handed out all evening. "My husband was fifty when he died."

"I'll put this behind Sophie's picture for safekeeping."

I introduced Bill to Louise's lemon scones. We sat away from the crowd to talk in a quiet place. Larry's booming laughter made us turn to see what was going on. A klatch of women, including Roseanne, stood around him.

"He seems like an affable fellow," Bill said.

"He's that, all right."

After the break, I talked with a guy whose goal in life was to eat at every McDonald's in the world. He got breathless telling me about the hot dog McNuggets he'd eaten in Wausau. He asked me if I liked to travel. I crossed my fingers and said no. Then came Sean, who went to the bathroom twice during our speed date. Frank tried to sell me mortgage insurance, and Chris asked me to tell him my testimony. That was nice. Herve didn't speak English very well, but he performed a mean sock puppet. When it was Larry's turn to come to my table, he was nowhere in sight. Roseanne's table was empty, too. All the way home, I batted away at the vision of Larry and Roseanne.

That's nuts.

~~~

Andrea selected a brown glass bead with a gold swirl and strung it on the jute necklace. "Out of ten guys, you gave your card to one. Let's see, that's a ten percent success rate. That has to be better than the national average. I think we should celebrate."

"And your friend Roseanne, how did she fare?" my mother asked.

I told Andrea and Mother about Roseanne leaving early and that Larry had never made it to my table.

"Roseanne and Larry? How cool is that?" Andrea said.

It wasn't cool at all. *Why do I feel like I'm being choked?* I mean, we were talking about Larry, right? Mr. Bluster? Mr. Do-funny-things-with-your-voice? I was so not jealous of Roseanne—not with Larry. *Get a grip!*

I needed to change the subject. A heap of macrame necklaces in harvest-colored jute filled the center of the kitchen table. "Are you building your inventory for Thanksgiving?" I asked.

"I always get a booth at the Harvest Home Festival," Mother said.

"Is that the festival in Santa Cruz?" Andrea asked.

"I don't know that one. I go to New Orleans."

My mother valued autonomy above everything else, and she shared few details of her life away from me, so I was forced to construct a life for her in my head. I imagined her sauntering each morning along sandy sidewalks to the pier, where a handful of benign craftspeople were tolerated and allowed to sell their trinkets. All day, I had her bantering with locals and pointing out the public restrooms to grateful tourists. As the sun dipped below the horizon, I pictured her stopping at the local market for fresh fish and a mango, or something even more exotic, for the next day's breakfast. She spent the evenings reading old books by candlelight. She did not stockpile jute necklaces and jet off to New Orleans.

"How long have you been doing that?" I asked.

She looked at the ceiling. "I think I started going in '98. No, it was '97."

"How do you get there?"

"I ride my broom, how else?"

"No, really, how do you get there?"

"I travel with a circle of friends."

"Do I know any of them?"

"Bré . . . Mibby, what are you trying to ask me?"

"It's just that I had no idea you went to New Orleans every year. You would think . . ."

There was a honed edge to Mother's question. "What would I think?"

Andrea spoke first, "Harvest Home is a Wiccan celebration of the aging goddess, isn't it?"

Mother looked from Andrea to me and back to Andrea. She spoke her words carefully. "Harvest Home is on the autumnal equinox. It's a time of balance; the day is equally light and dark. We celebrate the bounty of our harvests and prepare for the coming dark."

I had to ask. "Are you there to sell your necklaces or to participate?"

Hands around the table stilled and settled into laps.

"I go to sell my necklaces," she said. "And you don't have to worry; I haven't said a word to Ky. I knew you wouldn't approve. It's been so good to be here, to see how well you're managing, even during these difficult days. You have so many good people around you. Please don't . . ."

Within seconds my mind had distilled my choices down to two words—condemn or love. That night, I chose to simply love my mother. If there was a spiritual battle raging in the heavens over my mother selling necklaces to witches, the Victorious Warrior would have to go to battle for me. I was tired, and my mother, for the first time in my remembering, seemed willing to give me an exit date.

"Can you stay until Ky goes back to school?" I asked.

"I have a flight on the fourth."

AUG 25

Not much to write. My garden is in a serious state of neglect. Time for the weeds to know who's boss. Maybe next week.

In four short days the Dos Rios Garden Design contest would be judged. I was hopeful. Roseanne's garden was coming together. The perennials in the rock garden and the ornamental grasses around the boulders needed to be planted. After that, we would spread the cedar mulch. Larry whistled the same unrecognizable tune over and over. I was about to tell him to stick a sock in it when he said, "You're awfully quiet today."

I smoothed the soil around a Sonoran Sunset hyssop before I answered. "I'm thinking about what still needs to be done."

"That was some event Roseanne put on last night. Every one of those women gave me their card."

I didn't.

"They were just being nice," he said, but he was smiling to himself. There was that ego again.

I pressed the shovel into the soil. "I only gave out one card."

"To that old guy?"

"Bill isn't old."

Larry tipped a blanket flower out of its pot. "He has to be sixty."

"He's fifty-six." I tamped the soil around a hummingbird trumpet. "He's enthusiastic about life, and it's clear he loves his family."

"You learned all that in ten minutes?"

I lifted another shovelful of soil out of the hole I was digging. "We had lunch."

"Oh?"

"I met him at Piñon Mesa Country Club. A client lives around the corner, so it was pretty convenient."

Larry's voice stepped up an octave. "What's with you and old guys?"

"Age has nothing to do with it. He's a nice guy. He has his head on straight."

"You mean he's *safe,* don't you?"

"Safe? Like he's had all of his shots?"

"Safe as in a nice car and a stock portfolio, parental—you know, a guy with enough money to join a country club. Tell me, while you were eating your shrimp cocktail, were you looking around thinking you could get used to taking Louise there for lunch?"

How . . . ? I jabbed my shovel into the soil. "What are you implying?"

"You're looking for someone to be your father."

"I had a father—a very good father. You don't know what you're talking about."

"I'd say I've struck a nerve. A younger man would be too risky for you. You want to be taken care of."

"I want no such thing." I slid a creeping thyme out of its pot and crammed it in its hole. By the time I'd backfilled the hole, I had my verbal right hook ready. "You're the fine one to talk to me about avoiding risk. You hide behind your beard."

"Did Bill tell you that?"

"Your mom told me about Michelle."

Larry's eyes were two hard slits. "Her name's Melissa, and you don't know what you're talking about."

"You're not the only amateur psychologist around here. It's as plain as the beard on your face. You're hiding behind a mask. As long as you're behind all that hair . . ." And then it was clear to me. Larry hadn't been flirting with me at all. He'd been pushing me away. "Love is risk, right, Larry?"

"Are you through?"

"One more thing. Keep your nose out of my business."

"You can bring up the past but I can't?"

"Then let's not talk about the past. Let's stick with today. The shave is on me." I dropped my shovel. "Let's go."

His face reddened from his mustache up. "Okay, you've had your say. Pick up your shovel and let's get back to work."

I tapped my watch. "We're ahead of schedule. There's a walk-in barber by the college. I'll drive."

"I'd appreciate it if you'd drop it."

"What are you afraid of, Larry?"

"I'm not afraid of anything."

"Really?"

"Really!"

"Aren't you afraid you'll fall in love only to be left at the altar again?"

He threw his shovel across the yard. "Enough!" He ran his fingers through his hair and looked at his hands before he dropped them to his side. When he spoke, his voice was barely a whisper. "I think I better leave the rest of this to you." He walked briskly for the back gate and the Sweet Suzy truck. The slump of his shoulders nearly burst my heart. I called after him but he didn't turn back, so I ran to catch up.

"Larry!"

He turned. His eyes glistened with tears. I had to look away. "You probably don't know about this, but I actually met your Scott. My dad asked me to go on a men's retreat. I didn't want to go. I was working in Virginia. But Dad was insistent, so I met up with the guys in Estes Park. Scott drove over with my dad."

I remembered Scott going to that retreat. He'd come back changed. He started a men's accountability group and stepped in as a Sunday school teacher for the middle school boys. But the change I noticed most was that he started coming home earlier from work. Larry had been with Scott?

He continued, "At dinner one night, Scott told me how sweet and funny and hardworking his wife was." Larry's words, raw with disappointment, sliced right through me. "I thought I saw all of that in you, too."

AUG
27

*Harvested a few radishes—woody and bitter,
very disappointing. Foliage looks great,
though. Weeds still reign in the garden.*

Roseanne opened the glossy red door of Phoebe's new playhouse. "Would you believe Larry made all this furniture?" Roseanne's voice caught. "I never knew there were people like Larry . . . and you. Phoebe and me . . . we're going to be okay."

I patted the seat of a tiny blue chair to test its sturdiness.

"Don't worry, Larry sat on it. It's as solid as a rock," Roseanne said. "The playhouse came this morning. I'd just put Phoebe down for a nap when a giant flatbed truck brought it up the alley. All I could see was the roof of the playhouse over the fence. Did you see the cedar shakes? He cut them to scale and everything. Anyway, a crane lifted the playhouse into place, but Larry made it bigger than we'd planned. The driver dug up the rose for me so it wouldn't get squished, and then he replanted it. Do you think the rose will be okay?"

I assured her it would.

She ran her hand over the tiny table. "Feel this table. The finish is like glass. Larry won't let me give him any money. How will I ever repay him?"

We made our way out of the hot structure.

Roseanne continued, "All through the garden installation, he worked a full day delivering his Sweet Suzy stuff, and then he came here to work with you, and then he went home to his workshop to build the house and furniture. He's amazing. What a heart he has."

If Roseanne was trying to make me feel like a fool, she was late. I already did.

On the patio, she plumped a pillow on the chaise and told me to sit. "After all your hard work, you deserve to be the first to enjoy the beauty of the new garden. Sister friend, I feel like I've landed in a dream. It hasn't been that long since I would have described my life as a dank pit. Now look at it. It's beautiful . . . on the inside and outside. I'll be right back."

The glare off the red door hurt my eyes, so I closed my eyes to shut out the playhouse. I listened to water splashing in the fountain and breathed in the sweetness of the wet mulch. But I couldn't keep my eyes closed for long. Most of the plants were blooming, including the Coral Canyon twinspur with its pink fairy-hat flowers and the Coronado hyssop with its sunset-colored lanterns. Next year, they would almost touch and bloom from late spring to early fall. What a couple of showoffs. It wouldn't be long before the garden would be lush enough to screen the cozy niches and Phoebe would be riding her tricycle to the playhouse.

It is good.

Roseanne put a tray down beside me and put her cheek to mine. "I'm not at all afraid of the winter anymore. Goods things will happen for both of us, I just know it."

I wanted to believe her, but she didn't know how I'd hurt Larry. I didn't deserve good things.

"I have some great tuna salad in the frig. Can you stay for lunch?" she asked.

"I can't. Margaret and Walter are getting married this afternoon."

~⁓

Just as Walter and Margaret were introduced as man and wife, I heard a truck drive by, out of sight, in front of the house they would now share.

It sounded just like a Sweet Suzy delivery truck. My tummy fluttered. At such a poetic moment, I was sure I had been the only one to notice.

Margaret's daughter-in-law, whom I only knew as "the floozy," sobbed exuberantly as she joined her husband to congratulate the bride and groom. Margaret returned the girl's embrace and rolled her eyes when she saw I was watching.

"Do y'all think the daughter-in-law's crying because God hath wrought a wondrous love or because Colorado law makes Walter the sole beneficiary upon Margaret's homegoing?" asked Louise, not quite under her breath. The floozy paused her histrionics long enough to turn and sneer at Louise.

After the marriage license had been signed and pictures snapped, Walter and Margaret sliced through the zucchini bread. A bevy of neighbor girls delivered the bread with sliced peaches and crème fraiche. Despite the fact that neither Margaret nor Walter had ever met Larry, I looked for his coppery hair above the crowd. What was that all about?

"Who you lookin' for, sweet pea?" asked Louise.

I stood up. "I'm looking for the punch bowl."

"The invitation said no presents," Margaret scolded, but her eyes sparkled with intrigue.

Louise fastened a blindfold over Margaret's eyes. "This isn't a present, exactly."

"Then exactly what is it?" Walter asked.

"It's a surprise," Louise said. "Will you let Mibby blindfold you?"

When Margaret said his name as soft as a prayer, Walter turned his back to me so I could pin the dish towel in place. We led the new couple through the kitchen and to the bedroom.

"This is so exciting," Margaret said.

Walter felt his way down the hall. "It won't be exciting until I know where you're taking me."

"Us, Walter dear," Margaret said. "They're taking us."

A small smile played at the corners of Walter's mouth. "Lead on."

We had to stop for Walter to adjust his suspenders and for Margaret to whisper something in his ear. At the door to the bedroom, Louise said, "Y'all said you weren't going on a honeymoon, so we brought the honeymoon to you."

While Walter had scooped ice cream for the neighborhood children and Margaret supervised the loading of the flowerpots to be taken to nursing homes, Louise and I performed an extreme makeover of their bedroom. Honestly, it was mostly Louise, and she'd outdone herself with a Battenberg dust ruffle and a plump comforter and a matelassé folded at the foot of the bed. A mound of pillows with lace flounces and ribbons finished off the bed like whipped cream on pumpkin pie. Then we'd filled the room with long-stemmed red roses and enough burning candles to raise the temperature ten degrees.

Louise loosened Margaret's blindfold while I helped Walter. They took in the room with wide-eyed amazement.

"I've never seen anything so beautiful in all my life," Margaret said.

Walter's ears glowed red, but he was smiling.

"Louise," I said, "I think we best be getting along, don't y'all think so?"

SEPT

4

The weeds are shriveling thanks to my secret chemical cocktail. Next year, start applications earlier, even if it means doing so in the extreme heat.

"Ladies and gentlemen, gardeners all," Marta Cunningham, garden club president said, raising her arm to draw the crowd's attention. "On behalf of the homeowner, Mrs. Roseanne Mitchell, it's my pleasure to welcome you to the awards reception for the sixth annual Dos Rios Garden Club design contest."

Cameras beeped and whirred, and the small audience of garden club members clapped politely. Roseanne turned to smile warmly at the applauding crowd. Phoebe sat on her mother's hip. Mother and daughter wore matching sundresses of pink gingham and embroidered daisies. Phoebe twirled a strand of Roseanne's hair around her finger as she eyed the crowd warily. Larry stood beside them dressed in Dockers and a golf shirt. The work in Roseanne's garden had hardened his middle.

"Never in the history of the contest has the new-garden division been so difficult to judge. There were only a few points difference between first and second place. Both entries represent strong schools of design theory for arid climates. I must say, we discovered how passionately those theories can be defended when the judges go behind closed doors." Several onlookers laughed into their hands. "I'm happy to say we are all still speaking to one another." Another flutter of laughs.

"Seriously, look around you. You're standing in the future of garden design for our area. The designer balanced the requirements of water conservation and aesthetics perfectly. And so it is my pleasure to present this award for exemplary execution of sound xeriscaping principles in design and installation. Mibby Garrett, please step forward to claim your second-place ribbon."

"Second place," Ky grumbled.

I shot him a warning glare as I took the ribbon from Marta.

"Well done, Mibby." I started to return to my place beside Ky, but Marta stopped me. For my hearing only, she said, "Why don't you wait here while I introduce your associate?" And then to the audience, she said, "Mrs. Mitchell's garden placed in two categories, a grand accomplishment for a designer's first year in the competition. For his charming and beautifully crafted playhouse, I award Larry McManus of Orchard City first prize for outstanding achievement in garden structures. Congratulations, Mr. McManus!"

An intense man with a camera the size of a toaster said, "Hold that pose. Millie, move in toward Mr. McManus. A bit closer. Look at Marta. Smile." Once the camera flashed, Larry bolted back to Roseanne, and I returned to Ky and my mother.

Ky was indignant. "Mom, there's no way we should have gotten second place. All that other guy used were rocks and cactus and bleached skulls. And did you see the ore car? It's no wonder they didn't want to have the reception there. It's lethal, man." He expelled his disgust in a sigh that could be heard by all present. "This is so bogus."

I should have given him a lecture on gracious losing, but hearing him whine about the way *we* had been treated warmed me. Besides, when Ky was right, he was right. Ken Doddard's landscape design discouraged rather than invited human involvement, but the design still represented for many what gardens should look like in the arid west. Being critiqued by a peevish teenager wasn't going to change anyone's mind.

"You two don't have to stay," I said to Ky and Mother. "It's all downhill from here."

"Cool," Ky said and worked through the crowd. My mother threw her arm around my waist and put her cheek to mine. "I'm so proud of you."

We stood that way for a long moment. She kissed my cheek. "How long does it take to get to the airport?"

"Five minutes. Maybe you should stop by the Pampered Cow on the way home to say good-bye to Andrea. I think she has something for you."

"I'll see you in a couple hours then." And she kissed my cheek again.

"Excuse me, Mibby, could we have a word?" Christopher Stohl gestured me away from the refreshment table. He was accompanied by a man too conscientious about his shoes to be a gardener. Christopher introduced the man as Rod Kittenger, a golf pro developing an upscale golf course and housing development in Orchard City. Christopher made sure I understood that the man was also an old friend of the Stohl family.

Mr. Kittenger shook my hand firmly. "I hate developments that compete with the natural landscape for attention, don't you? What we got here in western Colorado is God's own handiwork. I want to build homes that respect what He designed. That includes the homes' landscapes and the common areas. Can you get on board with something like that, Mibby?"

I wasn't sure what he was asking, but I agreed with him in principle. "Sure."

"That's good, because I like what you've done here. You're a smart lady, and I like having smart people working around me. I'll have my architect get in touch with you." With that, Mr. Kittenger excused himself.

Christopher moved to follow him, but I caught him by the arm. "What's with the architect?"

"You've just been retained to design gardens for the most exclusive development project to hit Orchard City, but I can't talk about it now. Rod doesn't like to be kept waiting. Come by the garden center tomorrow." And he was gone.

As I watched Christopher trot to catch up with Mr. Kittenger, I struggled to keep my expectations realistic. Until I had a contract in my hand, there were no guarantees I'd see any design work from Mr. Kittenger. Still, his enthusiasm had cheered me.

Thanks, Lord.

For the next two hours, I answered questions, mostly giving common and botanical names for the plants I'd used in Roseanne's garden. Not surprisingly, I spent some time justifying my use of several less-known varieties of perennials. After a round or two of good-natured give and take, most folks asked me to write the plant name on a scrap of paper, and I knew I'd won them over. One plant I was sure to see all over town was the hummingbird trumpet, my star performer. My selection of mulching material proved especially contentious. There was no one as opinionated as a hardcore gardener.

Larry stood by the playhouse, welcoming people to step inside for a tour. Every time I looked his way, another knot of people stood around him, listening intently or laughing with him over some joke. When Roseanne wasn't refilling cookie trays or answering questions about her garden, she made sure Larry and I had something to drink.

"Do you want me to bring you a chair? You've been standing out here for a long time," she said.

My feet throbbed. I looked at my watch. "I only have to stay for another half hour. I can make it."

"Is everything okay? You seem—I don't know—far away."

Three women stood at a sociable distance waiting for our conversation to end. They looked ready to pounce. I recognized one of them, Janey Lindquist, the undisputed queen of succulents in the valley. By the conceited rise of her brow, I knew she thought my choice of Mexican bush sage was challengeable.

"I don't know what happened between you two," Roseanne whispered in my ear, "but before you go, you should talk to Larry."

I promised her I would, because I'd already promised myself I would apologize to him for my cruel remarks.

When Roseanne left to refill a cookie tray, Janey stepped closer and cleared her throat, "You know *Salvia leucantha* will never make it through the winter."

Some people are so predictable.

～

Larry opened the playhouse door for two women who bobbed and clucked like hens. When the second one wedged herself inside, Larry wiped his brow with a hanky.

I startled him when I touched his elbow. "Congratulations on your first place."

"I've gotten four solid orders for playhouses today. I didn't plan on going into the playhouse business, but I guess I am. Being in the wood-shop will keep me out of trouble this winter." His voice got soft and earnest. "I'm sorry you didn't get first place."

I'd had a couple days to get used to the idea since Marta called to tell me about the second-place finish. At first, I'd felt like Ky, but then Marta had suggested having the reception in Roseanne's garden. It was like giving her unofficial approval on a silver platter. Having that kind of exposure was better than winning.

"I've given out quite a few business cards," I said, "and a photographer from *Sunset* is arriving tomorrow to take pictures and to interview Roseanne and me."

"That's good."

The two women squeezed out of the playhouse and asked for one of Larry's cards. "My, you're a talented fellow," the lady in the denim jumper said.

Only a few people lingered in the garden. I swallowed hard to prepare myself to apologize to Larry, but he spoke first. "I've wanted to call. I just never . . . I feel real bad about leaving you to finish the garden on your own. Listen, I had no right to give you a hard time about Bill. You're a grown woman. You know what's best."

Do I?

"I hope you can forgive me," he said.

"I'm the one who should apologize. I said some pretty stupid things." He offered me his hand. "Friends?"

∼

Sitting in the airport waiting lounge, I remembered the day my mother left for Oregon when I was eleven. I'd pulled my suitcase from under the bed and threw open the lid. I crammed in all of my underwear, but no undershirts, and my favorite shorts and the three T-shirts that weren't hand-me-downs from Margot. My doll wouldn't fit, so I added a pair of pajamas and snapped the lid closed. I set the suitcase by the door and held Thumbelina to my chest. It was important that nothing put drag on the silver thread that tied me to my mother, so I lay on my bed to wait for her to come and get me.

Pipes groaned in the wall as Margot turned off the spigot in the bathroom. In my parents' room, drawers opened and were slammed shut again. Margot splashed her bath water. The longer I lay there, the harder it became to expand my chest to breathe. The front door opened and closed, opened and closed, opened and closed. And then it was still. The silence pressed my heart like a balloon between two strong hands. I jumped from the bed to return my suitcase to its hiding place before Margot saw it. She barged through the door with her hair wrapped in a towel and pulled Thumbelina from my arms. . . .

A tinny voice announced the boarding of the plane to Denver, pulling me out of my reverie. Beside me, Mother said, "You've been staring at that travel poster for twenty minutes. What are you thinking about?"

"The day you left for Oregon."

She straightened her skirt and read her boarding pass again. "That was a long time ago."

"I packed my bag and waited for you to come and get me. I thought you'd take me with you."

A groan as deep as a well came from my mother. I stifled the urge to apologize. Instead, I asked the question I'd been afraid to ask. "Why was it so easy for you to leave?"

"It wasn't easy. It was never, ever easy. My mother . . . " She said *mother* like she'd bitten into a pithy apple.

"Your mother? Didn't she die before I was born?" I asked.

"What do you know about my childhood?"

"You were born in Michigan, on a farm, but your daddy sold things. I don't remember what."

"Church pews. He sold church pews from Maine to California to Alaska."

"So he was gone a lot?"

"Our home was such a dark place. We weren't allowed to have toys. According to my father, make-believe was evil. If he'd ever found out that I sailed the prairie grasses to faraway lands with chocolate cities . . ." Mother shuddered. "My brother entertained himself by tormenting me. The night before I graduated from junior high, he cut a handful of hair to my scalp while I slept. Mother wouldn't let me go to graduation looking like that, even though I made myself a hat out of an old coat. There were worse things. . . .

"Mother had spells," she continued. "I suppose they call them something else now and have pills to take, but back then, they were spells. We watched her like we watched the sky for a coming storm. We got good at reading her face. When she looked half scared and half expectant, we pulled the shades down and took off our shoes. We ate with our hands so we wouldn't make any noise. One day, my brother came home from the field. When he'd left, my mother was baking a cake and whistling. He rushed into the kitchen for his piece of cake. That's where he found her, sleeping on the floor like a cat. When he crept out the kitchen door, he stepped on the squeaky plank by the buffet and woke her. She jumped up, grabbed him by the hair, and dragged him to the fireplace. He was twelve, big enough to break away. When I screamed for him to run, he put a finger to his lips. I ran to my room and covered my head with my pillow, but I could still hear the thud of the poker against his body."

Her voice cracked and she turned her face to wipe her tears away. Mother's story didn't surprise me. I'd seen pictures of her mother. She'd looked like an empty house. *But still . . .*

"Your mother didn't leave us for Oregon. You did," I said.

"Yes, but I lived in fear that something might trigger her wickedness in me. I could never be sure."

"So you left us?"

We waited in silence. Passengers bound to Denver said their good-byes and loaded their carry-on luggage onto the security scanner.

"You have things to do," she said. "You don't have to wait with me."

"All I ask is that you look back to see me waving."

≈

"What a load of—"

"No it's not, Margot. In her mind, leaving us was the most loving thing she could've done for us. It made her different than our grandmother." I'd come to the garden to talk to Margot on the phone in private, but now Blink stood before me with a new chew bone, whining plaintively.

"She was no victim, Mibby. Dad adored her. We adored her. She left because she wanted to, nothing more."

"She never hit us."

"Don't you remember tiptoeing around the house to keep her from leaving? How is that different? One false move and she was gone."

Blink looked at me from behind a lilac. When he saw me watching him, he cried pitifully and walked deeper into the shrub bed.

"Margot, what does it get us to hang on to the past? She's the only mother we'll ever have. Maybe it's time to forgive her."

Blink dug at the soil below the flowering almond but only until he noticed I was still on the bench. He trotted toward me, stopped just out of reach, and moaned. I waved him off, but he persisted.

"Forgive her?" Margot said. "Are you nuts?"

"Love doesn't keep a record of wrongs."

"Are you quoting Scripture at me?"

"It makes sense, doesn't it? No one can bear the full weight of their mistakes. The load would crush us. Now that we're adults and we don't depend on Mother to take care of us, maybe it's time to give her a fresh start."

"Has she gotten religion? Is that what this is all about? Are the two of you sitting around reading Scripture to each other? And now you're out to get me?"

Blink collapsed at my feet to gnaw on his bone.

"I honestly don't know what she believes."

"Right."

The dial tone hummed in my ear.

≈

Ky slammed his door, so I stomped down the hall to my bedroom and did the same.

There!

I'd just confiscated the modem—*again*—for excessive and unsupervised use, and his skateboard was back in my closet because I'd caught him building a ramp to jump over Blink.

My rational side tapped me on the shoulder. *Is this about Ky or do your feelings of inadequacy have more to do with your mother leaving and your sister hanging up on you?* Of course this was all about Ky. He'd completely disregarded the household rules and put Blink in mortal danger. Someone had to protect the dog.

I spread my collection of teenage parenting books across the bed and played eenie meenie miney mo to choose a book to bolster my sagging resolve. The first book to be eliminated was *The Encyclopedia for Parents with Teenagers*. Just reading the title made me yawn. Next to go was *Something's Gotta Give: Negotiating Through the Teenage Years*. Too fatalistic. The lucky winner was *Fly Your Teenager to Maturity*. Flying sounded fast.

In the chapter dealing with natural consequences, the author wrote, "Consistent repetition of negative behaviors points to a general lack of respect for the parent's authority. Job one is earning it back." I closed the book to read the title again. Under the block letters, a shiny yellow biplane tipped its wings to the reader. The passengers, a teenage boy in the front and his parents in the back, waved and smiled. They were the absolute pictures of frivolity.

I turned back to the text. "During preflight checks, the pilot checks the integrity of the plane's joints. In the same way, the parent of a rebellious teenager must check the soundness of the discipline plan and tighten as necessary." This wasn't helping. I already saw myself as a curmudgeon, and I didn't like it. Ky liked it even less.

I knocked on his door and spoke through the closed door, "Meet me in the backyard in a half hour." I knew better than to wait for an answer.

I pulled a shower cap over my hair and swiped at the cobwebs in the back of the garage with a toilet brush. It took a while, but I managed to wrangle the charcoal grill free from its place behind our camping equipment. I pulled it to the middle of the poop deck, loaded it with my entire library of parenting books, and doused the books with lighter fluid. I lit a match and called Ky on my cell phone from the backyard.

"Are you hungry?" I asked.

"Where are you?"

"Look out your window."

He lifted his shade. "Cool. What are you burning?"

"Don't worry; it's just a bunch of stupid books. I thought a wienie roast would be fun."

"Can we make s'mores?"

"I've got the stuff right here."

The phone went dead.

Minutes later, Ky lay beside me on the blanket I'd spread on the grass. "We should have waited for Andrea to get home," he said, licking his fingers.

"I wanted to talk to you alone."

He sat up.

"Relax, it's not one of those kinds of talks. I'm the one apologizing. I completely forgot what it's like to be a kid. With the heat and the drought, it's been a hard summer, and when I saw you disappearing into your computer, I panicked. I don't regret limiting the time you have on the Internet, but I do regret not doing it in a respectful way. You deserve that much."

Ky turned to look at me.

"And, son, we haven't talked about the night we fought over the CD. I never intended for you to get hurt. I let my anger get away from me. Can you forgive me?"

"Sure."

"Sure?"

"Sure. It's cool."

"Really?"

"Yeah."

That was easy. On to the next item on the agenda. "I'm so clueless about how to help you through the teenage years. It's a jungle out there."

"I'll be okay."

His confidence was contagious. "You will, won't you?" And then I remembered all the milestones of high school—sports tryouts and his first driver's license and dances and traveling with his baseball team and choosing a college and maybe a girlfriend or two. *Yikes!* "I sure wish your dad was here."

"You're doing okay."

"Really?"

"Sure. You're a little weird sometimes, but most mothers are."

"Thanks. It's good to know I'm inside the bubble on weirdness."

"Don't let it go to your head."

"Too late."

Blink trotted back from walking the perimeter of the yard and plopped down by Ky. The dog rolled to his back and offered his belly for a rub.

"I'm going to make you a promise, son. No, make that three promises. First of all, you can tell me anything. I can't promise that I won't get angry, but I can promise you I'll treat you with respect. That means no more sarcasm."

"Is that one or two promises?"

I bit my tongue. "That's one, actually."

"It's just that I'm expecting a call from Salvador."

"I'll try to make this quick."

"Thanks."

"Also, I'm going to trust you to learn from your own mistakes, but I'm going to love you enough to step in when you're heading for big trouble."

"That was definitely two promises. I heard a promise to trust and a promise to love."

Easy. "Ky?"

"Okay, okay."

"And last, I promise to enjoy you, even when you're less than enjoyable. We'll take time to be together for no other reason than to appreciate each other's company."

"Is that what roasting wienies over burning books is all about?"

"Yep."

"That's cool."

He lay down by Blink with his hands behind his head.

"I thought you were waiting for a phone call," I said.

"Salvador will leave a message."

I lay beside Ky in the fading light. We talked about the start of school in a few days. He admitted to worrying about getting to his locker between classes and remembering the combination, so he planned on carrying all his books. I suggested a lock with a key, which he dismissed as a dumb idea. The sky dimmed and Jupiter appeared.

"Mom?"

"Yeah?"

"I took the money out of your purse."

"I know."

"I'll pay it back."

"I figured you would."

"I'm real sorry."

"I know."

We lay there until a breeze stirred the ashes and a column of sparks rose above us.

"There's something else," he said.

"Shoot."

"Grandma let me go to the skate park while you were working."

The neighborhood owl hooted.

"Are you angry?" he asked.

"Yep."

"You promised . . ."

"I'm glad you told me."

"Does that mean you aren't going to trust me like you said?"

"It means it's going to be harder is all."

"And you should probably know—"

"Is whatever you're about to tell me going to require me to hire a lawyer?"

"No."

"Then let's pretend it never happened. I'm new at this no-sarcasm thing. It's going to take me a while to get up to speed."

A siren and the deep honk of a fire engine sounded in the distance. I took Ky's hand. "I'm going to pray for you."

" 'Kay."

"Lord, bless Ky as he starts high school. Help him to remember his locker combination, give him more cool teachers than dorky ones, and give him a good friend. Stay near to him. Increase his faith. Fill his life with love. Amen."

OCT

9

Planted the bulbs today and topped them with pansies to sparkle up the beds for fall— and next spring. I want it to be October forever!

Long fingers of light carried dancing shadows into the house, and the colors suppressed by the saddling heat of summer finally emerged—coralbells, delphiniums, red-hot pokers, pincushion flowers, purple coneflowers, and whirling butterflies. Even the roses encored their colors.

As the nights cooled, ash leaves like golden coins littered the ground, and the Engleman ivy blushed scarlet red. Maybe a flock of cedar waxwings would stop by again to dine on the clusters of red berries in the hawthorn. My favorite, the autumn purple ash, deepened its hue, and startling splashes of vibrant yellow appeared among its leaves. And finally, the globe willows paled in the cold. The optimism of a pair of sparrows previewing a birdhouse for next spring made me smile.

The days were warm enough for short sleeves, and the nights had cooled for deep, restful sleep. At least, that's what I'd heard from Louise. Autumn's elaborate display, to be completely truthful, only taunted me with the coming months of winter, when the days would only grow shorter.

I dropped wearily onto the family room sofa.

Take a nap.

Ky will be home soon.

Rest.

He'll be hungry, too.

Lie down.

All I do is toss and turn.

I'm waiting.

I lay down and closed my eyes. Within a breath, I was back on the storm-tossed ship, only this time, I crouched on the deck halfway between the mast and the hatch. A wave swamped the deck and I slid to the rail. The boat rose on a wave and the water receded, so I scrambled for the hatch and caught its handle. It swung open. I was off my feet but I clung tightly. If blessing came from being close to Jesus, I was determined to leave the storm behind. With the strength of dreams, I pulled myself up. I stooped to step through the hatch and into the golden light of a lantern. Toward the prow, a man wrapped in a blanket lay sleeping on a pile of nets. When my feet touched the hull, he awoke and rose to one elbow. He opened the blanket for me to join him.

You will arrive on the other side of the lake upright and whole, Mibby. Come and rest.

And still I hesitated. To choose rest was to trust God inside the storm. I didn't like storms. I wanted a storm-free life. But even more, I wanted to be upright and whole. I ran to lie with Him under the blanket like two spoons in the drawer. The wind buffeted the tiny boat, but now it was no more threatening than Mr. Toad's Wild Ride. I fell asleep thinking I should have taken a nap a lot sooner.

~⌒

My mouth started watering the moment I stepped into Chez Ami with Louise. The air was thick with chocolate and dark-roasted coffee and sweet cream. I considered ordering one of everything from the refrigerated case, but Louise ordered a sensible raspberry tart, so I limited myself to several *profiteroles au chocolat,* a couple lemon almond madeleines, and a coffee with heavy cream—and two packets of sugar. "Almonds are good for the heart," I said, taking a bite of a madeleine.

"Funny you should say that, sweet pea."

I worked the cream filling of a profiterole against the roof of my mouth.

Louise was still opening her napkin. "Sugar, if I'm pryin', you know you can tell me to zip my lips and I won't breathe another word."

Uh-oh.

"I haven't seen you and Larry together in a long time."

"Why would you?"

She stuck a single raspberry with her fork. "I would have sworn you two . . ."

"He's pretty chummy with Roseanne."

"Really?"

I dipped a madeleine in my coffee. "They spent most of their time together at the Dos Rios reception."

"That was ages ago. Have you talked to Roseanne?"

Roseanne had left several messages on my answering machine right after the reception but nothing recently.

Louise squinted at me over her coffee. "I'm not usually wrong about these things."

"There may have been a time . . . but now I'm content to see this season of my life as a time to draw near to God. I'm reading my Bible more and getting serious about making time in my day to pray. It's made such a difference. A man—any man—would be nothing but a distraction to me right now. I wouldn't be surprised if God has chosen the single life for me. Remember, you're the one who told me I needed to take a nap with Jesus."

"Oh, brother."

"What? This is monumental." So I told Louise how I'd come home from church that morning and felt God urging me to rest and how wildly the boat had churned under my feet, but even so, I was able to go into the hull and lie down with Jesus. "I even fell asleep."

"La-de-dah. Sugar, it's time to jump out of the boat and dance on the waves." She frowned down hard on her next thought. "I wonder . . ."

I stood up fast enough to wobble the small table. "*No wondering,*

Louise. I can't. I've worked too hard to—" A patio full of people looked back at me over their newspapers. I turned and started for home.

Louise matched my pace. "To shut down your heart? That's never God's plan. What's really going on here?"

"I'd rather not talk about it."

"You can tell me anything."

"Louise, you're prying, and you promised you wouldn't."

I pictured one of those little yappy dogs digging up the petunia bed until he found his bone. That was Louise. "Tell me," she said.

"Larry and I had a fight." Louise blinked, waiting for the rest of the story, so I told her how ugly I'd been to Larry about being dumped by Melissa and how he'd thrown his shovel and left. "We talked at the awards reception. I asked him to forgive me and he did, but I haven't seen him since."

"Do I hear you saying that since you kicked Larry like a dog, you don't deserve his love?"

I had to close my eyes against the truth of what she'd said.

"Sweet pea, Jesus already died for your sins. All that's left is to forgive yourself and live a life of love."

~

I nestled the last of the Tête-à-Tête daffodil bulbs into the shallow bowl I'd dug near the back porch steps. The south-facing bed warmed early in the spring, so the tiny daffodils would be blooming for Easter, I hoped. I tamped the soil over the bulbs and sighed. Blink cocked his head, but when he saw I hadn't unearthed his bones, he lay down again. And I joined him. After the summer's fierce heat, the benevolence of the October sun held me like a robin's egg that had fallen from its nest.

All around me, the perennials wounded by the intense summer heat still bore their scorched leaves, and yet they bloomed, long past their usual season, though their flowers were smaller and less numerous. A single Amber Queen rose bloomed on its central cane, taller than the rest and startling in its vibrancy, and a Stella d'Oro daylily reprised its flowers. To see these particular flowers so late in October was strange, yet hopeful. And hope was a very good thing.

I let myself imagine the kind of Mibby who would love Larry. I would have to rise while it was still dark to make him breakfast before he went off to the bakery. I would have to be content to watch him walk away with Ky to places I couldn't go. There would be times when I would have to console him over the betrayal of his brother and wonder if he still loved Melissa. On Sundays, Connie would invite us for dinner and always have a pie cooling on the counter. At the end of a work day, we'd both be tired, but Larry would help me make dinner and offer to do the dishes. If he didn't, we'd eat off of paper plates, the paper-thin ones that come a hundred to a package. I'd walk side by side with Larry, and sometimes he'd have to lean on me. And with a subtle swipe of my hand across my chin, he would know to brush crumbs out of his beard. When he got blustery, I'd have to listen to what he was really trying to say so I wouldn't hurt his feelings. We'd live in a smaller house, probably never have a new car, and vacations would be in tents along wild streams. The house would be filled with dahlias from July to September.

I took in the bulkiness of my home against the broad blue sky. I remembered my grandmother saying that a small home was easier to keep clean. She was right, of course. When I imagined Larry's voice saying good morning to me through the mist of my dreams, my heart fluttered, and then I cried for what I had carelessly thrown away.

When the tears stopped, I prayed, "Lord, I'm very sorry I missed the love you sent my way. Next time—if there is a next time—please mark him with a big red X."

OCT
23

Wind blew a storm in last night. Woke to rain and it hasn't stopped. Hallelujah! Planned on raking leaves—my heart's not broken. There's always tomorrow.

I dusted off the last pair of Scott's golf shoes and added them to the black garbage bag along with all of his other shoes and socks and belts and about forty white hankies. I cinched the bag closed, and for the umpteenth time that day, the tears flowed. Nothing is better for drying tears than a man's hanky, so I reopened the bag and loaded Scott's hankies into the drawer of my nightstand.

Scott's closet was empty, save for a pile of hangers lying on the floor like an old bone yard. His clothing now filled boxes and garbage bags around the bedroom, ready to be taken to the hospice thrift store. I would ask Ky to help me carry them out to the Daisy Mobile tomorrow or the next day. *No rush.*

Ky leaned into the room. "Coach is here to see you," he said and disappeared.

"What coach?" My eyes felt gummy, and my nose wouldn't stop running. "Tell him to come back later!"

"Is this a bad time?"

I recognized the voice and the green eyes and the broad forehead, but Larry had been to the barber. His hair was shorter and darker, more chestnut than copper now that the sun's lightening had been cut off, and his beard, trimmed close to his face, revealed a strong but nicely padded jawline. Raindrops speckled the shoulders of his jacket.

I thought of a couple smarty-pants comments about his new look, but I said, "It's good to see you."

"You, too," he said, "but if you want, I could come back another time."

I looked around the room. "I've done what I can for the day."

"Is there someplace I could carry these boxes and bags for you?"

"The Daisy Mobile is in the garage."

Larry picked up boxes that I'd marked *Dress Shirts* and *Suits*. "Lead the way."

I carried a bag of shoes. When he took the bag from me and loaded it in the truck bed, he said, "Are you sure you want me here? I'd understand . . ."

"I'm glad you're here."

"Because I didn't call or anything. I was afraid you'd say no."

How sad that Larry had to step back into my life so cautiously.

"I wondered about Bill," he said.

"From the roller rink?"

"I wondered if the two of you . . . if the two of you had . . . if you'd gotten together."

"He told me at our first, and last, lunch date that he didn't want another family, especially not a teenager. I haven't seen him since."

A small smile—at least I thought it was a smile—creased the corners of Larry's eyes, and my heart thumped in response.

"That's interesting," he said and walked with long strides toward the house.

That's interesting?

We wiped our feet on the rug, and I followed him back upstairs for another load.

"Did you call all the ladies from the roller rink?" I asked.

"Not one."

"Not even Roseanne?"

He picked up two more boxes and told me to add a bag on top. On our way out to the garage and back, we talked about his dahlia garden. He was waiting for the first frost to dig the tubers. "I don't lose so many tubers to mold since I started waiting three days after the first frost. I think the cold seals them."

Back in my bedroom, he said, "The funny thing about Roseanne is— Hey, how about those golf clubs? You're not going to get rid of those are you?"

"What's so funny about Roseanne?"

"You're keeping the clubs for Ky, aren't you?"

"He wasn't all that interested when I asked him, but I thought I'd keep them in the basement in case he changes his mind."

"Are *you* ready for them to be in the basement?"

"Louise says the bag is a breeding ground for black widow spiders, so yeah, I think the basement is a better place for the clubs."

He held the golf bag while I wrestled the travel cover on and zipped it up. With his head so close to mine, I could smell his Old Spice. My father had worn Old Spice. In the basement, Larry rearranged some boxes to make room for the golf bag.

He started up the basement steps.

"You were saying something about Roseanne?" I asked.

The rain fell harder. "We better get another load out to the truck."

Larry stood at the garage door looking out at my sodden garden. Against the gray sky, the mountain ash glowed a mandarin orange. "You were right about me hiding behind my beard," he said. He ran his right hand over his chin. "But I couldn't bring myself to shave it off completely."

"I like it." And I did.

Our eyes met. "So does my mom."

If Larry was here to tell me he was serious about Roseanne, I wanted to hear it before I let myself liken his eyes to something as cliché as jade or a lagoon or a pair of Granny Smith apples. *Cut to the chase.* "About Roseanne?" I prompted.

"Man, is she pretty or what? And what a great mother. I love watching her with Phoebe. She has a grace about her. . . . I've tried to explain it. . . .

I'm not that good with words." He smacked his lips. "She sure makes a great lemon cream pie."

This isn't helping.

"When I heard what her husband had put her through, I wanted to rescue her," he said.

If the ground was going to open up and swallow me whole, I wished it would get on with it.

"But when I pictured myself de-budding my dahlias, you were out in my flower beds with me. If I dreamed of traveling to an exotic place to walk along a beach or to hike up a mountain, I dreamed it was you with me."

My lips quivered, and the tears started to flow again. Larry wrapped his arms around me. His chest was broad and soft and safe. He patted my back. "You go ahead and cry. I'm going to finish this pretty speech I've been working on."

I cried harder.

"When the softball team scores a run, you're the one I want to see in the stands cheering. And when it comes to fighting, I can't think of a more worthy opponent or anyone I'd rather make up with. I've never seen a woman handle a shovel better than you, and your laugh is the sweetest song I've ever heard." He cradled the back of my head with his hand. "You're the kind of pretty that's nice to touch."

"I'm getting your jacket all wet."

"Go right ahead."

But I wasn't crying anymore. My bones had gone soft, and I was listening to his heartbeat.

"I know that I got pretty weird on you . . . talking about pink tomato festivals . . . and . . . Maybe I shouldn't remind you of all that. Anyway, I was wondering if we could keep each other company during the Bronco game tomorrow, just to see how it goes. Then I'd like to show you how good I am at grilling a steak."

"I'll bake a pie."

Thanks, Lord.

I was looking through the recipe box for my grandmother's lemon cream pie recipe when the phone rang.

"That you, Mibby?"

"Hey, Crenshaw, how are you tonight?"

"Not so good. Brenda and me had a fight."

"A bad one?"

"She don't want to see me no more."

"Did you tell her you were sorry?"

"I didn't do nothing wrong."

"What does she think you did wrong?"

"She says I made her look bad in front of the other waitresses, 'cause I said her section looked sloppy. I say that to everybody. I'm the boss!"

Where do I begin? "Do you love her?"

"Yeah."

"What's more important to you, being with Brenda or being right?"

The phone went quiet for a long time. "Being with Brenda, hands down," he finally said.

"Good."

"I guess that means I'm going to have to apologize to her, right?"

"Yep."

"First thing in the morning—"

"Call her tonight."

"Right."

"Crenshaw, how's the lemon cream pie at the Hop?"

ACKNOWLEDGMENTS

Dennis Hill, my beloved husband and resident expert on all things horticultural. Your love has given my creativity a safe place to grow. Thanks, honey.

Geoff and Matt, our sons, who managed to live through their teenage years fully male, yet with great dignity and amazing achievement. I got the best of Ky from you!

My critique group, Darlia Hill, Muriel Morley, Sharon Bridgewater, and Linda Callison. They never hold back criticism or encouragement. Thanks, sweet and gifted ladies. And special thanks to Muriel for reading through the entire manuscript twice. I promise to improve my hyphen use on book three.

My writing group, the Lord's Write Hands, gives me a place to grow as a believer and a writer.

Paul Sparks, known locally as Mr. Dahlia, walked me through his dahlia garden on one of the hottest days of the year and answered all of my questions. This might be the year you grow the record-breaker, Paul.

Françoise Evans, my expert on all things deliciously French.

Lynn Vrany, horsewoman extraordinaire, shared her knowledge as she unknotted my shoulder muscles. *Ahh.*

New Contemporary Fiction
from Lawana Blackwell

a table by the window

LAWANA BLACKWELL

a novel

Carley Reed makes a cross country trip to her grandmother's southern town, and the serenity of small-town living charms her into staying. Soon she realizes she has found the kind of life she always desired, but it's more than she bargained for when the unveiling of the truth about a mysterious murder threatens her newfound happiness.

◊ BETHANY HOUSE